DUDLEY PUBLIC LIBRARIES

The loan of this book may be renewed if not required by other readers, by contacting the library from which it was borrowed.

Sar
Texas
beauti
poodle

In her
much o
loves in
support

Nicole
dream
failed
writing
romant
to the
thems
Missou
somed

WHAT SHE DID

BARB HAN

COVERT COMPLICATION

NICOLE HELM

MILLS & BOON

First Published in Great Britain 2020
by Mills & Boon, an imprint of HarperCollins*Publishers*
1 London Bridge Street, London, SE1 9GF

What She Did © 2020 Barb Han
Covert Complication © 2020 Nicole Helm

ISBN: 978-0-263-28026-5

0420

WHAT SHE DID

BARB HAN

All my love to Brandon, Jacob and Tori,
my favourite people in the world.

To Babe, my hero, for being my great love and my place
to call home.

To my mum, Juanita, for being my biggest cheerleader.
And to my sister, Tonia, for always having my back.
Love you both!

Chapter One

"Skylar, it's time to go," Chelsea McGregor shouted up the stairs to her four-year-old daughter. She listened for the sounds of those still-small bare feet running on the creaky wood flooring of the new house in Jacobstown. Skylar's energy never ceased to amaze Chelsea. The kid had two speeds: full-out and passed out. And she was being way too quiet for this hour of the morning.

Chelsea called to her daughter again.

At least they'd made it through the first night in a new house. The move to a new town in Texas, a fresh start, had been the only light of hope in Chelsea's life since the first time she'd looked into her newborn baby's eyes. In that moment of pure bliss, Chelsea had had no idea what was going on at home. Anything of value was being cleaned out of her house while both her personal and business accounts were also being drained by the man who'd promised to love and protect her for the rest of her life.

Travis Zucker had robbed her blind, cost her her livelihood and, to be honest, her dignity. She'd been young and naïve in falling for a charmer. He'd charmed her right out of her life's work.

People talked about defining moments. That had been hers.

When Travis hadn't answered any of her texts while she was in labor, she'd gone from fearing her husband had gotten into a terrible car accident—because she'd thought there was no way he'd miss the birth of their daughter otherwise—to laboring for seventeen hours with her mother at her side, to shock followed by horror that she had a brand-new life to care for and no financial means to do it with. She and Skylar had moved in with Chelsea's mother, whose health had been declining for years. Linda McGregor had high blood pressure and cholesterol, diabetes, and arthritis to name a few. Staying on top of her medications and having the money to pay for them had been a challenge.

"Hey, Mom," Chelsea shouted up the stairs to her mother, who was helping Skylar get dressed for pre-school. "How's it going up there?"

Her mother appeared at the top of the wooden banister.

"I sent her down." Linda checked her watch. "Must've been at least five minutes ago."

"That's odd. I didn't hear her." Chelsea spun around and scanned the long hallway past the boxes that had been stacked and pushed haphazardly against the wall.

She immediately checked the hall bathroom but it was empty. Skylar might be playing a game. She loved hide-and-seek. Or she might be trying to avoid her first day at a new school.

Skylar had to be upstairs. There was only one staircase in the house. It creaked and groaned even under the weight of a child. Chelsea had already flagged a couple of random nails sticking out that would need to be addressed soon. Her to-do list was growing considering the place hadn't been updated or repaired in probably a good twenty years. None of the imperfections mattered. This house was a gift beyond measure.

"Where are you, little bit?" Chelsea tried to regulate her breathing as her stress levels climbed. She reminded herself that the man who'd taken everything from her wouldn't come back for their daughter. The fear was unrealistic. And yet it could be crippling when it struck. This was one of those moments.

Chelsea reminded herself to breathe slowly as she checked behind boxes, shivering in the drafty hall. There was a door to a small storage space underneath the stairs. It was possible that Skylar could've tiptoed downstairs and slipped inside. Chelsea had been in the kitchen making Skylar's lunch for her first day in a new school. A new month. A new house. A new lease on life.

Her mother had agreed to come live with Chelsea in Jacobstown. Chelsea had said she needed help with Skylar to convince her mother to leave Houston but the reality was that she was worried about her mother. Her health was a concern and Chelsea needed to be able to keep an eye on her. A group of doctors in Fort Worth had a great reputation and Chelsea figured a change couldn't hurt considering her mother's Houston doctors seemed to be running out of ideas and inspiration. They'd played around with her mother's medications, which had led to all kinds of side effects. Getting the balance right proved tricky.

A cold front had blown in during the night. Seventy-five-degree temperatures had dropped into the low forties.

Chelsea rubbed her arms to stave off the cold and called her daughter's name again.

Skylar didn't so much as make a peep.

Chelsea quickened her pace, knocking empty boxes out of her way as she locked her gaze onto the door underneath the stairs that had been made into a small coat closet.

"Hey, sweet girl. Are you in here?" Chelsea opened the door with her heart in her throat. Her calm words belied her panic.

There was no sign of Skylar.

Now, Chelsea was jogging through the rooms, double-checking the small powder room near the kitchen.

She returned to the bottom of the stairs and called up to her mother. "She's not down here. Are you sure she isn't upstairs with you?"

"I'll double-check her room." There was worry in her mother's voice, too.

Chelsea ran to the kitchen.

If Skylar was playing a joke, this wasn't funny anymore.

"Come on out of your hiding place." Chelsea drummed up her I'm-not-kidding tone. Her Serious Mom voice was nothing to mess with and maybe because she only used it as a last resort did it always work.

She listened for sounds of movement. When none came, her heart lurched. She stormed toward the stairs, panic slamming into her with the force of a tornado, threatening to rip her apart and smack her into the ground when it was done with her.

Chelsea broke into a run and by the time she hit the stairs her body was already trembling. She took the wooden steps two at a clip and then sprinted toward her daughter's bedroom.

What was it about her life that caused the walls to

come tumbling down around her just when everything seemed to be clicking?

"Skylar," she said so loudly it startled her mother.

"I can't find her." Linda squinted her eyes as her right hand went over her heart; habitual signs that she was out of options. It was also the expression she'd worn the few times Chelsea had asked about her own father.

At a young age, Chelsea had realized the topic brought painful memories to her mother. She'd since learned not to ask.

Once, her mother had asked twelve-year-old Chelsea to run and get muscle strain cream from her nightstand. When Chelsea had picked it up, accidentally knocking a book to the floor, a photograph had fallen out. The picture had been a younger version of her mother. Although, to be honest, Chelsea had barely recognized the woman with the carefree smile. She'd traced the beaming face with her index finger. Gone were the deep worry grooves from her forehead—a now-hardened face from years spent barely getting by on odd jobs. Her mother had had to sacrifice going to college to support Chelsea's father, whom she later found out had been an aspiring photographer. She'd made the connection years afterward that he had taken the picture of her mother.

Money had always been tight and Chelsea often wondered what had happened to her father. There'd been times when Chelsea and her mother had had to pick up in the middle of the night and leave all their belongings behind to avoid being forced out because her mother couldn't pay the rent.

The two of them had bounced around among well-meaning relatives for most of Chelsea's life. Chelsea had picked up on late-night conversations. Her father had gone out for milk and never returned.

She'd learned that in those first couple of years after her own father left that her mother believed he'd been injured somewhere and was unable to come home. And then, as time went on, she'd hear about a relative who'd seen her husband and then another sighting from a friend of a friend. Over time, her mother seemed to realize that he'd made the choice to leave. No explanation. No looking back.

Travis had been nothing more than history repeating itself. When he'd walked out, Chelsea had no such fantasies that he'd return. She'd accepted her fate and moved on.

She thought about Travis and the similarities. Unlike her mother, Chelsea had never searched for her husband.

The worst part for Chelsea during her childhood had been seeing the hope in her mother's eyes while on road trips—trips she later realized were voyages to locate Chelsea's father. Her mother would come alive for a few days. She'd stay up late and talk until Chelsea's eyelids grew so heavy they closed automatically. She'd splurge on eating at a restaurant, which Chelsea now realized was nothing more than a truck stop but had felt like five-star dining to a kid.

Before the day ended, her mother would produce a chocolate bar. The two would curl up in a motel room bed and break off piece after piece until it had disappeared. Looking back, Chelsea had also realized that every road trip she'd taken with her mother had ended at a photography exhibit.

At least one of her aunts had believed that her father had changed his name and was living in New York. A trip there at fifteen years old had amounted to a hot, sticky bus ride and a whole heap of disappointment. Her mother had quietly cried after she'd believed Chelsea had gone to sleep, just like all the other times.

Chelsea had started a successful food truck at nineteen and within two years owned three. She'd been so proud of her business, of her ability to financially support a mother who had given up everything to care for her only daughter. She'd met Travis two years later and married after a whirlwind romance because she'd found out she was pregnant despite taking birth control pills.

To have everything she'd worked for taken away was a hot poker in Chelsea's chest.

The thought of anything happening to her daughter was worse.

"Where could she have gone?" Linda threw her hands in the air, exacerbated.

"Maybe she slipped outside and is waiting in the car." Chelsea couldn't let herself think the worst.

She hurried to the front window so she could see her used pickup truck. She'd bought it with some of the small—but enormous in so many ways—inheritance money. Since losing her business four years ago, she'd gone to work in Renaldo Vinchesa's kitchen as a sous chef. It was pretty much the only job she could get after losing everything. He was notorious for being a womanizer despite being married with kids, something she didn't learn until she'd been on the job a few weeks. She'd rejected his advances, which seemed to make him even more determined to pursue her. He'd promised to leave his wife if Chelsea agreed to go out with him—an offer that had turned her stomach.

And then, when his wife left him, he seemed to turn

up the heat, pressuring Chelsea to date him or risk him smearing her reputation in the food service industry.

Vinchesa was powerful in the Houston culinary scene and his threats to ensure she'd never work in another restaurant weren't idle. He'd deliver on them in a heartbeat and, based on the texts she'd received from the couple of friends she'd made while working at Chez Houston, wheels were already turning in that direction.

Vinchesa had tried to corner her into staying put when she'd turned in her notice. Her aunt's inheritance had freed her. So she didn't mind a creaky old house, because it was *hers*. She didn't mind the elbow grease it would need to become ship-shape, because it would provide a home base for Skylar to grow up secure in. And she didn't mind that the heater had conked out in the middle of the night, because… Well, admittedly, that part had been awful.

What she did mind was her daughter pulling a Houdini.

Glancing down at the late-model pickup she'd bought, Skylar was nowhere to be seen.

"Where's my cell?" Chelsea's pockets were empty. Had she left it on the kitchen counter?

"I'll keep looking up here. You go down and check there," Linda said.

Chelsea turned to head toward the kitchen as her mother continued her closet inspection, picking up empty boxes and shaking them as though Skylar might tumble out of one.

A moment of I-can't-do-this struck. Chelsea hammered it down. She *could* do anything she wanted. She *would* pull on her big-girl pants and keep it together.

As she wheeled down the stairs and past the front door, the silhouette of a male figure appeared on the porch.

Funny, she hadn't seen anyone drive up, but then the house sat close to the road and she couldn't hear much over the howling winds picking up speed by the minute.

Heartbeat pounding at the base of her throat, she froze.

Three rapid knocks sounded at the door, followed by a masculine voice that sent warm vibrations rippling through her despite the frigid temperature.

A couple of thoughts raced through Chelsea's mind at that moment. She quickly crossed off the first. *That* voice did not belong to Renaldo. His was like fingernails on a chalkboard.

The other had to do with Skylar missing.

Chelsea bolted to the door and whisked it open.

Six foot three of male muscle under a gray cowboy hat stood on her porch. He looked to be in his early thirties with steel eyes and what she imagined would be a six-pack of pure power beneath his lightweight shirt.

The wind almost forced the door out of her hands but she held tight.

"My name's Nathan Kent and someone in this residence called in a fire." He examined her and then looked right past her. His voice would make reading a medicine bottle sound scandalous.

"A what?" Chelsea tried to ignore the inappropriate reaction her body had to the tall, gorgeous cowboy. She was confused because her cell was nowhere to be found and her mother hadn't made that call—

And then it dawned on her.

"Mom, she's okay," Chelsea called upstairs before turning back to the fireman. "Who called you?"

"A little girl by the name of Skylar was all Dispatch

could get from her. A truck is on the way. I happened to be passing by when the call came in."

"I'm so sorry," she said, spinning around to check the hallway in case the little culprit stood behind her. Relief flooded her that her daughter was okay. Skylar was a good kid, just scared, and she'd just learned how to call 9-1-1 at her old school when a fireman had come to visit her class. "My daughter's starting a new school today and we just moved in to a new house, and, as you can see, there's nothing on fire here." Chelsea motioned around awkwardly, not especially sure what to do with her hands. "I'm embarrassed that she wasted your time."

Nathan made a quick call to the Dispatcher, relaying the news this was a false alarm before tucking the phone in his front pocket. Chelsea expected him to pull out a citation book and write her a ticket or something.

Instead his intense expression softened when he asked, "Mind if I speak to the caller before I go?"

"She might not come out," Chelsea said. "I'm pretty sure she knows that she's in big trouble." Chelsea emphasized the last two words to make sure that Skylar heard them.

This probably wasn't the time to think about the fact that she hadn't brushed her hair yet or that she was wearing baggy sweatpants and a faded Journey concert T-shirt she'd bought from a resale shop because she liked the music and the shirt fit into her barely existent clothing budget.

Chelsea also didn't want to think about the fact that it felt like history repeating itself with her financial situation, too. She'd sworn never to let Skylar know what it was like to go without. At this point, Chelsea hadn't exactly broken the promise to her four-and-a-half-year-old daughter.

Liar, a little voice in her head accused her.

"Would you like to come in, Nathan?" Chelsea asked. If embarrassment could kill a person, she'd be flat on the floor by now. And she sincerely hoped the handsome cowboy/fireman believed the red flush to her cheeks, as she felt them flame even more when he stepped inside, was attributed to her reaction to the situation and not to the very real attraction she felt.

"Call me Nate," he said.

Chelsea chalked her reaction up to not having had time for a date in months. Her mother had become sicker in recent months, and working full-time while caring for a preschooler and aging mother left very little social time. Not to mention the fact that the last date she'd gone on had been such a dud that Chelsea had tried to convince herself she could swear off men until Skylar was eighteen. Fourteen years to go and she was already practically drooling over the first hot guy. Well played, Chelsea.

"The fireman's here, Skylar. I know you called. Mommy's worried and I want you to come out from wherever you're hiding right now." Chelsea softened her tone because, first and foremost, she was relieved her daughter was okay. Now that she knew Skylar was hiding and not stuck somewhere she couldn't call out for help, Chelsea relaxed below panic as she forced the door closed against the strong winds.

Nate stood in the front hall and Chelsea realized how bad her manners were.

"Can I get you something? A cup of coffee?" She looked him up and down. He wore jeans and a cotton shirt. The material on both was thin. He had to be cold.

He nodded. "Coffee, if it's not too much trouble."

"Follow me." She walked into the kitchen trying to think. "I know exactly where she'd be in our old house."

The hot cowboy leaned his hip against the counter and her heart stuttered when she thought about such a good-looking man standing in her kitchen.

He pulled his cell from his pocket and she noticed how graceful his movements were. He seemed like the type who would probably laugh at hearing himself described in that manner. Chelsea poured two cups of fresh brew and handed one over.

"What's your number?" he asked.

Her immediate reaction was to tense up.

He blinked at her like he was confused by her response. And then it must've dawned on him because he lowered his voice to church-quiet and said, "We'll hear it ring. But, if you're not comfortable—"

"It's okay." She whispered her number to him. This was turning out to be a red-letter day and Chelsea hadn't finished her first cup of coffee yet.

"My mother's upstairs. In fact, I'm surprised she hasn't been down here to check on things. I hope she heard me. She's most likely still looking for Skylar." The house wasn't that big. Had her mother had another episode? Chelsea's imagination was running away with her because Mother would've hollered if anything had happened. Chelsea excused herself and walked down the hall to the bottom of the stairs again, grabbing onto the wood railing that needed a few nails to steady it.

"Mom, can you listen for my ringtones?" she shouted upstairs.

"Who was at the door?" her mother asked, appearing

at the landing and scaring the hell out of Chelsea. Thankfully, her mother looked normal.

"Fireman," she responded and, before her mother could freak out, added, "Everything's fine."

"I'll keep an ear open," Linda said, giving a thumbs-up sign.

Chelsea hoped her mother was making the gesture because she caught onto the plan and not because she thought Chelsea should flirt with their guest. When Mom winked, it was pretty obvious which side she was on.

Hot cowboy or no, Chelsea couldn't be bothered with so much riding on her business getting off the ground. There was a lot of work to be done and she needed to focus on making sure the three of them didn't starve.

Plus, her immediate need was to find her daughter. Nothing overrode that.

Nate Kent entered the hallway and Chelsea didn't have to look to know he was there. She could feel his masculine presence. She turned and him gave the awkward hand signal her mother had just given her, with an even cheesier smile.

Chelsea took a breath and fisted her hand.

He seemed to get the idea because he tapped the call button.

A hush seemed to fall over the house and even the roaring winds outside calmed.

Chelsea listened, moving from room to room when no ringtones sounded. Her daughter was too young to change the settings on the phone. This couldn't be right. Skylar was hiding somewhere. She'd called 9-1-1 and asked for help.

The cowboy followed her until they ended up back in the kitchen.

"It's gone into voice mail."

Chapter Two

The look of terror on the brown-eyed, blond-haired mother punched Nate in the gut. The five-and-a-half-foot tall beauty had full lips, creamy skin and a flawless figure with just the right amount of curves. And those were things Nate had no business noticing.

"If she was okay, she would answer." Chelsea twisted her fingers together.

An older woman wearing a frock and apron came into the kitchen. "Any luck down here?"

"No." Chelsea looked frantic as she exited the kitchen and moved from room to room calling for her daughter.

"I'm Linda," the older woman said. She had permanent worry lines etched into her forehead and sad, light brown eyes. Maybe sad wasn't the right word. Deep down, behind her smile, she looked empty. She was thick around the middle and it looked like it took some effort to walk. But there was also a kindness and warmth to her that her daughter had no doubt inherited.

"Pleasure to meet you, ma'am. Name's Nate Kent." He offered a handshake that she took with a surprising amount of vigor for a woman of her stature.

His cell buzzed. He excused himself as he checked the screen and saw the call was from Dispatch.

"Are you still at the McGregor residence?" Patty Smart had turned seventy-eight on her last birthday and her mind was still sharp as a tack.

"Yes, ma'am."

"Good. I have a little girl on the line and she's quite distraught. Seems she's gotten herself in a fix." Patty's calm, sympathetic voice was a welcome relief. It meant the little girl was okay.

"Is she in the house?" He shot a knowing look toward Chelsea. Even wearing baggy jogging pants and a loose T-shirt, he could tell she had an amazing figure. Again, her shapely hips and full breasts were none of his business.

"Yes. She's in a closet under the stairwell," Patty supplied.

"We looked inside there." Nate was already circling back with Chelsea on his heels.

"Can you hold on, please?" Patty asked.

"Of course." Nate turned to Chelsea and whispered, "She called 9-1-1. I'm on the phone with one of the operators. Your daughter's here in the house and she's shaken up but all right." Nate was grateful he could deliver good news. As a volunteer fireman for Broward County, he'd seen a little bit of everything and not every situation turned out the way he'd like.

"Thank you." Chelsea's eyes closed for a second and she looked to be collecting herself as relief washed over her features. "If she's here, where is she?"

He nodded at the hall closet as Patty came back on the line.

Chelsea's forehead creased with confusion.

There could be a crawl space in there. He'd seen plenty

of oddities in these old houses. People created insulated spaces to hide money and, in some cases, bootleg whiskey.

"I'm putting the call on speaker," Nate said to Patty.

"Skylar said she's worried that her mommy is going to get upset with her for being bad. She didn't want to start a new school." Patty's grandmotherly compassion came through.

"She's safe. That's all that matters to me," Chelsea said.

"I'm sorry it took a minute to call. You must be worried sick. It took time to calm her down enough to understand what she was saying."

Chelsea was already inside the four-by-six closet with its sloped ceiling.

Nate peeked inside.

"She's not in here." Chelsea dropped to all fours and felt around on the floor.

"None of these houses have basements." Nate had no idea where the blond beauty had moved from. This was Old Lady Barstock's place.

Chelsea felt around walls. "There's nothing here."

"Can you tell Skylar to shout to us or bang on the wall?" Nate dropped to all fours and knocked on the walls, looking for a dead space.

And then he felt it. A ridge where there should have been solid wall. "Hold on. I might have something."

He ran his finger along the ridge. Chelsea moved beside him and her scent washed over him. She had that clean, warm and citrusy smell.

Refocusing, Nate pushed on the two-by-two box. The wall moved. Using both hands, he forced an opening. Almost instantly, sniffles sounded.

"Skylar, baby, are you in there?" Chelsea's voice had a forced calm that belied the wild look in her eyes.

"Momma?" A sob echoed as a scuffling movement sounded. The little girl's face appeared in the opening, round and angelic. Red, puffy eyes spilled tears when she saw her mother.

Nate backed away, ending the call with Patty after delivering the good news, giving mother and daughter space to reunite.

Linda paced in the hallway. "Was that her voice I heard?"

"She's okay."

The older woman clutched at her chest and it looked like her right knee gave out. Nate grabbed her arm to keep her from falling.

"Let's get you into a comfortable chair." He helped Linda into the kitchen and into a chair at the table.

Linda apologized several times.

"Don't worry about it. Happens all the time." It didn't, but he wanted to make her feel better. The family had clearly been through enough for one morning.

Nate didn't have children of his own but a few of his brothers did. He couldn't imagine the terror of one going missing even for a few minutes.

His family had been through a lot and that had made them even closer.

Their parents had died a short time apart, leaving Nate, his four brothers and one sister to run the family ranch. The Kent Ranch, known to most simply as KR, was one of the most successful cattle ranches in Texas. The family owned land across the state and into Idaho and Wyoming.

Then there was the growing problem of someone

butchering heifers on the family ranch. The gruesome killings had started out weeks ago with one heifer found near Rushing Creek with its left hoof hacked off before being left to die. There was no excuse for animal cruelty to any Kent, and Nate was no exception. His family had been working closely with local Sheriff Zach McWilliams, who was also a relative, to solve the cases. The cousins had been close from childhood, along with Zach's sister, Amy.

Everyone was on the hunt. There had been no new information or leads on the case yet extra patrols couldn't keep the killer at bay. His pattern of striking was unpredictable.

"I don't want to be any trouble," Linda said, settling in the chair.

"You couldn't be," Nate reassured her. He had basic EMT training but that's about as far as his skills went.

Linda's color had washed out, her pupils dilated.

"Are you taking any medications?" he asked.

The older woman issued a breath. "I forgot. In all the excitement, I completely missed my morning pills."

Chelsea came into the room, a little girl in her arms who looked like her Mini-Me but with black, kinky curls. Nate glanced up and his heart squeezed at the sight of mother and daughter. The little girl was still sniffling and softly crying, her face buried in her mother's long hair.

Linda put up a hand at Chelsea's obvious concern. "I forgot to take my medication this morning," Linda said.

"Where is it? I'll go get it." Chelsea was busy with her little girl, so Nate volunteered to do it.

"I keep them in the cabinet next to the kitchen sink." Linda pointed. "There's a lock on it so you'll have to finagle it open."

"A couple of my brothers are married with kids. I've seen most of these." He was able to open the cabinet easily. He grabbed three bottles with Linda's name on them and brought them to Chelsea's mother with a glass of water. He recognized one as a commonly prescribed blood pressure medication.

She thanked him and took the offering. She opened the bottles and popped three pills in her mouth. "I'll be back to normal in no time."

Nate noticed the concern on Chelsea's forehead. She had her hands full.

And so did he.

"Thank you for coming," Chelsea said to Nate. Her to-do list was piling up and she hadn't planned on Skylar being around for the day. Having her daughter home was going to throw a wrench in things. Part of her figured she should send her daughter to preschool, but the other part—the winning part—convinced her to keep Skylar home.

What Skylar had done was not okay. But the scare of being locked inside the crawl space had been bad enough for her daughter to still cling to Chelsea. There'd be no peeling those fingers from around Chelsea's neck, and maybe she was a bad parent for it, but she needed to keep eyes on her little girl after that shock, to see that her daughter was fine.

Chelsea, shaken up by the morning's events, was probably overreacting, but she also acknowledged that she'd uprooted Skylar from everything familiar.

Nate finished his cup of coffee and set it on the counter.

"There's no reason to rush him out the door," Linda

said with a little wink that made Chelsea's face flame with embarrassment.

Worse yet, he chuckled, and it was a rumble from deep in his chest.

"I'll walk you out." Chelsea didn't care how amused he was. She was mortified.

"Hope you feel better soon," he said to her mother.

"Maybe you could stop in later."

"Mom."

Chelsea, Skylar in her arms, led the way to the front door without looking back. She didn't want to give away her body's reaction to the handsome cowboy. Besides, it was most likely because of what had happened, but she had a creepy feeling that she couldn't shake. When she really thought about it, she'd woken with it.

A premonition? She didn't believe in psychic abilities.

She stopped at the door, hefting Skylar higher on her hip. "I think I've apologized like fifty times already, but I'm sorry about my mother just now."

"She was having a little fun." She was grateful for his good nature. He hesitated at the door. "I don't want to intrude, but it might be safer if I check out that crawl space before I leave."

Skylar lifted her head to look up. She'd always been a shy child, avoiding eye contact until it was absolutely necessary.

"It was scary," Skylar said, brown eyes wide and watery. A tear escaped, rolling down her cheek. She brought the back of her hand up to wipe it away.

Chelsea almost didn't know how to react. Her daughter rarely spoke to strangers, especially men she didn't know.

Nate's offer would take an item off Chelsea's growing to-do list. Accepting help was foreign to her, especially from a stranger. She had always been self-reliant. To be honest, she preferred it to depending on anyone else.

But she could also admit that she was in over her head.

"That would be great." She needed to get back to the kitchen to check on her mother, though she didn't like the idea of the crawl space being open. "Any chance you can board it up while you're here? I have a hammer and nails. I'm sure I can find a couple of boards."

"I was going to offer the same thing. Thought I'd check it out first to make sure nothing else was in there."

Chelsea must've tensed without realizing.

"In case there are any small critters in there that need to get out first," he clarified.

She wasn't sure she loved the sound of that, either, but it was a nice gesture. Being in the country would take some getting used to. "You must love animals." Wasn't his last name Kent?

He nodded and smiled. Those gray eyes of his shouldn't make her feel like her knees might buckle when he looked at her.

He was just a man. Okay, that wasn't entirely fair. He was more than a man. He was one seriously gorgeous cowboy with a familiar last name—why did she know it?

"You could say taking care of animals is in my blood."

"Do you have any?" Skylar asked, perking up.

"I live on a ranch where there are cattle, horses and pretty much every other wild thing you can find in Texas." Normally a man of his size and build would be intimidating to a small child. His gentle nature with Skylar made it easy to see why her daughter took to him.

Chelsea glanced at his ring finger and her heart gave a little flip when she didn't see a gold band. Not that it mattered, she quickly reminded herself.

Skylar's face lit up as the cowboy spoke. She leaned away from her mother and unclenched her hands from around her mother's neck. She rocked her body, indicating that she wanted to get down. Chelsea complied.

Her daughter had never recovered from a traumatic event so fast. Chelsea's head was spinning and she knew better than to look a gift horse in the mouth.

"Do you have a pony?" Skylar asked.

"We have three. Peter, Polka and Dot," he supplied much to Skylar's amusement. "Peter bites, so you have to watch out for him if you ever stop by."

"Can I come over now?" Skylar twisted her arms together and shifted from foot to foot.

"No, honey. Mr. Kent is working and you should be at your first day of school. Remember?" Chelsea couldn't help herself but to throw in that last part. Now that her own heart rate had settled below panic she was rethinking her position on keeping Sky home. If there was a chance she could get her daughter to school, even late, she probably should do it. Having even a few hours to focus would go a long way toward getting her restaurant ready for its opening in six weeks. *Six weeks?* Thinking about it made her lungs squeeze.

"What school do you go to?" Nate asked, squatting until he was eye level with the child.

Skylar looked up at her mother and blinked.

"Clemens Preschool. Have you heard of it?" It was an early childhood development program and the best part was that tuition was next to nothing—precisely what Chelsea could afford while she got her business off the ground.

"I know a few of the teachers over there. Mrs. Eaton—"

Skylar jump-clapped, which was quite a sight, considering she'd never jumped and clapped at the same time before. "That's my teacher's name." Skylar could barely contain her excitement.

Shock nearly knocked Chelsea back a step. Skylar's reaction had caught Chelsea off guard but then she'd never seen Skylar react to a man this way. Her little girl had never met her own father and there'd been no grandfather around to fill in the gap.

Chelsea's attempt to sign her daughter up for a coed soccer team had fallen flat when Skylar had refused to step on the pitch. In her daughter's defense, the coach had had a supersonic voice that boomed. He was Dad to seven boisterous boys and coached middle school football. He was big, round and loud. Skylar had been terrified of him.

"Your teacher brings in a special visitor every year around this time," Nate said. "A male frog by the name of Henry."

"Really?" Skylar's eyes were saucers. She was captivated. Her mother could admit to being enthralled by the handsome cowboy, too. The man most likely had a girlfriend or significant other. There was no way he was single and, even if he was, Chelsea had been there, done that, and the T-shirt had been stolen by her ex.

"That's right," he said. Chelsea already knew from checking his ring finger earlier there was no band, which didn't necessarily mean there was no relationship.

Besides, once this cowboy was on his way, Chelsea planned to have a serious discussion with her daughter about the proper use of 9-1-1. Although, in fairness, the little girl had been trapped between the walls. Chelsea shivered thinking about how badly this could've gone if her daughter hadn't taken the cell phone in with her.

A cold trickle, like when people said a cat walked over their grave, crept over her. She'd been on edge for days and it was probably because of the way she'd left things at her job in Houston.

Renaldo had made threats before telling her she'd regret walking out on him. He'd been outraged at the fact that she didn't want to date him and her quitting had seemed to infuriate him more. She would've walked out after the first time he'd made a pass at her but she'd needed the job and would need a letter of recommendation if she quit. She'd been forced to keep the peace.

Looking back she could see how naïve she'd been in believing his interest would blow over. She figured he'd lose interest and find another person to date. It wasn't like many of the other waitresses didn't see him as attractive. To Chelsea, he seemed like a spoiled middle-aged man used to getting what he wanted from people. There was absolutely nothing attractive about that to her.

Renaldo had made no secret of being put off by her rebuttals.

The man had an ego the size of Texas.

But was it dangerous?

Chapter Three

Nate had picked up a sidekick while he worked. Skylar was a cute little thing with big, rust-colored eyes and a shy smile. He'd been around kids enough recently, thanks to his brothers and their wives, to be halfway decent as an uncle. A few of his brothers had found true happiness with wives and kids. Don't misunderstand, Nate was all about the people he cared about being happy. And marriage was great for some people. He had no plans to rush into a commitment of that magnitude.

When he and his former girlfriend, Mia Chase, had hit the six-month mark of dating, her software job moved to Boulder. She'd told him how much she cared about him and that she didn't want the relationship to end. And that's when the ultimatum came to take their relationship to the next level or end it.

Nate had been honest. He hadn't been ready right then, but that didn't mean he would never be. He didn't share the part about something holding him back. It didn't matter. Mia had balked and it had become clear to him that she'd been expecting a different answer.

A couple of weeks after she'd left, he'd learned the move had been optional. She'd tried to back him against the wall to get him to the altar. Her plan had backfired.

To this day, he couldn't understand why she'd done it, but he knew for certain that he'd dodged a bullet. There wasn't much Nate despised more than a liar.

Besides, six months was a long time to spend with the same person. He'd been bored for the last two, but hadn't been able to bring himself to break up with her after she'd told him she was still dealing with the loss of her sister to lymphoma. That, he later found out, had also been a lie.

He hammered the last of the nails and backed out of the crawl space. "That should take care of it."

Chelsea had ushered her daughter into the kitchen and now stood next to him. She'd changed into formfitting jeans, a blouse and ankle boots. Her hair was slicked back in a ponytail, her brown eyes intent on him. "How'd you do that with Skylar?"

The little nugget, he knew, was in the kitchen, eating with her grandmother and happily chatting about how much fun her day at school was going to be.

"It's magic." Nate's work was done. It was time to take off. He put his hat back on and pulled down on the rim in front.

Chelsea was beautiful. And, under different circumstances, she was exactly the person he'd enjoy getting to know better. But family was sacred to him and he doubted a woman like Chelsea would be happy with what he could offer—a great time in the sack with mutual consent. Besides, the burn marks from his last relationship were fresh and he had no intention of jogging down that same snake-filled path any time soon.

"We're obviously new in town. Last night was our first night in a new house and this morning is not off to a good start," Chelsea said on what seemed like a frustrated sigh.

He already knew, thanks to Linda, she was single. He didn't want to like that fact as much as he did.

"Jacobstown is a great place to bring up a family. Small-town atmosphere. Nice folks," he told her. He also felt the need to warn her about the heifers. "Until a recent crime spree involving heifers, I don't think we knew what crime was."

Her eyes grew wide. "And now?"

"We've had a threat to our livestock. A few animals have been butchered by a man who has been cutting off the hooves of animals. In fact, he just picked up a name, Jacobstown Hacker. You might hear folks mention him." Nate didn't want to go into more details than that but people were on edge and she deserved to know the truth about what was going on.

Her face twisted in a mix of rebuke and sadness. "This sounds like one messed-up individual. Who on earth would get pleasure out of hurting innocent animals?"

"A twisted jerk." Nate couldn't agree more. "Do you have a pet?"

"I promised Skylar a puppy once we get settled," she said on a sigh.

"Might want to think about keeping it inside. There are coyotes to deal with in the country. Not to mention the Texas heat."

"Wouldn't have it any other way." Chelsea's eyes sparked but she didn't mention where she'd moved from.

"Folks from the city are known to drive out to these parts to drop off unwanted dogs. Not sure if you had your heart set on a specific breed, but you can save money if you're willing to care for anything that turns up." Nate thought it was a shame people did that to animals. A domesticated dog, especially a puppy, didn't have the survival skills necessary to outsmart a bobcat or a hungry pack of wolves. Get much farther out and wild boar roamed.

"That's awful." Chelsea frowned and he had no business looking at her pink lips or the freckle on the left side of her mouth.

"If you end up with more than you can handle, give my ranch a call. We have heated and air-conditioned barns for the horses with plenty of room to take care of strays." Nate gave her his personal cell number, just in case.

"I'll keep that in mind."

Part of Nate wanted to volunteer that she call if *she* needed anything. But he knew better. Go down that rabbit hole and what?

He had no idea. Chelsea seemed the opposite of Mia, but first impressions could be deceiving. He'd learned that the hard way, too.

Still fresh from his breakup and betrayal, Nate knew better than to jump back into the dating saddle—no matter how much his heart seemed to have other ideas when it came to the town's newest resident. Casual and consensual sex was another story altogether. He'd had plenty of that in the past few months since the breakup.

Lately, his opinion of it was changing.

"He was nice." Chelsea's mother winked at her.

"Don't get any ideas," Chelsea warned. She took her daughter's hand, ignoring the disappointment rumbling around in her chest that the cowboy had left. She didn't have time to mess around with an attraction. There was work to do and, for the first time in four years, she felt a twinge of excitement and a whole heap of nervous energy. But it was good.

"You look…" Linda paused. "Happy."

"Aunt Maddie did us a huge favor with this house and the business. There's enough money to get things off the ground. I know it'll be work, but I'm up for it." If she budgeted super tight, they should be okay. Her money was planned down to the penny. There wasn't a whole lot of play, which worried her about her mother's episode this morning. Chelsea hoped the health incident had been brought on by Linda missing her morning medication and not something more serious, such as her condition getting worse.

And just because she'd become expert at handling curve balls didn't mean she wouldn't mind an occasional straight path. What she needed was a fast track to success. But she knew building a business took time.

Shoot. That reminded her. She should've mentioned her business to the cowboy. He seemed like he knew everyone and it wouldn't hurt to start getting word out about her new pizza place that would open in six weeks.

Speaking of which, the delivery men would soon be at her restaurant site to install her fire pit and she needed to get a move on.

Chelsea checked her cell, making sure no one had called. And a little part of her wished Nate Kent would have. There was another text from Renaldo, this time asking if he could come see her new house.

Seriously?

"Ready, Sky?"

Her daughter's eyes brightened as she nodded. "Can we get him?"

"Oh, no, honey. The fireman has to work and be ready to help other people on a moment's notice." Skylar's confused face stared up at Chelsea and her mother laughed.

And then it dawned on Chelsea why. "You mean a puppy don't you?" Sky had been asking for a male puppy after reading a popular book about a yellow lab together.

"Uh-huh." Skylar nodded. "What else?"

Linda clucked her tongue and Chelsea refused to react. She wasn't giving in and letting her mother know how embarrassed she was. The woman would have a field day. She might be ill but her mind was sharp—a little too quick-witted for Chelsea's liking.

"Let's get you bundled up," Chelsea said to Skylar. "It's cold outside and the truck heater is taking another day off."

"Maybe *you* should take the day off, Momma." Sky's eyes were huge and they twinkled.

"I have important work to do." It felt good to say that. Even better to mean it.

Renaldo did not get to win. Not as long as Chelsea could help it. If he made good on his promise, she'd never work in another five-star restaurant for the rest of her career.

With the inheritance, she didn't intend to need to.

There was plenty to do and even more to worry about. But a light feeling filled her for the first time in longer than she could remember. Four years ago, she'd held her baby in her arms and wondered how on earth she'd be able to support her. Four years ago, she'd made a promise to that sleeping angel to figure out a way to come out on top. Four years ago, Chelsea had no idea the journey that was about to begin. She'd made it this far and, rather than focus on what she didn't have, she'd decided to be grateful for what she did.

Chelsea retrieved Skylar's winter coat from the same closet that had been a source of trouble this morning.

Hair prickled at the base of her neck. She tried to shake off the creepy-crawly feeling but failed. Maybe she'd have concrete poured into that crawl space to seal it off.

"Ready, Sky?" Chelsea turned to find her daughter skipping toward her down the hall, a wide smile on her face. To be a kid again and able to bounce back from every setback in life so fast. Chelsea could learn a thing or two about not holding on to the past, she thought as she wrapped the coat around her daughter.

"Can we go to the man's house?" Skylar's face lit up.

Chelsea didn't have it in her to dash the hope of her child, but she didn't want to set false expectations, either.

"Right now, we need to get you to school. We'll figure out the rest later." Those last six words had become her new mantra.

School drop-off went smoothly and Chelsea figured she owed Nate Kent a pizza on the house at her grand opening considering he was probably the reason. Skylar had met her teacher with an eager smile and most likely the strong hope that Henry would be showing up.

The delivery truck showed within minutes of Chelsea's arrival at what would be her new restaurant. The place needed a major overhaul, and would get it in the coming weeks. The location on Main Street would be perfect and she didn't mind some sweat equity if it meant she could have her own space again.

There was enough room for a dozen four-top tables for guests wanting to dine in. A small construction crew would show up tomorrow to knock out one of the walls to the outside to create a half wall on one side so customers could dine outside with a full view to the inside.

Three hours later, the oven was installed and Chelsea had cleaned out a corner in the back of the restaurant that would make a perfect office. She could have the same contractors put up Sheetrock, leaving space for a window so she could keep an eye on the kitchen.

She had another forty-five minutes before she had to leave to pick up Skylar.

Glancing around, she couldn't help but smile. She was dirty from head to toe from cleaning up the construction zone. But this was progress.

Chelsea picked up the broom. She had time to give the floor another sweep.

How crazy was it that a day could start out like this one had and turn into one of the most gratifying?

She finished sweeping, leaned the broom against the wall and then checked her phone. Another text from Renaldo had come in. If he thought she was going to answer any of these, he was eating fruit off the crazy tree. For a half second she thought about changing her number. It would be a hassle but it might be worth it.

If he kept on, she would have no choice. For now, she decided not to add any fuel to the fire and see what happened.

Lighter in step, she grabbed her purse and fished out her keys.

It was still light outside at three twenty-five in the afternoon, but not for long. Another couple of hours and it'd be dark. Part of Chelsea hoped that Skylar would be so worn out by her first day that she'd be ready for an early dinner, a hot bath and bed.

Chelsea laughed.

Yeah, right.

That was about as likely as Skylar getting a job and pitching in to pay the bills.

Locking the door to her place—her new restaurant—caused tears to well in her eyes. Happy tears.

She turned toward her pickup. She gasped and took a step back, only to be stopped by the industrial metal door.

Travis's flat smile was more like a sneer.

"Baby, you've been hard to track down."

Chapter Four

"I have no idea where you've been and what you've been doing, but I have a document that says I have no legal ties to you anymore," Chelsea said. Four years of anger, abandonment and betrayal welled inside her, threatening to bubble over. She fisted her hands and readied to draw her knee up, fast and hard, straight to Travis's groin if he took one step closer.

He seemed shorter than before but it was probably her perspective that had changed. At five feet, ten inches, with a decent build, he still paled in comparison with Nate Kent. Travis had sandy-blond hair and hazel eyes. Some people would consider him attractive with the defined jawline and runner's build. Not Chelsea. That ship had sailed the minute she'd seen behind the façade to the real man.

"A man has a right to see his wife and child—"

"*Ex*-wife," she corrected. "And you lost your rights when you disappeared with all of our money and left me with nothing to take care of a newborn."

"People make mistakes," he countered with one of those smiles that had made her heart flutter years ago. Standing there now, it was hard to know what she'd seen in him. She'd been young and naïve. He'd been a heck of a lot more charming when she hadn't known what a heartless jerk he'd turn out to be.

"Listen, baby—"

"Don't call me that. My name is Chelsea." She'd be damned if she let him get away with any of that sweet talk now. Besides, she'd never been big on being called *baby*. Kids could be manipulated. She was a grown woman, an ex-wife, and had the scars to prove it. No one—and that especially meant Travis—would ever be given the chance take advantage of her again. She was reminded of the old saying "Fool me once, shame on you. Fool me twice, shame on me."

If she fell for that easy charm and smile again, she deserved every moment of heartache that came along with it.

Travis stared at her for an uncomfortable moment before he made a show of glancing around. There was nothing genuine about the look in his eyes. She could see that so clearly now.

"Where's the little one?" he asked.

He didn't know if she'd given birth to a girl or boy. How on earth could a man not know something that important about his own child? "You would know if you'd showed up at the hospital four years ago. Move out of my way. I have plans."

His smile turned into a sneer as she tried to push past him. A dark cloud passed behind his hazel eyes.

"You're mad. I get that. But we had something special, bab—"

She shot him a look so harsh he stopped mid-word.

"Chelsea," he continued. "I did something I shouldn't have, but it can't be too late to be a family. Our child needs a father."

"We'll see about that," was all Chelsea said. She hadn't asked for child support in the divorce and she wondered if he'd even received the paperwork. Of course, he'd had to have by now. A wave of panic washed over her. She imagined the possibility of court battles for custody and the need for a lawyer. She'd never been anxious before Travis. Now she lived with her nerves on the edge. Being broke and bringing up a child on her own did that to her.

And it was great that he was now saying that Skylar was his in the first place. When she'd first told him the news about the pregnancy, he'd accused her of sleeping with one of her employees.

"There's not a judge in Texas who would deny me the right to see my child. You better get used to the idea of seeing me around, because I plan to be in both of your lives." He brought his hand up to touch her face, but she smacked it away before he made contact.

"Don't touch me, Travis," she stated as calmly as she could with her heart hammering against her ribs. She needed to talk to a lawyer to find out her legal rights. "What gives you the right to waltz back into our lives? Where have you been?"

"Alaska," he said. "I went to work on a pipeline so I could save money to pay you back and see if you'd give me another chance."

Okay, her ex was seriously delusional if he thought she would look at him twice let alone consider a reconciliation. He'd have to be delusional or drunk, and she didn't smell alcohol on his breath. If he had been in Alaska and that whole story turned out to be true, she might have to figure out a supervised visitation schedule. How many nights had she held her infant daughter and wished the little girl could grow up with a father?

Too many to count, a voice in the back of her mind said.

But before Travis got a chance with their daughter, Chelsea needed to know he wouldn't disappear again. Her angel deserved a man who stuck around, not someone who popped in and out of her life every four or five years when it was convenient for him.

The timing of his showing up again with Chelsea about to open a restaurant following receiving an inheritance was suspect. None of this exchange was sitting right with her. She figured she could do an easy enough internet search to check out his story. She could make some calls. She'd never filed criminal charges against him for draining their bank account and, technically, the money was as much his as it had been hers. She'd been crazy enough to trust him to put both names on the accounts. He'd showed an interest in her growing company and she'd had a vision of running a family business someday.

"You can start by paying your child the money you stole from us, Travis. Don't waste your time trying to win me back. If you stick around this time and prove you really want to be a father to your child, we can talk about you two meeting. Until then—"

Travis's sneer intensified as he took a threatening step toward her. He was so close she could smell his aftershave, which had been put on with gusto.

Instinctively, Chelsea turned her face to the side and winced. And then she caught herself acting afraid. She remembered that the best way to stop a bully was to confront one.

She turned her face toward his. He grabbed her chin and forced a kiss on her lips before she could push him back a step.

He came at her again, but this time she threw her right knee into his groin.

Travis brought his hands up to the door to brace himself and keep from dropping to the ground. He blew out a couple of sharp breaths as Chelsea tried to duck underneath his arm.

She managed to break away until he spun around and grabbed her by the arm.

"You're hurting me," she said through clenched teeth. She dropped down to her knees, breaking his grip.

"When did you get so mean?" Travis asked through labored breaths as she stood up and sidestepped him.

"Go away, Travis."

"Not until I see my child." He seemed to know right where to hit her. Four years ago, it was her financial security. Now, money paled in comparison to the need to protect her daughter from harm. She wanted to tell him that would happen as soon as hell froze over.

Checking into her legal rights just became top priority.

She stalked to her truck that was parked on the street, half expecting him to charge up behind her again. This exchange was making her late to pick up Skylar.

Chelsea made it to her pickup and jumped inside. She immediately closed and locked the door. And then she drove around the block a couple of times to make sure Travis was gone and hadn't followed her.

When she was certain he was long gone, she pulled over and let the school know she was running late.

Ten minutes later Chelsea pulled into the parking lot and found a space. It wasn't hard because it was empty. Surprising tears sprang to her eyes. Travis in Skylar's life should be a good thing. He was her father. Knowing what he'd done and what he was capable of doing slammed into Chelsea.

A car pulled into the lot and she watched it all the way until it parked. Relief flooded her when a female stepped out of the driver's side. Chelsea wished she'd taken note of what Travis had driven.

She hurried inside the building. There were two kids besides Skylar, and Chelsea was grateful that she wasn't the last one there.

"I'm so sorry to be late," Chelsea said to the head mistress, Mrs. Bartels.

"She had a great day," Mrs. Bartels informed her. "She was a little shy at first, but that all changed once she got comfortable with the other students."

Normally that kind of news would make Chelsea smile and ease the tension she'd been feeling.

"That's really good to hear," Chelsea finally said. "Thank you."

"Would you like me to walk you to her classroom?" Mrs. Bartels asked.

The female from the parking lot rushed in.

"Hello, Mrs. Stanley," Mrs. Bartels said.

"Hi, Elaine," the woman responded. "How'd he do today?"

Chelsea excused herself. She needed to see her baby, to know that Skylar was okay, even though she already did on some level. If there'd been trouble, Mrs. Bartels would've phoned. And, besides, Travis didn't know he had a daughter let alone where she was.

Skylar's eyes lit up when she saw her mother step into the room. Her little face broke into a wide smile. "Mommy!"

Chelsea made eye contact with the teacher, Mrs. Eaton, who smiled her approval.

Dropping to her knees, she welcomed the little angel who had flown over to her. Those tiny arms wrapped around Chelsea's neck brought an unexpected tear.

"I'm so happy to see you." She held her little girl a bit tighter.

"I had fun. I colored a picture of an elephant and rode a real bike." Skylar's enthusiasm for her day eased some of Chelsea's guilt for being away from her so long.

"It sounds like you were very busy," Chelsea agreed. She pulled back a little to look into her daughter's eyes. "And you get to come back tomorrow."

Skylar's face nearly burst from smiling so hard as she nodded. "Do you think he'll be here?"

A wave of panic ripped through Chelsea. There was no way Skylar could be talking about Travis. "Who?"

Her gaze darted toward Mrs. Eaton for an answer.

"You know," Skylar said, making eyes at her mother. "The fireman."

"Probably not, sweetie." Relief washed over Chelsea. "But all your new friends will be. Now go get your coat."

Before Skylar trotted away, she said, "He was right about Henry. My teacher has a frog."

Mrs. Stanley came into the room and the little boy who'd been sitting at the same coloring table as Skylar perked up.

"Hey, buddy," Mrs. Stanley said, bending to one knee. "Are you ready?"

He dutifully walked to his cubby and got his things. Skylar struggled with hers.

Chelsea walked over to help her daughter with her coat as a man's voice from the hallway shot through her. She sucked in a burst of air and spun around.

Mrs. Eaton looked at Chelsea, confusion stamped

on her forehead. A man in a janitor's shirt nodded and walked in to empty the trash.

"Sorry," Chelsea mumbled as she led Skylar out of the classroom, down the hallway and into the parking lot. It was dark outside now and she watched wearily as every car drove by while she buckled her daughter into the car seat.

CHELSEA PULLED INTO her driveway and her heart clenched. An unfamiliar truck was parked on the pad next to the house. Complete panic was a stalking panther coming up from behind. Chelsea used the rearview mirror to glance at her daughter, who was strapped into her car seat in the back.

What if Travis knew where they lived?

Chelsea cursed the wave of fear threatening to suck her under. She'd already dealt with him once today and wasn't sure she could take another round. She couldn't tell Skylar to stay in the truck alone and nothing in her wanted to go inside to see who was there.

She grabbed the gearshift, ready to put the truck in Reverse on a moment's notice. Maybe she could wait it out. She could park down the street and see who the truck belonged to.

"Momma, are we going inside?" Skylar looked at Chelsea with the most adorable albeit incredulous look on her four-year-old face.

"Maybe in just a minute, sweetheart. I'm not sure who that truck belongs to," Chelsea admitted.

"What if Nanna is sick again and needs our help?" Skylar asked.

In Chelsea's panic about her run-in with Travis, the episode with her mother this morning had slipped her mind. Well, that got Chelsea moving and her mind spinning.

"You're right. Let's go inside. But hold Mommy's hand and stay behind me until I say it's okay." Skylar was old enough to unbuckle her car seat strap. Chelsea held the door open so the little girl could climb out.

Every step toward the front door caused Chelsea's heart to pound faster against her rib cage. Tamping down her fears, she squeezed Skylar's hand once they got onto the porch.

Skylar took her mother's advice, hiding behind her leg.

Chelsea couldn't bring herself to put her key in the lock.

"Can I do it, Momma?" Skylar always wanted to be the one to do the honors.

Normally, Chelsea wouldn't have a problem letting her. The place had one of those old-fashioned skeleton keys and she was pretty sure the door, lock and key were original to the house. The place needed some updating once Chelsea got on her feet. For now, it was her own personal piece of paradise. The thought of Travis invading her territory made her downright furious. He'd taken so much already. He didn't get to take this.

Chelsea worked up enough courage to open that door and face whatever was inside.

The sound of a man's laugh from inside the house washed over her. The familiar timbre sent warmth spilling down her back. Nate Kent.

His laughter was quickly followed by her mother's.

Chelsea walked into the hallway. A chill hit her. The heater had better not be out. The weather was turning and January in Texas could bring all kinds of cold snaps.

Her nerves were beyond fried at this point, even

though her rebellious stomach freefell at the sight of Nate standing in her kitchen. Her mother was nowhere in sight but Chelsea could hear the woman's voice and Nate was angled toward the kitchen table. Thoughts of her mother's episode this morning struck hard.

"Is everything okay in here?" Chelsea asked the handsome near stranger. It had been an awful day and she didn't need to make it worse by worrying about her mother. But what if something had happened to her mother?

Nate turned to look at Chelsea, causing a hundred butterflies to release in her stomach.

Under normal circumstances, she'd like to spend time getting to know Nate Kent. But the "normal" ship had sailed years ago for Chelsea. And no matter how wonderful someone seemed at first or how good-looking—and this guy hit it out of the park with his looks—she'd never truly trust another man again. Travis had done a number on her. Part of her realized that by allowing that experience to color the rest of her life, she was letting him win.

"Hey, mister." Skylar darted around Chelsea's leg and ran toward Nate. She'd never seen her little girl be so welcoming to a stranger before and a part of her wondered if the fast friendship had anything to do with the fact that Nate was a man. Was Skylar missing having a male figure in her life?

Chelsea was grateful for her mother's help and presence in her daughter's life. Even while sick and requiring attention herself, the woman had been nothing short of a lifesaver. Linda McGregor had kept Chelsea from the staggering loneliness in those early days of Travis's disappearing. She'd loved Skylar with all her heart from the moment the child had been born. And she'd pitched in to care for the little angel, which had allowed Chelsea to get back on her feet.

Working nights had made it all possible. Chelsea left for work at four. Skylar ate dinner an hour later and was in bed by seven. She'd always been an early riser and Chelsea was pretty certain she didn't sleep for Skylar's first three years of life. Those early years weren't easy, but the Three Musketeers—as her mother had called them—had made it work.

Looking back, she kicked herself for not seeing through Travis sooner. He'd been charming and seemed genuine with his admission of falling for her even though he'd said he didn't think it was possible with his background. He'd told her about a loveless childhood where he'd been bounced around from family member to family member when his mother's "nerves" were shot. He'd said it was code for when she had to go into rehab again.

Chelsea had never met his mother, so she had no reason to doubt his claims. He'd explained that his mother and his family couldn't come to their wedding because his mother had gone off on a bender. Chelsea had fallen for his lies.

After he'd left her and she'd searched for him, she found out that his mother was married to a pastor in a small town outside Little Rock. Chelsea'd been working long hours as her business expanded or maybe she would've been sharper. Lack of sleep didn't always yield the best judgment.

Nate dropped down to his knees so he was almost eye level with Skylar, causing Chelsea's heart to give another inappropriate flip. It was probably his training as a volunteer firefighter that had him so good with kids and not because he had some instant connection to Sky.

Did part of her want Skylar to be able to connect with the handsome stranger?

She could admit that was true. Chelsea hoped her daughter would be able to trust men at some point. She'd always shied away from them and, deep down, Chelsea feared it would always be that way. There was something so totally different about Nate Kent, though. He was special.

With kids, that little voice quickly added.

"What are you doing here?" Skylar asked, fist planted on her hip like she was owed an explanation. Kids were so straightforward.

Chelsea sighed, wishing the same was true for adults.

"Your grandmother called and asked to see me," he answered.

Chelsea's cheeks burned from embarrassment because she suspected her mother was up to no good. "Mom. Is everything okay?"

"Better now." Her mother's cheeky smile told Chelsea everything she needed to know about what was happening.

Chelsea shot Linda a warning look when Nate's gaze dropped to Skylar.

"I was only saying this gentleman was a big help." Her mother gave a not-so-innocent shrug. "Someone threw a rock through the living room window and I was too scared to sit here alone until you got home."

"You should've called me, Mother." Chelsea held back from scolding the woman.

"I didn't want to bother you and this nice man did say this morning that I should call if I needed anything," her mother said.

"I meant it, too. It's not always easy being the new kid in town," Nate noted.

Especially one with an ex who seemed intent on bringing her down.

As she thought about the broken window, a question begged an answer.

Had Travis figured out where she lived?

Chapter Five

Chelsea tried to mask her panic as she shivered against the cold. "Someone threw a rock through the window?" She hadn't noticed any broken glass.

"Yes. At least, I believe it was a rock," her mother supplied. "It just happened."

Chelsea had already started toward the living room.

"I didn't want to upset you and I thought we could have this all fixed up before you got home so you wouldn't worry," her mother said. "It's no big deal."

Those words banged around in Chelsea's head. Sure, it was nothing to worry about if a couple of kids were playing a prank by tossing a rock at a window and running away. Her mother had no idea that Travis had resurfaced. Chelsea couldn't bring herself to mention him in front of Skylar. Instead of dwelling on the fact that a four-year-old had never met her father, Chelsea marched into the living room and scanned the floor for an object hard enough to break glass.

The window that had been broken was on the east side of the house, facing the parking pad. It was the bottom right panel. Chelsea didn't see that when she'd driven up. Dark grey clouds covered the sun even though it wouldn't officially be dark outside for another couple of hours.

The trail from the broken window to the location of the rock was an easy trajectory. Chelsea dropped down to her knees with a little more force than she expected. She started to pick up the rock, struggling against the onslaught of emotion threatening to unravel her tight grip.

"Hold on." Nate's calm, compassionate voice washed over her and through her and all she could think about was that it had been too long since she'd been on a date. Her stomach quivered at his voice and she could only imagine what would happen if he touched her.

Chelsea quashed the inappropriate thought.

"Whoever did this should be prosecuted. I'll call the sheriff." Nate palmed his cell phone as Chelsea stood.

"I'm hungry, Momma," Skylar said.

"I'll take her into the kitchen and fix her something to eat," Linda said, taking Skylar by the hand.

"Thank you. I'll be right in as soon as I figure out how to board this window up before we freeze tonight," Chelsea said.

Nate shot a look of apology and it dawned on her why. She couldn't touch that, either. There might be fingerprints.

"I'll stay right here," Nate said into the phone after providing the details to the sheriff.

Those words kept Chelsea from complete panic. She liked Nate and maybe it was because she needed her faith restored in men. After Travis, and then later her boss, she wasn't thrilled with the opposite sex.

"Thank you for sticking around," she said to Nate. "I promise we're normally pretty boring people."

He looked at her like he was looking through her. "Somehow, I doubt that."

She started to ask what he meant but he cut her off by putting his hand in the air.

"You're a great mother to that little girl. It's easy to see that she's loved and well cared for. If rumors can be trusted, you're about to open a gourmet pizza restaurant in town. You're smart. I take one look at you and can see that you're beautiful. I highly doubt that your life is boring," he said.

Did he just call her beautiful? Chelsea flushed red-hot. She hated that her cheeks always gave her away.

A knock sounded at the door, interrupting her embarrassing moment. Her mother would laugh if she'd heard the silence after Nate's remark.

"I'll be right back," was all she could muster to say as she held up her finger like she was telling him to wait right there.

Chelsea walked out of the room and to the front door. She stood at the closed door and for a split second feared Travis would be standing on the other side. Now that he'd returned, she wondered if she'd always have the feeling he could be on the other side of every unopened door. A chill raced down her back.

She tamped down her unease and opened the door. Thankfully, the sheriff stood on her porch.

"Good evening, ma'am. I'm Zach McWilliams." He stuck out his hand.

Chelsea took the offering and introduced herself. She could feel Nate's presence behind her and that frustrated her. She didn't want to have a visceral reaction to this man or any other.

"Come on in, Sheriff." She stepped aside.

"Thanks for coming, Zach," Nate said. She wondered if everyone in town was on a first-name basis. She liked the thought of neighbors who knew each other. That was a large part of the appeal of moving to a small town. She envisioned people helping each other and not throwing rocks through a window.

Nate and the sheriff resembled each other enough for her to do a double take.

Nate must've caught on to her confusion. "Zach is my cousin."

In her estimation, Nate won the genetic lotto between the two of them. Zach was good-looking, just not in the same manner as Nate. There was something extra special about Nate. She shelved the thought as she led Zach into her living room.

"Rock came through that window over there." She motioned toward the east-facing window.

"You're new here." Zach stated the obvious.

"That's right," she confirmed.

"That's no way to be welcomed to Jacobstown," Zach said. "We're normally a friendlier town than this."

Zach and Nate exchanged glances.

What was that about?

"WE'VE HAD SOME trouble at a couple of ranches." Nate picked up on Chelsea's hesitation.

"Oh, yeah? Like what?" She stopped in the middle of the room and folded her arms. A look of fear passed through her eyes.

Nate picked up on the look and decided to ask more about what caused it later.

"Animals have had hooves butchered," Zach told her.

"Nate mentioned that. Who would do that? Teens?" she asked.

"This is gruesome and cruel. It's happened enough

times and at enough places to put people in town on edge and make them worried there's more to come," Zach said. "It's way over the head of teens."

"Is that why you wanted to call the sheriff over my broken window?" She looked from Zach to Nate.

"Something like this is unusual here. Most folks are friendly and welcome strangers. No one used to lock their doors. Heck, half the town would leave keys in their car while they were parked to run into a store or into the county building. Not anymore. We have a panic mentality going on with a few and others are nervous. They aren't as accepting of new people. We're keeping an eye on anything out of the ordinary that happens. This qualifies," Zach informed.

There was something about this rock business that rubbed Nate the wrong way. Sure, people were on edge and, sometimes, they did something stupid. But folks in Jacobstown didn't pick on strangers. The town had a reputation for going out of its way to make others feel welcome.

Chelsea moving to town had nothing to do with the heifers.

"Are you from Texas?" Zach began the routine-sounding questions that Nate had heard from his cousin during investigations.

"Yes. Houston," she added.

Nate bowed his head and pulled out his cell, pretending he wasn't too interested in her answers.

"What about a spouse?" Zach continued.

"I was married once." Chelsea lowered her voice when she spoke. Nate glanced up and saw that she was staring at the floor. "I'm not anymore."

"Have you been in a fight with anyone or does anyone have a reason to want to harm you?" Zach asked.

A pair of footsteps came from the hallway. The heavy pair, Nate noticed, belonged to Skylar. Nate always marveled at how heavy someone three or four feet tall could walk in comparison to an adult.

Linda had her granddaughter's hand.

"I'll take her upstairs and give her a bath," the older woman said.

"Thank you, Mom." Chelsea looked to Zach as she shivered. "Any chance I can board up that window soon?"

"Yes, ma'am." Zach pulled out his phone and sent a text. "I just let my deputy know to drop what he's doing and come dust so you can cover the window."

Under different circumstances, Nate wouldn't mind offering to keep her warm. The thought was totally inappropriate given the current situation. Besides, he couldn't see himself trusting another woman for a while. He needed a cooling-off period after Mia.

Normally, Nate could spot a liar from a mile away. Mia had put on a convincing show. He was still disappointed in himself for allowing the relationship to go on as long as it had. He'd developed a soft spot lately that he didn't care much for. Mia had toyed with his emotions and used that weakness against him. Between that and the mutilated heifers, Nate had been in a lousy mood.

Little Skylar had changed that this morning. Being around Chelsea and her family was different than what he was used to. But then, Nate didn't normally do overnight stays or meet-the-families. Even more reason to be frustrated with his lapse in judgment when it came to Mia.

Zach's questions were a low murmur in the background. Nate's ears perked up when his cousin asked where Chelsea's ex-husband lived.

Chelsea's gaze shot up from staring at the floor to the staircase.

"I have no idea," she said, her voice low, like she didn't want her daughter to hear. "He disappeared while I was pregnant and I haven't seen or heard from him in four years. And then a few hours ago, he showed up at my restaurant out of the blue. No warning. He just appeared and started making demands."

Zach perked up with this information, too. Nate had a feeling their piqued interest in her response was for very different reasons.

"Did he say what he was doing there after all this time?" Zach's brow knitted together.

"Yes. He said that he wanted me back and wanted to see his child." Her tone sounded incredulous.

Nate couldn't help but look at her. What did he expect to see? For some strange reason, part of him wanted to know if she was still in love with her ex. Based on the tense lines across her forehead, the answer was *no*.

That shouldn't give him pleasure. This was a family, and that should always take precedence over everything else. If there was a way to heal one, Nate would be the last person to stand in the way. There were a few exceptions to that rule. A man who physically or emotionally abused a woman or child didn't deserve to have either.

"Did he say why he left in the first place?" Zach asked after taking down the name she supplied.

Chelsea looked like answering would put her in physical pain.

Zach apologized for the line of questioning before continuing. "I need to assess any threat to you, your daughter, and anyone else in town this person could see as a barrier to getting what he wants."

"He didn't give an excuse as to why he disappeared that day. I was in the hospital giving birth to our daughter while he cleaned out our bank accounts and bankrupted my successful small business. He did say that he wanted a reunion. I made my position clear on that." Her fisted hand on her hip coupled with the stress creases around her eyes made her stance clear to anyone who paid attention to body language.

"My apologies, ma'am. Can you tell me what happened next?" Zach asked.

"I got in my truck, made sure he didn't follow me and then drove to my daughter's school to pick her up. I was late on her first day." She looked to the right and high. She was being honest. Knowing if someone, anyone, was lying to him had taken on a new importance since Mia. He'd been watching for signs of truthfulness every time he listened to someone speak. Honesty meant even more to him.

"Approximately how long did it take to pick up your daughter?" Zach asked.

"Enough time for him to come here and throw a rock through the window," she stated. "He was my first thought."

"Is there anyone else?" Zach asked.

"My former boss threatened me if I quit. He's also sent a few texts since I moved, asking to come visit." She pulled her cell phone out and placed it on her flat hand. "I haven't answered because I'd like to move on from that part of my life."

She was beautiful. It was easy to see why someone would ask her out, but what Nate was hearing sounded like downright harassment. He clenched his back teeth. Give him five minutes alone with those jerks and they'd come out with a new respect for all women.

Zach took down the name and information of the kitchen boss she'd worked for. "What made you decide to move to Jacobstown?"

"This house was a gift," she said. "My great-aunt, Maddie Barstock, owned this house and the downtown property where I'm opening my restaurant. She left them both to me in her will. It seemed like a great way to start over, so we packed up and moved. She also gave me her business downtown."

"You and your great-aunt were close?" Zach asked.

"Strangely enough, we weren't. I mean, I didn't really know her. She and my mother weren't close and my mother's been sick the past few years. I didn't even realize I had a great-aunt on my mom's side."

"She must've remembered you," Zach stated. He looked up at Nate and it was clear the two were thinking the same thing.

"Didn't Ms. Barstock move to assisted living in Austin to be closer to family?" Nate asked.

"It's been a few years, but I remember hearing something like that." Zach pinched the bridge of his nose. It was a habit he'd picked up in the last couple of years when he tried to reach back in his memory. He seemed to pick up on the earlier conversation thread. "It'll be nice to have a new place to eat. That end of the square has been empty too long and I've had to watch out for teenagers there."

"I plan to put the building to good use," Chelsea said, and there was so much pride in those words.

There was something special about Chelsea and Skylar. Nate found himself wanting to help the single mother. With an ex showing up—an ex who was a criminal—and a former boss who seemed hell-bent on keeping tabs on her, she could use an extra set of eyes to keep her safe. Nate would be there as much as she wanted him to be because he'd also picked up on the fact that she wasn't the most trusting when it came to the opposite sex.

A knock interrupted the conversation.

Chelsea gasped and then apologized for her nerves.

Zach and Nate followed her to the foyer just in case her ex had decided to pay a visit, but Deputy Long stood on the porch when she opened the door. She let him in and he went right to work in the living room, wearing his gloves and using fingerprint powder to lift a print from the window.

"I'll check outside." Zach excused himself. Rain threatened and it was dark outside, making it feel much later than it was. Nate and Chelsea stepped out onto the porch.

Chelsea's little girl ran outside. "Momma, I can see my breath."

"Okay, sweetie. Go inside and I'll be right there," Chelsea said.

"Nanna said I had to go with her to her room to play." The little girl frowned.

"That's probably a good idea. Don't you agree?" Chelsea's smile twisted Nate's insides. She was being strong for her daughter and it sounded like she'd been through a lot. From her statement, she'd grown a business that had been bankrupted right under her nose. She'd then gone to work for someone else, who'd also turned out to be a total jerk.

And that brought Nate to another line of thinking.

Her ex was in town. He might be trying to scare her by tossing a rock through the window. Or maybe the chef had taken a ride to Jacobstown and was outside waiting for everyone to leave. He'd ask Zach to check into the whereabouts of the Houston chef tonight. It would be easy enough to call the restaurant where he worked. If the guy had taken the day off, he could've made the drive.

Reality crashed down. This wasn't Nate's case or his business. Once he helped board up her window and arranged for a replacement, his job would be done here.

In fact, it was late, but he was owed a favor by Bill Staller, a local contractor. Boarding up the window would let out too much heat. The house was old, drafty.

Nate excused himself. He walked over to his truck to make the call.

Bill answered on the first ring. "What can I do for you?"

"I need a favor." The truth was that Nate had kept Bill working for several winters. Bill had asked a dozen times to repay Nate in some way. Nate couldn't think of a better repayment than using the favor to help someone else. Of course, Nate would pay for the window. He wouldn't stick Bill with that price tag. Since the whole house needed energy-efficient windows, he'd pay to have that done, too. It was the least he could do for the struggling little family.

Chelsea seemed like the kind of person who had too much pride to admit she might need a helping hand.

Would she reject it?

Chapter Six

The sheriff had finished taking her statement. The window had been professionally fixed. The night had turned into the next day.

"I can't thank you enough for your help." Chelsea meant it, too. Nate Kent had already helped her daughter this morning and now this. It was too much.

"All part of the job," he said like it was nothing.

It meant a lot to her.

"I'm embarrassed to admit that I fell for a class-A jerk." Saying it out loud didn't make her feel any better, either. How many nights had Chelsea lain awake in bed tossing and turning, willing to give her right arm if she could just go to sleep and stop churning over her mistake? Dozens?

She looked over at Nate, expecting a reaction, a smirk, a look of disdain, or for him to look down on her. Instead, she found a sympathetic smile.

"I think we've all been there at least once in our lives," he said.

She gave him a look that said she didn't believe he'd ever fall into a trap like that.

"What? I'm no different than the next guy." He put his hand in air in the surrender position.

"Right." The sound that came out of her mouth was half chortle, half snort.

"What does that mean?" he asked.

Chelsea could tell that she'd insulted him. "I'm sorry. In no way was I trying to offend you. It's just that you're gorgeous and smart—" She shot him an apologetic look. "It's hard to see how you could have any problems."

She regretted the words as soon as they left her mouth. It was too late to reel them in. He was already on his feet, a storm gathering behind his eyes.

"Your mind is made up. In my experience, it would do no good to try to convince you otherwise." He walked into the kitchen and set his coffee cup down on the counter.

It had only taken a hot minute for her to make a mess of things.

"Is apologizing enough to stop you from hating me?" She realized just how shallow those words were, especially since he'd been nothing but kind to her. Stress was starting to show through and she didn't like the person on display. She'd like to blame Travis, but that wasn't fair. She was in charge of her actions. No one forced her to do or to say anything.

Chelsea was developing feelings for Nate that she didn't want. She was tired and her mother's health weighed heavily on her mind.

"I'm an idiot," she said to Nate's back as he started toward the door. "You're helping me and you've been nothing but nice to Skylar and my mother. I have no right to make judgments about your life. Especially since I don't really know anything about your life."

He didn't immediately turn around and that was the first clue at how badly she might've insulted him.

Pushing through her own walls proved more difficult than she expected. She walked over to him and placed a hand on his arm. "Nate, I'm the jerk here. Please don't be offended by what I said. It's not you. It's me."

He turned on that note and backed her up a step. "I think I understand what's going on."

"You do? Mind cluing me in?" she asked.

"You're scared." His hand rested on the counter.

She blinked at him. "Of what?"

"Not of *what...of who.*" He caught her gaze and held on to it.

"I'm not scared of you, Nate. If that's what you're thinking," she stammered. "You've been nothing but helpful."

His smile was devastating. Good-looking was almost an insult to say about a man as gorgeous as Nate. He had that animal magnetism she'd heard about but rarely seen. His piercing steel eyes and carved-from-granite jawline coupled with thick, curly, dark hair made for one seriously hot package. The man worked out. His body was defined in places she didn't even realize there could be muscles.

"If not me, then this." He brought his hand up to her chin and tilted her mouth toward his.

The truth was that she'd thought about kissing him far too often for her own good since she'd met him. It was uncharacteristic for her to have such an immediate and demanding reaction. If she had any sense, she'd push him away and let him walk out the door before things went too far.

But she *wanted* him to touch her, *wanted* to feel his lips moving against hers, *wanted* his hands to roam freely on her body. She tried to convince herself the only reason her body craved his touch was that she hadn't really been touched in too long.

That annoying voice inside her head called her out. *You want Nate.*

Nate was handsome and charming—but not in a polished and premeditated manner—and real. That same annoying voice reminded her there was something unavailable about him, too. Was that part of the attraction?

At this point, Chelsea didn't know or care. Her body hummed with desire for the handsome cowboy. She brought her hands up to his chest. Instead of pushing him away, which would be the smart move, she let her fingertips run along the muscled ridges.

His lips pressed against hers, causing a jolt of electricity to envelop her, pinging through her body and seeking an outlet. When there was none, the vibration hummed, gaining urgency as she gripped his shoulders.

She parted her lips to allow better access and he teased his tongue inside her mouth. Her lips fused with his in a bone-melting kiss. She'd heard about kisses so intense they weakened the knees, but the reality of one was far different, far more intense and pleasurable than anything she'd experienced.

There was so much passion in that one kiss that she melted against his strong, hard body. With her breasts flush against his chest, he released a primal groan. His hands dropped to her waist and he looped them around until they rested on the small of her back.

Her pulse skyrocketed as his large hands splayed across her back.

And this was a runaway train that needed stopping. Yet there was nothing inside Chelsea that wanted to stop kissing Nate. And that was a big problem. Panic gripped her because thinking about the effect of this kiss on her life was the equivalent of a bucket of cold water being poured on her.

She pulled back, forehead to forehead, giving herself enough space to let her ragged breathing stabilize before she stepped away from him.

The sizzle in that kiss had been missing from every kiss in her entire life.

Chelsea was in trouble. She didn't do curl-her-toes kisses anymore. Although, to be fair, this one had melted her bones more than curled her toes.

And there was nothing premeditated about it.

NATE STOOD IN the kitchen a second longer than he should have, locked in eye contact with Chelsea. Kissing her had been an impulse. One he should regret.

In the moment, he'd gone all caveman and ignored logic and better judgment. He hadn't made a mistake like that since he'd reached voting age. Letting his emotions run away with him wasn't something the adult Nate Kent usually did. That glittery look in Chelsea's eyes had him like a moth to a flame.

He tried to tell himself that he'd done it to erase Mia from his thoughts. Normally, bouncing back from a relationship wasn't a problem. It probably had a lot to do with the fact that Nate didn't *do* relationships in the first place. Had he let his guard down with Mia?

Ever since losing his parents and his family changing, Nate had felt off balance.

Time to correct his mistakes.

"Bill has your number. He'll call to make arrangements to replace the rest of the windows," he said to Chelsea.

"I'll get my checkbook," Chelsea said, holding up a finger.

"That's not necessary," Nate said.

"Oh? How's that?" The confused crinkle in her forehead was sexy as hell.

Nate forced his gaze away from it.

"It's covered," was all he said. He didn't want to go into detail as to why he felt the need to personally pay for new windows for the drafty old house. It could use more updates that he was fairly certain Chelsea would insist on covering herself.

"How? I haven't had a chance to set up homeowner's insurance," she stated.

"It's covered. There's nothing to pay." He hoped she'd leave it at that. He didn't know why he'd made the offer, except that when she'd spoken about her ex, he hadn't liked the look of fear in her eyes and he'd wanted to prove that not all men were jerks. "Have you thought about a security system?"

"Here in Jacobstown?" Again, the brows knitted. "I didn't think I'd need one."

"Never hurts to have a little extra security." He didn't want to say that she already had her hands full with a four-year-old and an ill mother. Linda had already told him how hard Chelsea was working to get back on her feet.

Nate wanted to offer a helping hand.

"I'll think about it." She had a lot on her plate financially, he could read it in her eyes. "I meant to mention this morning that the grand opening for the restaurant will be in six weeks if all goes well. You seem to know a lot of people."

Nate grunted and smiled at that one.

"I'd appreciate help spreading word about the opening," she continued.

"Not a problem. Folks in this town will know by morning that there's a new family in town and they'll probably know more about your business than you want them to by week's end." He couldn't help but smile. Living in Jacobstown was like that. Folks looked after each other. "Not a whole lot changes around here. They'll be lining up to experience something new come opening day."

"That's a relief." She blew out a breath.

"I'd best be on my way. Ranch work starts early in the mornings—" he checked the watch on his wrist.

Chelsea gasped. "You have two jobs?"

"Technically, just one, and it's more way of life than occupation," he said. He was glad her earlier tension had subsided some, unless he counted the chemistry pinging between them. That had been on overdrive ever since the kiss.

"What do you do on the ranch?" she asked, leaning her slender hip against the kitchen counter.

Lucky counter. It was easy to talk to Chelsea even though Nate wasn't normally a man of many words.

"Everything," he attested, which was true. He tagged and recorded calf births, rode fences and cleaned stalls, just like everyone else.

"Surely there's a primary responsibility. What's your job title?" she asked.

"Owner."

Chelsea seemed taken back by the admission. For the life of Nate, he couldn't figure out why.

"Is there something wrong with me owning a ranch?" He tried to hide the defensiveness in his voice.

"No. Not really," she said too fast. She'd picked up on his emotion. "It's just you work as a firefighter—"

"Volunteer," he corrected. He understood now. "I don't take a salary for that."

"Oh." The look on her face made her seem even more confused now. Like she couldn't imagine who would run a ranch *and* volunteer.

"This is a small town and we all have to do our part to keep it running. In fairness, I own the ranch with five siblings and we all work the cattle and the land. I volunteer as a firefighter because it gets me off the ranch and I like the distraction.

"Speaking of which, I'd better grab a few hours of shut-eye before my workday starts," he finally said.

Chelsea's face was unreadable. He couldn't tell if she thought he was crazy or noble. And, for some odd reason, it bothered him more than he wanted to admit.

"I can't thank you enough for everything you've done for us." There was a finality in her tone. Like the two would never see each other again.

"Not a problem," he said before leaving.

Inside his truck, he maneuvered around her pickup and out of the drive. On the street, he used the hands-free feature to call Zach.

"What do you think about the McGregor case?" he asked his cousin after perfunctory greetings.

"Wish I knew. I hope it's not someone from town," Zach admitted. "Could be her ex. I'm checking motels as we speak to see if he checked into one nearby."

"Throwing a rock through the window bothers me," Nate said.

"How so?" Zach asked.

"Her ex didn't seem to have a problem confronting

her head-on earlier. Why chicken out now and break a window in order to scare her?" Nate didn't believe the rock thrower was the same person.

"That crossed my mind, too," Zach conceded. "I'm heading over to the Last Bite Diner near the expressway. You want to come talk this through?"

"Yeah, sure. You headed there now?" Nate asked.

"On my way. I need a place to sit down and make a few calls. There won't be anyone else there at this hour," Zach stated.

Nate ended the call and headed west toward the diner. He was too wired to sleep anyway and that kiss kept overtaking his thoughts. He didn't want to remember how sweet Chelsea's rosy lips felt pressed against his. Or how much better coffee tasted on them. He forced his thoughts onto the road and away from the glittery look in her eyes that had sent him down that path in the first place.

The urge to kiss Chelsea had been a physical ache. Nate didn't want to get too inside his head about the pull toward her. She was an intelligent and attractive woman. She had a good head on her shoulders and had created a successful business. Under normal circumstances, she was the kind of woman he'd want to get to know better. Nate almost laughed. Okay, that wasn't entirely true. Under normal circumstances, he'd want a lot of amazing sex with no strings attached. An option that was clearly not possible with Chelsea, considering she had a child and he got the impression the woman didn't do one-night stands.

Another reason that kiss couldn't happen again. Nate didn't have more than one night to offer.

Kissing her had been bad judgment on his part. He wouldn't go down that road again.

Chapter Seven

Ten minutes later, Nate pulled into a parking spot at the diner. He'd been unsuccessful at not thinking about Chelsea's situation. Her ex showing up out of the blue troubled Nate. She said the two had been apart four years, starting from literally the day Skylar was born.

It made Nate all kinds of angry that a man would walk out on his own child. To never lay eyes on that child was another gut punch. If Nate had had a kid, he would be there just like his parents had been for him and his siblings.

Zach pulled into the parking spot next to Nate, jarring him from his thoughts. He turned off the ignition and stepped out of his truck. He rounded it and noted there was a car parked at the side of the building. Nate couldn't help but notice that Zach had seen it, too.

They both seemed to catch on to the fact that the plates were from Louisiana.

They greeted each other before walking into the restaurant.

A lone diner had positioned himself at the breakfast counter. He huddled over his plate, not bothering to look at the men. There was something familiar about him. He was of medium build and height, with light hair from the back. He had the carriage of someone who worked in an office all day rather than outside.

"Who is that?" Zach asked with an arched brow as he took a seat in the corner booth.

Liesel came over with a fresh carafe of coffee and set it on the table. "Howdy, boys. I know why you're awake—" she motioned toward Zach "—but what's got you up in the middle of the night, cowboy?"

The place was small and had its name on top of the roof in big red lights. Inside, there was a row of booths that stretched down the middle of the room, a counter on the right that ran the length of the place and a few tables to the left.

Liesel had worked at the diner since there'd been a diner, so maybe fifteen years. She kept tabs on most goings-on in Jacobstown given that people came through at all hours of the night. Jacobstown didn't have bartenders, it had Liesel. She poured their coffees.

"Thank you," Nate said as he picked up his cup. He took a sip and immediately thought about how much better coffee tasted when he tasted it on Chelsea.

"Why does he seem familiar?" Zach asked Liesel.

"Who? Him?" She glanced at the counter seater, like there was another option.

"Yes. I know him from somewhere," Zach added.

"That's the Barstock widow's boy, Reggie," she muttered. "He hasn't been around here in ages. He never did come visit his momma even when she died. Said he ain't staying, either."

"Oh, yeah?" Zach had the look on his face that Nate recognized.

His cousin stood, his gaze locked onto the lone diner.

"I apologize in advance for leaving you high and dry, Nate. You might be eating alone tonight."

"No problem here. I can always order to go and bring it to your office," Nate offered.

"BLT's the best here. Would you mind ordering me one with the sweet potato fries?" Zach said to Nate even though Liesel was standing right next to them.

"I'll make it two and be there to eat with you in fifteen minutes," Nate said. "But right now I plan to make sure this guy doesn't try any funny business with you."

There was something guilty-looking about the man at the breakfast counter that rubbed Nate the wrong way.

Zach walked toward the lone diner, stopping behind him. "Mind if I sit?"

"The whole place is empty. Can't you find another place to cop a squat?" Reggie didn't look up, didn't make eye contact.

"I'd like to sit here and talk to you. Or we could head down to my office if you'd be more comfortable there." Zach didn't waver.

"I didn't do nothing wrong," Reggie said.

There was something guilty about him. Nate couldn't put his finger on it, but the guy looked like he'd been caught with his hand in the cookie jar.

A picture was emerging. Didn't Chelsea say that she'd inherited the house and business from her great-aunt? A rock had been thrown in her window on her second night in town and Reggie Barstock, whose mother stood him up for the inheritance, makes an appearance?

Nate wanted to follow this through to its conclusion because he would like to be the one to ease Chelsea's fears. The look he'd seen on her face when she'd talked about her ex didn't sit well with him and his thoughts kept drifting to the little family on Sycamore.

"Who said you did?" Zach asked, leaning against the stool next to Reggie. "I thought we could talk. You're the Barstock boy."

Reggie, Nate knew, had been two grades ahead of him. That might as well have been in another town for how much interaction Nate had had with him. Reggie would've been in the same grade as Nate's older brother, Deacon, though. Nate made a mental note to circle back to ask Deacon about Reggie.

Maddie Barstock had been a saint. Her reputation had been golden. Her one and only son had been trouble, best as Nate could recall. The guy had disappeared after high school, which wasn't surprising. Some people felt confined by a small town where everyone knew each other. Especially if that person was up to no good. Word got around quick about who to avoid and who to hang around with.

Reggie looked up from his plate. "I'm not the talkative type."

"Are you sure about that, Reggie?" Zach stated. "Because someone damaged a new resident's property and you are the only person around who has motive, considering your mother used to own the place and you have no other business in town."

Standing, Reggie glared at Zach.

Barstock made a move for his pocket.

"Hands where I can see 'em," Zach took a step back and rested his hand on the butt of his Glock.

Reggie put his hands in the air. "I was trying to pay my bill." His tone sounded bitter.

"Where is your wallet?" Zach drew his weapon and took another step away from Barstock.

The air in the diner thickened with tension.

Nate thought about the fact that his gun was in the truck. He had an open carry permit and kept a pistol in his truck at all times. It was meant to shoot pests on the ranch and was easier than carrying a shotgun, not to mention more accurate.

From where Nate sat, he could see Zach's finger hovering over the trigger mechanism of his department-issued weapon.

"My back pocket." The bitterness was gone from Reggie's voice, replaced by trepidation.

"Lower your right hand and use two fingers to pull it out. Keep your hand visible to me at all times, Reggie. Do you understand?" Zach's commanding tone left no room for argument.

Nate had heard it used before and knew it was reserved for situations like this where Zach was uncertain of someone's motives. Not generally a good sign.

Nate glanced around, thinking he could take cover under the booth. He already knew where all the exits were, the one at the front door being the closest to him. He made eye contact with Liesel, who was frozen on the other side of the counter.

He nodded ever so slightly and she seemed to catch on. If the situation went south…duck.

Reggie did as commanded, pinching his wallet out of his back pocket.

"Keep your left hand in the air where I can see it," Zach demanded.

Now that Reggie had made an aggressive move, Zach

had every right to take him to his office and interrogate him.

Reggie pulled out a twenty and tossed it on the table. He looked at Liesel. "That about cover it?"

"You're square with me," she said, her hands in the air, palms toward him.

"Hands on the counter," Zach said to Reggie in that authoritative-cop voice Nate had heard on the occasional ride-along.

"What did I do?" Reggie barked the question, but seemed to realize that his best move was to do as he was told.

"Keep your feet apart," Zach directed, wanting to ensure Reggie wasn't a threat, which meant a pat-down to make certain the man wasn't carrying a weapon. He moved closer to Reggie, whose legs and hands were now planted wide.

"Look, man, all I'm doing is eating breakfast before I get back on the road," Reggie said.

"That your car in the parking lot?" Zach patted Reggie down as he asked.

"Yeah. So what?" Reggie quipped.

"Where are you headed tonight?" Zach finished the body search and straightened.

"I haven't decided," Reggie said.

"Did you pay anyone a visit while you were here?" Zach asked.

"That's none of your business," Reggie retorted.

"Everything that happens in my town is my business." Zach made sure of it. Especially since the hoof butchering had started and three years later there were still no leads. "You want to answer my question here or in my office?"

Reggie moved around the stool and Nate noticed the man had a slight limp. The hairs on the back of his neck prickled.

Zach had noticed it, too, based on the look he shot Nate.

"Did you do something to your left foot?" Zach's brow arched.

"It's my leg. It's nothing. Gout. I need to put it up." Reggie tried to blow it off, but Zach had zeroed in.

"You sure about that?" Zach asked. "Take five steps." He motioned the opposite direction of where Zach stood.

Reggie limped along a few steps before grabbing onto the counter stool. "That far enough?"

"Yes, sir." Zach didn't have probable cause to arrest Reggie, so the man would have to show up at Zach's office of his own free will. "Did you make up your mind about staying in town tonight?"

"I've decided to keep driving. I was just passing through town and stopped off for a bite. Is there something illegal about that, Sheriff?" Reggie turned around, slowly, careful not to put too much pressure on his leg.

It was impossible to tell if he was favoring his left foot or his leg. It had already been established the person butchering the heifers walked with a limp.

Reggie's mother had left him out of her will. She owned a home and a site downtown that Chelsea was planning to use for a restaurant. Nate needed to ask her about other relatives being mentioned in the will. He hadn't thought to do that before. They'd been so focused on her ex being the one who'd thrown the rock. Could Maddie Barstock's son have done it?

It was a minor crime, at best. The stuff of juvenile delinquents.

"Before you take off, I'd like you to stop by my office to answer a few questions," Zach said.

"And if I don't?" Reggie was pushing his luck.

There were literally hundreds if not thousands of traffic laws in Texas that no one could possibly know about. All Zach needed was one, like anything mechanically to be broken on Reggie's car, for Zach to haul the guy in.

"I noticed you taking up two spots out there. One of which is for handicapped drivers," Zach stated.

"I'm barely on the line," Reggie said defensively.

"But on it," Zach said.

He and Reggie locked gazes and stared each other down for a long minute.

"All I need is one violation to impound your vehicle and hold you in my office. We're going to have a conversation whether you like it or not. So, we can do this the hard way or the easy way. One is going to cost you money. You decide." Zach had laid down the gauntlet. He'd holstered his weapon and let his hand rest on the butt of his gun.

Reggie finally put his head down and said, "Fine."

"You need the address?" Zach asked.

"I already know it." Reggie limped past Zach and toward the front door.

"Good. Then, I'll follow you." Zach walked a couple of steps behind Reggie.

Nate made eye contact with his cousin. "I'll bring food."

Zach thanked him and then followed close behind Reggie before closing the door.

Liesel blew out a breath once the men were outside. Nate didn't dare take his eyes off Reggie. He had a bad feeling about that man, that limp.

Questions swirled like a swarm of bees. Could this man, who lived out of town, have come back to visit his mother's vacant home or business during the times the animals had been butchered?

Other questions popped into Nate's mind, like how well his brother knew Reggie. Was it possible that someone in the Kent family had done something to the man to make him want to exact revenge? If that was the case, why maim animals? They were innocent.

There was Reggie's mother to consider. Had she cut her only son out of her will? It seemed so. There would have to be a story behind that decision. Chelsea would have answers, but she wouldn't be awake for a few more hours.

Thinking about her brought up the memory of the kiss they'd shared.

Nate stuffed that thought down deep where it belonged.

"DID HE START talking on the way over?" Nate asked Zach when he arrived at his cousin's office and set the bag of food on the desk.

"Quiet as a church mouse," Zach stated. "I'm letting him sweat it out in there now."

"He didn't ask for a lawyer?" Nate was curious how this scenario was going to play out. He was also thinking about Chelsea more than he wanted to admit. She'd invaded his thoughts multiple times on the ride over. He'd tried to convince himself that it was purely out of concern for the sweet family, for the fact that they were new in town. Nate had no idea what starting over was like. He'd been fortunate to have a solid foundation at the Kent ranch. He'd always had a roof over his head and plenty of food on the table. Nate never took that for granted. He'd never had to worry about putting a child to bed hungry. He was pretty certain that was at least part of the fear he'd seen in Chelsea's eyes a few hours ago. It had hit him square in the jaw.

Nate opened the bag on Zach's desk and handed him a container. "Can you arrest him?"

"Have no reason to," Zach stated as he took the foam box and opened it. He grabbed a packet of utensils and pulled out a napkin.

"Care to elaborate?" Nate asked, taking a seat in front of Zach's desk.

"There's no doubt in my mind that he's guilty of *something* but I have nothing to hold him on," Zach stated. "There are no witnesses and I have no evidence."

"Did Long lift any prints earlier?" Nate asked.

Zach shot his cousin a look. "You know I'm not technically allowed to discuss the details of the case with you."

"When will you know if there's a match?" Nate asked, figuring that ship had sailed a long time ago.

Zach took a bite of his BLT and then checked his watch. "Couple of hours."

Nate wanted to be the one to tell Chelsea the news. He'd be overstepping his bounds, but he wanted to give her the relief that her ex was most likely not responsible for what had happened. He could only hope it wasn't the case. Based on his estimation, Reggie Barstock was a solid suspect.

"Can I ask you a question?" Zach caught Nate's gaze.

Nate wondered if the question his cousin was about to ask had anything to do with Chelsea. "Go ahead."

"What's got you so interested in this case?" Zach took another bite of his BLT.

"I took the yesterday morning about her kid. Nice family," Nate said by way of explanation.

"Didn't say they weren't." Zach took another bite and chewed. "We have lots of nice families in Jacobstown. Does your interest in this one have anything to do with the beautiful *and single* blonde?"

Chapter Eight

"I wonder if Deacon remembers much about Reggie." Nate set the empty container next to the take-out bag on Zach's desk.

"You didn't answer my question." Zach's eyebrow shot up.

"There's nothing to comment about. I took a call that was a gut punch. You know how that is. A single mom moving to a new place in order to start over. Seems like these ladies have had a rough go lately and I can't help but think how fortunate we are for being grounded here in Jacobstown despite what we've been through with the heifers recently. You know?"

It was more than Nate had planned to say, but he figured Zach wasn't going to stop asking until he got some kind of answer—and that was as good a one Nate could think up. There was more of a pull to Chelsea than he wanted to acknowledge or to admit to, which was most likely why he'd left specifics about her out of his explanation.

Granted, it was none of Zach's business where Nate spent his time, but the two had always enjoyed a close relationship and Nate had no reason to lie. Everything he'd said was true.

"Yeah, I know what you mean." Zach seemed willing to leave it at that. "I agree about asking your brother about Reggie. I saw that you picked up on his left foot giving him trouble."

"Might be nothing. Hell, ever since those incidences began, I've been on the lookout for anyone who favored his or her left foot after footprints confirmed a limp on that side," Nate admitted.

"Same here. We'd be stupid not to pay extra attention to anyone with a deformity or injury to the left side," Zach confirmed. "I've had my deputies scour through every document they could find for an injury that might be related. We tracked down a few names. I was especially looking for anyone who'd triggered an animal trap."

"You know we don't use those on our land," Nate said.

"No, but illegal hunters do."

Zach was stating a simple truth. As much as everyone on Kent Ranch worked to keep illegal hunters off the property, they couldn't keep all the criminals from getting close. Poaching was a lucrative industry. There would always be illegal hunters. Kids could be setting traps as some sort of cruel joke.

Nate nodded agreement. "What's the next move?"

"Dig into Reggie's background. If he has alibis for the dates in question, he's in the clear." Zach leaned back in his chair.

"I have a bad feeling about this guy. I just don't know how deep it goes yet," Nate admitted.

"Same here. He's up to no good. What do you know about the Barstock widow?" Zach opened a file on his computer.

"I know about as much as everyone else in town does. She kept to herself in her last years here in Jacobstown.

I think the Rotary Club used to check on her and there are a couple of widows in town who put meals together for anyone who's sick or can't get out. I know that she moved away a couple of years ago. I'd forgotten she had a son, to be honest." Nate wasn't aware of any other next of kin and he certainly would've remembered Chelsea if she'd been in town before.

"The only good news is that this is the first possible lead we've had in the Jacobstown Hacker case." Nate hoped for resolution before the guy became bolder and moved on to humans like everyone had feared recently when a man in Fort Worth killed joggers by hacking off their foot and leaving them to bleed out. He'd been careless and had butchered the wrong foot. But copycats could multiply and no one would rest easy until the twisted jerk maiming animals was behind bars.

"I need to dig deeper into her background, too." Nate knew Zach was referring to Chelsea McGregor. "A stranger shows up in town and brings trouble."

"Her ex is here." Nate ignored Zach's look and kept right on talking. "He's worth investigating, if not for the rock then for the trouble it sounds like he might bring."

Zach was already rocking his head.

"I already have that in motion, too." He glanced at the notepad on his desk.

His cousin looked tired from the inside out. He'd been busy between the heifers' hooves being butchered and other crimes that had found their way to Jacobstown in recent weeks. Several of which had involved his brothers and their wives. Zach cared about every citizen in his jurisdiction. His family was no exception. The McWilliamses and Kents were a close-knit bunch.

"How's Amy, by the way?" Nate asked, referring to Zach's sister.

"She seems a little lost after graduating." Zach's shoulders slumped.

"Amber's been busy at the ranch," Nate said.

"Those two used to be joined at the hip and now Amy seems restless." Zach smiled but it didn't reach his eyes, his worry evidenced by the near constant lines bracketing his mouth. "She's trying to figure out her next move. I told her she should move to a bigger city, like Austin or San Antonio. She said she didn't want to leave Amber."

"They were the only two girls in a family of boys. Makes for a tight bond. You think there could be something else going on with her?"

"Good question," Nate said.

"Hey, at least our sisters can hold their own in pretty much any situation." Zach laughed and the break in tension was a nice change.

Everyone at home, including Nate, had been on edge. It had started with their father's death and then the situation with the heifers had made it impossible to relax. There'd been more danger in town in the past couple of years than in Jacobstown's entire history. Good stuff had happened, too. It was all too easy to forget the good in times of strife. There'd also been marriages and babies. Several of Nate's siblings had found true happiness.

With Zach's recent reunion with a former girlfriend, Jillian Major, it was down to Nate and Jordon, the youngest brother, as the only bachelors left in the family.

"We haven't announced anything yet…" Zach glanced down at his phone. The wallpaper was a picture of Jillian touching her stomach.

"Are you telling me…?" Nate couldn't believe his ears. Stunned didn't begin to describe his feelings.

"We're having a baby." The love in Zach's eyes convinced Nate becoming a father was the logical next step for his cousin.

"It feels like you two just got back together."

Zach nodded and smiled. "I guess when you know, you know."

Nate had never experienced such a lightning bolt, but he'd heard tell of it from some of his siblings. They'd explained it was like a jolt out of nowhere and a sense of knowing they were in deep.

That annoying voice in the back of his head said he'd been hit with something when he'd met Chelsea, but that was ridiculous. He didn't even know her. Jillian and Zach had grown up across the street from each other. They had history.

Then again, that explanation didn't exactly hold water because a couple of his brothers had met and fallen for the loves of their lives without knowing each other before.

"Congratulations, man. I couldn't be happier for you and Jillian." Nate gave his cousin another hug then stepped back.

"Where are you headed?" Zach asked when Nate didn't return to his chair.

"Grab a few hours of shut-eye before work starts. Keep me posted on Reggie, will you?"

Zach nodded. "Keep the part about the baby between you and me for now. She wants to surprise everyone by inviting them to a barbecue. She doesn't want a lot of formality. Just family and a few close friends out at the lake house we're building." Zach's face softened some of the hard worry lines when he spoke about his fiancée.

"You can count on me," Nate said.

Besides, Zach wasn't the only one with a secret.

CHELSEA FIGURED THE Dumpster behind the restaurant would be full by the end of the day. She needed about five more of them to properly clean this place out.

Work was good and she enjoyed the feeling of progress on her new restaurant. She'd also been careful to lock the door behind her so there were no surprises this time. The contractor who could knock out the walls where glass would be installed was due tomorrow bright and early.

She blew on her cold fingers to warm them. It must've been hovering around freezing outside and she refused to turn on the thermostat until she got closer to opening day. It was imperative to keep expenses down so she could have a successful grand opening. Starting out in a financial hole was not the way to kick off a business.

Soon enough, the place would be ready and the doors would open. Money would flow, or at least she hoped it would. Excitement came in the form of tingly sensations in her stomach. She was so ready for life to take a positive turn and for her to get back on track after being shoved off on the first go-round. She'd never expected a second chance and had no plans to waste the gift she'd been given.

Travis had been a temporary setback. She wouldn't allow him to rattle her the same way he had yesterday. For one, the element of surprise was no longer on his side. She'd let her guard down temporarily. No more. She would be ready if he popped up again. And she planned to buy pepper spray in case he brought a bad attitude with him when he showed.

During the multiple trips she'd taken to the Dumpster

in the last few minutes, she'd checked both ways before exiting the building, like a young kid crossing the street for the first time. Luckily, there'd been no signs of Travis.

Chelsea locked the back door and walked into what would become her finished kitchen. A knock sounded at the front door. Her heart skipped a beat. The metal door hid the figure on the other side.

She considered not opening it.

Skylar was at school. Her mother was probably at the grocery store by now. Chelsea wasn't expecting a delivery. But then experience had taught her that didn't mean there wasn't one waiting on the other side of that door.

Taking in a sharp breath, Chelsea marched toward the door. The metal needed to go. She'd make a note to replace it with glass ASAP.

Another knock sounded, stopping her in her tracks.

"Chelsea." The familiar voice brought a wave of calmness over her. Nate Kent.

She couldn't get to the door fast enough.

"Come on in." She held it open.

"Sorry to interrupt." He glanced around as he stepped inside.

She closed and locked the door behind him.

"It's taking shape in here," Nate said.

"I still have a lot to do and not much time, but everything's on schedule so far." She couldn't afford to give up a day if she wanted to stick to her timetable.

Chelsea took an emotional hit seeing Nate again. She'd thought about the kiss they'd shared far too often for her own good last night.

Seriously, it was just a kiss. There was no need to get all weak-kneed just thinking about how impossibly soft his lips were for a face of such hard angles or how much better coffee tasted on them.

"There's coffee over there if you'd like a cup." She forced her gaze away from his mouth.

"You already have water?" he asked.

"I brought some with me." Nate looked just as good as he did last night. In fact, he looked almost exactly the same as he did last night.

"I don't mind a cup." He glanced around.

She pointed to the corner next to the new fire-brick oven where she'd set up a small folding table and put coffee supplies on it.

"Water won't be turned on for three more weeks. I bring in a jug to make coffee." She had a couple of foam cups, too.

Nate poured a cup and took a sip. "It's good."

"It's the blend I plan to serve." His approval sent a burst of pride rushing through her.

"I met up with Zach last night to grab a bite after we left your place. Ran into someone unexpected. Are you aware that Mrs. Barstock's son is in town?" he asked.

"Um, no. Wow. I thought he'd moved out west somewhere. He wasn't invited to the reading of her will, so I guess I figured he didn't come around anymore." Chelsea was shocked to hear the news.

"He's driving a car with Louisiana plates," Nate mentioned.

"There's another surprise." She could've sworn the attorney had said Reggie had disappeared out west. "He doesn't have a right to the property or business. My great-aunt was clear about that and her lawyer assured me that I was the sole inheritor. Her will is iron-clad."

"How well did you know your great-aunt?"

"I didn't. This whole inheritance came out of the blue for me." She motioned to the fold-up chairs tucked underneath the table with the coffee. She needed to sit after hearing this news. The ground had shifted just a little. "According to her lawyer, Aunt Maddie had me tracked down after she fell and broke her hip. She knew her son would throw her money away and she wanted it to go to someone who would know what to do with it. She hit a bull's-eye there."

"Looks like she made the best choice."

Nate's compliment made her smile. "Thank you." She looked Nate in the eyes. "What did he want?"

"He didn't say. Tried to convince us that he was just driving through town in the middle of the night on his way home."

And then it dawned on her.

"The rock in my window. You think Reggie was trying to scare me?" She smacked her flat palm on the table.

"Or make a threat. Zach is trying to get more information out of him while he finds out if there's a clear print from the scene." Nate took another sip of coffee. A little liquid spot remained on his bottom lip.

Chelsea was transfixed by it.

"When will he know for sure?" This sure changed things. Her initial reaction last night was that Travis had to have been involved with the rock throwing. Was it even possible he'd made his presence known then disappeared when he hadn't gotten what he'd wanted? Part of her hoped so. She never wanted to have to deal with him again for the rest of her life, and she had been clear about that.

If he came back and had a job and could show that he was responsible and ready to be a father, she'd consider allowing him to be part of Skylar's life. Anything less than that and Travis was just blowing hot air by talking to Chelsea. She wouldn't allow him around her daughter without a court order.

"Did Reggie seem upset?" she asked.

"You could say that. Have you ever met him?" Nate asked.

"No. I don't remember meeting my great-aunt, either, but my mother says I did when I was a kid." Chelsea ran her finger along the rim of her cup. "Her lawyer said she asked him to track me down. He apparently hired a PI to gain information about me. I guess Aunt Maddie was satisfied with what she saw. I did used to own and run a successful small business. Maybe that's why she thought I'd know what to do with her home and space.

"She must've also learned that the business's failure wasn't exactly my fault. I didn't mismanage the money. The business folding didn't have anything to do with me." Except, that part wasn't exactly truthful. Her business had failed because she'd trusted someone she shouldn't have. That part was very much on her.

"You must've made quite an impression." Nate focused on her finger rimming her cup and it sent a sensual shiver up his arm.

Chelsea's cell buzzed. Her heart skipped a beat as she jumped up and stalked toward the sound. She tracked it to where she'd left it on top of what would be a cabinet once it was hung.

"Hi, Mom," she answered with a glance toward Nate.

"Someone's in the house," her mother said.

Chapter Nine

"What do you mean? Like, *now*?" Chelsea's voice raised an octave as a look of panic washed over her.

Nate got to his feet and was by her side. She tilted the phone, giving him access so they could both listen.

"The back door stood wide open when I got here and I heard a noise upstairs, so I got out of there," Linda said.

"Thank heavens you're not still inside. Where are you now?" Chelsea asked.

"I'm in my car. I turned right around and walked out the door, got in my car and locked the doors." Linda sounded like a schoolkid who'd just shown her prize drawing to the class. "I figured this was the best place for me to call you."

"Stay where you are. I'm on my way," Chelsea said. "And don't hang up."

"I'll drive." Nate was already guiding Chelsea to the metal door leading outside, his hand at the curve of her back. It felt a little too natural for it to be there, a little too right. This close, he could smell her unique scent, a mix of wildflowers and dark roast coffee. It was fast becoming his favorite combination.

His truck was parked out front next to her pickup. He paused long enough for her to lock the door to her restaurant.

Chelsea rushed to the passenger side of his truck while he made a beeline for the driver's side. Normally, he'd open the door for her, but that courtesy would waste time and Linda had sounded scared.

The ride to her place on Sycamore took eight minutes, a record for cutting across town.

"We're almost home, Mom. Hold on a few more minutes for me, okay?" Chelsea shot a worried look at Nate.

On instinct, he reached out and touched her hand to comfort her. Those annoying jolts of electricity didn't seem to know when to let up because a few blasted his hand and vibrated up his arm.

Nate withdrew his hand and returned it to the steering wheel where his grip remained white-knuckled for the rest of the block. He pulled up next to Linda's parked sedan, essentially blocking her from the house. If someone charged out the front door, they'd have to get through Nate first.

"Call Zach," he said to Chelsea as he grabbed his pistol from underneath the bench seat. "Get your mother in my truck and lock the doors. Anything happens, I want the two of you to get out of here."

Chelsea started to argue but he was already dashing around the back of the house and out of earshot. He hoped she would be smart enough to listen even though he got the feeling she wasn't used to stepping aside and letting someone else take charge.

In this case, she'd be crazy to follow him, and she didn't strike him as someone who would take an unnecessary risk.

Nate slowed at the kitchen door, his pistol pointed in the direction he walked. He had the butt of it secured in his grip and his finger hovered over the trigger. A bullet waited in the chamber.

There were two known possibilities. Reggie had most likely been released by now. Zach hadn't had a reason to keep the man locked up. He could've decided to take matters into his own hands. He'd grown up in this house and something of his might still be here. It was possible that he'd returned to take it back. Or, he wanted Chelsea out.

The other known quantity was her ex. He could be looking for their daughter, trying to catch Chelsea unaware. That possibility sat a little sour in Nate's gut. It wasn't his place to interfere with a family, but there was no way he'd stand aside and allow a man to intimidate his ex.

A burst of anger shot through him that he had no business allowing. Rational thought took over. Nate reasoned that Skylar's father wouldn't likely break in while no one was home. What would he have to gain?

Nate crossed the kitchen, careful not to step too hard on the wood floors. An ill-timed creak could end this day very badly.

The kitchen was eat-in. He made his way around the table with four chairs. A vase of fresh flowers on the kitchen table brightened up the place. Nate had a feeling that Chelsea could make any space feel like home in a matter of minutes. There was something warm about her that made him want to talk to her and tell her all his secrets. The feeling was foreign as hell. Nate wasn't a chatterbox. And he didn't *do* talking, much less about emotions. He'd never been this much inside his own head in his life.

He made his way through the door separating the kitchen from the living room. There was a guest room off the living room. He'd noticed the layout yesterday morning. It was habit to memorize a house's layout in case he ever had to come back for an emergency.

The door had been open and the bed pushed to one side. There were boxes stacked in that room in random order, too.

A siren wailed in the distance. Backup was on its way. Nate blew out a sigh of relief. He continued through the downstairs before checking the closet underneath the stairwell with the crawl space. He was familiar with that area, too, of course. The minute he opened the door, a cold gust of wind blasted him. Damn.

The sirens stopped right outside. Within a few seconds, a voice sounded from the kitchen. "I'm coming in."

It was Zach.

"I'm in the downstairs hallway," Nate shouted. Zach had taught his cousin the protocol for hot situations long ago. Combine Zach's advice with Nate's volunteer firefighter training and he'd been told that he was handy to have around in an emergency.

A few seconds later, Zach was beside him.

"The bedroom hasn't been cleared and neither has the upstairs. The crawl space that I boarded up has been busted through," Nate informed his cousin.

"Okay. Good work. Are you ready to clear the rest of the house?" Zach would want to ensure no one was hiding in one of those rooms.

"Let's do it." Nate wouldn't be able to sleep without knowing the place was clear.

Side by side, they cleared each room. Nate checked the attic, just to make sure no one was hiding there. There were no basements in Texas to worry about, so once they cleared the upstairs, it was safe.

Nate followed his cousin outside to deliver the news to Chelsea and her mother. He let Zach take the lead.

"The place is clear. My deputy is on the way to see if he can lift prints off the door and the closet with the crawl space," Zach said.

Chelsea's gaze bounced from Zach to Nate. The terrified look in her eyes was a gut punch.

Zach briefed her as the same deputy from last night showed up.

"I'm sorry we didn't get a print yesterday. Maybe we'll get lucky this time," Deputy Long said before rounding the corner and getting to work.

"When he's finished, I'd like you to take a walk through the residence to see if anything's missing," Zach said to Chelsea.

"Half of our stuff is still in boxes." Chelsea sounded exacerbated. "How would I know?"

HAVING A SAFE home was important. Having the restaurant open on time was important. Having her sanity was important.

Chelsea saw her schedule blowing up before her eyes. It was shaping up to be a long day, and she couldn't afford to lose a day of progress at the restaurant.

The deputy finished his work quickly and a locksmith put a dead bolt on the back door as well as a new one on the front. It didn't hurt to ensure that Chelsea and her mother were the only key holders.

By lunch, Chelsea hadn't made it back to the restaurant. Nate had the closet patched up again in no time. Chelsea paid the locksmith from money she needed for the restaurant. She'd set the funds aside to buy tile floors. She'd have to go with painted concrete instead, a minor adjustment, but she was proud of herself for coming up with a contingency plan.

Reggie Barstock might be long gone. Zach had said the man had been released before the sun came up this morning. Chelsea guessed he could be responsible for the break-in. According to the sheriff, the lock had been jimmied. Chelsea had no idea what that entailed, except that it meant her new home had been easy to breach.

To Chelsea's thinking, Travis was up to something. Maybe he'd broken in to get information about her or his child. When it came to Travis, she knew to be suspicious. There'd been no sign of him, but that didn't mean he was gone. And how would he know where she lived? She guessed he could've asked someone. People would knew each other's business in a tight-knit community like Jacobstown.

Zach had promised to keep an eye out for her ex.

Wishing there'd be prints this time might be overly optimistic. The same person who threw the rock could be the one they were looking for now.

Chelsea was grateful that Skylar wasn't home to witness the break-in. She would never feel safe in the house. Anger pierced Chelsea. She *could* provide a safe home for her daughter, dammit. No one got to take that away from her.

By the time Chelsea got her mother settled and herself back to the restaurant, she only got in a half days' worth of work. She reminded herself that it was better than nothing. Surprisingly, Linda hadn't called more than twice and both times were in the first hour. Chelsea had texted her mother and was satisfied with the response she'd received stating that she was doing better knowing the place was locked.

Before she realized, it was time to pick up Skylar.

Chelsea was careful to make sure no one was parked out front near her pickup. She locked the metal door while checking side to side. No one would sneak up on her again, either. Her heart gave a little squeeze, reminding her that she missed Nate. A piece of her had hoped that he would stop by this afternoon.

Getting into her pickup, she locked the door behind her. She started the ignition and maneuvered onto the road leading to Skylar's school.

It was all good. Nate had a life on the ranch that he had to get back to. Shock didn't begin to describe her reaction to him owning the place. She was still trying to get over the fact. Using her phone, she'd looked him up last night and discovered that his family was one of the wealthiest ranching families in Texas. It struck her as odd that he was so well off.

Nate Kent was *one of* if not *the* most down-to-earth person she'd ever met. He'd mentioned that his parents were gone. She couldn't help but wish she'd been able to meet them. They'd done an excellent job with their children if the others were as grounded as him. Based on the couple of headlines she'd read, they were. They'd also been through a lot in the past few years and seemed to be stronger for it. With parenting skills like that, Chelsea wished she could ask questions.

Chelsea loved her own mother. Linda McGregor had been through the ringer and back. Her health was ailing. Chelsea couldn't help but feel responsible for her mother. Looking back, she couldn't remember a time when she hadn't felt like she needed to take care of the woman.

It was most likely the reason she felt so strongly about

making sure Skylar had as carefree a childhood as Chelsea could give her.

In the adult relationship department, Chelsea had touched that stove. It was hot. She'd got burned. And she was smart enough not to make the same mistake twice. At least she hoped she'd learned from her errors in judgment. The best way to take a hot pan off a stove was to wear an oven mitt.

Thankfully, Chelsea was the second parent at pickup. Skylar had noticed. The joy in her eyes made the day Chelsea had had sting a lot less. There was something magical about looking into her daughter's innocent eyes.

On the way home, they sang the song Skylar had learned at school. What was it about singing with her daughter that seemed to make the world's troubles wash away?

"Hey, Momma, look," Skylar said as they pulled up at home. Her daughter's voice had that excited pitch usually reserved for a first peek at an unwrapped birthday present.

Chelsea saw Nate's truck parked on the pad. Her first instinct was to panic. Her second was to check her phone, which she did the second she pulled up to the four-way stop sign. There were no stressful-sounding texts or missed phone calls from her mother.

Nate had boarded up the crawl space even better the second time.

"What's the fireman doing here?" Skylar asked.

Another rogue wave of panic washed over Chelsea. Was her mother okay? Had something else happened? Chelsea scanned the windows and saw that everything was intact.

"Let's go see for ourselves," Chelsea said to her daughter. The little flip her stomach gave at the thought of seeing him again belied her calm façade.

She took her daughter by the hand and walked to the porch. The door swung open before Chelsea could reach for the knob.

Nate standing there in her house looked a little too right.

"How's my mother?" Chelsea immediately asked, ignoring the flip-flop routine going on in her stomach.

Nate stepped outside and closed the door behind him. "I need to talk to you about something important."

He must've seen the look of fright in her eyes because he quickly added, "Linda's doing great. It's not about her."

"Hey, Mr. Fireman." Skylar beamed up at him so hard her little body vibrated with joy.

"Hello, Ms. Skylar." He smiled back at her and Chelsea's heart melted a little bit more. She couldn't afford to let her emotions run wild when it came to the handsome Mr. Kent. She needed to get a grip. Past experience had taught her that she couldn't exactly trust her judgment when it came to men. They didn't stick around and she had no time for heartbreak.

"What do you need to discuss?" Chelsea shored up her strength, ignoring the goose bumps on her arms.

Skylar let loose of her mother's hand and grabbed Nate's. He smiled down at her but tension lines bracketed his mouth.

He motioned toward the tire swing in the yard. Chelsea caught on. He wanted to talk in private and they could use the swing as a distraction for Skylar. Again, the man was good with children, but she wouldn't let that fact cloud her judgment.

"Hey, sweetie. Want me to push you on the swing?" Chelsea bent down to eye level with her daughter.

Skylar's answer came in the form of her squealing before making a run for it.

"Be careful," Chelsea shouted to the back of the little girl's bouncy ringlets.

She and Nate took their time walking toward the side yard. Her body pinged with electric current with him this close, but she was determined to ignore it.

"I brought a friend over to meet you guys and I'd like him to stick around for a few days until all this…*stuff*… blows over." She got the feeling he'd wanted to use a different word but had thought better of it considering Skylar was within earshot.

"Okay. What are we talking about here?" The image of a burly, unshaved nightclub bouncer struck her.

"He's big—"

"Do you really think it's necessary? Skylar might not be comfortable with a strange man in the house," she quickly said.

"Rofert isn't a man. He's a dog." He put his hand up to stop her from interrupting. "He's a stray who found his way to our ranch last year. He's a Newfoundland who showed up dehydrated and hungry, but we nursed him back to health. He loves children and I've never seen a more protective dog over the animals in the barn. He took on a coyote and came out on top when it tried to eat our barn cat."

"He sounds like a wonderful animal and I'm grateful for the thought," she hedged. "I'm not sure it's such a good idea for him to stay here. What if Skylar gets attached, and she will."

"She can always come visit him at the ranch. We can set it up that you're babysitting him for me while I work. It's not a lie." He'd thought of everything and she appreciated him for it.

But if the animal was as large as he said, affording food might be a problem.

"We can get by without him for a few days until everything calms down here. I don't want you to feel pressured to take him and that's why I wanted to talk to you first before Skylar met him. I promised her that I'd bring over a pony and he's the closest thing I've got that'll fit in my truck. If you don't want him here, then he'll come home with me tonight."

Nate's pleading look made her almost instantly cave.

She didn't have the money for a security system. A dog the size of a pony seemed like a good compromise.

"I'd rest easier knowing the three of you are safe," he stated. "And he's well behaved. He won't chew up your furniture or make a mess on the rug. Besides, Linda's home alone all day and she could use the company as well as the protection. He's great with kids. Heaven knows we have plenty now at the family ranch."

Those were all valid points.

Maybe if Chelsea shopped around, she could squeeze dog food into the budget for a few days. Skylar would love having Rofert around and it might help her acclimate to the new house if she had a buddy.

Plus, knowing her mother was safe would go a long way toward giving Chelsea the time she needed to focus on her restaurant. "What kind of food does he eat?"

"He's on a special diet. Don't worry about food. I'll supply it."

A loaner dog that came with its own food?

There was no way Chelsea could pass that up.

"I only came up with the idea because you mentioned getting a puppy at some point. I figured you weren't averse to dogs. What do you think?" The look of apprehension on the big, strong cowboy's face was adorable. It was clear that he wasn't trying to overstep his bounds.

"You might have a hard time prying my daughter off your dog when it's time for him to go home." Chelsea appreciated the way Nate had handled this situation. It could've been a potential powder keg if the conversation had gone down in front of Sky or she thought the dog was a present.

The wide smile on Nate's face caused a burst of pride to fill her chest. She reminded herself that pride could be dangerous.

"She'd be welcome to come see him anytime. Plus, he might get comfortable here and not want to leave if it's agreeable to you," Nate remarked. The smile on his face was a little too sexy.

Chelsea had never heard of a Newfoundland before. She'd never had a dog before. She and her mother had had to live off the good graces of relatives for most of Chelsea's young life, and the best Chelsea ever got for a pet was feral kittens the time she lived in the country. They'd lived underneath the trailer of one of her relatives. She'd sneaked cans of tuna outside to lure them close to her where she'd pet them and pretend they were hers. She'd daydream about living in house of her own one day and having a house full of pets. That dream came before the reality of vet bills and food costs that she'd seen living with relatives and their pets.

"How do you want to break the news to the little nugget?" Nate asked, motioning toward Skylar.

"Let's take her inside and see how she reacts," Chelsea said.

Chapter Ten

Chelsea opened the door and stepped aside, allowing Skylar an opportunity to see Rofert. "This is Mr. Kent's dog and he wants us to babysit while he works long hours for the next week or two. What do you think, Sky?"

The little girl took one step inside the house, locked eyes on the massive canine loping toward her from the kitchen and squealed. That kid's scream rivaled any tight-budget horror movie noise.

"What's his name?" Skylar jump-clapped, hopped and took off toward the large animal. Rofert had a thick brown coat, the color of coffee. His large head held noble brown eyes and soft floppy ears.

"Rofert," Nate advised.

"Can I pet him?" Skylar remembered her manners at the last second, right before she launched herself at the dog's neck.

For a second, Chelsea prayed that the animal was as forgiving as Nate had said and wouldn't be spooked by the overzealous four-year-old. But the large animal tilted his head down and let Skylar hug him. His tail wagged along with half of his backside and she figured that had to be a good sign.

"Like I already said, he loves kids," Nate said. "She'll be fine."

Chelsea's mother appeared from the kitchen.

"I doubt anyone wants to stop what they're doing long enough to eat, but supper's ready." Her mother motioned at Skylar, who was giggling and hugging the neck of the dog.

"You weren't kidding. He really is the size of a pony," Chelsea said to Nate.

"Just wait until you get to clean up outside after he eats." Nate's humor was a welcome change from the tension Chelsea had been feeling. But that dog weighed more than she did and she didn't even want to think about the shovel she'd need to use to clean up after him. Nate was right, though. Having a dog around would give her the feeling of much-needed extra security. She'd sleep better at night knowing they had extra protection. And the way he took to Skylar, he'd most likely sleep in her room.

This house had four bedrooms. There was one downstairs, which Chelsea planned to convert into a home office. There was no need for a guest bedroom, considering the only living relative she knew about was Reggie, aside from her mother who had a bedroom upstairs. She wasn't likely to invite him to stay overnight, so there wasn't much need to keep it like it was.

The room had been the dustiest one in the house. Chelsea figured Aunt Maddie hadn't had many people over. Chelsea couldn't help but wonder why she'd been selected by her great-aunt. The lawyer had stated that Reggie had turned out to be a disappointment and he and his mother hadn't kept in touch. Reggie might be a disappointment, but was he a danger?

Chelsea forced her thoughts to something more productive. "Thanks for the loan, Nate. I'm pretty sure you just made Skylar's week. You've done too much for us already."

His face cracked into a broad smile.

"It's common for people to help each other in these parts," Nate said, like it was nothing. "Guess it comes from being ranchers and farmers. We've always had to band together to survive. It's in our DNA."

"We could use more of that in the world," she said. "Speaking of food… Would you like to stay for supper?"

"I'm afraid not. Sorry. I have plans," was all he said.

"Oh. Right. I don't want to keep you." Chelsea ushered him to the door, embarrassed. Of course a man like Nate Kent would have a date, maybe a girlfriend. No, she reasoned, he seemed too honest to kiss her if he was in a relationship with someone else.

She stopped before opening the door and turned around. "Skylar, tell Mr. Kent 'thank you' for thinking of us to take care of Rofert."

Before he could tell her it was no big deal, Skylar was there, wrapping her arms around his legs in her biggest hug.

"When I grow up, I want to be a fireman just like you," Skylar stated. It was her most heartfelt compliment.

"I think Rofert would like that," Nate said, patting her on the back. Chelsea took note of how much he tensed.

It was probably just his training that made him so good with kids and not that he believed her daughter was exceptional or there was a special connection between the two of them. Chelsea's heart squeezed anyway. Seeing a man who was so good with little ones was such a nice change of pace.

"We'll take good care of *your* dog," Chelsea said to Nate.

Skylar unpeeled herself from the man's legs, spun around and charged toward Rofert. He barked and the sound was so loud it nearly shook the walls.

"He'll do that if anyone tries to come in night or day," Nate reassured Chelsea.

"A person would have to be crazy to break into a house with a noise like that coming at them," she said.

Nate's smile sent another jolt of electricity shooting through her. It was probably for the best that he couldn't stay for dinner. She didn't need the distraction or the eventual heartache.

When he left and she closed the door behind him, a little sense of disappointment rolled through her, causing her shoulders to sag. She tried to convince herself that it was the stress of the last couple of days.

Deep down, she knew it for the lie it was. Even so, if she fell for the first guy who was nice and gave her daughter a little positive attention, she might as well pack up and go home. Only, she remembered that she had no home to go to. Jacobstown was home. Maybe it would feel more like it when the boxes were unpacked.

Chelsea joined her mother in the kitchen. "Smells great in here."

"I cooked your favorite. Crispy beef tacos," Linda said. "Figured we should celebrate our new beginning."

"Thank you, Mom." The woman always had the sweetest of intentions. She'd done the best she could bringing up Chelsea alone. Her mother deserved better than what Chelsea had been able to give in the past few years. She wanted to do better by her mother. "I'll get Skylar."

The three of them ate at the kitchen table, chatting

about their days. Rofert positioned himself on the floor next to Skylar.

After dinner, the nighttime routine of cleaning dishes, giving Skylar a bath and reading a bedtime story kept Chelsea busy. Rofert stayed by Skylar's side, which posed a problem in the small bathroom. Chelsea had made it work. She was grateful for such a loyal companion and she'd never seen a bigger smile plastered on Skylar's face. Giving him back was going to be difficult, but Chelsea promised herself that she'd figure out a way to get Skylar a puppy as soon as she could.

Rofert loped into Skylar's bedroom at lights-out. The house was perfect with three bedrooms upstairs along with a small landing. The master bedroom was at the top of the stairs and Skylar's room was next door. Some people might not prefer to have their children so close. It was an absolute necessity for Chelsea.

The rooms were small but cozy and the entire upstairs shared a bathroom. And it was perfect.

Rofert slept with his head half in the hallway. The big, hairy dog comforted Chelsea and she was even more grateful for Nate's thoughtfulness.

Her mother had retired to her room to read and Chelsea took a long, hot bath. She went to her room and dropped down on the bed, too tired to take her bathrobe off. Instead, she curled up under the covers and fell into a deep sleep.

In the morning, she'd half expected to walk downstairs to find Nate Kent in her kitchen. She hid her disappointment when it was her mother stirring around in there.

"I'm making pancakes," Linda said proudly.

"Since when did you become such a great cook?" Chelsea teased. There hadn't been many home-cooked meals growing up. Her mother had been too tired to cook after being on her feet all day working odd jobs as they'd come along.

"I take after my daughter." Linda winked.

"I'm afraid she might be a one-trick pony." Chelsea made her way over to the coffee machine. Fresh coffee smelled like heaven. Skylar would be up in another half hour. Chelsea cherished her morning quiet time before the day got into full swing. She poured the steaming liquid into a cup and headed for the back door.

"Rofert still snoring at Skylar's feet?" her mother asked.

"Yep." It was going to be hard to separate those two when the time came. She'd offer to keep him if it wouldn't cost a month of groceries to feed him for a week.

Chelsea slipped on a pair of sneakers, unlocked the door and pushed open the screen door. She looked out onto the third-of-an-acre lot. There was room for Skylar to stretch her legs out here. Chelsea took in a deep breath and then exhaled. A rogue tear escaped at the thought this belonged to Chelsea. She could make a home for her daughter here. She could provide a stable place for her mother to live.

It was cold outside but Chelsea didn't care. She wiped away the tear and headed to the mailbox at the end of the gravel lane.

"How's the restaurant going?" a voice called out from her left. "I'm Gayle Swanson, by the way."

Gayle Swanson was a woman in her late sixties to early seventies. She wore a hot-pink and black jogging suit. Her head was covered in gray hair in one of those shorter, flattering cuts. Her face was filled with smile lines.

"I'm Chelsea McGregor." Chelsea walked to the chain-link fence and offered a handshake. The older woman had a surprisingly strong grip. She hoped this might be a friend for her mother. Linda needed more than Chelsea and Skylar. Her mother needed more to look forward to in life than helping take care of them. "It's nice to meet you."

"You getting settled in all right?" Ms. Swanson asked. "I'm not normally nosy, but it seems like there's been an unusual amount of excitement and I haven't had a next-door neighbor in years."

"We had some surprises at first, but everything is settling in all right now. Somehow a rock made it through that window." She pointed to the east living room window. "And someone broke in, but my mother interrupted them coming home from the grocery."

Gayle gasped. "That's awful. I'm sure sorry that's been happening. I saw that no-good Barstock boy around lately. I wondered if something was up. His mother and I go way back." She gave a pensive look. "She was older than me, so I kept an eye out for her in her last years at the house. I figured something must've happened to her when I saw the moving truck."

Chelsea nodded sympathetically.

"She said she had a beautiful great-niece who she would leave her home and business to one day. She must've been talking about you," Gayle observed with a point of her finger.

It was nice to speak to someone who knew her great-aunt personally. Chelsea's mother had no memories of Aunt Maddie to share. "I'm afraid I didn't know my great-aunt very well. This has all been a pleasant surprise. Did she say why she felt I was the right person to live here?"

"Said you were honest and hard-working. She saw a lot of herself in you."

Chelsea's chest swelled with pride. She thanked Gayle for telling her. "Did you also say that you saw Reggie around lately?"

"Mmm-hmm," she said with a begrudging look. "I don't know what happened to that boy. His mother was a saint for putting up with him as much as she did. She knew giving him the house and the store was out of the question. He'd sell 'em both bit by bit and blow the money gambling. He got mixed up with betting and got himself in some trouble. That's about all I know. Maddie didn't like talking about him. Said talk couldn't change a person and she'd tried everything in the book to set him right."

"I'm sorry." Chelsea'd had it rough and so had her mother, but neither would consider doing anything illegal. Travis hadn't technically stolen since he'd convinced her to put his name on the accounts. What he'd done was unconscionable and immoral, but not illegal.

"Well, you do what you can with your children and then you have to hope for the best," the older woman declared.

Chelsea liked Gayle. The woman had spunk. Her no-nonsense attitude was refreshing.

"Reggie's nothing like that Kent boy who's been coming around. Remind me, which one is the firefighter?" Gayle asked and there was a twinkle in her eye.

"Nate," Chelsea returned. It was impossible to hide the flush in her cheeks when she thought about him. "And, yeah, he's been helpful. My daughter pulled something and ended up getting herself stuck in a crawl space. Luckily, she had my phone and was able to call for help."

"She sounds smart as a whip," Gayle declared with a girl-power-fueled fist pump.

Chelsea smiled. "Maybe a little too smart for her own good sometimes."

"A girl can never be too smart...or too rich," Gayle quipped.

"I wouldn't mind more of that last part," Chelsea joked.

"Has that Nate been coming around a lot?"

The question surprised Chelsea.

"A few days ago, when we were having some trouble, but not now." Chelsea stuffed down her disappointment.

"He's a catch, that one. But then, from what I've heard, he's not the 'settling down' type. He'll go out with this one for a week and that one the next. He's easy on the eyes. I don't think I've ever seen him with the same woman twice." She held up a finger and wagged it. "Well, that's not true. I'm a liar. He was going with one for a few months. She got transferred with her job and that was that."

"Oh. Well. I better get back inside. My daughter's due to be awake any minute and my coffee's gone cold." Chelsea didn't like hearing gossip about Nate. Even worse if it was true. He'd tensed up the other day when Skylar had grabbed onto his legs for a hug. Now it made sense why. If Gayle could be believed, he never stuck around one place for long and he'd probably moved on from Chelsea in the same manner. Why did that feel like a physical blow? What Nate Kent did with his personal life was none of Chelsea's business.

"Nice meeting you," Gayle said. "Can't wait for your grand opening. It's about time we got a new place to eat in town."

"Thanks. I look forward to seeing you at the restaurant." Chelsea turned away to hide the embarrassment heating her cheeks. She'd been thinking about the kiss she'd shared with Nate far too much and a silly part of her thought he might actually be attracted to her. He was just being nice. Granted, that didn't explain the kiss. Although it could've just been for curiosity's sake.

She stalked in through the back door and was greeted by the warmest sight. Skylar's arms wrapped around the Rofert's neck. She'd thrown her leg over his back and was hopping on one foot down the hallway, coming toward the kitchen.

When Chelsea really looked, she could've sworn that dog was smiling, too.

"How was your walk?" her mother asked.

"Fine. Cold." Chelsea moved to the coffeemaker and poured a second cup. She set the mug on the counter and bent down to greet her daughter. "Good morning."

Rofert's tail swished back and forth, nailing the fridge. He was a beautiful animal even if he did shed like crazy. When that big face with those serious brown eyes looked up at her, she bent and kissed him on the forehead. She didn't care about Nate Kent's motives or lack thereof. She appreciated his kindness and that's as far as she could let her feelings go.

The next few days were a blur of early mornings and long, productive days at the restaurant. The quiet was a welcome change from the excitement of the first few days in town. Except that Chelsea hadn't seen or heard from Nate. Much to her surprise, she missed talking to him.

There were other, darker issues lurking. She had no idea when and if Reggie Barstock would turn up again. Travis hadn't made himself known, either.

It was probably too much to hope the two of them would leave her alone and go about their own business. A creepy feeling that she couldn't shake made her fear that neither would walk away so easily. It was too quiet, like the calm before a raging storm.

She pushed those unproductive thoughts aside. Life was getting back on track. Her little family of three, plus Rofert, was starting to get into a good rhythm.

The restaurant still looked like a construction site but the floors had been cleared of debris. There were no more stacks of half-broken and dirty bricks littering the space. An open concept was perfect for the restaurant and made for easier renovations. A contractor had built a wall inside with a swinging door for the cleanup area so dirty dishes wouldn't be visible from the main cooking and dining area.

A lot of work still needed to be done, but damn if progress didn't feel amazing. Chelsea had noticed that progress was everything. The destination was sweet, and every inch of progress toward a clear vision sometimes felt like she was already there.

Aunt Maddie had been a business owner and Chelsea felt a connection to her great-aunt through their entrepreneurial bond.

She tried not to think about the fact that it was Saturday night and she was alone working in her restaurant. She hadn't once given a thought to working weekends. What was going on with her lately?

Nate Kent, that little voice in the back of her head pointed out.

It was an annoying little brat.

THE CALL CAME over the emergency response radio at one fifty-five in the morning.

"Fire at 2312 Main. All emergency personnel to respond."

Nate scrambled out of bed and threw on his ready outfit of jeans and a pullover shirt that he kept draped over the chair next to his bed. He hopped on one foot trying to slip a sock on. While he was on his second sock, a bolt shot through him—2312 Main Street was the address of Chelsea's restaurant!

It was the middle of the night. Surely she was home sleeping in her bed, he reasoned.

The dispatch continued. *"A pickup with license plate BZWG 1234 is parked in front of the building. An unknown number of occupants is inside the building."*

Nate hopped into his boots, grabbed his cell and broke into a dead run toward his truck. He raked his fingers through his curls in an attempt to tame them. His truck was parked in the garage, keys in the ignition. He kept a bottle of mouthwash in the cup holder for just such occasions.

On the road, Nate took a swig of the mouthwash, rinsed and then opened the window to spit while at the four-way stop. Everything about this call was routine except that his gut was braided in a tight knot at the realization Chelsea could be in the restaurant, hurt.

He'd left her and her sweet family alone to avoid just that: anyone getting hurt. But the kiss they'd shared had burned its way into his thoughts and popped up at the most inopportune times. He'd finally returned Brenda Hunt's call and agreed to a date to prove to himself that he could go out with someone and be fine.

The date had lasted half an hour before Brenda looked him square in the eye and asked, "Do you really want to be here?"

An honest question like that deserved a real answer. He'd spared her the "It's me, not you" line even though in this case it was true. Brenda was an attractive brunette. There was no reason he shouldn't have enjoyed her company. But the comparisons had crept in. All that date had told him was that he needed to spend some time alone.

The ranch had been keeping him busy and he enjoyed the long days and hard work. Calves were due to be born in a matter of weeks and keeping watch over the heifers gave him a sense of purpose.

Nate gunned the engine, pushing his truck to its limit, lights on. His rotating beacon drew circles against quiet street after quiet street. His pulse had shot through the roof and all he could think about was Chelsea.

Even in the dark, he could see the thick cloud of smoke. The flames licking toward the sky.

Fires were indiscriminate creatures that took on a life of their own.

They didn't care about the wreckage left behind. There were no feelings in a fire. They didn't care if they made widows and orphans.

Skylar's sweet face popped into his thoughts.

And then Chelsea's.

A sense of foreboding crept over him as he neared the scene. A fire truck had just arrived, based on the sound of the siren. Confirmation came on the radio a few seconds later.

Nate parked alongside the fire truck and bolted for the rig. He had his equipment on in a matter of minutes.

Details were being given over the radio but there wasn't much other than the severity of the blaze.

A crew was working the hose, twisting off the fire hydrant cap at the corner and working quickly and efficiently to clamp on the hose. They had a steady spray going by the time Nate located his captain.

Nate already had his ax ready to go as he approached Steve Benton. "I'm ready to go in as soon as word comes."

"What's your rush?" Captain Benton asked.

"Chelsea McGregor is inside." His voice was calm although he felt anything but.

"How can you be certain?" Benton asked.

"That's her pickup. It would be just like her to pull an all-nighter to get back on schedule."

"She might've gotten a ride home with someone. I'm not sending a man in there until I know it's safe," his captain said.

Nate blew out a sharp breath. "I know her. She's in there. She has a daughter who needs her. If me going in means the difference between life and death for her, I'm willing to take the risk. I signed up for this job and I knew what I was doing." Nate was emphatic.

Captain Benton studied him carefully. "As soon as I give the all-clear, you'll be the first to go in. Right now we have a two-alarm fire and one engine to deal with it. The backdraft could take you and several others out if we tamper—"

"Like I said, I'm aware of the risks and I didn't ask anyone to come inside with me." Nate stood his ground. "I'm going in."

Chapter Eleven

Chelsea heard a voice in the distance but she couldn't move, couldn't respond. If only she could open her eyes... *Nate?*

It was probably wishful thinking that had her hearing his voice. She wished he was there, wished she could see him. She'd thought about him more than she cared to admit while she'd worked. His deep timbre normally washed over her, stirring a physical reaction. This time, he sounded concerned, and her body had a different kind of reaction to him. It went on full alert.

She wanted to shout to him, to tell him where she was, to stop him from being concerned about her. There was so much noise drowning him out. Crackling and popping.

Chelsea took in a breath and choked on it. She coughed. Everything burned; her eyes, her nose, her throat. Her lungs clawed for oxygen but came up short.

Out of seemingly nowhere something was being placed on her face. Then someone's arms lifted her like she weighed nothing. And then she took in a breath of air. She coughed like she'd just chugged water after being lost in the desert. Her lungs ached.

Time passed, Chelsea couldn't be sure how much before she finally took in a real breath. She heard several male voices telling her to stay awake. All she wanted to do was to sleep. She fought the urge.

"Skylar needs you," Nate said, his voice like a whisper in her ear.

Skylar's image popped into Chelsea's thoughts. She had to stay awake so she could get home to her daughter. Chelsea locked on to the thought.

By the time she could blink her eyes open, she was in the emergency room. Breathing still hurt and a headache threatened to split her head in two.

She forced her eyes to open and stay that way.

There he was, standing by her side, holding her hand.

"Nate—" Trying to speak caused a coughing jag.

"I'm here." He bent next to her bed while a nurse called for the doctor.

"Well, hello," the nurse said. "My name's Willow. I'll be taking care of you tonight."

Chelsea shook her head. She needed to get home. If word got home about the fire...*damn*, her restaurant had just gone up in flames. She'd cry if she could squeeze out a tear. Instead, she just felt deflated and drained of energy.

"It'll be okay," Nate reassured her, but he was wrong. Nothing was okay. Her livelihood had just gone up in flames. She'd been shopping around for insurance but hadn't settled on a company yet. Her to-do list was scary long. She'd been making progress, knocking off item after item.

And now this. *This.*

"Don't worry. Everything will work out." Nate squeezed her hand, causing all kinds of inappropriate volts of electricity to rocket through her. All she could think about was her mother and Skylar. How would Chelsea support the two most important people in her life now? That little voice tried to point out that Nate felt pretty darn important. She quashed the thought before it could gather steam and fought to stay conscious. There was something else niggling away at the edge of her consciousness. *What?*

Working all night at the restaurant by herself to make up for lost time was a mistake. It had left her vulnerable and almost cost her life. She couldn't imagine the fire had been an accident. If it had been set on purpose, who was to blame? This stunt went beyond trying to scare her. Her truck had been parked outside the restaurant. Was someone seriously after her? Had someone been watching her? Waiting for an opportunity?

Chelsea said a silent thank you for the fact the fire had been lit at the restaurant instead of at her home because it spared her mother and daughter.

"What were you doing there so late?" Nate asked.

"I'm so behind. I was trying to catch up." She squeezed her eyes shut trying to block the roaring headache forming between her eyes.

He must've been paying close attention and reading the signs because he quietly said, "Try to rest. I'm here. I'm not going anywhere."

For the next few hours, hospital staff came and went, asking questions and marking charts. Chelsea managed to sit upright and sip water on her own. Her eyes, nose and throat still burned, but her lungs ached less.

Dr. Newman was the on-call physician. He was a squatty-looking man with a ruddy complexion and easy bedside manner.

"You're lucky this man arrived when he did," Dr. Newman told her. "You took a fall that most likely knocked you out."

"That explains the horrible pounding going on back there." She gestured to her crown after lifting her oxygen mask. She already knew that she'd taken a blow to the head and that Nate had probably defied orders and probably good judgment when he'd burst through the back door. He'd gotten to her before she'd succumbed to smoke inhalation.

"We were lucky," Nate noted.

Chelsea would have to take the doctor's word on falling. Her memory was fuzzy. She didn't remember tripping or hitting her head. Now that she thought about it, she did remember hearing a voice and, for some reason, she thought she'd heard it before losing consciousness. A chill raced down her back.

She probably just had it mixed up with Nate's or an EMT's.

"Good news is that you can leave as soon as that drip finishes." Dr. Newman motioned toward her IV bag. "But you have to put your oxygen mask back on a little while longer."

Chelsea replaced the mask.

"We'll get you out of here before you know it," Dr. Newman said.

She liked the sound of that. She smiled at Nate and her heart performed that freefall routine whenever he was near. She'd missed him the last few days. She'd missed the comfortable way she had with him. Even from the start, and forget the fact that they were strangers, she'd felt at ease talking to him. Granted, her body reminded her he was very much male and she was all female every time the two of them were in the same room. But even with all that sexual chemistry pinging between them, conversation with him flowed effortlessly.

"Any chance you'll let me give you a ride home later?" he asked.

It was either that or wake her mother up in the wee hours of the morning, who would, in turn, wake her daughter, and then come to pick Chelsea up from the ER. She was certain one of those ride-hailing services used in the city hadn't made it out to these parts. Ordering a ride would be impossible and, since she knew only one person in town other than Nate, so far…

"I'd appreciate that. Thank you," she said, lifting her mask to speak. "The more I think about what happened, the more I could swear I heard a male voice *before* I blacked out."

"Head injuries can be tricky. Are you sure about that?"

"Not absolutely certain. And yet, that's what I'm remembering."

CHELSEA LEANED HER head back on the passenger seat of Nate's truck. An hour had passed since the IV ran dry.

"Zach will stop by in a little while to get your statement. Make sure he knows about the voice," Nate stated. She could almost hear the wheels churning in his mind.

"That fire wasn't my fault. I didn't do anything for it to start. I keep racking my brain for something…a kerosene lamp…*something* that could've started it. I didn't so much as bring a space heater. I was cold while I worked but being inside kept the winds from freezing me. I was saving money on heat, so I had the thermostat so low I had to work in my coat and gloves." She was probably going to catch the death of a cold because of it.

Nate's forehead creased with worry lines. He white-knuckled the steering wheel. "Did you say the male voice sounded familiar?"

"Yes. But thinking back, I couldn't tell you who it belonged to." Her mind started clicking. "I can't even be certain I'm remembering correctly except that it feels like I am."

"Do you know what Reggie's voice sounds like? No one's seen him around town but that doesn't mean he's not here," Nate said after a thoughtful pause.

"No. What would he have to gain if the restaurant is destroyed?" He'd come to her mind, too. But she hadn't worked out a motive yet or where she might've heard his voice.

"He might want to scare you or run you out of town. Any word from the lawyer on who gets the home and the property if something happens to you?" he asked.

"Aunt Maddie didn't say. But isn't that obvious? I mean, even to a man like Reggie? I own the properties now. They'd go to my next of kin," she stated.

"He might think he'd have a better court case if you weren't in the picture. Or maybe he thinks you'll abandon the properties and then he can make a play for them." There was another option that he wasn't stating.

"Or he could just hate me for being the one she left everything to and want revenge."

Nate nodded as his gaze intensified on the road ahead.

"I'll call Zach and ask if he can come right over. The fire marshal will investigate the fire as part of insurance requirements before payout. I'll see if we can put some pressure on the investigation and get a verdict sooner."

"What if I don't have insurance?" She pinched the bridge of her nose to stave off a threatening headache. "I was still trying to decide which company to go with."

"There might be an umbrella policy from your aunt. We'll check into it," he said to reassure her.

She sat there, trying to make sense of what had happened. Details were fuzzy. She wished she could pinpoint who the male voice had belonged to.

The back of her skull had a knot on it.

"My purse and my cell are back at the restaurant." She hadn't seen them since the fire.

"I know this sounds cliché and it might not be what you want to hear right now, but all those things can be replaced."

"You're right," she said as he pulled into the drive.

"No one called your mother because we didn't want her to worry." He pulled up next to the house and parked. "It's better coming from me."

A car was parked in the drive, causing Chelsea's pulse to skyrocket.

"It's Deputy Long. Zach sent him over to keep watch as soon as he heard about the fire," Nate stated. "He didn't want to take a chance with your mother and Skylar."

"What if it's my ex who started the fire. What if it's Travis?" she asked as she put her hand on the handle.

"What would he have to gain?" Nate gripped the steering wheel.

"My daughter." Travis had the most to gain if something happened to Chelsea. A wave of nausea nearly doubled her over.

She squinted through blurry eyes as she realized he was watching her.

"Let's get inside and get you in bed. Food will go a long way toward making you feel better," Nate said. His eyebrows were drawn together with concern.

Chelsea pushed open the door before he could get out and do it for her. He was at the passenger door before she could step out of the truck. She accepted his hand and then climbed out of the cab.

The sun was almost up. The lights flipped on in the kitchen. Her mother was awake. Thankfully, she was home and could explain everything before Linda worked herself up with too much worry.

Nate offered his arm and she took it, leaning much of her weight on him while ignoring the frissons of electricity pinging between them.

Linda was in the kitchen when Chelsea knocked on the back door. She swished the curtain over the top glass, saw Chelsea standing there with Nate, and immediately unlocked the door.

"What happened?" her mother asked.

Nate helped Chelsea to the kitchen table where she eased onto the chair.

"The good news is that I'm fine. The restaurant caught fire last night." Chelsea did her best to hide her emotions. Breaking down would only make things worse. Somehow, Chelsea would figure out a way to get the restaurant back on track. And hadn't she always been the strong one?

"I'm sorry, dear. You've been working so hard and I know how much the place means to you." Her mother's concern was genuine. It was odd for Linda to be trying to comfort Chelsea when normally it was the other way around. "If I know my daughter, and I do, you'll figure out how to fix it and make it even better than it was before."

A rogue tear slipped down Chelsea's cheek as she embraced her mother.

Nate busied himself making coffee and she appreciated him giving her space to talk to her mother.

Rofert barked from upstairs and she'd never seen a person move as fast as Nate to reach him.

Chelsea pushed to her feet and did her best to keep up. She didn't want Skylar waking up to a stranger. That bratty voice in the back of her head reminded her that Skylar was well acquainted with Nate. The little girl had asked for the fireman more than once in the past few days.

Chelsea had been able to distract her by bringing up the one male figure who could be counted on, Santa Claus.

Taking the steps three at a clip, Nate was at the top of the stairwell in no time. Chelsea's lungs burned and she had to stop and grip the rail, which slowed her down considerably.

Rofert barked again from inside Skylar's room.

Why was the door shut?

By the time Chelsea made it to the top of the stairs, Skylar was lying full-out on top of Rofert who was on his side.

"What happened?" Chelsea asked, out of breath.

"The door was closed and I'm guessing Rofert heard us downstairs. He must not have realized who we were," Nate explained.

"It's my fault," her mother called upstairs. "I'm the one who closed the door so I could get some sleep from all that snoring."

Chelsea leaned against the wall and slid onto the floor. All the stress she'd been under and now the fire collided in a perfect storm of crazy. No one could predict any of the things that had happened, were still happening.

As far as she could tell, there were two options. Laugh or cry.

She laughed to the point of tears.

Chapter Twelve

Nate listened as Chelsea recounted everything she remembered to Zach. Her first lucky break was his cousin finding and returning her cell phone and handbag intact. Somehow those had managed to make it out of the fire undamaged. It was a miracle and would save her time and hassle by not having to replace her ID, credit cards and whatever else she kept in her bag.

The first thing she'd done was dig inside her purse. She palmed what looked like a photo. The look of relief on her face caught Nate off guard at first. She'd gone for the photo without checking her wallet.

According to her, her whole life was practically stored inside her handbag. Based on Nate's knowledge of his sister and cousin, Amy, that was probably true.

Linda had volunteered to take Skylar to school and Zach had sent Deputy Long to follow them, just in case. This wasn't the warm welcome most folks got when they came to Jacobstown.

The attack at the restaurant was bold. Someone had gotten into the place undetected while she'd worked. To the best of her knowledge, Chelsea'd sworn that she'd locked the front and back door.

That part was unsettling to Nate.

Could someone have a key? That brought his thoughts back to Reggie. In fact, most roads led to that jerk. Nate's hands fisted thinking about Barstock. He'd worn a smirk that didn't sit well with Nate.

The fire marshal wouldn't complete his report for a few days. They'd know then if the fire had been started from inside or out.

Chelsea had also brought up her ex, Travis.

Nate would be remiss to rule Travis out as a suspect.

"Travis said he's been working for a pipeline in Alaska trying to earn enough money to win us back," Chelsea told Zach. "I haven't had time to check out his story and I've been relieved that it was quiet for the past week."

Nate had forced himself to stay away from the little family of three. He'd busied himself on the ranch. It seemed like there was always something to fix or clean out back home.

"I can run a check on him with his legal name and social security if you still have it," Zach offered.

"It's in here." She dug through her bag and fished out a wallet. She pilfered through it until she produced a social security card. "It was tucked in my wallet years ago from before he left. He'd asked me to hold on to it and must've forgotten he gave it to me. I kept it just in case I needed it. There you go."

Zach snapped a picture of the card. "Did he mention where he might be headed next?"

"Actually, he was pretty insistent that he intended to stick around this time," she reported. Her face twisted in a look of disgust. Her feelings for her ex were strong and Nate didn't blame her. Any man who would clean out bank accounts and disappear while his wife was in labor was a class-A jerk and didn't deserve a second chance unless he moved mountains to get it.

Nate would never treat Chelsea like that if the two of them were married.

He almost choked on the thought of marriage. Suddenly, his collar was too tight. He tucked his finger inside the top button and tugged to loosen it.

Chelsea must've yawned four times in a row. Zach stood and made eye contact with Nate.

"I'll see him out," Nate said to her.

"Great. I need a hot shower more than I need air right now."

Chelsea didn't need to go putting images of her naked in his mind. He'd thought about that kiss more then was good for either one of them. In fact, that kiss was a large part of the reason he'd kept his distance.

But she was in trouble and he couldn't turn his back while she was in danger. Someone was targeting her. And the jerk seemed ready to do just about anything to make sure she stayed out of the way.

Nate walked Zach out the front door and stopped on the porch.

"You sticking around?" Zach asked.

"Yeah, why?" Nate must've sounded pretty damn defensive based on the look he got from his cousin, raised eyebrow included.

"Hey." Zach's hands rose in the surrender position. "I'm just trying to see what kind of manpower I need over here to make sure this family is safe. If you're sticking around, I can use my resources elsewhere on the investigation and less on a protection detail. That's all."

"Got it. Didn't mean to overreact," Nate clarified.

"No problem. I'm glad you'll be around. These three

seem like good people and they look like they could use a friend," Zach continued.

Nate nodded agreement. "I'll give you a call if she remembers anything else."

"It's possible. Her brain could be blocking out the attack. Or, as her injury indicates, someone approached her from behind," Zach stated.

"Who else has a key?"

"I'm not sure. She could've left one of the doors unlocked." Zach looked away from the bright morning sun.

It was cold outside but the sun shining made a world of difference.

"Christmas is in a couple of weeks. Her ex might be getting sentimental about having his family back." Nate was thinking out loud.

"True. I thought about that possibility. She could've been killed in the fire."

"He might've been watching from somewhere, even planning to play the big hero and save her once the blaze hit fever pitch," Nate suggested.

"A twisted mind could think that, even if she died, a judge would grant him custody of his daughter and he'd get everything that little girl inherited." Zach rubbed the scruff on his chin. "I'll dig around in his background some more. Figure out where this guy's been during the last four years."

"Any word about Reggie's background?" Before Zach could play the I-can't-tell-you card, Nate put a hand up. "He's a relative of hers and if I'm going to stay here, I'd like to know what I could be dealing with. We both noticed him favoring his left foot."

"He's been brought in a few times in the past ten years for petty crimes. The best I can tell, he works odd jobs.

Nothing seems to stick, according to Chief Smith in Bossier Parish. I called in a favor to find out that Reggie's been on the chief's watch list for several crimes." Zach's and Nate's cell phones went off at almost the exact same time.

They locked gazes for a split second before each taking a call.

"What's going on, Deacon?" Deacon was brother number three in the Kent hierarchy and the next closest to Nate in age.

"I haven't seen you much lately and I just heard a rumor about Reggie Barstock and a bad left foot…" Deacon started. "Any possible connection to what's been going on at the ranch?"

"I'm at Chelsea McGregor's house talking to Zach about that right now," Nate admitted.

"I don't have to tell you the longer we go without figuring out who's responsible, the more people are starting to panic," Deacon said.

Recently, Deacon and his now wife, Leah, had gone through an ordeal with a copycat killer. Her coworker, a detective with the Fort Worth PD, had become fixated on her after losing his child to illness and his wife divorcing him. He'd known enough about the case to cover up his killings by trying to make it look like the Jacobstown Hacker was attacking women on a jogging path in downtown Fort Worth. The path happened to be the same one that Leah had used every night at around the same time. The killer had been targeting her.

"With everything going on, the town's nervous. I get that. I'm planning to stay over at the McGregor house until things cool off for her. You think you can handle things on the ranch if I have to be away for a few days?"

Nate realized he was needed but hoped for a couple of days to stay with the McGregors.

Deacon was quiet for longer than Nate was comfortable.

"She have a kid in Mrs. Eaton's class who just started a week or two ago?" Deacon asked.

"Yeah. I forgot all about the possibility of her being in class with Connor," Nate said. His mind hadn't been on the family lately. He'd been too busy being irritated with himself for falling down a trap with a woman so callous she could lie about her sister being ill. Maybe that was the connection he felt toward Chelsea? They'd both been lied to and deceived.

Granted, Nate had allowed it to happen. He should've kept his eyes open. The breakup with Mia had been his call, but he'd been trying to figure out how she'd outsmarted him for as long as she'd gotten away with it.

It hadn't taken that long to recognize her pattern. As soon as he'd figured her out, he'd given her walking papers. Nate figured the reason he'd allowed himself to think about settling down with one person was the happiness several of his brothers had found with their wives and kids.

But, hey, that kind of commitment wasn't for everyone. That was why he couldn't stop questioning his own judgment when it came to Chelsea. She was nothing like Mia. The two didn't even compare. Mia had been quick to try to lock Nate in while Chelsea seemed ready to put on her running shoes every time they bumped into each other in her small but cozy kitchen.

"Am I cutting out?" Deacon's voice came through loud and clear.

"No. Why? What did I miss?" Nate had no plans to

share that he'd been lost in thought over Chelsea. Deacon would have a field day teasing him about that slip.

"I was saying that I can cover for you for a few days. Wish I could offer more, but we're drowning right now and we need all the help we can get." Deacon paused. "I've heard good things about the little girl from Connor. He talks about the new girl and says she's quiet but nice."

Skylar had touched Nate's heart, too. Those big, round eyes, gap-toothed smile and curly locks could melt an iceberg. "Good to hear that she's making friends," he responded. "It's got to be hard to be the new kid in town."

"Yeah, we never had that growing up, but I saw it in Connor when he first came to live at the ranch." Deacon was in the process of adopting Leah's son even though Connor would always carry his real father's last name.

Connor's father had passed away from an incurable disease and, by all accounts, had been a decent man. Roger had died never knowing that his wife was pregnant because Leah had said she'd known it would break his heart. Roger had been abandoned by his father and had had a rough upbringing. By not telling him about his child, Leah had spared him the scars of feeling like he was abandoning his child. Roger never would have repeated the cycle of abandonment.

And that's why Deacon and Leah had agreed to keep Connor's last name the same even though he would have every right that came along with being a Kent heir. Connor's last name didn't matter. He was as much a Kent as any of them and no one would look at him any differently.

Nate had seen the way having a child had changed Deacon for the better. His brother was happy in ways Nate couldn't begin to explain. The same went for Mitch and Will. They'd found true happiness.

"Well, I've gotta get going, Nate. If you need any one of us we'll be right there for you," Deacon said.

"You know I appreciate it," Nate stated and he meant it. His brothers and sister having his back meant the world to him.

He and his brother exchanged goodbyes.

He thought about Chelsea and her mother. They'd done well without having much of a support network. Their love for each other was obvious. Linda was a hoot and she loved her daughter. There was something broken about her spirit, though. Nate figured there was a story behind it.

Zach wrapped up his call a minute later. "That Deacon who called you?"

"Yeah. How about your call?" Nate asked.

"Mine was from Patty. She's being flooded with calls after the fire with people wanting details. Everyone assumes the fire was arson and somehow connected to the heifers," Zach advised.

"Chelsea thinks she was hit before the fire started. That pretty much ensures it was arson, doesn't it?" Nate wasn't following the line of thinking about this crime being connected to the heifers.

"I'm with you. Captain Benton will probably rule arson." Zach lifted his hat and wiped sweat from this forehead with his arm sleeve. "Town's already in an uproar over the hooves."

"It's been a while, but someone who chops off a heifer's hoof isn't going to graduate to setting fires." The logic didn't work.

"You and I know that but try to tell Ray Royce that. Or Betty Orson. People worry and then that worry turns into panic. None of which will help us figure out who's behind any of this." Zach put his hat back on his head. "I have some calls to make."

A white van caught Nate's attention as it slowed in front of Chelsea's house. Nate and Zach exchanged glances.

A young-ish man popped out of the driver's side and opened the side door to the vehicle. He pulled out a large bouquet of flowers and balanced them on his arm while he pulled the door shut. When he turned toward them, Nate recognized the partially blocked face as Sammy Orr. Sammy was in the same grade as Amber, if Nate's memory served and he worked for the town's florist.

"Flowers?" Zach said almost under his breath. "Did Ms. McGregor mention dating anyone?"

"Not to me." Nate searched his memory. Nah, he'd know by now if she was seeing someone, wouldn't he? They'd shared one helluva hot kiss and he didn't make a habit of kissing woman already in a relationship. He wouldn't think too highly of Chelsea if she'd allowed that to happen while she was seeing someone else, either.

Sammy stopped short of climbing the couple of stairs to the porch. "I have a delivery for Chelsea McGregor. I'm guessing she's just moved in. Nice to see the Barstock house occupied for a change."

Nate took a proprietary step forward. The bouquet was massive. It almost completely blocked Sammy's face as he walked up. "Who sent them?"

"Someone by the name of Renaldo Vinchesa." The delivery driver shrugged. "Is Ms. McGregor home or can I leave these with one of you?"

"I'll take it," Nate said. The bouquet was filled with at least a dozen roses. There were other flowers that he recognized but couldn't name to save his life. The scent was sweet and romantic, and pretty much a slap in the face.

"There's a card in there," Sammy said.

Nate handed the bouquet to Zach and then fished out a ten to tip.

"Thanks," Sammy said with a quick smile and a wave.

Nate waved and clenched his back teeth.

The conversation he needed to have with Chelsea couldn't wait.

CHELSEA SAT ON the sofa in the living room, watching out the window. Rofert was asleep at her feet. There was so much comfort in having him around. She saw a delivery man hand off the biggest, most beautiful bouquet of flowers she'd ever seen. Her mind snapped in a couple of directions. None made sense.

Nate walked in the front door, his expression serious. He didn't seem any more amused than she was that the flowers had showed up. Oh. She realized why. He'd think they were from someone she'd dated in Houston. Maybe he thought she was still seeing him?

A piece of her was tickled that he seemed upset about them. Did he like her more than he was letting on? He'd kissed her and then kept his distance. She figured that he must've regretted it.

But the rest of her figured the flowers were from Travis.

"Who are those from?" she asked.

He set the bouquet on the coffee table and took a step back like it was a bomb about to explode. That shouldn't amuse her, either. It did.

"Renaldo Vinchesa."

"What?" Shock didn't begin to describe her reaction.

The timing of these flowers struck her as odd, especially after his threats.

She pushed up to standing so she could walk around the bouquet to find the card. Nate must've realized what she was doing because he stepped forward and located the card for her.

The note inside read "Forgive a fool. Best of luck with your new venture."

He'd signed the card and she could vouch for his signature. She'd seen it many times on purchase orders for the restaurant back in Houston.

She blinked up at Nate as she returned to her seat, card in hand. "He's my old boss."

"Yeah, I remember." His feet were positioned in an athletic stance, his arms folded across his massive chest. He was in a defensive position, like he was fortifying himself for a physical blow.

"We had a purely professional relationship," she clarified.

"It's none of my business." Those words felt like a physical blow.

Based on his stoic expression, he didn't believe her.

Chapter Thirteen

"Don't you think it's a little odd that he threatened me when I left the restaurant and now sends flowers out of the blue after someone knocked me in the back of the head and then set my restaurant on fire?" Saying it out loud made it even more horrific to Chelsea.

Her restaurant was in ruins. All the progress she'd made so far was down the tube and she needed to start earning money soon.

Worse yet, she didn't have the funds to buy another fire pit to cook the pizza or the cabinets that had arrived and had been waiting to be put up. She hadn't bought insurance yet. An umbrella plan was unlikely but her best bet. Her only bet?

Nate moved to the couch and sat next to her.

While she had his ear, she continued, "I can show you the texts on my phone if you don't believe me."

The sound of tires on the gravel drive interrupted them. Nate was up in a heartbeat, checking out the window. "It's your mother."

Chelsea let out the breath she'd been holding. Her pulse jacked through the roof at the slightest noise. Rofert stirred but Nate settled the huge dog down with a few words and a scratch behind his ears.

Chelsea bit back her second yawn in five minutes.

"I thought you were going to take a shower earlier." He eyed her up and down. "We can talk about your old boss after you get some rest. It was a long night."

"I was going to take a shower but…" She hated to admit the reason she hadn't done it already.

"Did something happen? A noise?" Nate's concern caused her heart to squeeze.

"I was scared to be alone in the house." She couldn't look him in the eyes while she felt so vulnerable.

He tilted her chin so she'd be forced to make eye contact. "You don't have to be afraid when I'm here. I'm not going to let anything happen to you."

The back door opened and her mother called out.

"In here, Mom," Chelsea said, the interruption breaking the moment between her and Nate.

"Hello, Nate," Linda said as she entered the room.

"Ma'am," Nate said.

"I better clean up." Chelsea pushed up to stand. She was weak and had to stop at the end of the couch to gain her balance.

"Take my arm." Nate wrapped one arm around her waist for support.

She held on to his muscled arm, wishing she could pull from his strength. He helped her up the stairs, one at a time, and to her bedroom. She welcomed the heat rushing through her body from the contact even though it was a bad idea to get used to it.

He turned his back, granting her privacy when she took off her clothes and put on her bathrobe. Luckily, that thing was so long it practically dragged the floor. She was keenly aware of just how naked she was underneath it when Nate stood next to her, helping her to the bathroom.

The past twelve hours had started taking a toll and exhaustion wore her to the bone.

"Will you wait upstairs?" Her fear was irrational, and she would find a way to get over it. For this moment, though, she needed to be around someone stronger than her.

"Yeah." His voice had that low gravelly pitch that sent sensual shivers skittering across her skin.

She closed the bathroom door and then leaned against it. The weight of last night's events hit her full-force and her knees threatened to buckle. Nothing could happen to her. Where would that leave her mother and Skylar?

Rather than get lost drowning in a vat of self-pity, Chelsea pushed off the door and started the water.

It was then she heard the floorboards creak and realized that Nate had waited for her. It was also then that she realized how much trouble she was in when it came to her feelings for him.

"I UPDATED ZACH on the situation with your former boss. He checked his notes and remembered you mentioning him on the first day he spoke to you," Nate said to Chelsea. She was fresh from the shower and had that clean, flowery, spring-like scent.

She sat next to him on the bed and her fragrance filled his senses, causing a reaction in places that didn't need stirring.

Nate needed to get a grip. He tried to convince himself that his reaction to her, naked and smelling like the first sunny day after a spring shower, was because he hadn't been out on a decent date since his relationship with Mia had ended.

But that wasn't entirely true. He hadn't been out seriously since Mia because no one had interested him and certainly never as much as Chelsea.

"Here." He lifted the covers. "Get into bed."

She shot him a look and he laughed.

"Don't worry. I don't go anywhere I'm not invited."

"That's not the problem," she said so low he almost didn't hear her as she climbed under the comforter.

He sat on the edge of the bed, feeling the same nerves as an inexperienced teenager.

"What is it about your mother's picture that made you have the reaction you did earlier?" He'd been curious about it, but the chance to ask hadn't presented itself.

Chelsea relaxed her shoulders a little, sat up and pulled the covers to just below her chin. She kept a piece of material in between the thumb and forefinger of her left hand.

She was a lefty? Curious. So was Nate. It surprised him that he hadn't noticed already. Especially since he'd noticed the right dimple on her cheek when she smiled. Then there was the freckle above her lip. Her soft skin and big eyes. He'd thought about all of those things more than he cared to admit.

"My father took that photo. My mother says he was creative and so talented." She shrugged but her eyes said the statement was anything but noncommittal.

"What happened to him?" Nate asked.

"That's the question of the hour. He literally went out for milk one day a couple of weeks before my second birthday and never came back. I don't think my mom was ever truly happy again." Her voice cracked a little, like the pain was still raw even after all these years.

"Sounds like a good reason to stay single," he quipped before thinking.

She frowned.

"I'm just saying I'd rather be single my whole life than suffer through a disappointment that punches a hole through someone's heart like that would." He realized in that moment that Chelsea had suffered through a similar fate.

Damn.

She shrugged again. "I guess. I've never experienced anything near that level. Not even when I was married. I cared about Travis, but I was young when we met and probably naïve. It didn't help that I was so busy working my food truck business that I didn't go out much. I didn't really know what qualities to look for in a person. Guess I wasn't looking for anything substantial. Then I got pregnant. Turns out you can't take an antibiotic and expect the birth control pill to work."

She gave him a look that was equal parts adorable and frustrated.

"It still hurt like hell when he took off. The weird thing is, I don't think I was all that angry that he left. I was frustrated for Skylar. But I was more upset about losing everything I'd worked so hard to build. It never occurred to me that anyone could be so cruel. I look at people in a different light now," she admitted.

"Who wouldn't? Being deceived is a sucker punch. Especially if you care about the person who pulled one over on you. You don't have to be in love for that to hurt," he said.

"How would you know?" She bit back another yawn.

"That's a story for another time. Right now, I just want you to get some rest," he returned.

Chelsea had slid lower so she was lying down again.

Self-control was not normally a problem for Nate. But

it was taking every ounce he had not to lie down next to her. She needed sleep. If she invited him into her bed, neither would get any rest. He could take the hit. She couldn't.

He started to get up but she grabbed his arm.

"Will you stay in here until I fall asleep?" she asked, releasing his arm.

"I'll do you one better. I'll stick around until you wake." There was a wing-backed chair in the corner of the room that he could get comfortable in.

He looked back at her in time to see her smile as she closed her eyes and released her grip on the blanket.

CHELSEA WOKE WITH a start, her lungs clawing for oxygen. A strong, masculine presence was by her side a second after she opened her eyes. It was dark in the room and she couldn't see anything.

"You're okay." Nate's voice soothed.

The mattress dipped beside her.

"What time is it?" She had no idea. She tried to sit up but her head hurt. She'd refused medication at the ER, wanting to have a clear mind.

"It's quarter to three in the morning." Nate used a flashlight app on his phone and set it beside her on the bed.

"What? I've been asleep that long?" Chelsea rubbed her eyes and glanced at the clock on the nightstand.

"Afraid so. Your mother has been taking care of Skylar."

"Have you been awake this whole time?" Didn't he sleep?

"I don't need a lot of sleep. Every once in a while, I stay in bed for a weekend and catch up," he said. "I didn't turn on the light just now because I don't want to wake your mother or Skylar. They've been through enough without causing more worry."

She gasped. "Did my daughter know you were in here?"

Skylar had rarely ever seen a man in the house unless something was in need of repair let alone witness one in her mother's bedroom. She would be traumatized.

"Yes," he said apologetically. "I told her that you had an accident while you were working the other night and I was making sure you were okay. She seemed fine with it, comforted."

When Travis had left, Chelsea had sworn her daughter wouldn't have men paraded in and out of her life. Once, Chelsea and her mother had stayed with a cousin of her mother's who'd had little kids and a different "uncle" sleeping over every few weeks. It had been confusing to Chelsea as a child and, as an adult, she saw it as inappropriate.

There was nothing wrong with a single mother having a sex life. Chelsea was beginning to want one of those herself. Especially with the feelings she was developing for Nate. But a parade of men through the house had always been out of the question. If her own mother had done one thing right, it was that.

"What is it? Did I do something wrong?" Concern had Nate's dark brows arching.

Chelsea needed to exhale and try to relax. "I'm sure one time won't damage Skylar's psyche. I hope."

"She saw that I was fully dressed," he said with a smile that was a little too sexy. "And she asked if I could sleep over all the time."

Chelsea wasn't sure if that was better or worse.

"What about Mother?" she asked.

"Linda had pretty much the same response," he informed her. "She asked what I'd like to eat for breakfast."

Had everything she'd built up in her mind about being single and bringing a man home been paranoia?.

Given the circumstances, she decided not to put too much thought into it. There were so many other things to worry about instead, like the fact that someone at the very least had assaulted her and possibly wanted her dead.

"My head feels like an ex-thrower used it for target practice," she admitted.

Nate picked up a bottle of OTC pain medication along with a glass of water from her nightstand.

"I thought you might ask for these," he said. That smile from a few seconds ago played with the corners of his mouth.

She opened her hand and he dropped a pain reliever on it.

"More?" he asked.

"I'll start with one. I don't want to be completely out of it in case Skylar needs me," she said.

"Zach texted earlier and a waitress from the Last Bite Diner said Reggie's becoming quite the regular customer. He's showing up at odd hours, though," Nate reported.

"In that case, is he Zach's primary suspect?" she asked.

"He was until your old boss sent those flowers." She still hadn't showed him the texts. She reached for her purse and thought her head might split in two.

"What are you trying to get? Let me." He glanced around the room and must've realized before she could get the words out because he made a move for the dresser.

"My purse is over there. My cell should be inside." She pointed to her handbag.

Nate retrieved it and set it down on the bed. The mattress dipped underneath his weight.

She located her cell, which was out of battery. The charger was on her nightstand. She plugged in her phone and it came to life a few seconds later.

According to the icon on the bottom left-hand side of her phone, there were thirty-seven new texts. She pressed the icon and scanned through the few names. Several were from vendors. And then there was Renaldo's name. She'd almost deleted his contact info from her list but figured she didn't want to be caught off guard if he called. She wanted to know it was him, so she wouldn't accidentally answer.

Twenty-three of the messages were from Renaldo. She hadn't read many of them since she'd moved to Jacobstown, figuring his attempts to contact her would peter out eventually. There was no use fanning that flame by responding.

They'd been stacking up. The oldest ones sounded the most venomous. She tilted the phone so Nate could read them.

I'll ruin you.
You'll never work again.
You're a spoiled bitch.
Answer me!
You won't get away so easy.
You better watch out.
I could be anywhere.

"This guy was your boss?" he asked.

"Yeah, for the better part of the last three years," she stated.

"Were there no other kitchens that would hire you?" He read each text and the intensity of his gaze increased with each one.

"I'm afraid not. He's influential. I thought the chance to work with him was straight from heaven at first. My food truck was gone in the blink of an eye. The truck repossessed. I had debt. There weren't many jobs available where I lived at the time and I had to be close to home. Travis took the only car we had with him. My mom had her sedan and that's how I got Skylar home from the hospital. Mom had to run out and buy a new car seat because he took off with the only one I had. Money was tight. Then I heard about this job with a famous chef. Nice restaurant. I didn't have a lot of options even though I'd heard he had a reputation. I expected to get hit on, but everyone said he was so much worse with me. Like he developed a fixation because I wouldn't flirt back. It got worse from there. I was done with men and had zero interest."

"You couldn't quit?" He quirked a brow.

"My reputation wasn't the best after losing my truck. People thought I mismanaged the business. No one has the patience to listen to what really happened. I was good at what I did, but I didn't have real restaurant experience. Renaldo had a lot of influence in the Houston area and I didn't have the money to relocate. Not until now," she admitted.

Nate flexed and released his fist. "I can think of a few things I'd do to a man who takes advantage of someone in a weaker position."

"It didn't help that my self-esteem was pretty shot. I was so tired from caring for Skylar as a baby. Then there was my mom. I couldn't just walk out, and Renaldo seemed ready to make my life miserable as long as I stayed. I threatened to quit and he said he'd ruin me." Thinking about it now sent anger shooting through her. "He had influence and I didn't. If I went somewhere else, I'd need a reference. He made it clear that he wouldn't give me one." She pinched the bridge of her nose. "I felt pretty damn trapped until I heard from Aunt Maddie's lawyer. I had hope for the first time in four years. This restaurant *had* to open. It *had* to work. Now, I don't know what I'm going to do."

Hearing the words brought her to the brink of a breakdown.

"It'll be okay—"

"How? The restaurant is gone now." Panic welled inside her.

"We'll figure it out. I'm not going to let that be taken away from you, Chelsea. I have a feeling you're going to be very successful and I want to offer seed money," Nate said.

Odd that his words were so reassuring when there was no real reason to feel that way. There'd been a fire. She could've easily lost her life.

"You would do that?" Could she allow him to?

"Yes."

"Why?"

"Because you're a decent person who needs a break. I have enough money to help you get back on your feet as long as you're not too stubborn to accept it." His offer was tempting.

She had her daughter to think about and medical bills for her mother. "I can't afford to be stubborn, Nate. But you have to let me pay you back."

"We can handle the finances however you want to." His words came out final-sounding.

"I need to figure a few things out first on the financial end."

"Agreed."

A burst of hope swelled inside her chest.

"We need to show these texts to Zach." Nate motioned toward her phone and she figured he was changing the subject before she had a chance to rethink his offer. "He'll want to see this. He'll also want to drive to Houston and speak to Renaldo personally."

"Look at the more recent texts," she said.

I've been a jerk.
Forgive me.
Chelsea?
Answer please.
I'm sorry.

"That last one could cover several scenarios." Nate pointed out the fact that it had come in two hours after the fire.

"Right. He's a hothead and lost his temper daily. I'm wondering if he'd be so stupid as to text me threats and then set my restaurant on fire." She couldn't fathom it, but then his actions had left her scratching her head. Why fixate on her in the first place? Why would anyone want to be with someone who didn't want them back?

Chelsea had had plenty of time to ponder that question as a child. Even as young as twelve she knew her mother had stopped living, like she was waiting for her husband to show up and make everything okay again.

Life didn't always hand "okay" to people, not even to

good people. In fact, pretty bad things happened to good people far too often.

"I've learned that people sometimes are that obvious with their words and actions. Only the most calculating ones don't get caught right away." Nate palmed her phone. "I'd still like a few minutes alone with him in a locked room. We'd see how tough he was then."

Nate was already taking screen shots of the texts. "I'm sending these to Zach so he'll have them first thing in the morning. He'll want to talk to this guy. The timing is weird, but Vinchesa doesn't sound like a career criminal who's used to covering his tracks. You'd be surprised at how many criminals give themselves away easily."

"What about the ones who don't?"

Chapter Fourteen

"Those can be scary as hell." Nate didn't want to think about the level to which someone might go to cover up deviant behavior. A smart person didn't get caught and that's exactly the type were dealing with when it came to the heifers. Even with advanced security measures in place like installing cameras near Rushing Creek and adding security personnel and patrols, the responsible person hadn't been caught. All anyone knew so far was that the killer was male based on his shoe print. He was good at making certain that none of his DNA was ever found at a crime scene.

"Do you think Reggie's that smart?" It was a fair question.

"He's a known criminal. Someone with a long history of committing petty crimes could wise up with experience. Someone like him learns the system from the inside. Gets smarter every time he gets away with something." It was the closest anyone had been to so much as making an educated guess about who might be responsible for the heifers. But would the same man be stupid enough to try to hurt Chelsea? Would he draw attention to himself now? And why would the two crimes be connected?

The probability was low.

"Reggie seems guilty of something. He's been coming in and out of town undetected for the most part," she surmised.

"True. We have no idea how long this has been going on and the last time Zach had him in custody, the man wasn't speaking. He has a Louisiana license plate but Zach discovered the address on his vehicle registration didn't match his driver's license."

"There are no witnesses to the fire. Right?" Chelsea asked.

"No one besides you. We're still waiting on unofficial word from the fire marshal." Nate figured he could lean on the captain for an answer. The conversation would go over better in person, which was why he hadn't called yet.

Chelsea took another sip of water.

"I don't want to wake the house, but is there any chance I can slip downstairs and make coffee?" Nate hadn't had a cup in hours and he could use the caffeine boost to help him think more clearly.

"Depends on how quiet you are," she replied. "My mother sleeps like a rock once she falls asleep. But that can take a minute. Skylar fights sleep until it pulls her under. Once she's out, she's out. Rofert knows you, so I doubt he'll bark."

That was all the confirmation he needed. "You want a cup?"

"Is that a serious question?" She smiled and he liked the way it softened the worry lines on her face. The break in tension was a nice change. It was easy to talk to Chelsea.

"In that case, I'll be right back." He stopped at the door. "Are you hungry?"

"I think there's yogurt in the fridge. Do you mind bringing it up?"

"Not at all." He disappeared down the hallway without so much as a floorboard creak.

He flipped the light on in the kitchen and went about making the fresh brew. As he stood there with his palms on the counter, waiting for the machine to spit out the brown liquid, a thought occurred to him. Had the attacker chosen to strike at the restaurant because Rofert was at Chelsea's home?

Wouldn't that make more sense than someone trying to destroy her business for no reason? And he was damn sure there'd been an attack. He believed that she'd heard a male voice before she'd blacked out.

If it hadn't been for the winds, she might've succumbed to smoke inhalation. She'd gotten lucky. And what about the person who'd called in the blaze? Nate needed to ask Zach about the interview. Zach had surely investigated that angle by now. It wasn't uncommon for a criminal to call in his own crime, especially once he believed his victim was dead.

At the very least, someone was sending a message to Chelsea. He was saying that he could get to her whenever he wanted. He could strike anywhere, any place.

Except home.

Rofert would've heard a noise if anyone had broken into the house. The locks were secure, too. Nate had seen to it that the best locks had been used. The windows had been replaced. Getting to Chelsea at home would definitely require more skill.

Another consideration was that the attacker only wanted to harm Chelsea. The person wanted to ensure no one else was hurt. That scenario pointed directly to her ex, Travis. Reggie wouldn't make that distinction. He'd strike where he could and Nate doubted the man would care about collateral damage.

Nate doubted anyone from town would have a problem with Chelsea opening up a new restaurant. People had been complaining about that building being vacant for years. He'd only heard good things from folks about her breathing life into it again. There'd always be one or two complainers.

And then, there could be nothing to it. She might've fallen and hit her head, knocking the heater off the table and starting the blaze. Nate didn't think Chelsea would lie. Her brain had been scrambled in the fall and she might be recalling events out of order.

He'd worked with enough head-injury patients to realize Chelsea could be remembering wrong.

The coffeemaker sputtered and beeped, a welcome sound.

He filled two mugs, grabbed yogurt and a spoon, and then headed upstairs, stopping at the top long enough to set one of the mugs down so he could scratch Rofert behind the ears. Rofert seemed happy as a lark.

The old boy might have a tough time leaving the sweet family when this was all said and done.

NATE WOKE TO the scent of bacon the next morning. And a pair of familiar voices. Amber and Amy, his sister and cousin respectively.

A moment of panic had him to his feet and out the door in two seconds flat. The sun was up for now. The news had predicted a turn in weather. Nate hoped everything was okay at the ranch.

"Amber," he said from down the hallway. He'd heard

Linda shout upstairs that she was taking Skylar to school a few hours ago. Nate had heard Linda return before letting himself nod off. All he needed was a couple of twenty-minute spurts and he was fine. He'd slept longer than that. He reminded himself not to get too comfortable in the single mother's home.

"Hey, Nate," Amber practically chirped. She met him at the door to the kitchen and gave him a warm hug.

Amy followed suit.

"What's going on?" He looked to Amy and then Amber.

"We heard about the fire and wanted to stop by to see if there's anything we can do to help," Amber said. His baby sister and cousin had hearts of gold.

"Good morning, Nate," Linda said. "I sure appreciate you staying over last night to keep watch over my daughter."

"Much obliged, ma'am," he responded.

"How *is* Chelsea?" Amber asked.

"Physically, she's doing better. The high winds probably saved her from having more issues with her lungs," he stated.

"My brother told us what happened. That's so scary," Amy interjected. "I'm sorry she had to go through that. It sounds like she's very lucky."

Nate wouldn't disagree with that statement. But first, coffee.

He moved to the pot and pulled a mug from the cabinet. He didn't think much about his actions until he'd poured a cup, taken a sip and then turned around. Both Amber and Amy's jaws practically hit the floor.

It hadn't occurred to Nate how comfortable he'd become in the McGregor house and that must be the action widening his sibling and cousin's eyes.

"I see Rofert has been keeping you company, Linda." Nate redirected their focus. He didn't want to discuss his comfort level at Chelsea's house with anyone. Hell, he didn't want to put too much stock in it.

"He sits by the door until Skylar comes back," Linda responded.

"Aw," both women said at the same time.

"I shouldn't be surprised, though. He loves kids," Amber related, shooting an affectionate look toward the oversize pup curled up against the back door.

"I made bacon, in case you two woke," Linda stated. "I'll just go check on Chelsea."

That's when the women whirled on Nate.

"So what's *really* going on?" Amber asked.

"Nothing, I slept in a chair." He rolled his head around, trying to loosen the crick in his neck. "I have the knots to prove it."

Amber stared at him like he had two heads. "What are you talking about?"

"Last night. Isn't that what you were…" His blunder occurred to him midsentence. "*You're* asking about the fire."

He glanced from Amber to Amy. "I thought you spoke to your brother."

"We did. But you know Zach. He doesn't say a whole lot if he doesn't think we need to know. We've been hearing rumors about her distant cousin and something about a limp on his left side. Is that true?" Amy had always had a spunky side and Nate could see the twinkle in her eye.

"Yes, her cousin has a bad leg. Zach is checking into his background and whereabouts over the past couple of years," Nate told them.

"Is that the same person who set the fire last night?" Amber persisted.

"No one knows for sure. I haven't spoken to the captain about the fire yet."

"It's arson," Amy said emphatically.

"How do you know?" Nate took another sip of coffee. Dealing with Amy and Amber's energy before he had a solid cup in him was proving interesting. He didn't want to give away information that was inaccurate, but felt everyone should be in the know so they could look out for one another.

"I overheard my brother. He seemed certain," Amy said.

"Then the initial investigation is probably iron-clad." He'd tell Chelsea as soon as she woke. He'd witnessed the distress lines on her forehead earlier and hoped more information would help ease some of her worry.

Nate downed the rest of his coffee and turned to fix another. It was then he noticed the bags of groceries on the counter along with a stack of plastic containers filled with cooked food.

"Did you do all this?" he asked Amber.

"Me and Amy and the rest of the Kent clan. We all figured they could use a hand while Chelsea heals." The compassion in his sister's voice warmed his heart.

Footsteps sounded from the hallway. A fresh-faced Chelsea walked into the kitchen wearing a jogging suit. Her blond hair fell around her shoulders.

Nate's heart clenched.

"GOOD MORNING." CHELSEA's gaze bounced from Amy to Amber. She saw the family resemblance and couldn't help but think the Kents had been blessed with amazing genes.

"We heard about what happened. I'm so sorry. I'm Amber, Nate's sister." She offered a handshake and Chelsea took it.

"I'm Amy, his cousin," the other one said. She shook Chelsea's hand next.

"Should you be standing up?" Amber asked.

"Rest does a lot of good, but I should probably take a seat at the kitchen table." There was no reason to push it.

"Coffee?" Nate asked. He'd been silently observing from the corner by the machine.

"Yes, please," Chelsea said, looking around. "My mother said you brought food. You really didn't have to—"

"It's nothing," Amber waved her hand like she was lazily swatting a fly. "The least we can do under the circumstances. We've been meaning to come by anyway and introduce ourselves. The ranch has been keeping us busy, but that's no excuse."

"This is too much." Chelsea choked back the emotion threatening to bring tears to her eyes. By and large, she was not a crier. Although she couldn't help but think a good cry might make her feel better if she could let out her emotions. Instead, she bottled them up inside until they threatened to choke her.

"We were helping your mother put groceries away when Nate came downstairs and we got distracted." Amy glanced at Nate before returning her gaze to Chelsea. "Is it okay if we finish what we started?"

Their kindness was a little overwhelming but Chelsea was grateful. "I wish there was something I could do to help."

She started to rise, but Nate put a steaming coffee mug in front of her.

"Fair warning. Once these two get something in their heads, they go all-in." He smiled. Seeing that man in her kitchen first thing in the morning made her heart want things she knew better than to allow. Nate was intelligent, handsome and built like she couldn't believe. In short, he was dangerous.

"It's too much." Chelsea could lose her business and she would figure out how to get a job to pay bills. She could lose her house and she would figure out some way to find shelter. But she could not lose her heart. That was the one thing she wouldn't gamble.

Looking at Nate, she hoped like hell she wasn't too late.

"You guys are lucky to have one another." Chelsea's gaze moved from Amy to Amber, appreciating how the two moved in sync with each other. It was obvious they were close and seeing them made her realize just how opposite she must seem to Nate.

He came from a wealthy, tight-knit family. Chelsea and her mother were as close as they could be. They loved each other, but her mother had always held back, protected herself, even with her daughter.

Chelsea didn't blame Linda for guarding her heart. Or maybe it wasn't guarding at all. Maybe it was just broken and the pieces had never fit back together in the right way. There was no doubt her mother loved Chelsea. Loved Skylar. But once her heart had been shattered, she'd never seemed to recover.

It was the kind of all-consuming heartbreak Chelsea would experience with a man like Nate. And all the more reason to keep her distance.

MEETING NATE'S FAMILY a few days ago and seeing their generosity had Chelsea wishing her daughter could grow up surrounded by that kind of love.

Chelsea pushed the unproductive thought aside. She was doing okay as Skylar's mother. Wasn't she?

Nate had taken to sleeping in the guest room downstairs even though she'd insisted that she was well enough for him to go home.

Having Nate sleep at her house was a stark reminder of the danger she'd been in. She was *still* in danger as long as the person who'd clocked her from behind and then lit her restaurant on fire was still on the loose.

The fire marshal's initial ruling was arson, noting that the fire had been started from the inside. Any DNA evidence linking a perp to the crime had most likely been burned at the scene, so Zach was no closer to figuring out who was responsible.

Chelsea had contacted the estate lawyer, Michel Green, who'd relayed that the restaurant had been covered under an umbrella policy left by Aunt Maddie. Thankfully, Chelsea hadn't lost everything and she had a certain pride from not having to borrow from Nate even though she deeply appreciated his offer. There'd be a delay in opening—the fire set back her opening to the end of February at the earliest—and that was definitely more stressful.

Money would be tight, but Chelsea figured she might be able to eke by until then.

Nate walked into the kitchen where she sat at the table nursing a cup of coffee.

"I just heard from Zach," he said.

"What did he have to say?"

"You're not going to like this." Nate held up his phone. "Travis has been in jail for the past three years. He was locked up on illegal possession of a firearm."

Chapter Fifteen

Chelsea could scarcely believe her ears. Granted, Travis had gone down a dark path, but real jail time? For weapons?

And then another thought dawned on her.

"He won't be able to get custody of Skylar," she said to Nate in an almost whisper.

"A judge could grant supervised visitation, but that's the best he'll be able to get based on other cases I've heard about," Nate confirmed.

Travis was far more dangerous than she realized if he was involved in weapons charges.

"What if I'm not in the picture?" she asked. "What if I'm gone?"

"That would be tricky. Skylar has spent her entire life with you and your mother. If Travis had a real job and could prove that his home would be more fit…"

"He would never be a better option than my mother." They both knew that her mother's health could be made into an issue.

All this time she'd been afraid that Travis would show up with court-ordered visitation or shared custody and he didn't have a leg to stand on with a judge. His threats the other day had been idle because he had to know it, too.

"I'm guessing that Zach has no idea where Travis is," she stated.

Nate shook his head.

Travis hadn't showed up since that evening at the restaurant as far as she knew. "He knew about the restaurant. I wonder how long he's been watching me."

"Good questions. Zach said he was released two months ago and has to see his parole officer on the second of every month," Nate advised.

"He must've just visited before he came to Jacobstown," she said.

"If he's responsible for the fire, he might skip his next appointment." Nate poured a cup of coffee and held up the pot. "You ready for more?"

Chelsea nodded.

He walked over and refilled her mug. He stopped for a second and looked her in the eyes. "He won't get to you or Skylar as long as I'm around. You know that. Right?"

"Yeah." The key was *as long as he was around.* He couldn't stick around forever. He had responsibilities on his family ranch. "At some point you need to go back to work. I feel bad enough that your family has sacrificed the extra set of hands this long. From everything I've read about running a ranch, it takes everyone in your family and then some."

"It's not the easiest way to make a living. It's a way of life. My family bought land a long time ago and got the associated mineral rights," he said. "We're fortunate and we know it. Our parents made sure we didn't take any of it for granted."

"I wish I could've met them. They sound amazing." She picked up her mug and rolled it in her hands. "I'm pretty sure I could benefit from a few pointers from them. I hope I'm not messing up being a parent too badly."

"You love your daughter more than anything else. Isn't that what kids need the most?" Nate had a point.

She wanted to give Skylar the world. But it wouldn't do any good if her daughter didn't feel loved. Chelsea loved her mother and the two had grown close over the years. She still remembered feeling like she wasn't enough to keep her mother happy. As an adult, she realized that her mother had been grieving losing her husband and the life she thought they'd have together. Chelsea came to realize that having her had probably kept her mother from completely falling apart.

Losing Travis in the way she had, facing the same fate as her mother, gave Chelsea even more resolve to make sure Skylar always knew she was loved. "I guess you're right. It's so easy to focus on my mistakes when it comes to parenting. It's this big, important job and I want to get it right."

Nate took the seat next to her and put his hand over hers. "I've been around a few babies recently and it's help me realize a few things. No parent is ever perfect. No kid is ever perfect. But honesty, forgiveness and genuine love go a long way toward a perfect relationship."

"Said like that, it makes perfect sense." Chelsea's heart pounded her ribs with him this close, touching her, but she managed a smile.

He leaned toward her.

Her mother's footsteps sounded in the hallway, heading for the kitchen.

Nate stood and grabbed his cup of coffee from the counter. "Morning, ma'am."

"You know you can call me Linda," she said.

"My apologies. It's old habit," he said.

Chelsea took a sip of coffee, enjoying the burn. She needed a reality check. Falling for Nate was out of the question.

"WE'LL GO TO Houston with Zach first thing tomorrow morning to interview Renaldo." Nate made sure Chelsea was settled in bed before he shut off the light.

"I need to be here with my mother and Skylar," Chelsea said.

"I'm not going without you. We have a pilot who can fly us down and back. You'll be home before supper." Nate had no plans to let Chelsea out of his sight until the case was solved. He wanted to be there when Zach interviewed Chelsea's former boss if for no other reason than to have Zach's back. He also planned to make sure someone watched her house to protect Skylar and Linda.

"In that case, I'd like to hear what he has to say." She pulled the covers up and settled in. "I'm guessing Zach couldn't pinpoint Renaldo's location based on the texts."

"No. So, he wants to interview him and get a feel for whether he's honest. We'll wait at a nearby café while Zach speaks to the suspect. That's as close as Zach will allow us to get." There were too many variables for Nate to feel comfortable. First, there was Reggie. Nate didn't like anything about that man. Everyone was keeping watch for him, though. And the benefit to that kind of scrutiny was that it would be much more difficult for him to show up unannounced.

Word had gotten out about Reggie's limp and that he'd been in and out of town doing who knew what.

Travis was more of an unknown quantity. He'd been in jail for three years and his first act after release was to hunt Chelsea down. Then again, he might've been keeping tabs on her from prison if he'd had access to a computer or friends on the outside. Controls were in place to prevent computers being used for devious reasons but convicts were cunning and could find ways around them.

Chelsea hadn't exactly been in hiding for the past four years. She'd been working and taking care of her family. Nate couldn't help but think someone as honest and hardworking as her deserved a break. Life had thrown a lot at her, but she was still standing. He admired her courage.

At seven o'clock the next morning, the airplane waited on the tarmac. A checklist had been run through and Nate received the text that all systems were go.

It took an hour, give or take, to fly to Houston. They arrived at Renaldo's downtown apartment building by 8:53 a.m.

Nate couldn't help but notice that the modern building was extremely tall and that the glass had a blue tint that looked like it reflected the sky. There were sharp angles at the top. It was the kind of building Nate expected an entire apartment to be decorated in shades of gray: light gray walls with a dark gray sofa. The place would be all about the lines.

He couldn't imagine living in such a colorless environment but it suited some people. He was more of an outdoor campfire guy. A house with a fireplace and comfortable furniture was more his style. He liked being able to sink into a chair rather than perch on the edge of one like a bird.

There was a café across the street from the building by the name of Roasted Bean. It was the perfect spot for Nate and Chelsea to set up and wait for Zach.

The trio split up after confirming that Renaldo's vehicle was parked in the attached garage in the space assigned to apartment 1101.

Chelsea had been fidgeting in the airplane. She'd twisted her fingers together on the ride over and now she was tapping her toe on the concrete flooring while they waited in line to order coffee.

It was understandable.

She kept glancing across the street.

"You want to grab a table by the window while I order?" he asked, figuring she needed something to do besides stand there.

"Yeah, sure." She'd healed from her injury and the headaches had subsided. "He should be in there, right?"

"His vehicle is parked in its spot. There's a high probability he's in there." Plus, from what Nate knew about the restaurant business, a chef's world didn't get started until at least 3:00 p.m. and would run late into the night. An executive chef like Renaldo wouldn't likely arrive until 3:30 p.m. He would most likely have already been up and shopping at five o'clock this morning as the freshest produce and meats would be put out then.

Renaldo might be arrogant but he hadn't risen to his position in the restaurant business by being lazy.

By the time Nate got the drinks and sat, his cell buzzed. He checked the screen. It was Zach.

"No one's answering the door," Nate reported to Chelsea.

She groaned. "He might've gone back to sleep, in which case he'll be wearing ear plugs."

"I'll let Zach know," Nate said not wanting to ask how she knew the man's sleeping habits.

"Hold on. There he is." She pointed across the street. A man wearing expensive jogging pants and a T-shirt with bare feet came running from around the side of the building. "Security must've called up and warned him."

Nate bit out a curse and bolted out the door. He made a beeline for the shorter, medium-built guy with long hair and loose curls.

"Stop!" Nate shouted, hoping that Chelsea had stayed inside the restaurant and texted Zach. Nate should've told her to do just that but he hadn't wanted to risk Renaldo getting to his vehicle.

Renaldo wasn't nearly as fit as Nate.

Nate shot across the street and dove into the man, knocking him off balance.

"Where do you think you're going?" Nate said as he tackled Renaldo.

The chef screamed like he was in a horror movie being chased by a psycho with a chainsaw in his hands. The few people on the sidewalk cleared the way darn fast.

Nate landed on top of Renaldo, who skidded on the pavement.

There was no use throwing a punch. Nate used his heft to pin the man on the concrete.

"Freeze. Put your hands where I can see 'em," Zach commanded in that cop voice reserved for ordering criminals around.

Nate put his hands in the air and so did Renaldo. Of course, Nate kept his knee in the man's chest, which probably helped him be more compliant. If the jerk made a wrong move, he'd be picking his teeth out of the concrete as far as Nate was concerned.

"Let's take this inside," Zach said after a quick patdown to ensure Renaldo wasn't carrying a weapon. "I'm guessing the security officer at the front desk told you I was heading upstairs."

Renaldo nodded.

The lobby of the apartment building had several chairs nestled together to the right of the main desk. The security guard shot an apology at Renaldo. No doubt his job depended on him alerting residents, but Nate figured Zach would have a few words for the man when all was said and done. Phrases like "obstruction of justice" came to mind. Although, to be fair, this guy most likely made the call as a heads-up and hadn't expected the chef to make a run for it.

Zach stood with his feet apart, hand resting on the butt of his gun as he instructed Renaldo to take a seat. Nate had seen the defensive position many times with his cousin while on a call. Civilians were allowed to ride-along with the sheriff. Nate had accompanied his cousin several times.

"Where were you last Tuesday?" Zach asked.

Nate's cell buzzed. He glanced up at Zach, who gave him a nod to indicate it was okay to leave.

The text was from Chelsea, as expected. He dashed across the street. Obviously, she wouldn't want to risk being seen or letting Renaldo know she was in the area. Being connected in any way wouldn't help, especially if he'd had nothing to do with the attack or fire.

"Are you all right?" she asked, worry lines etched across her forehead.

"Yeah," Nate said. "But the chef got a few scrapes and bruises out of it."

He was trying to cut through the tension with the joke but it fell flat. He could see how uncomfortable she was with her old boss nearby. Her toe was tapping again and she was sitting on the edge of her chair.

Nate took a seat. "Zach is interviewing Renaldo right

now. If he had anything to do with the fire, Zach will figure it out."

"I almost want it to be him. Is that weird?" She blinked a couple of times before taking another sip of coffee. Caffeine was probably the last thing she needed but he acknowledged that it gave her something to do.

"No. You don't want Travis to be involved because that's unthinkable. No matter what else your relationship is with him, the fact remains that you're the mother of his child. As much as you don't like him personally, if he was sincere about wanting a relationship with Skylar, you'd figure it out," he concluded.

"Exactly."

"Because you love her. You have to keep in mind, he's never met her. He didn't hold her in his arms late at night like you did. He didn't rock her to sleep like you did." For all intents and purposes, Nate reasoned, the man was a stranger to his own kid. Another in a long list of reasons why Nate didn't much care for the guy. Mistakes, he understood. Dating the wrong person, he understood. He would never understand a man who could turn his back on his wife and child. That just wasn't in a Kent's DNA.

"You're right. I'm still trying to figure out what he wants with her and why he even showed up in the first place." She glanced left to right, scanning the coffee shop.

Yeah, the guy could show up and force his way into her life at any time. Chelsea seemed keenly aware of that fact. And she'd most likely be looking over her shoulder the rest of her life, wondering if Travis would be there when she turned around, given the way they'd left things after their exchange at her restaurant.

Knowing her ex had been behind bars for the past three years had to be yet another blow. Especially since he'd lied and said he was working. He probably hadn't wanted to show his hand to her because he'd wanted to threaten her with custody.

Again, what did Travis have to gain?

It was anyone's guess where the guy had disappeared to. Selfishly, Nate wanted Travis to be far away. As long as he was wishing, why not go all-in? Nate wished Travis would settle somewhere else, start fresh and leave Chelsea alone.

That scenario wasn't likely with a guy like Travis. Not if he smelled money. He'd cleaned her out once and Chelsea didn't strike Nate as the type to get taken a second time. It made sense as to why she was so guarded with him.

She'd been burned big time. And just like a frightened or abused animal, it would take a boatload of patience to get her to trust anyone again.

Nate looked up in time to see Zach crossing the street.

His cousin wore an intense expression as he pushed open the door and walked inside the café.

"What happened?" Chelsea asked.

"He's guilty of something." Zach took a seat.

Chapter Sixteen

"Renaldo said he was with a friend at her place on the night in question." Zach's frustration was written across his features.

Nate had listened quietly as Zach recounted the story of the conversation between him and Renaldo.

"You don't believe him," Chelsea stated.

"He called her on the phone and I could tell she was scared to say anything against him. I need to talk to her face-to-face. See if she'll fold under the heat. You guys feel like taking a ride?" Zach asked.

"Did he mention the friend's name?" Maybe Chelsea had heard of her.

"Danielle French." Zach leaned forward.

"She works at the restaurant. She's a waitress," Chelsea said. "He goes through a variety of women and it does seem like he's with a different one every other week, but they weren't dating when I left the restaurant."

"The address he gave is not that far away." Zach held up his phone, revealing the map feature with an address on it.

"Let's go," Nate said.

They pulled into the Rancho Verde Apartment Homes' lot twenty minutes later. The place was on the outskirts of downtown, more in the suburbs. The structure was not as nice as Renaldo's upscale complex. This was more like a typical Texas apartment building. A front gate, which Zach got through by waiting for a car to exit, was supposed to keep loiterers away. It was easy to bypass.

There was a sprinkling of three-story buildings spread out across several acres. There were mini parking lots for each building and clusters of mail centers and laundry facilities.

The apartments were considerably less expensive, which wasn't a surprise given the pay difference between a near celebrity chef versus someone waiting tables.

Zach parked and exited the sedan. The way the buildings were set up, Chelsea stood behind Nate, using his heft to conceal most of her.

A female answered the door on the second knock, but Chelsea didn't recognize her voice.

"Ms. Danielle French?" Zach standing there in uniform would probably make anyone nervous, but this person's voice cracked when she tried to respond.

"No. I'm Cindy Staten, her roommate. Why are you looking for Danielle?" The words sounded rehearsed and a little forced.

Chelsea figured the roommate had been forewarned of this visit, just as Renaldo had been. Between his threatening texts and then his sudden change of heart with the flowers and apologies, she presumed he was trying to look as innocent as possible. Most innocent people wouldn't give it a thought. Whereas he was going out of his way to appear above suspicion.

"Is Ms. French home?" Zach asked.

"Yes. Hold on. I'll get her—"

Cindy returned a few seconds later with a woman presumed to be Danielle.

"Ms. Staten?"

She nodded, a skeptical look crossed her features. She was attractive. In her mid-twenties, she had blond hair and blue eyes, and was the kind of person who seemed to want everyone to like her. Chelsea also noted that Danielle was easily impressionable. She was exactly the kind of person an older man like Renaldo could manipulate.

"Where were you last Tuesday night?" Zach pressed on.

"I was right here," Danielle supplied.

"Yes, she was here with her boyfriend," Cindy concurred. "Why? Did something happen?"

"Who is her boyfriend?" Zach ignored the question.

"He's her boss. His name is Renaldo," Cindy responded.

"And he was here?"

"Yes. Well, yeah…" Cindy paused as her voice trailing off.

"What does that mean?" Zach prompted.

"He wears really expensive, like, Italian leather shoes and they were parked next to the front door all night. I didn't actually *see* either one of them. I came in late and left early the next morning. His shoes were here when I got home and were in the same place when I got up the next morning," she told him.

Chelsea figured questioning her was useless. The shoes could've been left there for days. The so-called girlfriend could be covering for Renaldo. Or maybe he'd threatened Danielle. Who knew? This felt like a dead end.

Chelsea's phone buzzed. She glanced at the screen and then showed it to Nate. The call was from her mother.

He took her hand and led her outside, away from the apartment, without so much as making a noise.

When Chelsea was clear of the building, she returned her mother's call.

"Everything okay?" Chelsea's pulse skyrocketed at the thought she was more than an hour's plane ride away and something could be wrong back home.

"I'm feeling light-headed," Linda said.

"Did you take your medicine?" Chelsea didn't mince words. This had happened before when her mother had forgotten to take one of her yellow pills.

"I think so," her mother said. "It's probably nothing, but I was wondering if you could pick up Skylar later. I'm going to fix myself a cup of tea and get to bed." Her mother coughed.

She could be coming down with something.

"Okay, Mom. Yeah, sure, I can pick up Skylar. Don't worry about it. Get some rest and I'll check on you when I get home before pickup." Chelsea started to end the call. "Mom?"

"Yes, honey."

"Are you sure you're okay? This is nothing I need to worry about. Right?" Her mother knew the difference between needing medical attention and having a virus. The problem was that she downplayed everything and Chelsea believed her mother didn't want to be the cause of concern for her daughter.

"I have Rofert here to keep me company and I'll be better once I get a cup of chamomile inside me. A nap will do a world of good. There's plenty of food in the fridge, so there's no need to cook. I ate some of the chicken and mushroom risotto the young ladies brought over. It was so good." Linda sounded tired but all right.

"That sounds delicious. I'll heat up a bowl when I get home for me, Skylar and Nate. Keep your phone on your nightstand in case you need to reach me. Then you won't have to get out of bed," Chelsea recommended.

"Will do, honey. Be careful on your way home from picking up Skylar. They said on the news the weather might turn," her mother said.

"Thanks, Mom." Chelsea ended the call and turned to Nate.

"I need to get home as soon as possible. Mother isn't feeling well and I don't like being so far away." Chelsea gripped her phone as she looked up to see Zach coming their way.

"Roger that." Nate, who had been fixated on his phone, glanced up and locked eyes with his cousin. "What's the verdict?"

"Both of them lied but I can't prove a thing," Zach stated. "He's covering his tracks, but it could be that he's an overall jerk. He's in the middle of a divorce and probably figures he can't afford bad publicity. I don't like him."

"CHELSEA NEEDS TO get home. Her mother might be getting sick," Nate said to his cousin. He could see the worry behind Chelsea's eyes even though she did her best to maintain composure. She'd been uncomfortable ever since they'd landed and he'd picked up on her nerves. He didn't want to overthink why he was so attuned to her moods.

"I have everything I'm going to get from these people today. If I need to come back, it'll be with a local policeman and a warrant." Zach would need to inform Houston PD and get them involved should he find evidence against Renaldo.

"What did the girls say?" Nate was curious as they walked toward their rented vehicle.

"The two gave exactly the same story," Zach noted. "And that's why I'm not buying it. Usually in an interview people give two versions of the same story but these two sounded like parrots. Only people who have rehearsed a story beforehand use identical words and tell the story in the same way."

"I wonder why they'd cover for him," Nate said.

"We did pretty much anything Renaldo asked or we'd risk losing our jobs," Chelsea stated.

Nate flexed and released his fists, thinking that he should've gotten in a few shots before he'd let the chef stand up.

"Even lie to law enforcement?" Zach asked.

"He might be holding something over Danielle's head. I never gave him any leverage over me, but others did," she reflected.

"Like what?" Zach asked.

"A couple of wait staff got caught using drugs in the meat locker," she said. "Renaldo had them do all kinds of favors for him so he wouldn't report them."

"Does Renaldo use illegal drugs?" Nate asked.

"Not that I know of. He's high on himself as far as I could tell. That, and the feeling of dominating everyone around him." Renaldo had been a jerk and acted like a spoiled brat when he didn't get his way. "He liked to catch people doing things wrong. A cook had an affair with one of the married waitresses. Renaldo had a field day with that."

"And you? Did he try to catch you doing something wrong?" Nate asked.

"I never gave him anything to work with," she admitted. "All he could hold over my head was my job and my reputation. Both were important to me. The kitchen is all I've ever known and I'm damn good at it. I didn't want anyone to take that away from me."

"Were there sexual advances?" Zach asked as they made it back to the vehicle.

Chelsea had a good laugh over that question even though it wasn't funny to Nate. "Yes."

"And?"

"A lot of the waitresses gave in. I mean, he was considered good-looking. He has enough money to seem impressive to those without. He lives in a fancy downtown apartment and drives an expensive sports car. Most of the women he hit on were flattered."

The three of them climbed into their rented sedan. Nate took the driver's seat, Chelsea got in on the passenger side.

"What about you?" Nate started the engine of the rental as he glanced at Chelsea. "Did he manipulate you?"

"I didn't let him get away with anything," she stated.

"Where does he stand on your suspect list after speaking to him?" Nate asked Zach as he settled in the back seat.

"Right now he's at the bottom of a short list," Zach admitted.

And that left Travis and Reggie.

"Rumors are circulating that Reggie was heading up north. There was too much heat on him here."

"Can we rule him out?" Nate asked.

"Possibly."

THE FLIGHT HOME was quiet and bumpy. A weather system was coming. Chelsea worked her purse strap between her fingers for most of the time they were in the air. Zach studied his notebook or his phone. Nate acknowledged that he was getting behind on work at the ranch. And yet all he could think about was helping Chelsea get her restaurant off the ground.

The plan landed while he was still chewing on ideas. Chelsea was too proud to ask for help and he didn't want to overstep his bounds. But he did want to find a way to be of service. He'd figure out something. The number of bachelors in the family was dwindling fast. Especially since his cousin Zach had recently told him of his engagement and pending nuptials.

The thought of Chelsea struggling against her deadline to open the restaurant alone sat heavy on Nate's chest as he thanked Zach for flying to Houston to investigate Renaldo. Again, the thought of a man abusing his power by forcing people to do things they didn't want to do caused tension to cord Nate's muscles. If he kept thinking about it, he'd end up with a headache.

Chelsea rode with Nate while Zach took off in his cruiser, promising to get back to them as soon as he had news to report.

"I'm needed at the ranch before the weather system hits," Nate told her. He'd been keeping an eye on the reports. "We need all hands on deck to secure the animals in the barns before the front comes in. I'd like to take you to the ranch with me."

She shot him an apologetic look. "I should probably check on Mother and schedule a few contractors before I pick up Skylar."

Chelsea looked surprised that he didn't put up an argument.

"I'll do my best to get back before supper," he said.

He wasn't sure how long he'd be, considering his head had been out of the ranching business lately.

Nate pulled up next to Linda's car at Chelsea's house. He got out and walked her to the back door, linking their fingers.

The urge to kiss her had been building all morning.

"Before you go inside, I'd like your permission to kiss you again."

Chelsea turned around and locked gazes with him.

"You sure that's such a good idea?"

Chapter Seventeen

"It's a terrible idea," Nate said with one those devastating smiles of his.

Chelsea fisted Nate's shirt. She'd been thinking about the kiss they'd shared far too often. This was going to be the worst of bad ideas and yet she couldn't stop herself. Her gaze drifted up to his lips.

And then she looked into his eyes—another grave mistake—because the hunger she saw in them caused heat to swirl low in her belly. The feeling of a hundred butterflies releasing caused her stomach to drop.

Yeah, she was in deep trouble with Nate because this kiss was going to mean a lot more than she wanted it to.

She'd rather do emotional breezy with white-hot passion with him. The kind that burned intensely for a few hours before flaming itself out.

The fire between her and Nate spread.

Ignoring the fact that this heat could cause devastation like she'd never known, Chelsea pushed up to her tiptoes and pressed her lips against his. His tongue delved into her mouth, causing more of that heat to rocket through her body. His mouth fused to hers. His breath quickened, matching the tempo of hers.

Chelsea had never experienced the kind of all-consuming passion that she did when she was with Nate. He was more than just ridiculously hot. He was intelligent and kind, which made for a potent combination. It was also impossible to resist for long.

His hands looped around her waist, pressing her body flush to his. His hands splayed against the small of her back and her stomach turned summersaults.

Every time she took in a breath, her breasts felt heavy and swollen with need, a need to be touched.

Desire built inside her and she was perplexed by how one kiss could stir up such a reaction in her body.

She pulled back long enough to ask, "Do you want to come inside?"

"Is that a real question?" Nate asked.

He linked their fingers after she unlocked the back door.

Once inside, he stopped her long enough to feather a kiss on her collarbone. She grabbed his hand and tugged him into the hallway where she stopped him midway to kiss him on the lips.

Their breath quickened as they moved to the stairwell. Anticipation building with each step toward her room, her bed.

The floor creaked and Chelsea froze. A few beats later, she squeezed Nate's hand and led him to the top of the landing.

Her mother's door was closed and, after a quick peek, Chelsea realized the woman was sound asleep. Skylar was still in school.

Chelsea led Nate to her bedroom.

It didn't take but a second to close and lock the door. She turned to find him standing right there. He took her hands and lifted them until they pressed against the door above her head. He dipped his head and captured her lips. And her knees struggled to support her weight with the heat in the kiss.

His tongue dipped inside her mouth and warmth pooled between her thighs.

With her back against the door and Nate flush with her front, she thought about how amazing he would feel on top of her, crushing her into the mattress with his weight. She wanted to feel him inside her.

Her breathing quickened, matching the pitch of his as he toed off his boots and she stepped out of her tennis shoes.

Chelsea wiggled her hands free of his and dropped them to the hem of his shirt. He helped her by shrugging out of it and then she tossed it onto the floor. Hers joined his a moment later.

He groaned a deep guttural noise when he saw the teal lace of her bra. Then he palmed her breasts as she angled for her bra snap. A moment later, that joined the growing pile on the wood floor.

"You are perfection," he whispered in a low, husky voice that sent trills of electricity shooting through her body.

She figured this wasn't the time to point out the stretch marks that he didn't seem to notice or care about as he dipped his head and captured a nipple in his lips.

Her body hummed with need as her fingers dropped to the waistband of his jeans. She fumbled with the buttons at first but his strong hands joined hers and he stepped out of the denim a second later. In his boxers, she could see his stiff length and another rocket of desire fired through her. Her mind tried to convince her that it had been too long since she'd had mind-blowing sex but her reaction was all Nate Kent.

He had buckets of sex appeal.

She dropped her hand to the erection tenting his boxers and his body stiffened with her touch. His gaze locked onto hers. There was so much hunger in his eyes, he made her feel like the sexiest woman on earth, flaws and all.

A few seconds later, she stepped out of her jeans. He hooked his fingers on either side of her hips and her panties joined the pile on the floor.

By the time they reached the bed, they were bare, naked, skin to skin.

The silky skin of his erection pressed against her belly. He looped his arms around her and kissed her so thoroughly her knees actually buckled. Strong arms kept her upright.

"You're beautiful," he whispered in that low, husky voice that trailed along her skin. "And smart."

He feathered a kiss along her collarbone.

"And sexy."

More kisses along the nape of her neck.

Chelsea pushed him back a step, causing him to sit on the edge of the bed. She joined him, wrapping her legs around his midsection, feeling the sexiest and most empowered she'd ever felt with a man.

It was Nate. He had that effect on her. She felt smart and beautiful and appreciated by him.

Chelsea wrapped her arms around his neck and tunneled her fingers into his hair as she kissed him.

She settled on top of his erection, slowing enough to allow the tip inside. She moved her hips until he was a little deeper inside. His tongue swirled in her mouth. And then her pace picked up.

She ground her hips and he groaned a sexy noise.

He brought his hands up to her breasts and rolled her

nipples between his thumbs and forefingers as she slid on top of him until he reached deeper insider.

Bucking her hips, a well of need sprung as he matched her tempo.

Chelsea gripped his shoulders, digging her fingernails into his skin as he brought her to the brink of ecstasy.

Before she could jump off the cliff, he twisted her around until she was on her back, his weight pushing her deeper into the mattress. She loved the feel of him on top of her as he thrust his sex deeper inside her.

She matched his pitch as she felt his muscles tense. He was on the edge with her.

Faster. Harder. Deeper.

He drove himself inside her until her muscles clenched and released as she reached the peak of ecstasy.

He dove off the cliff with her, drawing out the last spasm.

And then he collapsed next to her, chest heaving.

By far, that was the best sex she'd ever had because it had felt like so much more.

"This changes things between us," he said so low she almost didn't hear him. "I'm falling for you."

Chelsea wasn't sure how to respond so she pretended not to hear him.

A few minutes later, Nate kissed her before getting dressed and walking out the door.

Why hadn't she said something to him?

Why couldn't she go there with him?

Why hadn't she stopped him from leaving?

A BRANCH SCRAPED against the window, startling Chelsea. The winds had picked up in the past hour and the cold front seemed to be moving in earlier than expected. She glanced at the time. She wasn't due to pick up Skylar for another half hour.

Rain droplets pelted the window behind her, making it sound like someone was tap dancing on the pane.

That couldn't be a good sign.

Rather than wait for the front to worsen, Chelsea decided to pick up her daughter early. *Better safe than sorry*, was her thought when it came to unpredictable Texas weather.

Brutal winds blasted her windshield and pea-size hail crashed against the hood. Debris blew around on the streets, which were empty, as most people were already hunkering down for the storm.

Chelsea realized half the kids had already been picked up by the time she got to the preschool. A moment of gratitude washed over her for not being the last one there.

Skylar ran to her mother and launched herself into the air. Chelsea put her arms out just in time to catch her. At close to forty pounds, Skylar was getting harder to hold.

"Momma!" the little girl exclaimed and Chelsea's heart nearly burst. Skylar had her father but a selfish part of her was grateful that she wouldn't have to deal with sharing custody. She was selfish enough to want every birthday, every Christmas, with her angel. Granted, if Travis had turned out to be the standup father Skylar deserved, Chelsea would figure out a way to make peace with being alone every other year for special holidays.

But Chelsea would be grateful for what she had.

"Are you ready to go, sweet girl?" Chelsea set Skylar down and bent to her level.

"Yes." That little girl's smile could melt even the worst day.

Skylar packed up her princess-themed backpack as Chelsea thanked Mrs. Eaton, her teacher.

Hand-in-hand, the two walked out of the preschool. Wind pelted them the minute they stepped outside. Chelsea squeezed her daughter's hand a little tighter as she clutched her coat closed with her free hand.

"Ready to run?" she asked Skylar.

"Mommy? Who's that man?"

Chelsea looked up in time to see Travis in front of her pickup, leaning against the hood.

Her heart clutched as icy fingers gripped her spine.

"Can we talk about it later?" Chelsea had no plans to deliver the news he was Skylar's father.

She gripped her keys a little tighter. "Let's go home, okay?" she said to Skylar.

"Okay," came the response along with a giggle.

Chelsea hurried her daughter toward the pickup.

"We need to talk," Travis said as they approached.

"I'm sorry but I don't have anything to say to you." Chelsea she stalked past Travis, glaring at him. "Please stay away from me."

"We both know I won't," he declared.

"Do you care about me at all?" she asked, incredulous.

"Baby, I still love you," he stated.

Fire ants crawled across her skin as she opened the door and secured Skylar into her car seat.

Chelsea shut the door as Travis gripped her wrist.

"Ouch. You're hurting me," she said to him, forcing a smile to hide her reaction from her daughter who watched through the window.

"I saw you with that fireman." Travis seemed to grind out the words.

"Let go of me." Chelsea jerked her arm away from him, breaking his grip.

"You're my girl." Travis's voice sent a chill down her spine. In his twisted world, he believed those words.

"I belong to *me* and *my daughter*. None of which is your business, Travis," she stated as she stalked to the driver's side.

She grabbed the handle and opened the door just a little when it was jerked out of her hand and slammed shut.

Travis pushed her up against it and then his mouth was next to her ear. "Hear this. You are still my girl. That child in there belongs to me. And I have every intention of getting my family back."

Chelsea planted both hands on the vehicle and, using all her strength, pushed back.

Travis was caught off balance and stumbled backward a couple of steps. Chelsea rushed into the pickup and locked the door behind her. He banged against the window with his fist and she thought he might actually break the glass.

Skylar screamed.

"It's okay, sweetie. That man won't hurt us." Chelsea's heart squeezed at the thought of telling her daughter *that man* was her father.

This was not the man she'd known. Travis had changed so much. Was it jail that had made him so cruel? Sure, he'd stolen from her, but he'd never wished her harm. This was different. *He* was different. And she was very afraid of what he'd become.

The engine cranked up and she squealed her tires out of the parking lot. Her hands shook as she reminded herself to take a few deep breaths.

The weather system had arrived, full force, as nickel-size pieces of hail pelted the windshield. Back at the preschool, she'd barely noticed the freezing rain while distracted by Travis.

Travis. Chelsea had racked her brain dozens of times in the past four years for missed signs. When she'd first told Travis she was pregnant, he hadn't been thrilled by the news but he'd come around. She'd been the one concerned because they hadn't been dating nearly long enough and he'd lost his job and had been down about it.

After being told about the baby, he'd accused her of having an affair and then walked out, disappearing for eighteen hours. His phone had been turned off. Chelsea, certain he'd leave her, convinced herself that she could have the baby on her own. Her business had started flourishing. It wouldn't have been easy but she'd been prepared.

And then he'd come back. He'd said that he'd needed a little time to think about being a father. He apologized for his initial reaction to the news and managed to convince her that he was excited about the baby. He'd kissed her belly and she'd wanted to believe him so much that she'd ignored all the signs that he wasn't telling the truth. The slight twitch at the corner of his mouth was his telltale giveaway.

Chelsea had ignored it. She'd wanted, no *needed*, to believe that Travis had wanted to be a good father. She couldn't allow herself to believe that her family history was repeating itself. She'd refused to think that she could be that naïve or stupid.

It had taken experience and hardship for Chelsea to realize that none of Travis's failures had been her fault. She hadn't been able to fix him any more than she could make him love his daughter.

The similarities to her family background had not been lost on her when Travis hadn't showed up at the hospital that early April morning—

An old Jeep roared up behind her, flashing its lights.

She checked her rearview and saw that Travis was behind the wheel. And then he tapped her back bumper.

Chelsea bit back a curse.

"Mommy, I'm scared," Skylar stated before crying.

If crying would help, Chelsea would have no problem doing the same. But she had to be strong for her daughter.

"It's okay. I get scared sometimes, too. Let's make this a game, okay?" Chelsea was searching her brain for something to say as she banked a last-minute right turn. But Travis followed.

"Close your eyes, cover them with your hands and count to one hundred as loud as you can," she said to Skylar. Her own heart rate climbed and she prayed the distraction would work. Anger burned through her. It was one thing to try to hurt her, but to bring harm to their daughter was unforgivable.

"One, two, three…" came from the back seat.

"Good, girl. Keep it going." Chelsea made another quick left-hand turn and then another. The roads were getting slick so she couldn't risk going too fast.

Another pair of quick turns yet the Jeep was still behind her.

Chelsea glanced around, unfamiliar with the surroundings as she continued to make left or right turns, trying to lose the Jeep.

This was not the time to realize she didn't know how to get to the sheriff's office from here. Her cell was on the floorboard, the contents of her purse being dumped out on the last turn.

She approached a bridge that warned of a lake and had no choice but to slow to a crawl. She wanted to turn around but couldn't manage it with Travis on her bumper. How on earth had they gotten to this place where her ex, the father of her child, was trying to harm her? Didn't he realize that his daughter could be hurt?

Chelsea white-knuckled the steering wheel, seeking an outlet for the rage building inside her. She had so much anger. She switched lanes and he followed, tapping her bumper again. He might be scaring her but there was no way she was going to let him win. Not this time.

The roads were bad. She wanted to gun the engine but couldn't risk the slick roads. Chelsea pushed slightly harder on the gas pedal and then switched lanes as Travis roared up to her back bumper.

What was he thinking?

Desperate, Chelsea scanned the road. Was there a turnoff? Would it be safer for her and Skylar if Chelsea pulled over?

Travis had to know that there was no way she was letting him get anywhere near Skylar. As far as Chelsea was concerned, the man would never meet his child after pulling this stunt. Her heart hurt for the fact that Skylar would never have a real father.

Of course, when she thought about an amazing man whom she'd prefer to have as her daughter's father, Nate Kent came to mind.

"Sixty-five, sixty-six…"

She heard Travis gun his engine, trying to slam into her on the bridge, but he'd only succeeded in spinning out. The Jeep banged against the guardrail. He must've hit the ice patch she'd managed to avoid.

Chelsea continued to creep along the bridge, her stress levels through the roof as her heart pounded her ribs.

She checked her rearview mirror but no Jeep came whirling up to the bumper. At least the heater in the pickup was solid, she thought distractedly.

Chelsea continued to drive but felt like she was crawling, looking for a good place to pull over. When nothing appeared, she took a risk and reached for her cell. She got it.

"Ninety-six…"

"New game, Skylar. Mommy wants you to take her phone and call 9-1-1."

"Is the bad man gone?" she asked.

"He is for now."

Chelsea knew the reprieve wouldn't last. With shaky hands, she handed over her cell.

She was almost across the bridge when a patch of ice caught her off guard and the pickup slid out of control before landing in a ditch.

Chapter Eighteen

"Everything all right?" Nate picked up on the controlled panic in Chelsea's voice over the phone.

"I told Skylar to call 9-1-1." Chelsea sounded confused as to why he was on the other end of the line.

"My phone rang and I answered it." It was all he could think to say. "Are you guys okay?"

"It's okay, Sky." Chelsea's voice sounded like she'd moved her mouth away from the phone. Then came, "I'm stuck in a ditch. The roads are slick and my tires spun out at the end of a long bridge over a lake. I don't know where I am exactly."

"Stay put. I'm on my way." He knew exactly where she was. He didn't want her to move an inch until he got there. It was also freezing outside. "Do you have enough gas to keep the engine running and the heater on?" Nate had already thrown on his coat and slipped into his boots. He was in his truck before she could answer.

"Yes. But there's a problem." Her voice was low, almost a whisper. "Travis."

"Where?" The answer was the only thing that mattered.

The temperature had dropped a solid twenty degrees

outside. Hail littered the roads. Winds blasted the windshield. Conditions were worsening by the minute.

"I managed to get away from him a few minutes ago. He's on the other side of the bridge and he's probably trying to get to us." Again, her voice was barely above a whisper and he knew why. Skylar was within earshot.

"If we don't get out of here now, he might get to us," she said. Again she lowered her voice. "I'm scared, Nate."

"Is the road clear behind you?" He didn't want to ask outright if she could see Travis.

"I think so."

"Unless you see someone coming, I want you to stay right where you are. It's nineteen degrees outside and too cold for the little bean in the back seat." His truck was slipping and sliding already and he'd barely left ranch property. "The roads are going to slow me down. I'm a half hour away."

"I'm praying either you or Zach will get to us before Travis does." The line was quiet save for the hum of the truck engine. She dropped her tone to almost a whisper. "He was in a jealous rage and I barely got away from him."

The thought that Travis had said he wanted to be a family again with Chelsea and Skylar didn't sit right. As far as Nate was concerned, Travis had had his chance. Leaving Chelsea destitute with a newborn didn't qualify as a man worthy of a family. It would be one thing if Travis had straightened out his life and come back to her honestly. Nate would never stand in the way of a decent man trying to atone for past mistakes. Travis was doing the opposite.

Nate ran a mental checklist of anyone he might know who lived near the lake. There weren't many houses out there as of yet. A development was planned but construction wouldn't start until next year.

Best as he could recall there were two families who lived near Elm Fork Lake. Nate wasn't close to either of them. Was there anyone he could call who could get to her faster?

Nate's truck tires slid on an ice patch. He turned the steering wheel into the spin until the truck tires caught traction again. He realized calling anyone else wasn't an option. There was no way he'd put his family in danger. Each one would risk life and limb to help someone in crisis.

At least she'd called in the emergency to Zach. He or one of his deputies might be able to get to her in time. Nate feared he'd be too late.

"Someone's coming, Nate. I'm not sure if it's him." The panic in her voice sent a fire bolt of frustration swirling in Nate's gut. He needed to get her.

"Describe the area around you," he said.

"There's a clump of trees on this side of the bridge. Across the bridge is all lake." Her tone grew louder and her voice cracked.

There was one obvious place to hide that he knew about in that area. Too obvious? "Where's the vehicle?"

"Slowly making its way. It's still far but it won't be too long before it's here," she said, the sound of panic rising.

No one would willingly drive across an icy bridge unless it was the only way home or they were determined to follow someone else. That second option was a gut check and most likely the right one.

"Can you get across the street without the driver seeing you?" he asked.

"I doubt it," she responded.

Nickel-size hail pelted his windshield and this was just the beginning of the weather front about to batter the town. It was predicted to get a whole lot worse.

First, he needed to come up with a plan. It was clear that he wasn't going to get to Chelsea and her daughter before the driver of the vehicle on the bridge. Send them into the woods where they might lose cell coverage and they could get lost and end up freezing to death? Tell them to stay in the pickup and a jealous ex could get to them?

The fact that domestic abuse was a leading killer of women was not lost on Nate. He'd heard Zach talk about it too many times for it not to resonate.

"Doors are locked, right?"

"Yes." She paused. "He's halfway across the bridge. What should we do?"

Before he could answer, he heard the sweet sound of a siren.

"Can you hear that?" she asked. Her tone picked up, too.

"Help is on the way." Nate was halfway there and not nearly close enough. All it would take was one bullet to end Chelsea. Travis could disappear with his child over the border and both mother and child would be lost to Nate forever.

The thought hit him harder than expected.

Was he in love with Chelsea? He couldn't deny that he'd never felt this strongly about anyone else before. Skylar had his heart, too.

So, yeah, he was in love with Chelsea and he wanted to be a family. But did she? *Could* she open up and let herself love another man after what she'd been through? Mia's betrayal paled in comparison to what Travis had done to Chelsea and Nate wanted to shut it down for good. There was no doubt in his mind that Chelsea had feelings for him. The kind of chemistry they had was rare.

Even though it had only been a couple of weeks, it felt like he'd known her his entire life. It struck him as odd but he figured it had to do with being kindred spirits. Down deep, where it counted, the two of them knew each other. He'd known Mia for a year before they'd dated. Being around someone for a long period of time didn't always equate to knowing them. There was something honest and pure about Chelsea despite what she'd been through.

Nate respected her a helluva lot.

There was no way of knowing if Chelsea could open up to him, though. Being able to go there again with anyone was a whole different matter and only Chelsea could decide if she was up for the challenge.

"It's going to be all right," he said to a quiet Chelsea.

It was as though she was holding her breath, afraid to speak.

Nate pressed the pedal as hard as he could, pushing his speed to the brink of losing control. He *had* to get to Chelsea and Skylar. There was no other option.

The sound of Skylar's sweet little voice in the background singing the nursery rhyme that Chelsea had told her daughter to sing was a punch in the chest.

It was smart to distract the little nugget.

"There's an SUV with lights and sirens pulling up behind the Jeep," Chelsea informed him.

Nate's stress levels calmed with the news. He kept his voice the same timbre as before, just like he'd been trained to do in emergency situations. "Help is there. I'm probably ten minutes out."

He was making better time than he'd initially calculated.

The sound of a shot split the air.

The air was suddenly sucked out of the cab of Nate's truck. He bit out a swearword. "What happened, Chelsea?"

"It's the deputy who came over. Deputy Long. He walked up to the driver's side and then he was shot. He leaned his hands on the vehicle and I thought everything was fine, but then he took a couple of steps back before he dropped to the ground. Nate, the Jeep is coming. What should I do?"

"Is Skylar out of her seat?" Nothing inside him wanted to give this advice.

"Yes."

"Get out of there. Run to the tree line and make a zigzag pattern. Don't just run straight. Turn a lot so you'll be hard to track and even harder to hit. Be as quiet as you can as you move through the woods." He paused at the sound of her pickup door creaking open and then slamming shut.

He heard rustling noises and what sounded like blasts of wind. Skylar's sweet voice was more of a whisper as she finished singing the song.

And then all he could hear was the sound of the wind.

"Chelsea…?"

No response came.

IT WAS SO cold that Chelsea's lungs hurt every time she took a breath. She cradled Skylar against her chest. At least her baby was warm with her face burrowed inside

Chelsea's coat. She was grateful Travis hadn't come after her. He'd been busy wrestling with the deputy.

Chelsea pushed her burning legs as she hugged her daughter.

It was almost impossible to process the fact that a law-enforcement officer had been shot. Chelsea couldn't begin to allow that knowledge to sink in. Or that Travis was responsible. She couldn't fathom how wrong his life had turned for him to be capable of such an act.

It was crazy to think that her ex would go to such lengths to hurt her. She'd underestimated the potency of jealousy and anger mixed with desperation. When she really thought about it, Travis's life was over. Once he was caught, and she could only pray that would happen soon, he'd spend the rest of his life behind bars. All she could wonder was why.

Why track her down?

Why try to kill her?

Why ruin any chance he had for a future on his own?

Of course, at this point she had to consider his intention might be to kill her and take Skylar. He could easily slip across the border with their daughter as Chelsea had heard happened in custody cases far too many times.

For four years she'd wondered if he'd ever show up again. Unlike her mother, Chelsea hadn't looked for her husband. There hadn't seemed to be a point because there'd be no going back after what he'd done. But she'd always feared that he would show one day ready to take her daughter away.

Chelsea made a right turn, ran for a while and then made another. She'd been changing her course, just like Nate had said to do. Every once in a while she stopped to listen in case someone was calling for her, or worse, chasing after her.

The wind cut right through her coat.

Another right turn and this time she had to slow her pace for a minute to catch her breath. Running was one thing but carrying a little one while darting through trees, being slapped in the face with icy branches, wore her thin. At least hail wasn't a problem in the thicket. There were enough evergreens to keep a canopy overhead.

She'd managed to drop her cell phone before she'd reached the trees earlier. How long had she been running? Where was she?

She'd long ago lost feeling in her toes and feared frostbite might be setting in.

She'd wanted to give up more times than she could count but couldn't. Nothing inside her could surrender to Travis.

And then Chelsea heard her name. The strong, masculine voice trilled through her, bringing with it the first sense of hope since this whole ordeal had started.

"Nate," she said barely above a whisper.

"Mommy, I hear the fireman," Skylar said. "He can help us."

"That's right, sweetie." Chelsea spun toward the voice, drew up what little energy she had left and sprinted toward the sound.

She knew he was taking a risk in calling her name. He was not only letting her know where he was but was also giving away his location. Did that mean Travis was out of the picture? Had he taken off or, better yet, been arrested?

There was no way Chelsea was taking a chance. She pushed forward, her toes feeling like needles were pressing into them with every step.

Another shot fired.

Chelsea froze.

"What's that noise, Momma?" Skylar asked.

She tried to speak but no words came. And, for a split second, the entire world stopped spinning. Time stopped. She was no longer cold. The wind stopped blowing and everything went perfectly still, eerily quiet.

A second later, as though someone flipped a switch, the world restarted.

"Nate," she whispered before taking off in the direction of the shot.

"Go back to the road," Nate shouted. "Run. He can't catch you."

Was Nate lying in a ditch somewhere? Bleeding out? How on earth was she supposed to leave him in the woods? He could be dying trying to save her. She'd never forgive herself if she didn't try to help him. But she wouldn't put her daughter at risk, either. The decision to run to her pickup or Nate warred inside her.

And then it occurred to her that he didn't *want* her to go to her pickup. That was too obvious and Nate was too smart to give away her location.

Chelsea spun around and ran toward the place where she'd heard the shot.

NATE CROUCHED LOW to the ground, listening for the sounds of Chelsea's footsteps over the blasts of wind. Travis had turned back to the road the minute Nate had yelled for her to go to the vehicle.

Travis must not've realized that his shot had gone wide and missed Nate, who'd been dramatic and played the part of victim. Thankfully, he must've pulled it off. Travis had retraced his steps. Deputy Long, who'd been shot but was alive, would be ready for Travis this time. Travis wouldn't catch the lawman off guard.

Leaving Deputy Long had been the most difficult thing that Nate had ever done. The deputy had been shot in the neck, but the bullet had missed a major artery. His bloodied uniform had made things look worse than they were. By the time Nate arrived, the deputy had already called for an ambulance and had insisted that he would be fine. He'd sent Nate into the woods to help Chelsea and Skylar. Long had promised that he would be ready if Nate was able to flush Travis out.

Time was running out. Nate needed to find Chelsea before she and Skylar froze to death. They'd been out in this weather for nearly an hour now. He scanned the woods as hail pelted his face in the clearing.

And then he spotted movement to his left. He eased behind the tree trunk in case Travis had figured out the ruse and circled back.

"Nate." Chelsea's voice was barely a whisper and the sweetest sound he'd heard in a long time.

His heart fisted as he popped to his feet and saw the look of exhaustion on her face.

Nate tore toward her, taking Skylar from her arms. The little girl was cold and Chelsea was shivering.

"Pull my coat off and put it on," he instructed Chelsea.

"You'll freeze," she said.

He could see by the determined look in her eyes that arguing would do no good. She wouldn't take his coat.

"Let's get you both to a heater." Nate knew the fastest way back to the pickup. It took fifteen minutes, which was five minutes too long in his book.

As soon as they broke from the trees, he saw his cousin's SUV. He took a risk running toward Zach but Skylar's teeth had started chattering. Nate bolted for the vehicle and was almost surprised when no shots were fired.

Zach, outside the vehicle, opened the passenger door and Chelsea immediately climbed in as Nate handed Skylar to her mother.

"Get them out of here," Nate said to Zach.

"You belong in the vehicle. I need to check on my deputy," Zach stated.

The door had barely closed before the first shot rang out.

"Please. Take care of them." Nate dropped to the ground and scrambled to his own vehicle. He knew his cousin wouldn't leave the scene when he had a deputy down. Zach would ensure Chelsea and Skylar's safety.

A ping sounded, a bullet whizzed past Nate's ear.

Damn. That was a little too close for comfort. He dove, rolled and then popped to his feet behind his truck. He could climb in the cab, but then what?

Nate palmed his handgun.

He slowly looked around the side of his vehicle. Another shot was fired. He drew out two more as Nate counted shots.

Travis's gun was empty.

The man could reload, if he had more ammunition, and that would take a minute or two. Nate seized the opportunity and bolted for the area from where the shots had been fired.

The shooter looked up and Nate immediately recognized Travis Zucker from the photo Zach had once showed him. The panicked look on the man's face said he knew he was outmatched. Adrenaline must've kicked in because his hands shook as he tried to reload. That played to Nate's advantage because bullets dropped to the ground.

Nate got his own burst of energy, so he propelled himself at Travis.

The guy was small but quick, rolling out of the way at the last second.

Nate tried to adjust midair but collided with the hard ground. Bullets littered the cold, unforgiving earth as he scrambled to his knees and jerked right. Travis was trying to flee.

Nate managed to grab an ankle. Travis used the butt of his rifle to slam Nate's hand, trying to use the weapon to force Nate to let go. It landed on his index finger and hurt like hell. Travis kicked but Nate's grip was steely. There was no way in hell Travis was getting away when Nate had the man this close.

He took another jab, this time to his wrist, and feared it might've fractured. Pain shot up his arm and his fingers went completely numb. Sheer force of will caused Nate to dig his fingers into the skin of Travis's ankle deeper.

"Get. Off. Me." The words came out through labored breaths.

"Give up, Travis. You're going to jail. Why make it worse?" Nate growled as he pulled his left hand up to grab the man's calf.

"Not. Happening." Travis slammed the butt of the gun into Nate's skull.

His vision blurred and pain shot down his neck, but he had the presence of mind to grab hold of the weapon. Now he and Travis were in a dangerous game of tug-of-war.

Nate doubled down and let go of Travis's ankle. It

didn't take long to yank the rifle out of Travis's hands but he stomped on Nate's head.

Nate had had enough. Rising, he threw the rifle as far as he could, knowing full well where it landed.

And then he grabbed Travis, first by the wrist as a fist flew at Nate.

Nate brought his knee up at the same time he jerked Travis's arm down. When knee met face, Travis screamed in pain.

Capitalizing on the moment, Nate threw Travis to the ground face-first and thrust his knee into the man's back to pin him down. He grabbed Travis by the wrists and yanked his arms behind his back.

Nate's cell was long lost, so he shouted for help. He didn't have any wire or cable with him to tie Travis up. Hell, he'd leave the man tied to a tree and let hungry coyotes and cougars do the rest if it were up to him.

But then death would be too easy a way out for Travis. And there was always that rare chance the man might figure out an escape.

Travis needed to suffer. He needed to see what real justice looked like. Living the rest of his life behind bars for attempted murder, attempted capital murder and a host of other offenses, including domestic abuse and violence would teach him a thing or two about how to treat other people, especially someone who'd cared about him at one time.

Nate shouted for help again. His wrists hurt like hell and he was developing a massive headache. Thankfully, the cold was probably keeping his wrist from swelling.

He listened for a response but got none.

If he spent much more time outside, he'd freeze. Nate needed to get Travis to the road.

"We're going for a walk." Nate took off his belt with a yank and used it to bind Travis's hands together.

And then Nate forced the man to stand and walk toward his reckoning.

Chapter Nineteen

"Get down. Face down," Nate demanded as soon as he walked Travis back to the pickup.

"I can't. My hands," Travis complained.

Nate found it interesting the man could be a bully with someone smaller than him. With Nate, he was just a complaining punk. Of course, give the man an opportunity and he wouldn't hesitate to capitalize on it. Cowards usually hid behind weapons.

"On your knees or I'll help you," Nate said. "Don't test me."

Awkwardly, Travis complied.

Nate gripped the back of the man's neck and pushed him to the ground behind his pickup.

Travis grumbled some kind of complaint or threat that Nate couldn't make out. He didn't care, either.

In the rear of his truck, he located cable wire. He used that to bind Travis's hands behind his back.

"What are you, a cop?" Travis asked.

"You wish. I have no rules keeping me from beating you until you drop," Nate retorted as he tightened the bindings.

"Ouch. That hurts, man. Don't be a jerk," Travis said.

Nate didn't bother to respond. He texted his cousin

that Travis was in his custody and it was safe to come back to pick the scumbag up.

"Tell me one thing…" Nate said to Travis.

"Why should I?" Travis shot back.

Nate shrugged. "Be a man just this one time and tell me why you tried to burn down her restaurant."

"Who said I did?" Travis countered.

Nate picked Travis up by his wrists.

Travis released a string of swearwords as he winced in pain.

"Why?" was all Nate asked.

Travis looked up at Nate. "Because she didn't want me."

"So you tried to kill her?" Nate asked.

"Scare. I only meant to scare her just like when I threw the rock in her window," Travis admitted. A look of anguish crossed his features. "Thought it might make her want to give me another chance."

"She could've died, you idiot." Nate could hardly believe the man thought she'd want to be in the same room with him.

"Yeah, well, I got in over my head. I was blinded and figured if I couldn't have her no one should." There was a dead quality to Travis's eyes now. Nate had seen it before in men who'd crossed a line they could never come back from.

"You almost made your daughter an orphan. That's not just stupid and cruel, it's criminal." Nate had no sympathy for the man. He figured Chelsea would appreciate knowing that Travis hadn't actually been trying to kill her. He was sick and twisted, but he hadn't wanted her dead.

"I never did truly believe that kid was mine," Travis stated. "I would've claimed her anyhow."

Shock didn't begin to describe the blow Nate took on that one.

"Really? Why not?" Zach's SUV was a dot in the distance, growing bigger.

"She was on birth control and there was a guy she worked for that kept flirting with her."

Was he kidding?

"Did you think to get a DNA test?" Nate asked, incredulous, though it explained why the man had ruined her business and abandoned their child.

Travis stood there, anger scoring his forehead as Zach made a beeline toward them.

"You're going away for a long time, Travis."

CHELSEA'S HEART SQUEEZED when she saw Nate. The thought of anything happening to him had nearly broken her in two.

An ambulance had arrived and loaded Deputy Long inside. The EMT gave a thumbs-up sign to Zach, who said that meant his deputy was going to be fine.

"Momma, it's the fireman," Skylar said, pointing to Nate.

"Yes, it is," Chelsea said, fighting tears of relief.

"I'm hungry. Is it dinnertime yet?" Skylar asked.

Chelsea couldn't help but smile at her daughter. Kids had a unique ability to live in the moment. That was most likely why they were so happy. Ten minutes after a stressful event, they moved on. Especially if a toy was thrown into the mix.

Zach forced Travis to spread eagle, his chest against the hood of Deputy Long's SUV, before handcuffing him.

Nate walked toward Chelsea and her heart pounded her ribs.

"Momma, the fireman's coming here." Skylar clapped. Thankfully, they were warm inside the SUV thanks to Nate. If he hadn't showed up when he had, she and Skylar might still be wandering around in those woods. Chelsea shuddered thinking about what might've happened. She didn't care so much about what happened to her but thinking something might've happened to her daughter...

She couldn't even go there hypothetically.

"I know, sweetheart." Chelsea tried to mask her over-the-top reaction.

"I like him," Skylar stated with all the pomp and circumstance of a four-year-old.

"I do, too," Chelsea said softly. She hadn't been certain that she could allow herself to really fall for someone again. But there she was head-over-heels for Nate Kent. And now that this big mystery was solved, he'd go right back to his life and she'd go to hers. Why did that suddenly sound so empty?

Nate opened the driver's side door of his truck as Skylar climbed in back. Chelsea she scooted over so he could slide in beside her.

"You're freezing," she said to him as he rubbed his hands together before blowing on them.

Nate leaned toward her and gave her a quick kiss.

"What did you think about being in a cruiser?" he asked Skylar, who was beaming at him.

"The policeman let me push a button to turn on the lights," she said proudly.

Yeah, Chelsea was in trouble, all right. She had feelings for Nate, feelings that wouldn't go away easily. Her daughter had taken to him the first time they'd met.

A weight pressed on Chelsea's limbs.

"You should stop by and check out the fire truck some-day. We have so many more lights to play with," he said.

Skylar's face lit up.

"You want a ride home?" he asked Chelsea. "We'll get your pickup towed once the cold front blows over tomorrow afternoon."

"That would be great," she said.

"I'll get Skylar's car seat." Nate hopped out of the vehicle before she could stop him. She had no idea what she was going to say to him. She just didn't want him to leave.

THE RIDE HOME was quiet. Zach was transporting Travis to jail where he'd be locked up a very long time. Chelsea felt safe. Skylar sang in the back seat and played with the baby doll Nate had brought over from the ditched pickup. Chelsea and Nate sat in companionable silence.

At home, Chelsea checked on her mother then ate dinner with Skylar and Nate.

She put her daughter to bed, grateful that he'd waited around. He was standing in her kitchen, pouring two mugs of coffee, looking like the sexy man that he was.

"Thanks for hanging around tonight," Chelsea said to him as he handed a fresh mug to her.

He didn't respond and she figured he was choosing his words carefully. He'd been nothing but considerate and she assumed he'd let her down easy.

"I spoke to Travis…" Nate started to say.

"What did he have to say?" She rolled the warm mug in the palms of her hands.

"That he thought you were having an affair with one of your employees." There was no suspicion in his eyes and she appreciated him for it. Thinking back, Travis had become a little fixated on her friendship with Collier Stead.

"He brought it up a couple of times before he disappeared, but I couldn't believe he'd think that," she said.

"He doesn't know you very well, does he?"

"Not if he seriously believed I'd cheat." She stared at Nate. "How do you know that I didn't?"

"You're one of kindest and most honest people I've ever met. You're loyal to a fault. You wouldn't have an affair." His certainty caused warmth to rocket through her. "You're also beautiful, but that's a whole other conversation."

Her cheeks flamed.

Being with Nate made her feel beautiful.

"How do you know all this when I've only known you for a short time?" she asked. He was spot-on, though. She'd never cheat.

"I've felt a connection with you like I've never felt before, Chelsea. I know you've been through a lot with men, and it might be hard to trust, but I know you. And I think you know me, too," he stated.

"If anyone had told me that I could fall for someone this hard, this fast, and it would turn out to be real, I wouldn't believe them." It was true. "I feel like I know you from somewhere down deep. Is that weird?"

"I feel it, too," he said. "But you have a lot on your plate. You're building a restaurant almost from the ground up. You have a daughter who needs you every day, not to mention your mother."

This was the part where he let her down easy. And it was suddenly hard to breathe.

"That's all true," she confirmed.

"I might be throwing you a curveball…" He walked to her and dropped down on one knee. "That's why I think we shouldn't wait to get married."

"What?" She was pretty certain she hadn't heard him correctly.

"We can go through the motions of dating, steal time here and there, but I love you and I want you to be my wife. I want you and Skylar to be my family. Forever. And I don't see a good reason to wait. But if you do, I understand. I'm ready to do whatever it takes and if that means waiting, going slow, I will. I want to be in your life any way you'll allow. I'm patient and I can hold off until you're ready to trust me one hundred percent with your heart."

Chelsea's heart leaped for joy. Life had gotten really good at throwing curveballs at her. Finally, it tossed her one she wanted to catch and hold onto.

"I love you, too, Nate." She did. She loved him with her whole heart. "I can't think of one reason to wait to be your wife."

"Is that a yes?" A wide smile broke across that beautiful face of his.

"Yes." She set her coffee mug down as he stood. She wrapped her arms around his neck. "I will marry you."

Nate kissed her so hard it robbed her breath.

He pulled back and pressed his forehead against hers. "I've been waiting for you my whole life," he said. "Linda felt like family from the first time we met. With you and Skylar, I've found home."

Home.

Chelsea couldn't think of a better word to describe the way she felt about Nate.

And she finally had a real place to call home.

* * * * *

COVERT
COMPLICATION

NICOLE HELM

To my husband, the best dad I know.

Chapter One

Moving back home to his grandmother's ranch was not
what Cody Wyatt had envisioned for his adult life.

Despite being the youngest of six, despite having five
bossy, obnoxious older brothers, Cody had never excelled
at people telling him what to do. He accepted it from
his grandmother—she'd raised him and his brothers, had
saved him and his brothers. There was no challenging
Grandma Pauline.

But he was pretty sure he was going to punch Dev's
lights out if his brother kept criticizing the way he took
off a horse's saddle.

It wouldn't be the first time he'd gotten in a physical
fight with his brothers, but rarely did he get frustrated
with Dev.

With six brothers, certain smaller relationships existed.
The oldest, Jamison had saved all of them from their father's biker gang and secreted them out to Grandma—
their late mother's mother. Jamison had tried to father
him, and Cody had allowed it and chafed at it in turn. He
looked up to his oldest brother, but there were so many
years between them, and such a feeling of *responsibility* on Jamison's shoulders that Cody hadn't understood
when they'd been younger.

Brady and Gage were twins, their own playmates and

companions—operating on their own frequency. Cody loved them, respected them, but they were two sides of the same coin who spoke their own darn language half the time.

Tucker, closest in age to Cody, idolized Jamison. Tuck shared that core goodness about him that Jamison had, with a little less martyrdom weighing him down.

But Dev had shared that angry thing inside of Cody. A darkness the other brothers didn't have or didn't lean into the way Dev and Cody did, or had. That darker side had almost gotten Dev killed years ago—and Cody had vowed to hone it into a different kind of weapon.

It was a little harder these days now that he was back at the ranch after his last mission with the North Star group. Too many truths about his involvement in the secretive operation had been revealed.

He missed North Star and his confidential work there. It had become vital to the man he'd built himself into. But he'd also been very aware his time with North Star was temporary, just as everyone else's was. It was what made the group effective in taking down large, dangerous organizations.

Like his father's.

The Sons of the Badlands hadn't exactly disbanded last month when their leader had been arrested and their second-in-command had been killed. But they were weaker.

Cody had to let other people dismantle the remaining membership. While he sat on the sidelines herding cattle with his brother.

It just about ate him alive.

He glanced over at Dev, who was rubbing down his horse after an afternoon in the saddle moving the cattle to their new pasture, his two ranch dogs at his feet. Dev kept his expression carefully blank, but even if Cody hadn't been around much the past few years he knew that meant Dev was in some serious pain.

"So, he's really going to stay there?" Dev asked.

Cody didn't ask for clarification. As weeks passed, they all waited for word that Ace would somehow wiggle out of a trial or sentencing. But he was in jail at least.

"For now."

Dev made a considering snort. The dogs sniffed the air, cocked their heads, then both got onto their feet and loped out of the barn. Cody figured Grandma had put some scraps in their bowls.

Dev squinted toward the horizon. Three figures on horseback were coming closer. Duke Knight and his two daughters. Well, Rachel was his biological daughter, Sarah was one of his fosters. The only one he and his wife had managed to legally adopt before Eva Knight had died.

Sometimes Cody thought losing Mrs. Knight had been the beginning of all their problems—even though the real start was the moment they'd been born to Ace Wyatt, head of the Sons of the Badlands.

Thanks to Jamison, Cody had had a pretty normal childhood, getting out of the gang just shy of his seventh birthday. He'd also had his brothers. The Knights had been the kind of ranching neighbors that were more like family. All their daughters—fosters or biological—had been the Wyatt brothers' playmates.

Sometimes more. As had been the case with Liza and Jamison, before Liza had run back to the Sons.

Then later, Cody and Nina.

Cody didn't think about Nina much anymore. He'd erased her from his mind. Or had, until he had to come home.

She seemed to exist like a ghost here at the ranch. All the what-ifs. All the whys.

But it didn't matter. She'd left him. Disappeared and begged him not to follow.

So he hadn't.

"Guess they're coming over for dinner," Cody forced himself to say. It wasn't easy to sit in Grandma's kitchen with Duke Knight, who still blamed him for Nina's disappearing act.

But they pretended it didn't matter, because otherwise Grandma would whack them both with her biggest wooden spoon.

"Not normal," Dev replied.

Which was when Grandma appeared in the barn. But she wasn't dressed to work, and she looked pale.

"Come inside, Cody."

He shared a look with Dev, who shrugged. Grandma seemed grave, which wasn't like her. She usually gave orders with an ornery glint in her eye. This was muted.

Cody had learned a long time ago not to react to most situations. He'd interned in the CIA, and he'd been trained by the North Star group. Not to mention how much he'd learned from looking up to Jamison, who might have saved Cody from the Sons at seven, but had been stuck there until he himself was eighteen.

Cody couldn't access all that training and habit in the face of his very grave grandmother. He was stiff as something like fear actually made his heart beat too hard in his chest.

Still, Cody followed her toward the house. When he saw the ambulance lights he hurried to it, passing up Grandma's slower gait. A woman was on a stretcher being loaded up into the emergency vehicle.

A woman whose face had him stopping in his tracks.

Grandma caught up to him, sounding a little out of breath.

"Why is Ni—" Before he could say her name, Grandma hit him. Hard.

The EMT closed the doors and Cody stared at his grandmother.

"I'll explain soon enough. She isn't who you need to see right this moment," she said, somehow graver than she'd been. Cody might not understand what was going on, but he understood what his grandmother wasn't saying.

That was Nina, and she was in danger. The less talk right now, the better to assess the danger.

"I've already called Gage," Grandma said. "He'll take care of everything at the hospital, but she was hurt too badly for me to patch up. She needed a hospital."

Cody stood, frozen in the spot even as the ambulance began to pull away. Maybe his eyes were playing tricks on him. Maybe that wasn't Nina. Maybe…

"Follow me."

Grandma strode into the house and Cody didn't know what else to do but follow. The sight of Nina, pale and bloody, made it feel as though his brain had short-circuited. Nothing made sense, and all he could do was follow his grandmother into the house.

Through the kitchen, up the stairs, then to the room Liza and her half sister, Gigi, stayed in when they came to visit.

Liza and Gigi weren't there. They'd moved into a house in Bonesteel with Jamison, but another little girl was. She was huddled in the corner, clutching a doll. A doll that had blood on it. Just like her clothes.

"She's unhurt," Grandma said, just standing in the doorway with him.

"Who is she?" he asked, though something felt all wrong. Something clawed at him, dark and painful.

"Nina knocked on my door. She'd been hurt—there was so much blood I called 911 right away. I tried to help her, but she'd been shot in the stomach. I couldn't fix that. Not the way she was bleeding."

"Who is this, Grandma?" Cody reiterated, though the idea of Nina being shot in the stomach... What on earth had she gotten herself into?

"Nina said I needed to hide her," Grandma said, nodding to the girl. "No matter what, I needed to hide her. She just kept begging me not to let anyone know she was alive."

"I don't understand."

"I think you do, Cody. The last thing Nina told me before she passed out was that the child's name is Brianna. And that *you* had to protect her."

The little girl looked up at him with scared eyes and a bloodstained face. She looked vaguely familiar, but Cody couldn't place her. Not with the way his heart thundered in his ears and his body felt like lead.

"She won't let me touch her," Grandma said sadly.

"What makes you think she'll let me?" Cody managed to croak. Even knowing what his grandmother would say, sensing what all this meant, he couldn't get his brain to jump into gear. Couldn't seem to add up all the facts laid before him.

Grandma shook her head. "You're her father, Cody. I'm about sure."

NINA OAKS STRUGGLED to swim out of the black. There was beeping, and her baby was not here with her.

Brianna. Brianna.

Take care of her. He has to protect her.

When she opened her eyes, there were familiar ones staring back at her.

But not the ones she'd expected to see. Or maybe *hoped* to. Maybe someday she'd learn how not to hope, but she was beginning to doubt it.

She remembered, suddenly, everything. The break-in. The masked man. Hiding Brianna.

The masked man had shot her, but then she'd managed…

She closed her eyes against the memory. She'd been shot. She was in a hospital. And Brianna…

"Gage," she croaked. She supposed any Wyatt brother would do, even if it wasn't the one she really needed to talk to. They knew her. They'd protect her. They were her only hope.

"Hello, Mal."

She scrunched her face up against the pain, and the wave of confusion. "That's not my name. Gage, you know who—"

He placed his hand very gently on her arm that had an IV hooked up to it. "I know your name is Malory Jones," he said, his gaze on her, his words rote and devoid of emotion. "I found you on the side of the road. We're going to get you patched up. Don't you worry."

That wasn't what happened, but even in her foggy brain she knew better than to argue with him. He looked bigger than she remembered, but she supposed it was just the uniform. She was used to seeing him at Grandma Pauline's. Not in tiny hospital rooms.

Malory Jones.

He knew who she was. She had to believe Gage knew who she was. It hadn't been that long. Only about seven years. She hadn't changed. Not really. Not to look at anyway.

"I don't remember…" She had to remember things.

Get everything sorted in her head so she could make a plan. So she could...

Brianna. He has to keep her safe.

"That's all right. It'll be clearer when you're not getting pumped full of drugs. Right now you just keep quiet and focus on healing. Quiet is the best thing, *Mal*."

He was keeping her identity a secret. She couldn't quite remember things. "Gage, I need to know..." Even with what she couldn't remember, she knew she couldn't utter Brianna's name. She had to keep her daughter's existence a secret.

But she desperately had to know Brianna was all right. Nina remembered being shot. She dimly remembered grabbing a jagged piece of the lamp that had been broken and using all her strength to lodge it in her attacker's neck. She remembered the blood, and his screams, and she remembered crawling to Brianna's bed and getting her daughter out of the house before anyone else could come after them.

Then she'd had to burn it down, to keep Brianna's existence a secret. Burning it all away to cinders was the only way to escape the Sons' detection.

"Gage... Gage... Please." She felt a tear trickle down her cheek. She didn't remember past the fire. She didn't remember where Brianna was.

Gage crouched down so he was eye level with her as she lay in the hospital bed. "Listen. Everyone's fine and safe now. We'll get you patched up." He reached out and brushed the tear away. "Everyone is fine. *Everyone.* Okay?"

He meant Brianna. He had to mean her. She nodded. She tried to breathe and believe. She would do anything for her baby. Suffer anything. Nina had to believe she'd gotten Brianna to safety.

To the Wyatts.

Cody. She was almost certain she hadn't seen Cody. And almost certain she wouldn't be able to avoid that eventuality. Or what it meant.

He wouldn't understand. She wanted him to be able to, but he wouldn't. He was too good and brave and sure. He'd believe he would have been able to stop everything and that she should have come to him.

Nina didn't believe that, even now. Even coming to him and his family and tasking them with keeping her daughter safe.

Cody would be dead if not for her. Brianna would be dead if Nina hadn't done what she'd done.

Cody would never forgive her, and she would never be able to believe it could have been different.

The door opened and both her and Gage looked over to the man who stepped into the room.

Furious energy pumped off him. Tall and rangy and ready to attack. She should have been afraid.

But she'd seen all of that in him all those years ago— loved his dark side and being the one to lighten it.

There'd be no soothing anymore.

"I need to talk to her," Cody ground out as Gage slowly got to his feet.

Gage moved in front of Cody, trying to block his route to her bed. "Not here," Gage said, putting a hand on Cody's chest. "Not now."

Cody's hazel eyes blazed with furious, righteous anger. She would have expected nothing less.

Still, she closed her eyes and let the encroaching black win rather than face it. And him.

Chapter Two

Grandma had told him not to come, but after hours of getting nowhere with the little girl, Cody hadn't been able to stop himself. There had to be an explanation. It had to…

It couldn't be true.

But Nina had looked at him when he'd walked into her hospital room, pain in her expression. And something that wasn't apology but was close enough it was hard to deny Grandma's interpretation of the situation.

The little girl who wouldn't let anyone wash the blood off her was his.

His.

And Nina had kept her from him. For seven years.

Gage nudged him out of the room and Cody let himself be led because she'd closed her eyes anyway. Not in a pretend kind of way. In an unconscious kind of way.

"Go home, Cody. I'll take care of things here."

Cody wanted to laugh. Take care of things. What was there to take care of? What did any of this *mean*?

"The more you stay, the more you give away. Which means the more danger she is in," Gage said in a fierce whisper. "I know you don't want that."

"I don't know what I want."

"As soon as she's able to be moved, she will be. Just leave. We have to be careful right now."

"Why are we acting like—"

"What exactly do you think a woman—your ex-girl-friend—showing up at the ranch with a bullet hole in her body means, Cody?"

"He's in jail," Cody returned in the same guttural whisper his brother was speaking in. "And we're in a hospital so I don't—"

"He's in jail. They *all* aren't. Someone put a bullet in her. Someone who's likely still looking for her. Whatever secrets—"

"Yeah, she's got some secrets all right."

"Look. I only know what Grandma told me. I can't imagine… I'm not saying you don't have a right to be angry. I'm not saying you shouldn't want answers. I'm saying this isn't just delicate, it's dangerous." Gage put his hand on Cody's shoulder, as if he could steady him through this. "Not just for you. For all of us."

"What would you have me do?" Cody ground out.

"Go home. Watch over everything there. I'll handle this, and when she can be moved, we'll figure it all out."

Cody hated that answer. He wanted to argue with Gage. He wanted to install himself in Nina's hospital room and demand all the answers he needed.

But Gage was right. Cody couldn't find a way to out-reason everything Gage had said.

"Go home, Cody."

Cody turned and did just that. It didn't seem to matter—all the rage and fury inside of him had frozen at the sight of Nina pale in that hospital bed looking at him like he was her absolute worst nightmare.

And her total salvation.

He drove back to the ranch in that frozen state. The name Brianna kept circling around his head, but he couldn't seem to put together a discernible thought.

When he walked back into the ranch kitchen, Grandma was at the sink, washing dishes.

"You should be in bed," Cody said, noting that it was nearly midnight. Hours upon hours of…

"She keeps hiding under the bed any time the door opens or closes," Grandma said on a sigh, ignoring his admonition. "I called all the girls—out of desperation." She turned off the water and proceeded to dry her hands on a kitchen towel. "She hides. She's good at hiding, but all the girls are up there now doing what they can."

The girls. Duke Knight's army of daughters. Up there with—

With…

"Cody. Whatever this is. Whatever has happened. You need to put it away. Your feelings don't matter until that little girl is safe."

"That little girl…" Cody closed his eyes. He couldn't believe she was his. Couldn't believe Nina would hurt him that way. She'd broken up with him all those years ago, but he hadn't been surprised by that. Nina had always been sweet, good. He was not that. No good for her—Duke Knight had always been sure to tell them both.

He'd been at his CIA internship and she'd left him a message that it was over. It had hurt. It had been out of the blue, but in the end, it had only seemed right.

So, no, losing Nina hadn't been any big surprise. But this?

This was bigger than anything. Than everything.

A daughter. His.

Couldn't be true.

"Go up there. Talk to her. See if you can figure out what's going on without scaring her."

Cody could have argued. He almost wanted to. But they

needed to know what was going on, and Brianna seemed to be the best option.

"Be quiet though," Grandma ordered. "Gigi is asleep in my room."

Cody nodded and headed upstairs. When he reached Liza and Gigi's usual room, all the lights were blazing. Every Knight girl past and present was assembled in the room, Brianna in the center.

The blood was gone. Her hair was damp so they must have given her a bath. She was wearing some too-big clothes, but she looked… Tired, but also calm.

"You got her to take a bath."

All heads turned to him, even Brianna's. Her eyes were blue, like her mother's. But instead of Nina's light blond hair, her flyaway strands were a dark brown. Like his.

She didn't look like either of them fully and yet somehow he knew…

"Once we all showed up, she decided to give it a go," Liza offered, a small, sad smile on her face.

"Because they're the princesses," Brianna said. "I knew I was safe with the princesses, and they said Mommy will be okay."

Cody gave Sarah a questioning look, but she didn't say anything while Rachel held the girl in her lap and Liza braided her hair.

"The princesses?" Cody questioned, still standing in the doorway to the room.

"Mommy used to tell me about the princesses. Princess Rachel can't see very well," she said, reaching up to the scar across Rachel's eye that had been put there by a cougar when Rachel had been little. Brianna touched the lighter skin and the darker skin gently, reverently before turning to the other women around her.

"Princess Sarah doesn't want to be a princess. She

wants to be a knight. She's a warrior." Brianna smiled at Sarah, who wasn't dressed so much as a warrior or a knight as she was a rancher, but it didn't seem to make much difference to the six-year-old.

"Princess Cecilia always wanted a badge." Brianna pointed to Cecilia's tribal police badge, since Cecilia was still in uniform. She must have come straight from her shift at the reservation.

"Princess Felicity protects the animals and the forests." Felicity didn't have her park ranger uniform on, but she had clearly had some kind of conversation about it with Brianna.

"What about Liza?" Cody heard himself ask, feeling unbalanced and yet firmly rooted to the spot. To her blue eyes.

"She's not a princess." Brianna smiled big and wide. "She's the queen who keeps everyone safe, even when she was far away."

Liza finished the braid as she gave Cody a heartbreaking look filled with tears that didn't fall.

"And who am I?" Cody asked, his voice cracking somewhere in the middle of that question, though he barely even noticed it. He felt fuzzy and distant.

Brianna cocked her head and studied him. "You're my daddy. But you don't know I'm your daughter, because the bad men made us run away. Even brave knights need help sometimes."

"What bad men?"

Brianna kept her gaze on his, but there was no more smiling. "All of them."

"I NEED YOU to get me out of here."

Gage, who had barely left her hospital room as far as Nina knew these past few days, gave her a doleful look.

Nina sat up in the bed, ignoring the pain in her body. "I'm okay. I know I'm not good but I'm good enough to get out. I have to. I *have* to."

"You were shot in the stomach."

"And they've stitched me up. Gage. I can't just lie here much longer. I need…" She didn't want to say it. They avoided the topic of Brianna. Nina knew her daughter was safe with the Wyatts, but that was all she knew. That was *all* she knew.

For seven years—since she'd found out she was pregnant—she had existed solely to take care of Brianna. To keep her safe and healthy and completely off the Sons' radar.

I need Brianna.

Brianna needs me.

Even though she knew her strong, amazing girl was being taken care of by Grandma Pauline and the Wyatt brothers. Probably Duke and the girls too.

Her heart ached—there was something painful about Brianna meeting them all without Nina there to be with her.

Still, Brianna knew about them. About Nina's foster parents who'd given her a real home. Love and safety and three square meals. School and chores and a real life. Brianna knew about Nina's sisters—sort of.

Nina had always made it sound like a fairy tale so if Brianna ever talked about them to strangers, people would think they were fictional. But Nina had given her daughter stories of the people who'd given Nina the kind of life she'd never even dreamed of when she'd been growing up poor and hungry in her biological parents' drug-infested trailer.

Her sisters, the princesses. And the brave Wyatt brothers, knights in shining armor.

"I need to get out," she repeated to Gage.

"I'll see what I can do, but I need you to know everything is fine."

She wanted to tell him it wasn't, but he couldn't understand. He wasn't a parent. He didn't know what it was like to...

She remembered more and more every day. Killing the man who'd shot her. Driving as far as she could with a towel wrapped around her bleeding midsection. Then walking when she'd been afraid she'd crash the car. Brianna in her arms, trudging toward the one place she knew she could find help.

She didn't remember Grandma Pauline or the ambulance ride and wondered if she ever would.

It didn't matter.

She'd gotten her baby to safety, and Gage seemed to understand how important it was for no one to know Brianna was alive. For no one to know who Nina really was.

The longer she stayed, the easier it would be for someone to figure it out. Surely the people who'd tried to kill her knew she was hurt, and if they were who she thought they were...

They'd start looking into the Wyatts. Probably already had.

"We're not safe. The longer it goes on. I have to get—"

Gage gave her a sharp look. "We've got it covered. Trust me."

"Please." She knew crying wouldn't sway him one way or another. Not because he was cruel or unaffected by tears, but because—unless things had changed in the past seven years—the Wyatt brothers were actually quite uncomfortable with a woman's tears, something they couldn't fix or control.

But Gage took the seat next to her bed and leaned

forward. "Do you think I don't understand? That I don't know exactly what they're capable of? I may not know why they decided to target you after so long, but I know what all of this is. Everyone is being kept as safe as possible."

She wished she could explain to him it wasn't a lack of trust or belief. It was just she *needed* to see her daughter. She needed to hold Brianna and tell her things would be all right. She needed the time she hadn't had after she'd been shot to explain to Brianna that everything was going to be okay.

But Nina didn't have the words and when the door opened she could only sag in her bed as one of the nurses peeked her head in. "Mrs. Jones? Your husband and daughter are here."

Nina sat back up, wincing at the pain in her side. "My…"

Cody stepped inside. He had a hat pulled low and was different than he'd been the other day, but she could hardly notice it because he was carrying a little girl with red hair.

"Do you need another dose of pain—"

"No," Nina snapped, because it was taking everything in her power to keep from sobbing and jumping from the bed. Even with a wig and ill-fitting clothes, she knew that bundle. "I'm all right."

The nurse nodded and stepped back out. Before Nina could say anything, before she could hold her arms out for Brianna to come to her, Cody shook his head sharply. He nodded to Gage. "Watch the door."

Gage was clearly not in on this, or in approval. He stood slowly. "Cody?"

"I've got it covered. Watch the door."

Gage scowled at his brother's order, but something

passed between them and he eventually nodded and stepped outside.

Cody didn't say anything. He began to prowl the room, inspecting things, putting little devices on the walls, all while carrying Brianna. Who didn't say a word. Who held on to Cody like he'd always been her very-present father.

But the whole time, Brianna's eyes stayed on Nina. So she smiled. Big and wide with so much pride and love for her girl.

Nina watched as Cody kept moving around. "What are you—"

He held his finger to his lips and kept doing things she couldn't see or understand. Once he was satisfied with *whatever*, he crossed to the bed and sat Brianna down on the side of it.

Nina grabbed Brianna so fiercely the wig tumbled off, but it didn't matter. Brianna wrapped her arms around Nina's neck, and no matter that Nina's whole body hurt, she didn't adjust Brianna's grip.

"Oh, my baby. Baby girl." She couldn't say all the things she wanted to say. Apologies. Questions. Too many sobs clogged her throat. She couldn't let those out, so she just held on.

"Are you going to die?" Brianna whispered. "Daddy said no, but I want you to tell me."

Daddy. Twin feelings paralyzed Nina. A joyous relief that finally Brianna knew her father. A cold fear that… That they'd always be in danger from here on out.

Too late now.

Nina tugged Brianna's arms off her neck so she could look in her child's familiar blue eyes. "I am not going to die. The doctors fixed me up. I have to heal, but I'm not going to die." *Not here. Not now.* She looked up at Cody. "*Daddy* is right about that."

Chapter Three

It was hard enough to handle how easily Brianna had started calling him Daddy. She had no qualms, no questions. Because Nina had told Brianna about him, and so Brianna recognized him as the man from her mother's stories. She trusted her mother's stories.

Cody hadn't been told anything. Somehow he already loved that little girl after a few short days, but that didn't make it easy or simple to wrap his head around the facts.

It was just the way it was. What was he going to do? Tell a six-year-old to not call him that? She called him Daddy and he answered and his own feelings on the matter would be dealt with internally and in his own time.

But Nina looking at him while she called Cody Brianna's daddy broke something inside of him. He didn't know what, or how to fix it. He could only stare at her and wonder... How...

How?

He'd wanted to come alone, but Brianna needed some reassurances. While the "princesses," as she called the Knight girls, had opened her up some, enough to let them all take care of her—anxiety crept in with every passing hour she didn't see Nina.

So he'd brought her. Now he didn't know what to do. Not a sensation he was used to.

But he'd searched for listening devices, installed a few frequency busters in case someone was trying to listen in. No one could hear them in this room while they discussed this, so discuss it they would.

Before he could figure out what question to ask first, Nina pinned him with a desperate look.

"Cody, you have to get me out of here. It's too dangerous. They're looking for me."

"Who's looking for you?" he asked, trying to access his old self. The self that had investigated mysteries and ordered missions. An old self that didn't get emotionally involved in cases even when they involved his father or the Sons.

"Who do you think?" Nina replied, still holding on to Brianna with a death grip.

"Why would the Sons be after you after so long?"

"Cody…" Her eyebrows drew together, as if he was the one missing information. "They've always been after me."

"What does that mean?"

She let out a shaky breath. "I…" She glanced nervously at Brianna. "Back then…"

"We can talk about it later." As much because he didn't want Brianna overhearing things that would hurt her or scare her as the fact he didn't want…

He didn't want to have to go back over that breakup seven years ago and see all the signs he must have missed. All the things he'd ignored because he'd been hurt. Because it was becoming increasingly clear to him that the breakup seven years ago hadn't been as *inevitable* as he'd assumed.

"You need to get me out," Nina said in a fierce whisper. "You need to."

"Ace is in jail."

Again confusion took over her features. "How can

that… How can that be? It was one of his men who shot me."

"You're sure?"

"Yes." When he kept his gaze steady on her she wilted a little. "No. I mean, I didn't see him. He was dressed…" Again she looked at Brianna, clearly not wanting to get too far into it. "Who else, Cody? Who else?"

"I don't know what you've been doing these past few years."

The hurt that chased over her face was too hard to watch, so he turned his attention to Brianna. "We need to go."

"I don't want to."

"I know, but your mom needs to sleep to get better."

"I'll sleep with her."

Cody had to scrub his hands over his face. What had Nina gotten him into? Them all into?

Was it Nina, or was it you?

"Grandma Pauline was going to make a cake," Cody managed to say, though he had to admit he didn't sound very excited about it.

Nina rolled her eyes at him, but when she turned her attention to Brianna, she smiled big and bright. "Go on. I'm going to get better as soon as possible." Nina picked up the wig she'd knocked off Brianna's head. "And you get to play dress up and eat cake," Nina said, fixing the wig back on.

"The princesses gave me new toys."

"The…" Nina smiled, though it was sad around the edges. "And they'll protect you." Nina looked up at Cody, something indescribable in her expression. "And so will all those brave knights."

"You need a knight," Brianna said, her forehead pleated with worry.

"I have one," Nina replied easily, still smiling. Cody wondered if Brianna saw through it as easily as he did. "The man who was in here when you got here? That's your daddy's big brother. He's been keeping me safe, and he's going to keep doing that. Okay?"

"Why aren't *you* keeping Mommy safe?" Brianna asked, frowning at Cody.

Cody found himself speechless, which wasn't something he'd ever had a problem with until the past few days. But his daughter looking at him with such accusation when he hadn't even fully come to grips with the fact he *had* a daughter.

"Your daddy's job is to keep *you* safe," Nina said. She looked up at him, imploring and desperate. "And to get me out of here as soon as he can."

Cody didn't appreciate being put on the spot like that, but he was beginning to—somewhat against his will— come to her way of thinking. If it was the Sons who'd hurt her, for whatever reason, it wouldn't take much longer for them to come sniffing around the Wyatts, and it would eventually lead them to this hospital.

"We'll do our best. All us knights." Cody forced himself to smile and hold out his arms for Brianna. She gave Nina a kiss on the cheek and one last squeeze, then reluctantly went to him.

"Can't I walk?" she whined.

"We're trying to keep your age a secret, remember?"

Brianna sighed. "I'm tired of secrets," she mumbled.

Cody didn't say anything, but he met Nina's gaze. Regret. Fear. Sadness. Hurt.

It all echoed inside of him. So he turned away. "We'll do our best," he muttered, opening the door. As he stepped out, he pulled his hat back low and looked at Gage, who was standing there guarding the door, thank God.

"What do you know?" Cody asked Gage on a whisper.

"She's been living in Dyner," Gage said, keeping his voice low and their heads bent together.

Dyner was a small town at the edge of Valiant County. She'd been that close. *That* close. Granted, Cody had been living in Wyoming so it wasn't as if they would have run into each other, but…

"She killed a man—the man who shot her. He was a member of the Sons. It's not going to take long for one of the nurses to put it together when Tucker comes to investigate."

"He can't—"

"Why do you think he hasn't yet? But this is his job, Cody. He's the detective. He can only bend so many rules without losing his badge."

Rules. It was why Cody hadn't been able to follow his brothers' footsteps. He'd wanted to be a cop too, except for the rules. They too often didn't help people who needed to be helped.

Cody looked down at Brianna in his arms. She had her head leaned against his shoulder. She wasn't crying, but she looked like she might start at any moment. "We have to get her out."

Gage pulled a face, but he didn't argue. "Got any bright ideas?"

"Not yet, but we act now. One way or another."

Nina had been brought up by the Knights to believe in right and wrong. Good people followed the rules and the world would reward them if they did.

She didn't believe that anymore. Seven years of keeping her daughter's identity a secret, of moving and hiding and living in fear would shatter anyone's fairy-tale views.

Sneaking out of the hospital was wrong, and it felt

wrong, but she knew she had to do it. Gage had created a slight diversion, and Cody had taken out her IV and done something to the equipment so it wouldn't alert the nurses she'd removed the ports.

Then Cody had left with Brianna, leaving Nina to find a way to sneak out as soon as Gage gave her the go-ahead signal.

The Wyatt boys had made it easy, and she'd walked right out of the small local hospital as if she was actually supposed to.

When she saw Cody standing next to a truck, his hat pulled low, pretending to puff on a cigarette, her heart beat hard against her ribs reminding her she was alive.

No matter the aches, the pains, the fear that she actually wouldn't survive all this, she was alive. She had to keep living and trying for Brianna, no matter what hurt— body or heart.

He opened the passenger side door for her, dropping the unlit cigarette and crushing it with his boot. She slid inside and smiled back at Brianna in the back. Somehow they'd found a booster seat for her.

"How…"

Cody slid into the driver's side seat. "It's Gigi's. Uh, Gigi is Liza's little sister. She's only four, so we had to adjust it for Brianna, but it worked for today."

"Liza. I haven't seen her…" It had only been Nina's second year with the Knights when Liza had come to live with them. Liza had been sixteen, and the Knight girls had all been significantly younger. There'd been a big uproar because she and the oldest Wyatt boy had finally gotten out of the Sons.

Nina remembered that summer. Remembered how scared she'd been that if the Knights added another girl, they might send her back.

Nina had been the last foster, and the other girls had been together for years before the Knights had asked her to come home with them. But Nina had been afraid. Afraid to get too close. To settle in.

Then Liza had come and made Nina even more afraid. But instead of sending Nina back, or having less room, something about Liza had made them a family. A real family.

Then Liza had disappeared three years later. Back to the Sons everyone said. But Nina had known she'd only gone back to save her sister Marci. No matter what the Wyatt brothers had thought.

"Liza's back then."

"More or less. She lives in Bonesteel with her little sister and Jamison."

"Jamison. But…" Jamison had been the most devastated by Liza's disappearance. And the most angry. Granted that was all fifteen years ago.

Cody shrugged. "Got back together last month when she left the Sons."

The words *got back together* hung between them, heavy and uncomfortable as Cody pulled out of the hospital parking lot.

"Gage will stay back for a few hours," Cody said, his voice cool and devoid of emotion. "Then he'll make an excuse that he got a call, but not to bother you. It should buy us some hours."

"But they know Gage. They know you."

"If it's the Sons, they know us anyway. If it's not? That'll take longer."

"It's the Sons," Nina said flatly.

He shifted a glance in the rearview mirror, so Nina did the same. Brianna was fast asleep.

"She hasn't done much of that," Cody said. "She

wouldn't do anything until the girls—the *princesses*—all got there. They gave her a bath and she ate a bit. She's very talkative and seems…okay, but she's not sleeping or eating enough. She's been too worried."

Nina nodded, her stomach tying in knots. "We can't stay at the ranch."

"You can. You will."

"Cody—"

"You came to us for a reason, Nina. I assume in part because it's my fault if the Sons are trying to hurt you. But also because you knew we could keep you both safe. You're going to have to trust me to make those decisions. And my decision is you're at the ranch for the time being."

"You still think you're invincible," she said, before she could think better of it and temper the bitterness out of her tone.

He gave her an enigmatic look before turning his attention back to the road. "No one's invincible. But some people will do whatever it takes to make things right. *Whatever* it takes."

Chapter Four

Nina had kept it together. For Brianna's sake. For her own. Because letting her guard down with Cody would surely mean all kinds of trouble.

But when Cody pulled up to Grandma Pauline's ranch, and Duke Knight stood there waiting, she absolutely lost it.

He'd been her one true father figure, and she didn't realize until this moment how desperately she'd missed having someone to lean on. Someone who loved her, no matter what. A strong, sure presence. Always.

Brianna was still asleep so Nina let herself cry as she got out of the car and practically ran for him. He met her halfway, enveloping her in a tight hug. It didn't matter that her stomach hurt. He still smelled like horses and leather and home.

When he pulled her back, his dark eyes were full of tears. "You're lucky you're still healing, girlie, because I have a heap of lectures waiting for you."

His voice had gone raspier, and there was more gray at his temples than there had been. He was the absolute best man she knew. From taking her in when she'd been a shy little mess, to keeping all his daughters—biological and foster—strong and whole through Liza running away, and then his beloved wife dying shortly after.

Breaking up with Cody had been hard, but leaving her family had been a sacrifice she probably wouldn't have been able to bear… If she hadn't found out she was pregnant. It had made the ache for home greater, but it had made the stakes so much higher.

"Took three of us just to keep him from charging off to the hospital."

Nina inhaled and turned to find Dev. She let out a breath. Seven years had changed him. Not for the better. He was skinnier, edgier. She'd watched him slowly climb out of the near-death experience he'd suffered ten years ago, but it had left a forever mark that only seemed to deepen with time.

"Hi, Dev."

"Let's get inside," Cody said. "We can't be too careful."

Nina managed to look at him. Brianna was curled up against him. He made carrying her look easy when she was having a harder and harder time hefting Brianna's ever-growing frame.

Nina doubted inside was any safer than outside. If the Sons had finally come after her, it was because of her connection to the Wyatts. Grandma Pauline's ranch would be the first place they looked.

She let Cody usher her inside as Brianna yawned and woke up. With time to think more than panic, Nina could see that her coloring had been off, but the nap in the car had helped some.

"Come here, baby." Nina held out her arms.

Cody shook his head. "You're not supposed to be carrying anything."

She opened her mouth to argue, but there were too many men in the kitchen looking at her like she'd break.

Grandma Pauline bustled into the kitchen. "Now, you'll sit and you'll eat," she said by way of greeting, already making a beeline for the stove. Though she patted Nina's shoulder as she passed—which was often as close to a hug as Grandma Pauline ever got.

Slowly, Nina lowered herself into a chair at the kitchen table. She placed her palms on the scarred wood. Grandma Pauline's table had been a second home, which had been a miracle for a girl who'd been born into such a terrible one. To be brought to a place surrounded by so many people who cared. So many places to go when she was afraid or upset or lonely.

To have to leave it, all because she'd fallen in love. Even after seven years of living on the run, she couldn't find a way to make herself believe it had been a mistake. That she'd fallen in love with the wrong person. Cody had understood her better than anyone back then. And he'd given her Brianna.

The child he was setting down on the ground, as if he'd been born to be a father to her wonderful girl.

Brianna crossed the floor and seated herself on Nina's lap. Nina held her close and tight and tried to breathe through all the horrible and wonderful things pressing against her chest.

"Have you met Duke?" Nina asked Brianna through a tight throat, turning Brianna to face where Duke took a seat next to her.

Duke nodded slowly and Brianna bounced in Nina's lap, causing Nina to wince in pain.

"Grandpa Duke already gave me a present," Brianna said happily through bites of a cookie Grandma Pauline had sneaked her somehow.

"Grandpa," Nina echoed, touched beyond measure. Duke was her daughter's grandfather. It opened up a yawning, painful regret she knew would eat her alive if she'd let it.

It *hurt* that she'd lost her family seven years ago, but she had to remember why she'd done it. To save Cody. To save Brianna. She couldn't focus on the regret. She had to focus on the present.

Getting out of the hospital had been a start, but if the Sons suddenly wanted her dead—whether because they'd finally tracked her down or for some other reason—they wouldn't stop. Even if Ace was in jail, which she didn't quite believe.

The only way they'd stop now that they'd shot her was if they thought she'd died in that fire.

All things Nina didn't want to discuss in front of Brianna, no matter how much Brianna had gleaned from living her entire life knowing bad men were after them.

At the sound of little feet, Nina turned to the entryway of the kitchen that led out into the living room. A little girl scurried in, grinning broadly at everyone.

Behind her at a slower pace, a tall brunette appeared.

"Oh my God," Nina breathed. Cody had mentioned Liza, but Nina didn't know how to handle these onslaughts of memory and reality.

Brianna slid off Nina's lap and ran over to the little girl standing next to Liza. The two girls hugged like they were the best of friends and Nina could only stare at Liza. They'd been sisters for such a short time, but she supposed time didn't matter when you'd grown up with so few people in your life who'd loved you or cared about your well-being. The ones who did, no matter for how long, mattered.

Nina slowly got to her feet, in part because this all felt so surreal and in part because her side hurt.

"You've looked better, kid," Liza said, her voice scratchy at best.

Much like with Duke outside, Nina didn't try to hold

herself back. She moved forward and grabbed onto Liza, squeezing as tight as possible. She let it all go. Let herself remember what it was like to have a family, to depend on someone else.

Liza's arms were gentle, likely she was being careful because of Nina's injuries. Liza was older, and she'd always seemed to know everything. Looking back, Nina knew it wasn't true, but she wanted to believe in Liza's all-knowing powers for a while.

Liza cleared her throat and pulled away. "I'll watch the girls. You all have your war council. Then we can catch up."

Nina looked back at the table where Duke, Dev, Cody and Grandma Pauline were now seated, looking very much like just that—a *war* council. She let out a shaky breath.

For seven years she'd run. She knew that coming home to the Wyatts would mean only one thing.

Now it was time to fight.

CODY HAD NOW watched Nina fall apart while facing two people from her past.

She hadn't fallen apart when she'd seen him in that hospital room—him, the person she'd kept their daughter a secret from for so long.

It burned. Brianna being kept from him for so long was the kind of betrayal a person didn't just *set aside*.

Unless said daughter was in mortal danger, he supposed.

So, no. Betrayal couldn't be focused on right now. Survival came first—it always did. He might have been saved from the Sons at the age of six, but he'd always known the cost and importance of survival.

Nina returned to her seat at the table, wincing as she

sat. Whether out of pain or the fact everyone's attention was on her as Liza led the girls out of the kitchen with the promise of a tea party.

Nina inhaled and let the breath out slowly. He knew he should speak first. Lay out what they knew, but all he could seem to do was stare at her. She looked exactly the same. Same freckles, same dark blue eyes. Her hair was a little longer than it had been back then, but other than that, nothing about her had changed.

Except the woman he'd known, would never have kept his own child from him.

Unless she'd finally understood what it meant to be a Wyatt, and that she never wanted that mark on her child.

He had to get his head on straight. Daughter or not, Nina back here or not, there were lives at stake and he'd dedicated his life to saving lives from the Sons. No matter how he felt about said lives.

"We can't stay here," Nina finally said, her expression pained. "They'll already be looking for me here. Gage was in my hospital room. They're not going to view that as coincidence."

Cody looked down at his hands, clenched into fists. Carefully, mindfully, he unclenched his fingers and placed his palm against the scarred wood. "True," he replied evenly. "But they'd have to track you to that hospital. I'm not convinced they did."

"Fine. But they'll check here. You know they will."

He had no doubt, but he had protections for that. Protections he'd made before he'd known Nina had his child.

Your child. Your child.

Daddy.

One by one, he pressed his fingers into the wood, focused on the feel of it. Focused on the smell of Grandma Pauline's chili soup simmering on the stove.

"Why don't you start from the beginning," Duke said gently, and there was a warning in the look he shot Cody.

Cody could look down pure evil, could even hold his grandmother's censoring gaze most of the time, but he did not know what to do with the *blame* in Duke's dark eyes.

"Which beginning is that?" Nina returned, and her voice was sharp enough he knew without looking her way she was throwing that question at him as a kind of challenge.

"Someone shot you. Start there," Cody replied, facing her with the blankest expression he could muster under the circumstances.

Your daughter. Your daughter.

"I was living in Dyner."

There was a collective noise around the table, almost a sound of pain. Duke and Grandma were horrified she'd been so close. So close and they hadn't known.

"We'd been there about six months," Nina continued. "Brianna needed to start school, and I didn't know where to do it where she'd be safe. Being close seemed the best option. The Sons wouldn't think I'd come back toward home."

It was smart, if a gamble still. But everything about outwitting the Sons was a gamble.

"It had been about two years since I'd had a…run-in, shall we call it. I'd been living in Oklahoma then. Someone broke into my apartment while we were gone. Luckily I…" She trailed off and rubbed her hand against her chest.

Grandma was immediately on her feet, gathering bowls and serving up chili and crackers and glasses of milk. In Grandma's world, the first thing you fixed about a person was the state of their stomach—then they could deal with their emotional affairs.

"The reason I ran in the first place was I knew they

could never know Brianna existed. So, I've been very careful. I don't leave evidence of a child around. Brianna learned to put her things in hiding places—not that we ever had many things to begin with. But I just knew… I knew I had to keep her a secret."

Cody wanted to get up out of his seat. He wanted to prowl the kitchen. He wanted to *break* things.

Instead he leaned back casually in his chair. "So what you're telling me is that no one knew Brianna existed— not just me." He shouldn't have said that last part. Not *now*. But…

"Yes, that's what I'm saying," she returned, and her weak attempt at coldness failed miserably. "I hadn't had any run-ins for two years. We were living under a fake name. I worked at a gas station while Brianna was in school. It was a ramshackle little place, family run. They paid me under the table. They were nice. Even let me rent this small house they owned for less than…"

Nina seemed to lose herself in her memories and Cody had to fight against his own impatience.

"I'm sure glad to hear you had some nice people looking after you," Duke said, reaching out and patting Nina's hand. Complete with another glare in Cody's direction.

She smiled. "We've been lucky. Really. Until…" She took a deep breath and looked down at the chili soup Grandma had put in front of her. "Until that night. Morning I guess, but really early. I heard something—I thought it was Brianna. She sleepwalks sometimes."

His daughter sleepwalked sometimes. His daughter. And all she'd had for six years was Nina and danger.

"It wasn't Brianna. It was a man busting in my front door. He lifted a gun." Nina shuddered. "I did the first thing I could think of and threw my phone at him. It must have surprised him enough because the shot missed me and hit a lamp. It shattered into a million pieces and I dived to grab a piece of it and hide behind the couch."

Cody did stand then, his chair scraping violently against the floor. He couldn't...

"Sit down and eat, boy," Grandma ordered sharply.

He only looked at her with one furious sneer. "I will not. I cannot." He strode for the door. He'd come back and do his duty, but he needed to pound on *something* first.

"I fought him off, and that's when he shot me. But I used the shard and jabbed it in his neck. I'm pretty sure I killed him," Nina said all in a rush, as if hoping to get it all out before he stepped outside. "Then I grabbed Brianna and set a fire and—"

"You set a *fire*?" Dev asked incredulously.

"I had to hide any sign of Brianna being alive," Nina replied. "We were careful, but she still existed. If they came after me, knew it was *me*, and found the remnants of a child... I didn't have time to get her things. I'd been shot. So, yes, I started a fire."

When Cody turned to look at her, some combination of shock and horror dulling some of his fury to just plain confusion, she was looking up at him with what seemed pleading eyes.

But she wasn't begging. She was reciting everything she'd done to keep their daughter alive and unknown to his father's gang.

"Then they still don't know she exists," Dev said.

"I don't think they do. I hope to God they don't." She kept her eyes on Cody the whole time. "Which is why we can't stay here. They will look for me here and they will find her."

Chapter Five

Cody didn't walk out the door as Nina half expected him to. She'd clearly knocked some of the fury out of him by detailing the lengths she'd gone to in keeping Brianna a secret.

But she wasn't so sure this was better. She couldn't work out what stormed in his eyes. It wasn't just anger, and it wasn't just blame. It was oceans of hurt, and Nina didn't know how to fix any of it.

"I need to speak with Nina alone," he finally said, his voice a scrape against the quiet room.

"Hell n—"

Nina reached across to Duke, squeezing his hand. "He's right. We have some things to discuss privately."

"Well, it's not happening now," Duke said, withdrawing his hand and standing. He pointed at Cody, and it was only then Nina realized Duke was holding on to his temper. Barely. "You did this."

Nina tried to protest, but no one was listening to her, least of all Duke and Cody.

"You don't get a second alone with her. You fix my daughter being in trouble for seven years first. Then you can talk about what *you* need."

"Duke."

He whirled on her, anger and hurt vibrating in his big,

tough frame. "Oh no, little girl. I held my tongue back then, but I have learned from my mistakes. One of those was ever letting a Wyatt boy near any of my girls."

"You wait just a second," Grandma Pauline said, getting to her feet.

"I have held my tongue, Pauline, but this is a step too far."

"That girl has been shot—brought her child no one knew about here by the skin of her teeth—and you have no right to stand here and place blame."

"I'll stand here and place blame where it belongs."

Nina seemed to be the only one who noticed Cody slip out the door. Which felt all too much like they were back in high school. Duke had never expressed his displeasure about her dating Cody, but there'd often been fights. Jamison, the oldest Wyatt brother trying to play father to the rest—the rest taking exception—Grandma Pauline wading in and laying down the law.

Cody had never been built for it. He was an introvert, she'd always thought. He had to work his way through his problems on his own. He couldn't shout them out. It just didn't work for him.

She supposed it had been part of the attraction. All she remembered of her parents was dramatic yelling and arguments and blame. A wild, out-of-control abandon to everything.

The Knight house had involved shouting too, though she'd learned to live with it—because the arguments always ended in forgiveness and love. The Wyatt home was always chaos, noise and shouts, but with that same undercurrent of love and caring.

But even when they'd been teenagers Cody had been controlled and separate from that most of the time. She knew he felt deeply, wanted to act, but he contained it all very carefully.

Her heart squeezed as Grandma Pauline and Duke's argument turned into downright hollering. She glanced helplessly at Dev.

Dev nodded to the door, a signal for her to take the escape. He'd stay and clean up the aftermath.

It wasn't the first time Duke and Grandma Pauline had had a heated argument. It wasn't even the most vicious fight she'd watched them have, but it still made Nina's stomach cramp to think it was over her.

She got out of her seat and walked to the door, slipping out of it just as Cody had done. Now they could have their private conversation while the older generation fought over if they should.

Cody was standing over by the barn. He had one booted foot on the lowest rung of one of the pasture fences. He didn't have his hat on, and his dark hair moved with the slight breeze.

Though he didn't move or react to her approach, she knew without a shadow of a doubt he was aware of exactly where she was. She'd seen enough of the "cop" versions of his older brothers to know what that kind of feigned distractedness really meant.

Full and utter attention.

So she decided to speak first even though she didn't know how to broach the subject they really needed to discuss. "I guess we'll always be teenagers to them."

He didn't say anything. If they *were* teenagers, she would have reached out. Brushed her hand down his rigid back. She would have said something soft and sweet to break him out of his solitary brooding.

But they weren't teenagers anymore and she was the cause of his pain. She *knew* she'd never be able to explain it to him in a way he'd accept, but the words bubbled up anyway.

"I didn't have a choice."

He gave her a look so scathing she practically stepped back. She swallowed and recentered. She couldn't make him feel the way she wanted him to. So she'd have to be as honest as she could be and let him figure out how he wanted to feel about it without wishing for a certain reaction.

"I know you'll never believe me. You'll think there was something you could have done to save us, but there wasn't. It was so much better for you not to know—for everyone I love not to know."

"She's my daughter."

"And she knew you. She knew everyone. Kind of."

"But I didn't know her." He turned to her, and everything about him was contained and controlled, except the red-hot fury in his eyes. "I never would have let Ace touch her."

"I couldn't let Ace know she existed, regardless," she responded. She might not have self-righteous rage behind her words, but she had something more important. A desperate love and all-encompassing need to protect her child. *Their* child. "I know that hurts you. I'm sorry it had to, but I absolutely did what had to be done to keep her safe." She could tell him about the threats she'd received, but it wouldn't matter to him right now. She didn't even blame him for that. How could she?

She'd kept Brianna from him for almost seven years, and their daughter was a *joy*.

"She has your cowlick," Nina found herself saying, pointing to the crown of his head. "It's a lot more annoying when you're a girl."

"Do you think this helps?" he demanded, his voice so low and pained it almost sounded like a growl.

She wanted to reach out and touch him and knew she would absolutely in no way, shape, or form be welcome to. "Do you think it hurts?" she asked gently.

He turned away from her. "This *all* hurts."

"I'm sorry. I didn't want to come here."

He whirled on her, that control slipping a small measure. "You think that makes it better? That you didn't *want* our help? That you were shot, and our daughter could have been—"

"She wasn't, was she?" Nina demanded before he could finish all the horrible thoughts she'd entertained herself with in that hospital bed. "Because for seven years my entire being has been about protecting her, including this," she said pointing to her aching stomach. "I took a bullet for that child and I'd take a hell of a lot more."

His eyes flashed with a true violent anger. He lifted his chin and looked at her with a detached disdain that made her shiver. He said nothing.

"You have to understand what this all means. You have to understand that Brianna and I can't stay here."

"For now, it's all you can do." Then he simply walked away, as if that was that.

Nina was left with nothing but an ache so deep that she couldn't even blame it on a gunshot wound.

CODY DIDN'T HAVE a plan yet, but there were some things he had to do. Far away from where anyone could hear him.

He walked into the barn, but then walked right out the other side and kept going. Dev could return any moment to do chores or head out to the pastures. Cody walked toward the far fence that marked off the north side of the property. It was a pretty spring day, but he hardly noticed.

He knew every inch of this land, thought he'd understood every inch of himself. But he felt lost today. In emotion. In fear. He couldn't seem to harness either fully no matter how hard he tried.

You'll think there was something you could have done to save us, but there wasn't.

He would have done anything. Everything. The fact Nina didn't believe that... It shouldn't matter. They'd broken up a long time ago.

But he found himself wondering how much of that had been *her* decision.

He shook that thought away. Clearly she'd found out she was pregnant and wanted to make sure Ace Wyatt never got near her child. She'd succeeded for six years until somehow, someway, his father had found a way to...

It didn't make sense. Why the Sons would be after her if they didn't know about Brianna? But he had to believe they wouldn't have bothered shooting Nina if they knew Brianna existed.

So what *was* this?

Once he was far enough away from the house and the ranch areas to be sure he wouldn't be overheard, Cody pulled his phone out of his pocket and dialed.

"I'm going to change my number," was the woman's greeting.

"Nothing wrong with checking in."

Shay laughed, and he missed that. Not *her* laugh specifically, but the teamwork that could prompt that reaction out of someone even when nothing was funny. He'd spent the past four years immersed in the world of the North Star group—not the youngest Wyatt brother, not left in the dark.

And for all those years Nina had been running away with *his* daughter.

"Cody, if you check in every five seconds I can't get anything done."

"So, there's been nothing new?"

Shay sighed. "Ace hasn't had any visitors at the jail. No contact as far as we can see, outside of his lawyers. We're watching them too, but so far nothing out of the ordinary. We've been looking into the attack on this Oaks woman, but the fire pretty much took out any evidence."

"No chatter?"

"Nothing. Especially nothing that points to the Sons or Ace."

"It had to be him." Cody *knew* his father was behind this. There were no other options. But without evidence…

"Maybe it was, Cody, but I don't have any evidence. We work with facts. You know that."

"You'll keeping looking?"

There was a pause on the other end, and this was what he was afraid of. Not being part of the group anymore meant he couldn't push for information. North Star might be after taking the Sons down, and they had targeted Cody for a reason—he was a Wyatt.

But that didn't mean they would go after this thread. With Ace in jail, they had bigger leads to follow.

But Cody knew that if someone was after Nina in particular, no matter *who* it was, it linked to him.

"I can keep you up-to-date, Cody, but that's all I can do."

He wanted to press her, but it wouldn't do any good. He understood the North Star group too well. It wasn't personal for them. It couldn't be.

It would just be a hell of a lot easier if he had their help. "Thanks, Shay."

"Stay safe, Cody."

He ended the phone call and blew out a breath. He

shared Nina's concerns about them staying here, but until he knew where the threat was coming from—and with Nina recovering from her injuries—it was safer than running.

Besides, there were *some* protections here. Ones no one knew about—since his grandmother would throw a fit, and his brothers would want to know details he couldn't give them. But his time with North Star hadn't been a waste—and not just because Ace was in jail.

Cody turned toward the sound of an engine. A police cruiser stopped on the gravel. His eldest brother stepped out, hat shielding his face from the sun and Cody as he walked toward him.

"Jamison." It was strange. He'd spent most of the past few years staying away from the family and focusing on North Star and bringing down the Sons. When he'd crossed paths with Jamison last month, it had been as an agent.

The past few weeks when Jamison had come home had thrust him back into the role of baby brother. It had grated.

Until this moment, when Cody felt something like relief wash through him. Because here was someone who would know what to do. Not about the case, but about this horrible feeling inside of him he couldn't seem to control.

Jamison studied him, as if he could understand everything just from a look. "So."

"I have a daughter." It was such a stupid, pointless thing to say since Jamison surely knew, and yet Cody hadn't really said it out loud like that yet. Somehow, his oldest brother brought that out of him.

"So I hear. Hell of a thing."

"Yeah."

"Liza tells me Nina's recovering."

Cody nodded.

"Look, um…" Jamison cleared his throat and slid off his hat, rubbing the back of his neck. "I have some inkling of what you're feeling right now."

"Liza didn't show up with your kid in tow."

"No. She didn't," Jamison agreed easily. "But there was baggage. And I thought, well, we'd deal with the threat and Ace, and then I could figure that all out. It isn't going to work that way. I think, especially with a kid in tow."

"She calls me Daddy."

Jamison made a pained expression as if he understood. Pain and joy and a million conflicting emotions. How could Cody do anything but put them away until he'd secured his daughter's safety?

"I think you should go see Ace."

Cody could only stare for a full thirty seconds at his brother. Age had etched lines onto his face, but it was the same face it had always been——a little harder, a lot more determined and holding far more responsibility than any one man could contain.

Except Jamison had always managed.

"I don't think me seeing Ace right now would be a good idea."

"I know. But you held yourself back that day. You didn't end his life and you could have."

Should have.

"If you see him, talk to him, we might be able to get a handle on what he knows about what happened to Nina," Jamison said in his rational, cop voice.

"I can't right now, Jamison. I can't…" It burned to admit a weakness. "I don't have the control I need."

"Okay. What if we send Nina?"

Chapter Six

Nina sat in the living room of the Wyatt house with Liza, Brianna and Gigi playing with plastic ponies on the rug. Grandma Pauline and Dev had gone out to do ranch chores, and Duke had returned to his neighboring ranch.

Not before he and Grandma Pauline had fought over where she and Brianna should stay. But Grandma Pauline had the trump card: six grandsons who were all law enforcement or had been. Duke had Sarah and Rachel living at home—who no one wanted to bring into this mess.

Which brought home the fact she hadn't seen any of her sisters. Duke and Liza were the only ones from her life with the Knights who'd come to see her.

Nina shouldn't be surprised, and she had no right to feel hurt, but she was both and a little miserable with it. That and the aching pain in her stomach. She knew she could take more pain medication, but she'd deal with the pain over the loopy exhaustion that consumed her as a side effect from the meds.

"You can always go lie down," Liza offered gently.

"No. I'm tired of lying. I'm really tired of thinking." She picked at the arm of the couch. "I haven't seen any of the other girls."

Liza winced. "Well, Cecilia's had to work. And Felicity too, of course. They don't live at the ranch."

"But Rachel and Sarah do."

"I'm sure Rachel will come around. Sarah… Truth be told, she's not exactly sold on *me* being back yet, and I've been here two months. We may have had our reasons for leaving, Nina, but…"

"I know." Aside from Rachel, who was Duke and Eva's only biological child, they'd all grown up in varyingly tragic circumstances before being taken in by the Knights. They each had their own childhood scars. Being abandoned by the sisters they'd learned to love would be a particularly difficult blow.

"I had to, Liza."

"I don't doubt it." Liza smiled sadly. "The problem with doing things we have to do is that sometimes no one else can understand that need." Liza looked down at their two girls—because even if Gigi was Liza's half sister, she was a little girl Liza was taking care of. "It's really hard to understand when you don't have this kind of responsibility. So, they're struggling, but I understand you did what you had to, Nina. Really."

Nina nodded. She knew Liza was right. As much as she appreciated Liza saying she understood, it didn't assuage all those other things she felt at her sisters not coming to see her. Maybe she should go lie down as Liza had suggested.

But she heard the back door slam and low voices in the kitchen. A few moments later, Cody and Jamison strode into the living room.

Nina thought Cody's mood might have calmed some before he returned. But there was absolutely no change in all that angry energy that swirled around him.

Nina smiled at Jamison. It was such a strange parade of so many people she'd loved and had had to ruthlessly cut out of her life. She didn't know how to cope with it all.

The years were on Jamison's face. Or maybe it was all the responsibility he hefted on his shoulders that made him look so hard. So much older.

Everything about that hard face softened as Gigi squealed and ran over to him. He lifted her into his arms, and it was clear that Liza's half sister adored him. And that he adored her.

"Missed you, mite," he said in a low tone as Gigi snuggled into him.

Even back when Nina had been desperately in love with Cody, so sure they'd spend their lives together, children had never been a part of her future plans. No matter how much Duke and Eva had loved her, she'd lived under the specter of her parents' choices. She'd been determined to choose the opposite of all of them.

As much as Brianna had become the center of her whole life, sitting in the Wyatt house, her daughter on the floor, Jamison holding a little girl… It didn't feel real.

But Jamison spoke, and it was in that same calm, comfortingly in-control tone she remembered. "Hi, Nina. How are you feeling?"

"I'm all right." She was dead exhausted, but there was so much going on. So much to think about.

Jamison and Liza shared a glance that had Liza getting to her feet. "Hey, girlies, what about if we go visit the horses?"

Brianna jumped to her feet. "Can we feed them?"

"Well, we'll have to ask Uncle Dev."

Jamison handed Gigi off to Liza, and they exchanged a brief kiss, like some kind of perfect choreographed dance that made Nina's chest ache and her eyes search for Cody.

He was looking at the floor.

"You girls go get your shoes on," Liza urged, shooing them toward the kitchen.

"Are we sure it's safe for Brianna to run around outside?" Nina fretted.

"It's safe," Cody said, his voice hard and final. But that eased her nerves some. Cody wouldn't promise safety where there was none.

"What's going on?" Liza demanded of Jamison.

"We're just going to talk to Nina," Jamison replied.

Liza folded her arms over her chest. "About what?"

Nina had to smile at the warning and protectiveness in Liza's tone. Maybe Sarah was still getting over the betrayal of her leaving, maybe all the girls were, but Liza understood. Someone really understood and wanted to protect her. That was nice.

Jamison turned to Nina. "How would you feel about going to visit Ace in jail?"

Nina's gaze immediately flew to Cody's, but aside from a set jaw and the same furious eyes, she couldn't read his feelings.

She supposed his feelings didn't matter. "What would be the purpose?"

"To see if he has a reaction. To see if he gives anything away."

"Ace isn't stupid," Liza scoffed.

"No, but he's beyond arrogant. He certainly gave some things away when he had us that he shouldn't have."

"He *had* you?" Nina demanded, her gaze whipping to Liza.

Liza shrugged. "I had to get Gigi out from under the Sons, and Jamison helped. Then Cody rescued us."

"It wasn't me," Cody said gruffly.

Liza rolled her eyes. "I'll take the girls out, but don't agree to anything you don't want to do, Nina. Don't let these two push you around." She moved onto her toes and brushed a kiss against Jamison's cheek. "And you don't be pushy."

She walked out into the kitchen, and Nina noted that Jamison and Cody both waited to speak until the sounds of little girls' voices faded and the door closed.

"It's completely up to you, Nina," Jamison offered into the silence. "The problem we're running into is we're not quite sure why the Sons targeted you so violently after such a long time of not."

"It's possible they just couldn't find me."

"In Dyner?" Jamison replied with a raised eyebrow.

"It's possible."

"It's possible," he finally agreed. "But the man shot you. Maybe he was acting out of turn, but I doubt it. Not if he led with shooting. There's something more to this than just wanting to hurt you because you dated Cody once upon a time."

"Brianna?" she asked, fear icing her insides.

Jamison shook his head. "There's nothing to point to the Sons or Ace knowing about Brianna."

Cody still hadn't spoken, which poked at her irritation. "Don't you have anything to say?" she demanded.

He met her gaze, but only shook his head.

She wanted to punch him.

"I wouldn't," he said, his voice low and lethal against the dead quiet of the room.

Nina realized she'd curled her hands into fists and her thoughts on his behavior had been written all over her face. She lifted her chin and slowly released her fingers. She looked at Jamison and tried to come up with a bland expression.

"So what would you have me do?"

"We'd arrange for you to visit Ace. I'd be with you. We'd let Ace lead the conversation. See if he makes threats or shows his cards about what he does know. He'll try to get in your head, make you afraid, but that might give us some answers. Or some clues to follow."

"And if he gives you clues?"

"We see if we can connect him to your shooting and add it to the charges against him. We also find out how he's controlling things from the inside. Ideally."

"And if things go less than ideally, we go in there and get nothing."

"It's possible. Liza's right. Ace isn't stupid. He's spent a lot of time evading just what he's facing now. But he's facing it, because of Cody."

"It wasn't just me," Cody insisted again.

Jamison glanced at Cody. "But he'll put the blame square on you."

Something passed between the brothers that Nina couldn't read, which was irritating enough. But Cody just standing on the sidelines while Jamison handled all this irritated her even more.

"So, it's a test of sorts."

"Yes, a test where the risk is minimal. I don't think there's a chance this doesn't connect to the Sons, which means there isn't a chance Ace doesn't know exactly who you are. I know you won't bring up Brianna, and neither will I. We're not trying to find out if he knows Brianna exists. We're just going to see if he'll let anything slip. If he doesn't, we're in the same exact place we are right now."

Nina nodded. She didn't want to face Ace again. The last time had been scary enough. And clearly neither Cody nor Jamison knew that Ace had been the one to come to her to make sure she broke things off with Cody and disappeared.

She should probably tell them, but the words wouldn't

form. If Cody could stand there being stoic and silent, she would find a way to be the same.

"I'll do it," she offered, lifting her chin and fighting away the nerves that already threatened. "On one condition." She turned her gaze to Cody. "I don't want Jamison to come with me. I want you to."

CODY HAD SPENT a lot of time learning how to control his reactions. You didn't get to be part of North Star if you were a hothead who couldn't manage his temper. And there'd been a lot of tests to make sure Cody could handle taking down the Sons when it was personal for him.

He didn't understand why Nina broke all those pieces of control he'd honed for so long. He tried to convince himself it was just about being kept in the dark about his daughter's life for six years—but there was an annoying part of himself that knew it was more than that.

It was just her.

Whatever they'd been in their adolescence, it hadn't been ordinary. It hadn't left him. It had marked him, and for a man who had an evil gang leader of a father, nothing so simple and ordinary should mark him.

But she had.

Cody knew Jamison was waiting for him to answer. He knew Jamison would back him up whatever he said—but that only made the decision worse. He had to make the right one, not the one he wanted to make.

"All right then," he said, against his will, against his better judgment. He already didn't want Nina talking to Ace. It would be worse if he was there.

It was also a necessary step. They couldn't just hide out here forever. Brianna would need to go to school. She deserved a normal life. Something had to be figured out and there was no doubt in Cody's mind that Ace was the key.

"I'll make the arrangements then," Jamison said with a nod. He glanced at Nina then back at Cody. "I'll just go see what the girls are up to."

Code for *leave you two alone to talk this out*.

There was no way to talk it out. No way to make this work. There was only the slog of doing, but there was no point in explaining that to Jamison.

"Did he come all this way just to ask me that?" Nina asked after Jamison left. She sounded as exhausted as she looked. He bit back the urge to tell her to go lie down.

"I assume he came all this way because Liza and Gigi are here and he's used to having them underfoot in Bonesteel."

Her mouth curved. "They're so sweet together, the three of them."

Cody could only grunt. It was a strange thing to see his brother, and Liza for that matter, be so domestic. They didn't seem suited for it at all, and yet they seemed happier than he'd ever seen either of them.

Maybe it was just because Ace was in jail, and Liza's dangerous father was dead, but Cody had the uncomfortable feeling it was about things far more *personal* than all that.

He forced himself to look at Nina and focus on the task at hand. But all he could think was he'd created a child with this woman, and the uncomfortable truth he'd admit to no one was that he hadn't exactly been with anyone else.

He'd been recruited by North Star, and that had left him in dangerous situation after dangerous situation. There'd been some flirtation with Shay, but they'd both taken their positions in North Star too seriously to risk their jobs by acting on said flirtation.

So.

"There are some things I should tell you before we see Ace."

If there'd been any warm and fuzzy memories threatening for purchase, those words doused them in ice-cold water.

Nina clasped her hands in front of her, sitting in the armchair where Grandma Pauline did her crocheting. Nina's complexion was near gray and what she really needed was rest.

"It'll take Jamison some time to set up a meeting. We have time to go over a game plan. You're not looking so hot. I didn't break you out of the hospital so you could run yourself ragged and have to go back."

She stared at him, eyebrows drawing together. "You've changed," she said as if it came as some surprise.

"You're damn right."

"At first I thought it was just because of Brianna, but it's not. Is it?"

Brianna had changed him. Just her existence shifted something inside of him. He didn't know quite what yet, or what to do about it, but being a father—missing six years of that fatherhood—it meant things were different now.

If only he could get a handle on it all.

"You were never sweet, Cody. But your certainty and your plans weren't built on anger."

He kept his gaze stoic, but his words were more caustic than he'd wanted. "Weren't they?"

"Okay, maybe they were." She seemed to mull that over. "But you had more in you than anger."

And what had happened? Nina had broken up with him. She'd been the one bright spot. Ace had almost killed Dev, and his brothers had been determined to back away from Ace. Let him wreak his havoc as long as it wasn't on them.

Cody had been left with no anchor if it wasn't trying to end Ace—if it wasn't having that shared goal with his brothers. So, he'd had Nina, and then she'd left. And he'd known it was because of who he was. Who he came from.

What was left when his shared purpose with his brothers had been taken from him and she'd left him? Nothing but work, and work was bringing down the father who'd made him. So it was all anger. For more years than he cared to count.

But it seemed Nina couldn't let him even come to grips with all that before dropping another one of her many disastrous bombs.

"He came to see me. Ace did. Back then."

Chapter Seven

Nina knew she needed to say more, but her throat seemed to close up. There was a trickle of fear in admitting it to Cody—in seeing the way his eyes flashed with a new somehow brighter fury than he'd been carrying around for days.

"What did you say?" he asked, his voice as dangerous as a blade.

"When you were doing your CIA internship," Nina managed to choke out. "I was going to classes at the community college and living in a little apartment in Sioux Falls. I worked at a coffee shop and…" She felt a wave of dizziness wash over her and knew she should have taken his or Liza's suggestion to lie down seriously.

Everything hurt and now she felt nauseous with it, but she could hardly stop. "Ace walked in. Like he was any other customer. I only knew him because of the pictures you'd showed me of him." Before that moment, she'd thought it sweet, if a little unnecessary, that Cody insisted she knew what Ace looked like and made sure she hid if she ever saw him.

Then he'd walked into that coffee shop and she'd known Cody had been right all along. She'd frozen, not run away like Cody had always told her to. Ace's gaze had landed on her and Nina had known a true fear she hadn't had since she'd been a little girl unable to wake up her unconscious parents.

It had been worse somehow in that coffee shop because she thought she'd been safe and happy up until that moment. At home, her first home, fear was all she'd ever known.

And suddenly it had come back.

"I was the only one behind the counter, so I couldn't run away like you'd always told me to. He ordered coffee and a scone." She could still see it all in her mind's eye, like a movie.

Ace had smiled at her, treated her like any other customer might. Still she'd known. And the more he'd acted normal—paid his tab, sat down at a table and pretended to enjoy his scone and the scenery—the more she'd turned into a jumpy, scared mess.

"He didn't do anything. Just ordered and ate and left, but when I went out to my car after my shift ended, there he was."

Nina left out the detail where he'd been holding a knife. Not threateningly exactly. He'd played with it, but Nina had known it was a threat no matter how out in the open they were.

"It was still light out, though not by much. People came and went. No one… I guess I could have run away or yelled, but he didn't do anything. He just talked."

It seems my youngest son has a soft spot for you, Nina Oaks—for you and the law. I don't plan on allowing him any vulnerability.

"And what did he say?" Cody asked. She knew him well enough, even seven years later, to realize he was trying to sound tough and unaffected while he was anything but.

Nina paused. It was so long ago he hardly needed *all*

the details. "Nothing much. It wasn't threatening so much as a warning. He didn't want you distracted, he said. He pretended to be a concerned father. I knew he wasn't, and he made sure I knew that whatever he *said*, his true intent was to threaten me into staying away from you."

"That was why you broke up with me." He lifted a negligent shoulder. "So?"

"No, that isn't why I broke up with you, Cody." She wouldn't let it hurt that he'd think she was so weak as to have a threat work on her. She'd been too stupid at the time—too sure Cody would handle it.

Until...

He gave her a disbelieving look, which didn't surprise Nina in the least.

"I went back to my apartment and started packing just like he told me to. I thought I could get home or at least to Bonesteel. If I could get to your brothers, I knew they'd help me out and I thought... I had it in my head once you heard, you'd come home."

"I would have."

Nina nodded. "I know. So I was packing up all my stuff and I realized when I started throwing my toiletries in a bag that I hadn't... Well, that I might be pregnant."

"Why did that change anything?"

Everything. "I had to stop thinking about myself and what I wanted and focus instead on what my own child would need."

"You decided *my* own child didn't need me," he said, his control slipping bit by bit. "*You* decided that you'd protect her on your own," he said, pointing a finger at her. "*You* made those decisions and what do you want me to say *now*? What do you want me to feel?"

She shook her head, tears filling her eyes. "I don't know. I can't... I just wish you could understand that

I didn't want to. I loved you more than anything. I just didn't see a way she could be safe if anyone with the last name Wyatt knew she existed."

"I would have protected her. Why is it different? You thought I'd come home if I knew my father had threatened you, but you didn't think I'd do everything in my power to keep my own child safe?"

"What did he care about me, Cody? I was a nobody, doing nothing special. But he threatened me. Just because you loved me. What would he do to a child who was half yours? Part his?"

"Brianna is nothing of his," Cody replied so viciously she flinched.

"To us," Nina managed to return though she was starting to shake. "To her. But to Ace? He'd consider her his."

"If I'd known any of this, I would have killed him when I had the chance."

Her heart twisted. He believed that, but she knew it wasn't true. Whatever had happened, whatever little she knew about it, she knew Cody wouldn't, maybe *couldn't* kill in cold blood. To protect someone he loved? Sure. But not just to end something.

A tear slipped over her cheek, but she had to get this out. She didn't think they could ever get on the same page—for Brianna—if they didn't really get this out. Maybe he'd never understand, but it had to be out in the open.

"If you'd known, you would have wound up dead before Brianna was even born." She hadn't wanted to tell him this part of it. It was cowardly, she knew, but she wanted to protect her heart—the one that had never stopped loving him. "I don't think you understand I was trying to protect *you* as much as her."

His face went slack a moment before he pulled himself

back together, as if he sucked in all those emotions and shoved them behind a blank facade. Locked them up and hid them away—far away from her.

"Go take a nap, Nina. I'll let you know when I have the details for the meeting."

Then he walked away. Again.

And she was too tired to go after him.

CODY WORKED HIMSELF to the bone on ranch chores the rest of the day. He checked in with Shay but only reached her voice mail. He tested all his security—that no one on the ranch knew he'd set up.

Grandma believed Ace wouldn't step foot on the ranch because of some curse she'd put on him back when her daughter had still been alive and not totally convinced of Ace's evil. Cody's belief in curses didn't extend far enough to think his father could be scared by one.

So, years ago, on a variety of visits, he'd slowly begun installing a complicated and extensive network of security measures around the entire property.

He'd never even told Jamison about it. He supposed he should now. It was the day for telling people things.

He'd never tell Grandma. She'd skin him alive. Once upon a time he'd thought her invincible, but these days, whether it be her age or his, he understood all too well she was also a target. Maybe Ace did believe in her curse, since he fancied himself something of a god, but that only meant he'd find a way to make Pauline pay.

Because Ace Wyatt was determined to make every one of his sons pay for the betrayal of leaving, the insult of going into law enforcement, which he thought was the lowest occupation known to man.

You didn't cross Ace.

Worst of all, Ace had the patience to make you wait

years, or even decades, before he decided it was time for retribution.

Cody kept thinking about the day he'd saved Jamison and Liza from Ace's clutches. He'd had a gun, held it to Ace's head. He could have pulled the trigger. He could have ended everything.

But all he'd been able to think in the moment, thanks to Jamison, was that'd only make him like Ace.

Sometimes Cody feared it was in his DNA, in his bones, to be too hard. To be cruel. To be evil. Maybe it was.

But he chose, time and time again, not to give in to it.

Cody stood outside, looking up at a starry sky, freezing and yet not being able to bring himself to go inside. Because if he continued that choice of good over evil, he had to find a way to handle Nina. To be kind. To find some form of understanding.

He just kept playing the conversation over and over in his head. The way she'd cried. The way she'd clearly left some things out to spare his feelings.

This terrible thing inside of him wondered if she was right. If she'd told him about being pregnant and being threatened by Ace, he would have gone off half-cocked and probably gotten himself killed.

Had she really made the right choice? He supposed they'd never know. Cody had to live with that decision either way.

He blew out a breath and slipped inside. He heard Grandma and Dev talking in low tones in the kitchen and bypassed it, instead heading upstairs. The bedroom Nina was staying in had the door closed with no light coming from underneath it.

He inched down the hall toward voices. When he looked into the open door to the room Brianna and Gigi were sharing, he found Liza on one of the small beds—a girl on either side of her. She was reading a story complete with dramatic theatrics, and the girls were eating it up.

When she finished the book and looked up, she smiled at Cody. "It's getting late, girlies. Come on, Gigi. Let's go brush your teeth."

Gigi grumbled, but she got out of her bed and followed Liza out into the hall. Cody smiled weakly at Brianna, who looked so small with her hair wet and her pink sparkly pajamas.

"Maybe you'd let me read it to you?"

Brianna smiled brightly at him, holding up a book. "Will you do the voices?"

"Uh… Sure. I guess. I can't promise I'll be as good as Liza."

"Even Mom isn't," she said in a conspiratorial whisper.

Cody couldn't help but smile at that. Gingerly, he slid onto the bed next to her. He took the book she handed him and began to read. He felt foolish, but he tried to do voices for the dragon and the princess. The more Brianna laughed, the easier it was to get into it.

When he finished the story, Brianna was snuggled into his side. "I'm glad we're here," she said.

Cody gave her a gentle squeeze. "Me too."

"Did you know when Liza and Jamison get married that Gigi will be my aunt?" she laughed, then looked up at him as her expression sobered. "Can we all live together now? Forever? Uncle Dev is going to teach me how to ride horses."

Cody didn't know how to answer the question. Not by a long shot. "I can teach you to ride horses."

"Really? Uncle Dev said you're not very good."

"Uncle Dev is full of sh— Full of…it." *Uncle Dev.* This was his life. And weirdly this life he'd never planned to have—the ranch and living under his grandmother's roof—was exactly the life he wanted to give her.

"I don't know what's going to happen yet, Brianna. The one thing I know is I'm going to keep you safe, no matter what. Whether I'm with you or not, I want you to know I'm doing everything I can to keep you safe. I promise you that, and I do not break my promises."

"The bad men are coming again," Brianna said, looking down at her book.

Cody noted it wasn't a question, and there was a weary resignation to her voice. Too resigned for a girl of six.

But he'd been, hadn't he? He'd known exactly the kind of danger his life held for him at this age. He should keep her here, resigned and weary so she didn't get any ideas. So she didn't make any mistakes.

He couldn't bear it. "What did your mom tell you about the Wyatt brothers?"

Brianna lifted her face, mouth curving just a hint reminding him so much of Nina's smile he almost couldn't breathe. He'd loved Nina more truly and fiercely than he'd ever imagined possible, and no matter how the years passed he couldn't convince himself it had been an illusion or even teenage idiocy.

"She always told me stories that you all were brave knights."

Cody nodded. "And brave knights always win, Brianna. In the end, good wins."

He hadn't always believed that, but now that he had a daughter, he had to. For her.

Chapter Eight

It was happening too fast. Nina had hoped to have weeks before she'd have to confront Ace. But Cody had tersely informed her they'd be going to speak with Ace tomorrow.

That had thrown her for a loop this morning, made her edgy and irritable. Even more so when no one would let her do anything. Grandma Pauline insisted she sit whenever she walked into the kitchen. Liza shooed her away from the laundry. Even Brianna wouldn't play with her, telling her to lie down —she was going to feed the chickens with Gigi and Grandma Pauline after breakfast.

So Nina wandered the house achy and irritable. When she heard low male voices, she moved toward the kitchen.

The Wyatt brothers sat around the kitchen table. They made quite a sight together. Tall, broad men—Gage was in his uniform, Tucker had a gun holster strapped to his chest. Dev was in ranch clothes, Brady and Jamison in plainclothes, as was Cody. They all looked incredibly grave.

"She'll have to have a script of some kind," Tucker was saying, spreading his hands out on the table. "We have to be careful and meticulous."

Gage shook his head. "A script would be too obvious. She'd sound stilted and Ace would smell a rat."

"He can't smell a damn thing past his ego," Dev muttered irritably.

Nina stood in the entrance to the kitchen and blinked. They were making plans. About her. *Without* her.

"What is this?" she demanded.

No one responded. Cody lifted a hand and offered a dismissive wave.

She wasn't sure she'd ever wanted to punch someone as much as she did in that moment.

"If we don't go the script route, then we should practice," Tucker was saying, looking around the table to meet each of his brothers' gazes.

But not Nina's.

"What? Like role-play?" Gage returned with a snort.

"It's an effective training tool," Cody retorted, clearly unamused. "Practicing what you're going to say can give you a confidence. It can prepare you for the different ways a conversation can go."

"Nothing's going to prepare anyone for Ace," Dev said gruffly.

"I *have* faced Ace before," Nina noted.

"He's going to eat her up and spit her out and give us nothing," Dev continued bitterly without even glancing at Nina.

"I am right *here*."

Gage smiled up at her. "Of course you are, darling."

He didn't seem to register the killing look she sent him. So she did the only thing she could think to do.

She walked over to Grandma Pauline's dinner bell, which she knew didn't get used too often anymore. Never with a tableful of people already sitting down. She grabbed the wooden spoon off the hook—as this wooden spoon was specifically meant for striking the bell for stubborn, hardheaded men.

She struck the spoon against the bell as hard as she could.

It echoed and clanged and all six men flinched and looked in her direction.

"Is that all it takes to get your attention then?" she asked sweetly.

"We don't have much time to plan," Cody said.

"No, *we* don't. As I'm the main player in this little act, shouldn't I have a seat at this table? Or am I too feeble to handle the particulars of what *you* are asking *me* to do?"

All six men shifted uncomfortably. They looked at Jamison as if to say *you handle her.* She stared him down, slapping the spoon against her palm just like Grandma Pauline did when she was waiting for an explanation of poor behavior.

"He's our father," Jamison replied calmly, though he eyed the spoon suspiciously. "We know him as best as he can be known. It should be our plan, Nina."

"But I'm the one who has to put the plan in play, which means I deserve a spot at the table."

Both Jamison and Cody's mouths firmed, but Tucker stood. "She's right, of course." He smiled and motioned for her to take his seat.

She didn't smile at him, since it felt all too placating, but she took the seat because she deserved it.

Then they all looked at her expectantly and she realized she hadn't thought *this* part through. She'd just been mad that they weren't including her. She didn't actually have any ideas.

"So?" Cody asked, and she didn't miss the edge of irritation in his voice.

She smiled sarcastically at him, brain scrambling for something intelligent to say. She made a big show of clasping her hands together in front of her on the table and cleared her throat. "Well. I haven't heard everything you six have cooked up without me. Why don't you fill me in on how far you are first?"

"We haven't gotten anywhere," Gage said, and he was grinning at Cody like he was amused at his brother's clear irritation. "We've argued."

"How like you all," Nina returned. Which earned her a chuckle from Gage and no one else.

"We need a game plan," Cody said sourly. "We're trying to agree on one."

"Before you plan any games, which this isn't, you need to start with the goal."

"The goal is to get Ace to talk, without realizing he's given us anything," Jamison said.

Nina nodded. "We're trying to figure out what he knows. Which means the first step is giving him a darn good reason I'm going to see him. He shouldn't think we're trying to get information. He should think we're trying to prove something. If *I'm* coming to see him out of nowhere, it has to be solid."

"He shot you. Isn't that enough?" Dev replied.

Nina shook her head and noticed Cody was doing the same. Well, at least they were on the same page with some things. "*He* didn't shoot me. In fact, I killed the man who did. Right?" She looked at Tucker for confirmation even though she had no doubts. But he was the detective on the case.

Funny how life worked.

"There was a dead body in what remained of the house, yes."

Nina nodded, making sure she held the gaze of every man at this table. She'd learned something in seven years—you never got to show you were afraid. If you did, people took advantage. The Wyatt brothers might think they'd never take advantage of her, but this was about bringing their father down. She was only a pawn. A piece.

She wouldn't let them walk all over her when she had her own wrongs to right.

"We need more than the attack. We need something… something that feels like revenge."

"Well, there's the obvious," Brady said, speaking for the first time.

Cody frowned at his brother. "What's the obvious?"

"Seven years ago Ace warned you off, right?" Brady said to Nina. "Didn't want you seeing our boy here. Then, for whatever reason, seven years after you disappear, he— or someone in the Sons—targets you."

Gage nodded, though Nina didn't understand at all what they were getting at. She glanced at Cody, whose face had gone hard.

"What? What's so obvious that I'm missing?"

Gage and Brady looked pointedly at Cody. He sighed heavily. "We go there to prove something to Ace." He didn't move—not one inch. She wasn't even sure he breathed he was so still, but there was a shift in the air around him. Around them. "That he didn't succeed—either time."

For a few moments, Nina could only stare. Then she could only laugh, though it hurt her stomach something awful. "You're…" She laughed some more, unable to stop. Made worse by the fact the Wyatt brothers looked at each other in some mix of confusion and unease.

It took her a few minutes to really get ahold of herself enough to speak. "You expect Cody to be able to go in there and convince anyone that he's shooting daggers at me because we've reconciled?" She shook her head. "I don't think anyone's that good of an actor, let alone him."

"You'd be surprised what I can pretend when my daughter's life is at stake."

"Except that cold, disgusted way that you say that proves otherwise, Cody." And it hurt, no matter how she wished it didn't.

"Why don't we leave you two alone and—"

"You will not move," Nina snapped. "We will finish this before Brianna comes back inside. She understands more than I'd ever want her to, but she doesn't need the details. Cody, you think you can pretend we've somehow found a way to reconcile, then that should be the road we take." She wouldn't let herself crumble just because her feelings were a little hurt. "We're there to rub it in his face. Maybe even act like we're thanking him for bringing us back together. The more smug we are, the more likely he'll be to want to burst our bubble. It's the best chance to get him to slip up and give us a clue."

No one spoke or reacted for a few seconds. So she looked at Jamison. He was their leader, no matter that the younger ones might not admit it. They all looked to Jamison for the final decisions because once upon a time he'd saved all his brothers from hell while he'd been stuck there himself.

Eventually, he nodded. "It's a good plan."

"You should practice," Gage offered, and though he was trying to hold back a smile, Nina didn't miss that he found the whole thing *humorous*.

She scowled at him.

"Have, if not a script, an idea of how you're going to lead the conversation," Tucker said, with a little more tact than his brother. "Practicing will help make it seem natural."

Cody smiled, a complete and utter fake smile Nina didn't buy for a moment. "Goody."

THE BROTHERS WENT their separate ways, leaving Cody alone with Nina in the kitchen. Which was the last place he wanted to be right now.

"You should rest." She didn't look as pale as she had yesterday, but she certainly wasn't 100 percent. She'd been shot. Gone through surgery and been broken out of the hospital far too soon. "You should let Brady check you out."

"We should..." She wrinkled her nose. "Practice isn't the word I'd use. We should plan."

"Brianna and Gigi will be back any minute. There's no use practicing if you're only going to keel over because you aren't taking care of yourself."

She made a snorting sound. "Trust me, Cody, if there's one thing I know how to do it's take care of myself. I didn't have anyone else to do it for me."

"Which sounds like a 'your choice' type deal."

"Yes, my choice. Certainly nothing to do with my boy-friend's psychotic father."

"Right. Well..." He had nothing pithy or even snippy to say to that. Nothing at all to say to the truth. He could be angry. He could mourn the loss of six years, but he couldn't quite bring himself to believe it wasn't all necessary.

Because Ace had put a target on his back the day he'd been born. Cody had just been too old when he realized it.

"Cody." Her voice sounded so soft, so entreating. When she slid her hand over his, it was as if the years fell away. "I don't blame you. Not for Ace. Why would I?"

Why wouldn't you?

The kitchen door opened, and Brianna clattered inside, already halfway through a story about chickens. She skidded to a stop in between the chairs Nina and Cody both sat in.

"Grandpa Duke said I could go over to his ranch and meet all his horses and he has three dogs and two cats and—"

"No." He knew he'd been too harsh when Brianna's face crumpled, but it killed him that she was so excited about something that absolutely could not happen.

He glanced at his grandmother and Liza standing in the door with their arms crossed over their chests in exactly the same way. Then he met Nina's hurt and confused stare.

"We have to stay on the property," Cody said, and no matter how he told himself to be hard, to be strong against that vulnerable cast to her expression, he found himself gentling the words against his will.

"And why's that?" Grandma demanded.

He might have lied if not for the fact Brianna was looking up at him with big blue eyes as if the world rested on his next words.

"I have safety precautions here. I'll know if someone's coming. Here. I don't know about Duke's property." He pulled Brianna onto his lap so he could be eye level with her. "I am sorry, sweetheart, but we've got to stay here for the time being."

"I like it here. I love it here. It's the best place we've ever lived." She threw her arms around his neck, squeezing tight as her voice wavered. "We can stay here forever. I don't have to go anywhere. Please don't make us. I love it here. Right here."

He flicked a glance at Nina, who looked like she'd been stabbed.

Cody rubbed Brianna's back and tried to find something reassuring to say. "We're good here. Everything's all right," he murmured. She sniffled into his shoulder.

He didn't dare look at Nina or his grandmother. He was sure it would break that last thread of control he had.

"Can I go watch TV?"

"Let's watch Peppa!" Gigi announced enthusiastically.

Brianna sighed heavily, muttering about baby shows, but she slid out of Cody's lap and took Gigi's hand. They disappeared into the living room, and all Cody could do was stare at his empty lap.

"We'll go keep an eye on them," Liza said, looking meaningfully at Grandma.

"Humph," Grandma muttered before following Liza out to the living room.

"Look. I'm sorry. I should have found a better way of… I don't have this…" *Hell.* "I snapped at her and I shouldn't have."

When he looked up at Nina she was barely holding back tears, but she was shaking her head. "It isn't that," she said, her voice squeaky and weak. "I… I didn't realize how miserable she's been."

"She hasn't been—"

"All you said was she couldn't go next door and she begged to be able to stay. She hasn't been happy if she's desperate to stay here."

"Nina…" He didn't know what to say to her. He shouldn't want to comfort her. She'd hidden their child from him. If Brianna was unhappy it *was* Nina's fault.

Except he knew too well what a truly scary childhood looked like. "It isn't something you should blame yourself for."

"When you're in it—deep in it—you don't see. I worried about her safety. I worried about everything, but I didn't spend enough time worrying if I'd given her a childhood."

"Trust me, Nina. Having been the six-year-old who wasn't safe, you had your mind on the right thing. She knows you love her. If she didn't, she wouldn't trust any of us. But she does. Sure, the way she's been raised has left its scars on her, but that happens to everyone. We know better than most how much worse those scars can be."

"You don't have to try and comfort me." She shook her head and stood, wrapping her arms around herself. "I know what I did to you. I know—"

"You don't know everything," he returned, irritated that she was throwing his justified anger in his face. "If my mother had done half of what you've done, my childhood would have looked a lot different, especially at the age of six." Something cold and discordant slithered up his spine, but he pushed it away.

"That's different."

"How?"

"Your father was Ace."

"My father *is* Ace."

"But you aren't. You aren't him. I wasn't saving Brianna from you. I don't know that there was any other way, Cody. I really don't. But it wasn't about you. I just didn't know any other way to keep you both safe. I never… I really never thought you'd believe me."

"I don't want to."

"That's not the same as not actually believing me."

"I don't know about forgiveness, Nina. I don't know how to forgive what I've lost." He didn't know how to do any of this, but Brianna was his. "But I can't blame you, *hate* you for what you did. I don't even think it was wrong. You're probably right. I would've gotten myself killed."

Her jaw dropped and she stared at him like he'd lost his mind.

He probably had. "I *can* admit when someone else is right."

Her mouth curved. "Well, that's new."

He almost—*almost*—laughed. It would have felt good.

It would have been nice to laugh with her. But there wasn't much to laugh at here. Tomorrow they'd visit Ace. Nina was in danger no matter who they saw or what they did.

"Jamison was a lot younger than I am now when he was getting me out of the Sons and away from Ace. He had a lot less help too. I would have thought I could do the same, but I wouldn't have thought it through the way Jamison spent our entire childhoods doing. Looking back, I know it wasn't so simple for him. I was the only one he got out before..." That cold, needling feeling was back.

"Before what?"

"When we were seven... Ace considered seven the age of testing. That's when he'd been left and..." It couldn't be. It couldn't... "On my brothers' seventh birthdays he left them each in the middle of the Badlands with no supplies, no nothing. Every birthday you had to spend the amount of days you were old on your own out there. To prove you were worthy of the Wyatt name, to prove you belonged."

"That's awful. How can a seven-year-old be expected to survive on their own?" Nina said, hugging herself tighter.

"They did. They did, but Jamison got me out before..." Cody's gut roiled. "When's Brianna's birthday?"

"What?"

He took Nina by the hands, fear and panic and utter horror beating through him. "When does she turn seven?"

"In three weeks. I—"

He dropped her hands as the icy weight of horror took all the strength out of him. "Ace knows."

Chapter Nine

Nina practically staggered as Cody let her go. She couldn't process his words, but his clear panic had her heart beating so hard in her head she could hardly make out what he was saying.

"I have to get everyone back here. We have to reformulate." He moved for the door, but never quite finished a movement.

"How does he know, Cody? How is this possible?" It wasn't. It couldn't be. All along, everyone had assured her there was no way Ace had known about Brianna.

"I don't know. Hell. I don't know." He ran a shaky hand through his hair and it was how utterly affected he was that scared her down to her bones. "But it isn't a coincidence. Jamison got me out the day before I turned seven. The timing of Ace coming after you *now* not making sense? It makes a whole hell of a lot of sense now."

"But he didn't know. The man who shot me didn't know Brianna was there. All this time…"

"We don't know what he knew, Nina. You killed him." Cody scraped his hands over his face. "And if the timing… Ace loves his damn timing. The man wasn't meant to take her. He was meant to scare you."

"Why would Ace want to do that?"

"I can't understand everything Ace does, but if there's

a why it's usually to screw with you. End of story. I have to stop Jamison before he gets too far. And Tuck. They have to come back and we have to—"

"No. Too many voices. Too many opinions. This is about Brianna, Cody. Which means it's down to us."

"I'm not leaving my brothers out of this. The only reason we ever survived in the first place was—"

"Jamison taking everything upon himself to save the younger ones."

Cody opened his mouth as if to argue, but there was nothing to dispute. She knew the story. You couldn't know the Wyatts and not know how Jamison had slowly and methodically managed to rescue each one of his brothers out of the Sons' camps and gotten them to Grandma Pauline's ranch before finally managing to get himself out, with Liza, when he was almost eighteen and she sixteen.

Nina also knew Cody carried around a certain amount of guilt—she'd always likened it to survivor guilt. He'd been the youngest to get out. He hadn't had to survive what his brothers had to—like this awful seven-year thing.

Nina sank into the chair again. Ace knew about Brianna. "How could he know? Why would he have waited?"

"The reason Ace has done everything he's done is because he has patience. And a plan no one else knows. He left Dev alive for a reason, Nina. It wasn't out of the goodness of his heart. It wasn't a miracle moment of having a conscience. It was a warning, at best. And I think we all know deep down it wasn't the end. We'd only hoped it was."

She didn't know how to process all this. How to accept that she'd failed. "So, what you're telling me is these six years were a waste. That we could have all been together. It wouldn't have mattered."

He turned to face her, some of that panic or restlessness fading into something a lot closer to shock. "Was that ever what you actually wanted?"

"Of course that's what I wanted. Do you know how… I was so happy, you know, that moment I took that pregnancy test." She could picture it. The gas station bathroom, all her stuff packed up in her car heading back to the Wyatt and Knight ranches. Heading home. "For a brief shining second I thought… I never expected I'd have kids, but I was thrilled. And then I had to deal with reality." Now she had to as well. There was no time for Cody's feelings. There was only protecting their child. "What are we going to say to Ace?"

"If he already knows—"

"We still have to figure out what this is. What he's trying to do."

"I know what it is. It's revenge. It's Ace's sick, twisted view of the world. To him, his sons were property, his celestial reward or whatever. We betrayed him—time and time again. I put him in jail, Nina. Me. So I know what he wants. He wants to hurt me. And he'll do it in the way he considers himself hurt—through my child."

Nina wouldn't let herself panic, though fear beat through her and threatened to tighten around her throat. She'd been here. She'd faced *this*. "If that's true, all it means is we change our game plan. She's here. She's safe. Nothing has changed."

"Nina." The look of desolation on his face nearly snapped her weakening grip on control.

"I know. Trust me, I know." Her voice wavered so she took a second to firm it. "It feels too big. It feels too… awful, but I have been doing this for six years—with no help. No nothing. I kept her safe."

"Or he let you think that," Cody replied with utter disgust. As much as she knew that disgust wasn't directed at her, it was too much to bear. Was it true? Had she kept Brianna safe all these years simply because Ace wanted some warped revenge on his own bizarre timeline?

She looked down at her shaking hands, felt the tears trickle down her cheeks. It was almost surreal, how her body reacted when her mind seemed to just go numb.

There wasn't time. She'd been here before—whether Ace had "let" her escape or not, she'd felt in that moment the same as she did now.

Except there was no one to lean on then. She looked up at Cody. He was stricken and close to crying—but he wouldn't. The fear was there, all over his face. A lack of certainty in the way he held himself poised to move but never did.

Neither of them spoke as the horror of Ace knowing Brianna existed stretched out around them, growing beyond reality into that horrible place she couldn't go.

What if…

What if…

"I can't lose her," Nina managed to say, wiping her wet face with her palms.

"I haven't even had her," Cody said, his voice hoarse and anything but strong.

He was right. He was too right. He hadn't had enough of Brianna. More important, Brianna hadn't had enough of Cody.

Nina couldn't think about how, if Ace truly knew about Brianna's existence, Nina could have had those years of Cody and Brianna together—regardless of what might have happened between *her* and Cody, Brianna would have had her father.

But there was no going back. She'd learned to never finish *what-ifs*. She'd learned to keep going forward. She had learned that once she let the panic out, she had to rein it back in and move forward anyway.

She stood, though a few tears still slipped out, though her legs and arms shook. She crossed to Cody and she took his hands in hers. He'd likely never felt a day of true panic in his life, so she'd have to teach him that parenthood was forever a new panic—and you let it out, and reined it in.

When he met her gaze, she was all too familiar with that particular kind of devastation.

"Maybe Ace knew all along. Maybe that's the only reason Brianna and I survived. But that doesn't mean we couldn't have survived. What it means is Ace gave me six years to practice." She squeezed his hands. "This time, I don't have to do it alone. We have to work together."

ALONE.

It was a strange word to hit him sideways, at an even stranger time. They had so many bigger issues at hand than *alone*.

But that's what he'd been since Nina broke up with him. He'd graduated, gone into North Star and dedicated his twenties to bringing down the Sons and his father. He'd succeeded at neither and he'd kept a good distance between him and his brothers. The people he'd met in North Star had become something like friends, but they hadn't worked together exactly. Everyone had their own specialty. They worked in teams and as a unit, but not for any one reason. Only for one target.

They weren't his brothers. They weren't family.

Now this woman was holding his hand, telling him that teamwork was somehow the answer here. She didn't mean like it had been in North Star. She meant like it had been when he was a kid.

And she was right. He knew she was right because what had saved each of his brothers and himself from the Sons?

Each other.

He would happily go on, singularly trying to keep Brianna safe, but it didn't work. He knew what worked against Ace.

He looked down at Nina, awed, because he never would have realized that if she hadn't reached out to him and said *together*. If she hadn't looked him straight in the eye and *understood* this horrible clutching, all-encompassing fear that left all his normal faculties dimmed.

"Nina." His voice was still rusty, but he forced himself to keep talking without trying to hide it. "Brianna is ours, but this fight isn't. This fight is bigger than her."

"There is nothing bigger than her to me, Cody. Nothing."

Nina tried to pull her hands away, but he gripped them before she could let go. "I understand that. I do. But there is to Ace. Because I am just one of six betrayals. He wants us all to pay. Piece by piece. He wants his symbolic timing and his mind games."

"I don't care what he wants."

"Exactly. You said you're not alone this time—we can win this time. Okay, you don't want to do it alone? Then let's really not do it alone. And I don't just mean my brothers. I mean all of us. Wyatts. Knights. We don't just formulate a plan to keep Brianna safe. We formulate a plan to make her future safe. All our futures safe from him."

"How? How? It's been all these years, Cody, and...he knew. He knew." She shook her head against that truth. "The more people involved the more people get hurt like this."

"Maybe he knew about Brianna. Maybe he'll target

her to hurt me. Those things are likely." He had to accept it, like he'd done in North Star when things hadn't gone as planned. You couldn't get emotionally involved. You had to be able to accept failure and move on to the next mission.

But his daughter wasn't a mission and there was no failure he could accept here.

"But I am the reason Ace is in jail. Not because I did anything special, but because Jamison, Liza and I worked together. Now imagine what could happen if you put all fourteen of us together."

"Sixteen," Nina corrected. "Gigi and Brianna are part of this too."

Cody nodded. "Together."

Nina nodded in response. He could see her fears and worries parade across her face, but she nodded. She agreed.

They had a lot of work to do.

"First things first, we need to get everyone here."

"The girls…" Nina trailed off, her expression taking on a new pain. "Sarah and Rachel especially. They don't want to see me."

"When you were in the hospital, and Brianna was bloody and wouldn't speak or let us bathe her, who came over and helped? All of the girls. Brianna trusted them because of your stories. Maybe they don't want to see you, Nina, but they all rallied together to help that little girl. They'll keep doing that. That's what family does."

"I didn't," she said, and everything about how blue her eyes got with tears filling them was heartbreaking and painful.

"You did what you thought was right."

She made a scoffing sound. "Be careful, Cody. That sounds an awful lot like forgiveness."

He heard a peal of laughter from upstairs, Brianna's laughter. Nina had kept him from that for six years, but in this moment he didn't know how to focus on anger. He'd done questionable things to survive Ace, why shouldn't Nina?

"Maybe after this I'll manage to find some. Now. We need to round everyone up."

He instructed Nina to tell Liza the whole story and send Liza over to the Knight ranch to get Duke and inform all the Knight girls. Cody called his brothers who'd left and asked them to turn around. He'd found Grandma and Dev in the barn and brought them up to speed.

It took a few hours to collect them all, but it worked out for the best because it was after Brianna's and Gigi's bedtime. Cody himself had set up a high-tech listening device and camera in the girls' room, though Liza had pointed out drily it was just a baby monitor on steroids.

Grandma had made a big platter of ham sandwiches, an array of sliced fruits and vegetables, and was frosting brownies as they spoke. It had taken Cody twenty-eight years to realize feeding them was how Grandma dealt with stress, fear and worry. He saw it clearly in this moment, with everyone he considered family pressed together around Grandma's kitchen table.

"I think we still need to pay Ace a visit," Cody announced. "We should act like we don't have any suspicions he might know about Brianna."

"Nina isn't going to visit that sociopath," Duke announced.

"Nina will make her own decisions like she has been for the past seven years," Nina replied.

Cody had made her lie down earlier, but he wondered how much she'd slept based on the bags under her eyes.

She needed to rest if that bullet wound was ever going to truly heal, but this was hardly a time for resting.

"You can't get anything out of him," Duke said resolutely. "It's a pointless exercise that plays into his hands."

"That isn't exactly true," Jamison countered, a lot more diplomatically than Cody would have. "Ace's biggest flaw is ego. He thinks he's a god of some kind. He believes he knows better than everyone—which is how he's able to be patient and ruthless when it comes to payback."

"For years that man has left you alone." Duke looked at Jamison, then Liza. "If you two hadn't gone interfering—"

"And left Gigi there?" Liza demanded. "Don't play that card, Duke."

Duke shut his mouth and crossed his arms over his chest.

"Personally, I think if Cody and Nina go in acting like they've won, he won't be able to resist telling them how they've lost," Tucker said equitably.

"And in telling us how we've lost, we might just get an idea of what his plan is," Cody continued. "If we don't, we haven't lost anything."

"That you know of," Duke replied darkly.

"It's a risk," Cody returned, holding Duke's angry gaze. "But so is sitting here just hoping he doesn't come after Brianna."

"I say you take that girl and Nina and move to Saskatchewan or some such place and keep them away from danger instead of throwing them headlong into it."

"Brianna deserves her family," Nina said quietly.

"You didn't think that seven years ago," Duke pointed out.

Cody opened his mouth to order Duke to back off, or shut up, or *something*. But Nina shook her head and held up a hand to ward him off.

She looked at Duke, met his gaze head-on. "I was barely twenty-one and had been threatened by the leader of a powerful biker gang. I'd also spent the first eight years of my life in hell, so I figured whatever I gave Brianna would be better than that—especially if it meant everyone else I loved was safe. I can't say I was wrong because I did the only thing I knew how to do in the moment."

She took a deep, shaky breath and let it out. "But I wish I could have given her this sooner. If it's true that Ace knew all along, I could have. Which means he has to pay. And I want to be the person collecting. Not just for my daughter, but for the years he cost me with you."

Silence shrouded the room, a rare feat with fourteen Wyatts and Knights in the same room. Footsteps sounded above, and the monitor crackled with the sounds of movement.

"Let me," Cody murmured as Liza and Nina both stood. "You'll win Duke over better if I'm not here for a few minutes," he whispered to Nina before exiting the kitchen.

He went upstairs and found Brianna standing in the hallway.

"What are you doing up, Brianna?"

She looked up at him solemnly. "Drink of water."

But he could see questions in her eyes. Fear. He crouched to be eye level with her. "Did you hear anything you want to talk about?"

She shook her head, but when she stepped forward and wrapped her arms around his neck he knew there had to be something. Maybe not right now, but she sensed things weren't right. She'd likely overheard *something* over the past few days.

Not to mention she knew her mother had been hurt and her entire life had changed. She had every reason to be frightened no matter how much she liked living at the ranch.

He lifted her as he stood. "Come on. I've got something for you."

"A present?"

"Sort of." He walked to his room, carrying her weight easily—and reveling in how she held on to him. He had a daughter, and she loved him, no questions asked.

He moved into his room and set her on the bed, then went to his dresser, where he'd been keeping what he'd been working on for her. It wasn't perfected, but he had no doubt the necklace would do what he needed it to.

"This is a very special necklace," he said, holding out the piece of jewelry. It was sturdy, made more for purpose than because it was pretty—though he'd tried to give it some pretty touches so she'd want to wear it.

"Is it magic?"

He didn't want her to believe in magic, because some day she wouldn't anymore. But for that same exact reason, he desperately wanted her to believe in possibilities.

"Yeah, I guess it is. But it's emergency magic only. See, if you open it up…" He opened the locket for her and showed her the tiny device he'd attached inside. "See that button?"

She nodded.

"If you push it, I get a notification. It's only for emergencies though. If you're in trouble—real, scary trouble—hit that button and I will come find you."

She chewed on her bottom lip, running her fingers over the edges of the now-closed locket. "Who's Ace?" she asked, keeping her gaze on the necklace.

Cody closed his eyes against the wave of pain. He hadn't expected that question. It was easy to talk about bad men in broad strokes. A little harder when the evil in question came from your own father.

"Ace is a very bad man, Brianna. He wants to hurt us. I know that's scary to hear, and I hate scaring you, baby. But I need you to know he's very bad, and no matter what anyone says, he doesn't ever want to help us."

She finally looked up at him. "Why does he want to hurt me if I don't even know him?"

That question was worse by far. Still, she'd asked it of him—her father—which meant he had to find an answer. "Some people only understand how to be mean. That's why…that's why I—and all your uncles too—became police officers and the like. We wanted to help people instead of hurt them."

She half smiled at him. No surprise since fear and danger were all around them. Even if he'd lied to her and told her nothing was wrong, she would have felt it. She would have known.

He had to hold on to that, and the fact he had a daughter who loved him.

Which meant for the first time he had to go after Ace and also care about what happened to *him*. Because he wouldn't leave Brianna, and he wouldn't lose her.

"I know we haven't known each other that long, but I want you to know I love you, Brianna. More than anything in this world."

She crawled off the bed and wrapped her arms around his neck, snuggling in as he pulled her close and stood.

"I love you too, Daddy." She leaned her head against his shoulder, her whole body relaxing. "I know you'll keep me and Mommy safe."

No matter what.

Chapter Ten

Nina looked at herself in the mirror. No amount of makeup seemed to hide the exhaustion that had marked itself across her face. She was pale, and looked weak.

Maybe that could work in their favor. The point was to make sure Ace underestimated them, because if he did, he would give them something they could work with.

Nina closed her eyes and gripped the sink. She didn't want to take the pain pills for her aching side because they made her too fuzzy, but the over-the-counter pain-killer wasn't doing much of anything to take away the dull, throbbing ache.

She breathed, steadily and mindfully, trying to find some peace for a few minutes of meditation.

It didn't work. At all. But she didn't have any more time. She had to face the music.

Not alone though. She'd barely slept all night turning that over in her head. She wouldn't be the scared young girl in a coffee shop parking lot this time. She'd have Cody at her side and the Wyatts and Knights fully behind her.

She was older, wiser, and had people supporting her.

And had so much more to lose this time around.

Which was not a particularly meditative thought, so she left the bathroom and headed downstairs. Jamison and Cody were in the kitchen with Grandma Pauline and a furious-looking Duke.

None of the sisters. They'd all come over last night, but none of them had really addressed her. She noted that there was an uneasiness between them and Liza too. Nina and Liza had left and cut ties.

It wouldn't easily be forgiven, but that didn't mean they wouldn't help.

"Ready?" Cody asked, getting to his feet.

Not even close. "Yeah."

It had been decided they wouldn't arrive together. Cody and Nina would drive in one car, trying to give the appearance to anyone who might be watching their moves that they were a happy couple.

Jamison would borrow the Knights' truck and also drive to the jail. Gage would already be there in his cruiser on his shift. Tucker had specifically made an appointment before theirs so that he could be in the jail for investigative reasons in his detective role while Cody and Nina were visiting Ace. Brady and Dev would stay home at the ranch and make sure nothing out of the ordinary was happening on the property while Liza and Grandma watched the girls.

Duke took her by the shoulders. "Just remember, you did this on your own for seven years. You can handle that monster. We'll find a way to destroy him yet."

It was the exact opposite of what he'd said last night, but that was why Duke had been such an excellent foster father. He might express his opinion, he might loudly disagree, but if anyone was going to go through with whatever he didn't approve of, he turned all that disagreement into support.

She smiled and nodded. He gave her a squeeze, then

let her go, and she followed Jamison and Cody out the door to their vehicles.

If the drive felt interminable, she could blame that on nerves and the pain in her stomach. She'd also blame it on Cody's silence and stoic expression.

Even when they finally arrived, Cody said nothing. He led her into the jail, nodding at Jamison in the parking lot, then Gage in the lobby.

When he finally spoke, it was to the woman at the front desk. They filled out the necessary paperwork and were led to various places. Out of nowhere, Cody took her hand and linked it with his.

She stared at it for a moment, surprised by the contact, the warmth and how much that simple gesture steadied her. She wasn't so sure she liked that reminder that she was stupid enough to still be in love with a man who'd never forgive her.

She thought about last night, but shook it away. Cody had been shaken by the realization Ace knew about Brianna. He didn't actually mean anything he'd said about forgiveness.

It would hurt too much to hope for that and not get it, so she had to pretend like it wasn't possible.

They were finally led to a narrow corridor that, unlike the rest of the jail, reminded her of a movie. A small room, rows of cubbies with plastic partitions between this side of the room and the other.

They were led to one of the cubes and told to sit, so they did. After a few minutes of waiting, a door on the other side of the partition opened and Ace was led inside.

He looked exactly like Nina remembered him. Like he hadn't aged, like he hadn't been affected at all by jail.

He smiled as he approached. Nina no longer felt weird holding Cody's hand. It was a lifeline and a reminder Ace couldn't do anything to her in this moment. Because she had Cody.

"Well, son. Isn't this a nice reunion?" His gaze turned to Nina. "What's it been, Nina? Seven years?"

There were many plans in place. They'd gone over them ad nauseum last night. *Pretend they were back together. Pretend Brianna didn't exist. Pretend Cody didn't know anything about why she'd left him in the first place.*

So much *pretending* made her tired, but it was the only option. She shifted her gaze away from Ace and to Cody. Cody withdrew his hand, because he was acting like he didn't know Ace had met with her all those years ago. But also pretending to Ace that he wasn't affected by the pretend bombshell.

God, she wanted a nap. To be far, far away from Ace's dark stare.

"Well, if you were trying to prove to me that you have power even locked in a cell, I'm not very impressed," Cody said. He didn't even sound rehearsed, though they'd all discussed their opening line, edited it until it felt perfect.

Or as flawless as it could be in this situation.

"Do you think everything comes back to you, Cody?" Ace asked, tilting his head and smiling at his youngest son. "That you're singular somehow in my attentions, we'll call them."

Cody only smiled blandly. "I'm the one who put you here, Ace. I almost took your life."

"But you didn't. Because you don't have it in you." He sighed gustily, giving Nina a look that seemed to say *kids these days.* "Which is a shame. The only one of you brave enough to kill me is the only one fit to take my legacy and make it yours."

"None of us want what you have, Ace. No one wants

to be a murdering evil psychopath. So you'll have to devise a new plan."

"I haven't killed anyone, Cody. I have no idea what I could have done from here to make you think I'm trying to prove I have power." Ace held up his hands, some attempt to look harmless—honest. *What a crock.* Nina supposed it only failed because they both knew what Ace was so capable of. "But it's so nice to see the two of you together. How did that happen?"

"You tried to kill her. I saved her life."

Nina was amazed at the way Cody could sound smug, when she knew he wasn't. Amazed that he could come off a shade too cocky and sure when she knew he wasn't any of those things in this moment.

Ace's expression went sheepish. "Sorry, son. I've been locked up for weeks now. Perhaps you should see a therapist. I hear they're very helpful in curbing obsessive disorders. You and that little group of yours seem to have *quite* the obsession with me. What were they called? The North Pole?"

"I haven't the faintest idea what you're talking about. But delusions *are* your MO."

"Now this one…" Ace turned his gaze to Nina and smiled again, ignoring Cody's words completely. Nina had to fight the urge to look in the opposite direction from his empty, evil gaze. Ace scared her to her bones, but she had to face him. "Did she ever tell you about our little visit in Sioux Falls?"

"Of course," Cody snapped. Again, Cody's acting amazed her. He appeared both frustrated with the question and vaguely distrusting of her, all while putting on a certain veneer as if he was attempting to fool Ace.

Ace rested his chin on his palms and stared at Nina.

Her hands shook, so she shoved them under the table where he couldn't see.

"And what did you tell Cody, sweetheart?"

"I told him w-what happened. That you came to the coffee shop."

"And when I told you to run, you ran. Right?"

Nina looked at Cody. She wasn't nearly as good at acting as he was, but she hoped her true desperation at the situation translated to a despair about what Ace had just said.

"You see, unlike your brothers, Nina has always done what I told her to do. It's why I like her so much. In fact, I downright approve of this little romance."

"You like anyone you can control, Ace," Nina shot back. Though she still shook, and fear still felt like ice in her gut, it also made her mad. This was the man who'd cheated her out of so much. "But I'm not a little girl anymore."

"No, you're not. Are you? But on the subject of little girls… I suppose we should discuss yours."

"WHAT DOES THAT MEAN?" Cody demanded. Ace wasn't giving him anything he didn't already know, but Ace's MO was also to wait until the person's weakest point. Until everything fell apart. Then strike.

Cody had to fake falling apart, no matter how it galled him to act weak in front of his father. It *was* an act. Nina had told him everything.

He hoped.

"How's Gigi?" Ace asked, changing the subject with an easy grin. "Jamison getting good and bonded with that girl who will come crawling back to the life she was born into once she has a choice?"

"Gigi will never crawl," Cody replied, letting emotion bleed into his voice. His father would see emotion as a weakness, a place to strike. "Least of all to what we saved her from."

Ace's smile made Nina shiver next to him. "Come on. You know everyone comes crawling back to what they know. Everyone." He turned his attention to Nina, studying, calculating.

Cody wanted to jump in front of her. He wished she'd never come. But here she was and they couldn't give away more than they wanted to.

"Sweet, quiet Nina. What *have* you been up to?"

"Nothing," she said a little shrilly. "Nothing except getting shot because of you. I killed your lackey, you know. He's dead."

Ace laughed. "If I knew what you were talking about, and I of course don't, I'd have to make it clear how little I care what happens to any flunky who can't follow directions."

Cody watched his father's expression carefully. Of course it was no outright admission of guilt, but what it did tell Cody was that screwing up was not Ace's plan, as Cody had thought it might have been.

But it made sense the man Nina had killed had failed. Ace had to know how protected the ranch was. He wouldn't have wanted Nina to move there.

Ace's plan had actually backfired. He wasn't quite so powerful from jail as all the Wyatt brothers half believed he could potentially be.

"Must be hard to find good help when your second-in-command gets blown to hell," Cody offered. He tried not to relish the killing, because it would make him too much like Ace, but he felt no guilt for being part of the team that had set explosives that took down Tony Dean and a slew of Ace's other top men in the Sons.

"Yes, isn't it funny how you caused the death of numerous men with your explosives, yet *I* sit in here."

"I find it hilarious," Cody returned, flashing a grin. "Especially when I think about the condition of those twelve girls I saved from the men I blew up. The difference is I can admit that I did it, because the law is on my side, Ace."

"The law." Ace snorted derisively, shifting in his chair. Cody was getting to him. "Morons write laws, and mindless weaklings enforce them. That I raised such spineless, pointless fools is my greatest regret. I was created in the ashes, in abandonment, and I thrived in an unforgiving land devoid of law."

Cody sat back while Ace went off on his tirade about how he built himself from nothing. How their mother had failed them with her inferior genes, and if he'd known he would have killed them all in the womb.

It was downright boring to Cody, slightly satisfying that he'd worked his father up into such a lather. But when he looked at Nina, he watched horror and pain chase over her face. That gave him no pleasure.

"Maybe you can wrap this up in under ten minutes. We do have things to do."

Ace's eyes were manic and bright, but when they landed on Cody that cold chill of foreboding that had preceded a beating in his childhood stole through him. Cody held as still now as he had then.

"When am I going to meet my granddaughter, Cody?"

"Never," he spat.

It was when Ace grinned that Cody knew that momentary high of getting to his father had just cost him getting anything else. Because he couldn't pretend he didn't know about Brianna, or that there was a rift with Nina over it.

Cody stood abruptly. Better to get out than give his

father anything else. Better to retreat and let his father think they were weak. "We're done."

"When did she finally tell you? After she got shot? When she had no choice?" Ace made a *tsking* sound. "Your mother tried that on me too. Look where it got her."

Cody all but hauled Nina to her feet and started moving her toward the door. He wouldn't let his father poison her.

"I've watched her all along," Ace called after them. "I have baby pictures, Cody. Do you?"

Nina made a pained noise, so Cody basically pushed her out of the room, following quickly behind. She sagged against the wall, and he wasn't in much better shape himself.

"He won. He did. He got the better of us," she said, sounding close to tears.

"Maybe at the end, but we got what we came for." He had to hold on to that instead of his own idiocy.

"How?"

"We know that he meant to kill you and take Brianna, but the man he sent failed. He failed. You and Brianna have moved to the ranch, which is ten times safer than anywhere else you've been." He took her hands, waited for her to look him in the eye.

The blue of her eyes was vibrant with tears, and it made him feel even weaker himself. When he spoke, his voice was rough.

"You saved her, and yourself. That was no accidental scare tactic. Everything you did that day saved Brianna. If nothing else, you should take some pride in that."

She swallowed. "How can I—"

"Baby, you are the reason you're both alive." Though he shouldn't, though it broke something inside of him he'd been building for probably all these past seven years, he wrapped her in his arms and held her close. "Now I'm going to keep you both safe. No matter what."

Chapter Eleven

The words echoed in her head as Cody went through the rigmarole of getting them back to his car. Nina felt mostly numb.

Everything Ace had said at the end erased any satisfaction in the little piece of information they'd gained. It even erased any pleasure she might have gotten from knowing she'd saved Brianna's life.

Ace had pictures of Brianna. He'd *watched* them. Nina had left everyone she'd loved for nothing.

Nina buckled her seat belt in a painful fog. She didn't dare look at Cody. She'd cry *again*, and she was tired of crying. Tired of hurting—physically and emotionally.

"I know what he said… I know that hurts, Nina," Cody said as he turned on the car. "But he *wants* you to hurt. He's twisting the knife on purpose, and he's an expert."

Cody gripped the wheel, and she could see the tension in him despite how gently he spoke.

"What would have happened? If I hadn't thought I could keep Brianna a secret from him. What would we have?"

"You can't think like that. Because it didn't happen that way."

Nina looked out the window, desperately blinking back

tears. Just because it didn't happen that way didn't mean she didn't ache over those what-ifs.

"I wouldn't have finished my internship," Cody said into the quiet. "I wouldn't have worked for the past six years to dismantle the Sons, which means it's very possible Ace wouldn't be in jail right now. Gigi would still be stuck in the Sons, or worse, dead or trafficked. Liza and Jamison would sure as hell be dead."

"You don't know that."

"Not for sure. But I don't know the opposite to be true either."

"My sisters won't even talk to me."

"They were there last night."

"Because of you."

"Because of you and Brianna. Don't wallow. We don't have time for it."

She scowled at him. "Wallow? I lost seven years of my life I could have given Brianna, and she would have been safe. And happy. Don't wallow? How *dare* you."

"See, if you're ticked off, you're not sad." He smiled at her, and there was a hint of the boy he'd been. A hint of what they'd had.

As much as she'd loved Duke and her sisters, she'd never felt like they fully understood her childhood pain. Looking back now, she realized they probably had, but they'd all been young and self-absorbed and sure in the belief they were unique and alone.

But Cody had always seemed to understand. After all, so much of his childhood had mirrored her own. Negligent, dangerous parents. Fear and death. Then a loving, overwhelming family neither of them could always believe was real.

"I just want to go home," she said on a sigh, closing her eyes and wishing for some kind of respite from all this.

"You mean the ranch."

She shifted uncomfortably. She already thought of it as home. Even though she hadn't lived there growing up, it had been a part of her childhood. She liked Grandma Pauline cooking Brianna breakfast. She loved having the Wyatt brothers as part of the fabric of Brianna's life.

But it wasn't permanent, was it?

"I need ibuprofen, a nap and my daughter."

"Will do."

"Then what?" she asked, a fresh wave of exhaustion bringing back the threat of tears.

"We keep you both safe and see what we can do to figure out how Ace is getting messages to the outside. If we can cut him off completely, then we have nothing to fear."

Nina didn't say what she thought about that, because the truth was she'd always have *something* to fear. Jail wasn't permanent and cutting off ways of getting messages wasn't either. There was no conclusion to this that wasn't temporary.

Except Ace dead.

She thought over what Cody had said—that he'd had a chance and hadn't taken it. She wondered what she would have done in that position. Could she have ended someone's life when it wasn't strictly self-defense?

To protect her daughter from a lifetime of fear… She thought maybe she could.

Would Cody have done something different if he'd known about Brianna?

She pushed those thoughts away, because Cody had one thing right. There was no use wishing things had been different when they weren't. There was no way to change the past. Only ways to survive the future.

She let herself doze, but an odd noise from the car woke her with a start. She glanced at Cody, whose face was grave.

"Don't panic," he said, his voice too deadly calm to be any kind of comfort.

"Don't panic about what?"

"Someone's tampered with the car," he said through gritted teeth. "I need you to call Jamison."

"Cody, I—"

He had a death grip on the steering wheel and she realized that, whatever was wrong with the car, he was fighting to keep it on the road. "Call. Now. Tell him exactly where we are and that someone's following us."

A million questions piled up in her brain, but she understood this was no time for them. She fumbled through her purse and grabbed her phone. She had Jamison's number programmed in, but when she tried to dial the call failed.

"No service," she said. "I'll keep trying."

"Text instead. It might go through eventually if you try to text. Give him our exact location, say the car has been tampered with, and a white Ford F-150 is following us. I can't make out the plate or the driver." He swore as the car jerked and made an awful grinding noise.

Nina did everything she could to type a clear message, but the car was shuddering now. Her fingers shook no matter how she inwardly scolded herself.

"Whatever you've got, hit Send and hold on."

Nina did as she was told even though she hadn't finished the car description. She hit Send, grabbed on to the arm of her seat.

Then they were flying off the road, and all Nina could do was squeeze her eyes shut and pray.

CODY FELT SOMEONE pulling at him. He heard the faint sound of a woman's voice.

Nina.

His eyes were open, he thought, but he couldn't see anything. Everything was a dim kind of gray. His head throbbed, and he realized the side of his face was wet. He was pretty sure with blood.

He couldn't move his body at first. Couldn't seem to fully find himself in the present moment. He tried to speak, tried to tell Nina he was okay even though it was very much not true.

He'd crashed. That much he could determine. He took stock of his body. He was still in the car, he was pretty sure. His body hurt, but nothing seemed broken. Except he couldn't see.

"Cody. Cody. Please talk to me."

"I can't see," he finally managed to say, though his voice was raw, and speaking sent a wave of pain through him. He leaned back and away from the air bag that had deployed.

"What?" she breathed. She had to be close. Her voice was soft but audible. He couldn't see. He didn't know where he was. But Nina was talking so she had to be okay, right?

"Are you hurt?" he demanded.

"No."

She was lying. He didn't have to see to hear it in her voice. "Nina."

"Nothing serious. Nothing like… You're covered in blood, Cody. You need help. Serious help."

"I'm fine."

"Cody, you're not looking at me."

There was no point trying to hide it from her. "My eyes are open, aren't they?"

"What do you mean? Of course they're open. Cody, what is wrong?" Hysteria tinged her voice.

"Nina, it's okay. Listen to me. You can't panic, all right?"

"The entire side of your face is covered in blood. And you're *asking me* if your eyes are open. I need to call an ambulance."

"No. No ambulance. I can move. I just can't see exactly."

"Cody. God." She sucked in an audible breath. "You can't see anything?"

He shook his head, winced. "Just gray. Some shadows, but… I can't see. I crashed."

"You crashed." He could hear the way she was fighting against the hysteria, struggling for control. "You won't be able to get out your side. It hit a tree and it's blocked. We'll have to crawl out the passenger side."

"There was a truck following us. Are they coming?" He heard her move though he couldn't see what she was doing.

"I can't see much of anything. Between the air bags and the broken windows. It's hard to say. But we can't move. You have a head injury, and God knows what else. You're not supposed to move."

"Well, I can pick between dying from my father's goons or moving a head injury. I'll take moving a head injury."

She made a pained noise, but he couldn't worry too much about offending her. There had been a truck following them.

"Okay. Okay." He heard her suck in a breath and let it out. "Can you unbuckle yourself?"

He moved and though it was tricky between the pain

and dizziness and not being able to see, he managed to unlatch the belt. "Get the gun out of my glove compartment."

He could hear her following instructions, but his vision wasn't magically clearing up. He couldn't focus on that. He couldn't get lost in the now when surviving the next moment was paramount.

How are you going to keep her safe if you can't see?

He'd just have to find a way. "You know how to use it?"

"I can figure it out. Where's the safety?"

He held out his hands and she gingerly placed the gun across his palm. He rubbed his fingers over the gun, pointing out the necessary features.

"It's been years since I've actually done it, and even after Grandma Pauline and Duke taught us, I was never a very good shot."

"Well, unless my sight magically reappears you're all we've got." He handed the gun back to her. "Now, I want you to crawl in the back. I'm going to go out first and—"

"You can't go out first, Cody. You can't *see*."

He opened his mouth to argue. He was the first to jump into a bad situation, the first to risk everything for the safety of others. That was his training and a promise he'd made to himself a long time ago.

But he couldn't see.

"They might be waiting for us to get out. They might grab you, or even hurt you the minute you step out there," Cody replied, but he knew he was only delaying the inevitable. If she wanted to get out of the car, he had no way to stop her.

"I think if they wanted to hurt us they could have done it already if they're out there. I'll carefully creep out and see if I can see anything. You stay put."

Stay put. *Stay put?* He'd never stayed *put* in his entire life. But he didn't have much of a choice since reaching out yielded him nothing but air. He could hear movements, but he couldn't see.

The simple fact lodged like panic in his gut, so he closed his eyes. One step at a time. Always take everything one step at a time.

The first was to get out of the car.

"I don't see anyone," Nina said. "We're in something of a ravine. They had to have seen us go over, but if they're watching from the road, the car is positioned in such a way we should be able to get out without detection. The car is cover. Let's try to get you out. Now you'll have to crawl over the console. Can you—"

"Just tell me if I'm heading the wrong way," he interrupted through gritted teeth. He moved his body and used his hands to feel his way over the console and into the passenger seat. His body throbbed, but the pain there had nothing on the pain in his head, which led him to believe the head injury was the only major injury he'd sustained.

Once he felt the edge of the seat, he got himself into a normal sitting position on it and carefully slung one leg outside, feeling around for the ground. Once he gained purchase, he managed to launch himself onto his feet.

The wave of dizziness threatened to take him down, but Nina's arms came around him.

"I can't call for help. My phone was crushed in the crash. I don't think… I don't think my text to Jamison sent in time," she said, her voice cracking at the end.

"Mine's in my back pocket."

"Don't. I'll get it," she said when he tried to reach for it. "We need to get you cleaned up," she muttered as she slid his phone out of his pocket. "How do you have service? I'm calling 911."

"You can't call 911. Call Jamison."

"You can't see!"

She really needed to stop saying that. He huffed out a breath. "We can't call an ambulance, but I know someone who can help. Go into my contacts." He wavered on his feet feeling unaccountably weak. But then he talked her through finding the hidden contacts on his phone and had her call Shay. She put the phone in his hand and he held it to his nonbloody ear.

"You've got to stop—" Shay answered.

"I've got a serious problem, Shay. I need help."

"I can't help you, Cody. I've done everything I can and—"

"I've been in an accident. I'm pretty sure one or more of Ace's men will have us soon enough. We just need some extrication."

"Extrication. We?" He could hear her mutter something irritable. "Coordinates?"

"Hold on." He turned toward Nina, only knowing where she was because she still had her arm around him helping him stay upright. "Where are we?"

"I don't… I don't know."

"Are you okay?" Shay demanded in his ear.

"Little hurt."

"How little?"

Cody paused.

"That bad, huh?"

He ignored that and explained to her where they'd been driving. About where he thought they went off the highway.

"Hang tight," Shay said, and he could hear her typing away on the computer she was likely hunched over. "I'll see what I can do. We've got a place not far from there. I'll send you a map."

"I can't…see."

"You can't *what*?"

"I'm sure it's temporary, but at the moment I can't see. At all."

"I can read a map," Nina muttered.

"Who is that?" Shay demanded in his ear.

"Nina."

Shay swore. "I'll send the map. Have her follow it. I'll see if I can get anyone out to you."

"A doctor of some kind wouldn't be turned down."

"Ask for the moon why don't you. Get moving. Run into trouble… Hell, I don't know. Just—"

"We'll figure it out. A map and some help and we'll figure it out."

"Turn on your locator."

"Yes, ma'am."

"Things are really bad when you ma'am me. Be careful, Cody." She disconnected and Cody held out the phone. He talked Nina through turning on his locator that he should have deleted after North Star had kicked him out but hadn't.

Thank God for that.

"Cody."

"If you tell me I need an ambulance one more time—"

"Someone's coming," Nina said in low tones. "And they've got a very big gun."

Chapter Twelve

The man picking his way down the ravine took his time, and fear paralyzed Nina for longer than she wanted to admit.

Cody was *blind*, and so bloody and weak she wanted to break down and cry.

But much like that night when someone had broken into her house, she couldn't let fear win. She had to protect the people she loved. She'd killed for Brianna, and she had no doubt she would kill for Cody.

But that didn't make it easy, and it certainly didn't lessen the fear.

"How many?" Cody demanded.

"I only see one. How many were in the truck following us?"

"I only saw one, but there could have been more. You're going to have to shoot him before he gets any closer."

Nina swallowed. She'd always been a terrible shot, but she had to try.

"Use the car as a shield. Don't open yourself up to getting shot back," Cody was instructing. "You've got a few bullets, so just keep pulling the trigger till you hit."

"And if I don't?"

"We fight."

Nina looked at Cody. He couldn't fight. He was blind,

weak, probably from the loss of *all* that blood. She *had* to shoot this person. Which meant she couldn't shake or be frozen like she currently was.

"Talk me through it."

He didn't even hesitate. He nodded. "Find a place where you can see him, but you're hidden as much as possible behind the car."

She did so, and it took too many seconds for her to realize he couldn't *see* that she'd done it. She had to tell him.

"How do you aim?"

"Look for the white circle, then you're trying to get that lined up with the open square. Get it on our guy. Take a deep breath, then pull the trigger. Keep shooting till he stops moving."

Luckily the terrain was uneven at best, which kept the man's progress slow. He was dressed all in black and was much bigger than the man she'd killed in her house back in Dyner.

"Breathe. Breathe and count. Whatever keeps you calm and steady," Cody was explaining in a calm, quiet voice. "You can do it."

She took deep breaths and let them out. She still shook, but as she lined up the sight to the man who got closer with every second, she focused on Cody's quiet, steady words behind her, talking her through it over and over again.

The first shot shook her some, and didn't hit the target. The man didn't even stop his forward movement as he lifted his own gun and pointed it toward the car. She swore.

"It's okay. Just line up and try again. Make sure you've got cover."

She glanced quickly at Cody. "Get lower," she instructed. Because she was their only hope. She knew

Ace's men would kill her. They might leave Cody alive since he was Ace's son, but he wouldn't be treated well.

Brianna needed both her parents for once in her life.

The sound of the other man's gun firing pierced the air only a second before the crash of a bullet hitting the car scared a scream out of her.

"Are you okay?" Cody demanded.

"I'm fine. I'm fine," she muttered, lining up her sight. She focused on the fact that she had to save them, for Brianna, and shot again.

This time the man staggered. He didn't fall, but by the way he looked down at his leg she was pretty sure she'd gotten a hit.

"Hit?"

Nina nodded, then remembered Cody couldn't see. "He's still moving, but he's definitely hurt."

"Shoot again."

She did so, once again focusing on Brianna and doing what she had to do. This time when the bullet landed, the man staggered back and fell to his knees.

"You have to kill him, Nina. It's the only way."

She nodded, and though the shakes had taken her over again, she breathed. In and out until she was steady. She aimed for the man's head.

He fell back immediately. Nina could barely hold on to the gun, she was shaking so hard. "Oh God. Oh God." Somehow in the course of a week or so she'd killed two men.

"It's okay. Focus, Nina. We've got to get to safety. Look at my phone." He explained to her where to find the map the person he'd called would have sent and though she struggled to control her limbs, she managed to do what he told her to do.

"I can't read this," she muttered as the map came into view all lines and blinking dots she didn't understand.

"Press the arrow in the corner," Cody instructed.

She did so and nothing happened. "Now what?"

"We move. The red blinking dot will show us where we're going."

"What is all this high-tech stuff?"

"I'll explain once we have some shelter." He made a frustrated noise. "You're going to have to lead me."

She'd killed two men. They were stranded. Brianna was at the ranch. Safe. Thank God. At the ranch.

"Your brothers are going to come looking for us."

"Send them a message. Brianna is their first priority. Text. Quickly. Use code."

"Code?"

"We can't be too careful at this point. Someone might have followed Jamison and Tucker too—which seems likely if only one man came after us. So text Dev. Type this exactly. 827 period B#1 dash 672."

"What does all that mean?" Nina asked as she typed it all in just as he'd said.

"Dev will know. That's what's important. Now…" He trailed off, frowning.

"You're going to have to hold my hand, I guess," Nina said. It was the only way she could think to lead him. "The ground is really uneven here though, so we have to go slow so you don't fall."

He muttered a few curses under his breath. She reached over and took his hand. She swallowed against fear, against the pain at seeing him so hurt. "I have to watch the map, so you have to inch forward slowly feeling the ground before you take a step. I can't carry you if you twist an ankle."

"I won't twist my damn ankle."

Nina studied the land in front of them, then the map. It'd be a miracle if they made it ten feet, let alone the length of this map's route. A miracle if no other men with guns showed up. A miracle if they survived.

But she'd killed two men. Two men who'd tried to kill her simply because of who she'd fallen in love with as a teenager. Simply because of the father of her child.

Who was blind and bloody and weak at the moment.

Which meant she'd find that miracle no matter what.

IT TOOK HOURS. Cody didn't need a clock or sight to know that. It was interminably slow progress, and Nina's constant encouragement was starting to fade and sound hopelessly empty.

But she kept leading him forward, kept muttering over the map.

He fell twice thanks to the rocky terrain. The second time he got up, he almost passed out, but somehow Nina managed to hold him up while he breathed through the wave of pain trying to take him under.

"Oh, there's something ahead," Nina said. "A cabin." Her voice was raspy. They were both dehydrated. He knew he had lost blood too rapidly, but they didn't have time to fix that. They had to get to safety.

But if Nina saw a cabin it had to be the place Shay had mentioned on the phone.

Nina stopped on a dime. "Someone opened the door," she whispered.

"Describe."

"Uh, medium height. It's a woman, I think. Blonde. She's wearing all black. No weapons that I can see."

"Shay."

"Who?"

"The woman I called. She's here to help."

"She's coming this way. Are you sure she's going to help us?"

It took only a few seconds, but soon he heard Shay's voice.

"Lord, you weren't kidding. You need some *help*."

His knees almost gave out when he felt Shay's hand take his free one. Somehow he and Nina had made it. Alive.

So far. There was still a way to go, but this was such a huge step.

"Come on. We'll get you inside and cleaned up ASAP," Shay said, her voice no-nonsense and sure, which was a great relief.

"She needs to get checked out too," Cody managed to say despite how raw his throat felt.

"I'm fine," Nina insisted as they kept moving. God he wanted to lie down.

"We'll get you both looked at," Shay returned reassuringly. "Jennings wouldn't approve any of the medical team to come with me, so I had to go for the next best thing."

"Holy hell, brother, what did you do to yourself?"

"Brady?" Cody nearly collapsed at the sound of his brother's voice, but strong arms were holding him up. Not Nina's slim ones or even Shay's capable ones, but his brother's.

"Brianna—"

Brady quickly cut Nina off. "Everyone's at the ranch and accounted for except you two. Tucker and Jamison had tails, but no tampering on their car. Probably because they'd parked next to Gage at the prison. They lost the tails and got home. Everyone, including the Knights, are staying at the ranch until further notice, and Brianna is absolutely under someone's watch 24-7."

While Brady explained that to Nina, he helped Cody

sit down. Cody could feel his brother's hands on his face and Cody tried not to wince or give away how badly everything hurt.

"I'm not sure I've got the skills for this," Brady said in practically a whisper. Cody assumed he was trying to keep Nina from hearing.

"Let's get him cleaned up." Shay's voice. "I can maybe call Betty and see if she can video chat us through making sure he's repairable."

"Of course he's repairable," Nina snapped.

Someone took his hand, and it only took a second or two to realize it was Nina. She murmured encouraging words to him as Brady and Shay spoke in low tones about the extent of his injuries. The pain while they cleaned up his face was nearly unbearable, so he focused on Nina's hand in his and the fact everyone else he loved was keeping Brianna safe.

"I can stitch you up," Brady finally said. "But we don't have any local anesthesia. The real concern is the loss of sight. That could be caused by bleeding in the brain."

Nina's sharp intake of breath next to him had him squeezing her hand. "But it's not the only cause."

"No. It could be permanent or temporary damage to the part of your brain that controls sight."

"Which means my sight could return as it heals."

"*Could*, Cody. Not will. This could be serious."

"*Could be* but not *is*."

Brady muttered curses under his breath.

"How would we get him to a hospital?" Nina asked gently. "I think it's paramount Ace doesn't know he's been hurt, especially this severely."

"We don't *know* it's severe," Cody interrupted.

"We know it's possible though," Brady returned.

"Let me call Betty. She's our resident doc. We can do a

secure video chat and she can lead Brady through a more thorough examination. Then we'll decide what kind of interventions we need."

"I don't need any—"

"And you'll shut the hell up, Cody," Shay snapped.

He grunted irritably while Brady and Shay murmured in low tones, before he heard a faraway voice. Presumably Betty on the video call.

"Well, someone did a number on you. And you thought being part of North Star was dangerous, huh?"

"I'm Ace Wyatt's son, Bet. Life is dangerous."

She snorted derisively. Everyone involved with North Star liked to give him crap that he was Ace Wyatt's son, and Cody had become something like immune to the barbs. He was who he was.

He found he wasn't so sanguine about what and who he was with Nina holding his hand.

Shay and Brady poked and prodded his face while Betty asked them questions.

"Cody, no sight whatsoever?"

"I can make out some shadows. Sort of."

Betty made a considering noise. She'd patched Jamison up after their last run-in with Dad, and Brady was a skilled EMT, who most definitely could have become a doctor if he'd had the opportunities normal kids did. There was no reason to believe they couldn't patch him up.

He had to be okay. He might not have cared so deeply about surviving a few weeks ago, but he had a daughter now.

"Any other situation, I'd already have you in a hospital. But we're all versed in how dangerous Ace can be, and apparently jail hasn't put an end to his reach. Not that any of us thought it would be that easy."

No, Cody hadn't thought it would be, but he'd hoped.

"Brady—what kind of supplies you got?"

Brady and Betty discussed logistics, and eventually ended the call. Even though Cody couldn't see, he could practically feel everyone looking at him, determining his fate.

He really didn't appreciate that feeling. If that didn't make him antsy enough, he heard a door open and close. Footsteps. Low voices. And he had no clue what was going on around him.

He always relied on all of his senses, on being in control of a situation. If he was in charge, no one could get the better of him—most especially Ace.

"Breathe," Nina whispered, and it was only then he realized panic was winning, and no matter what the situation he could not let that happen.

The door opening and closing sounded again, then clanking and thumping noises. "First things first," Brady offered. "Sedatives."

"No."

"I've got to give you stitches—in your face. I'm going to knock you out and you're not going to argue with me over it. Now, Shay and Nina let's move him to a bed. But I'll need good light and help from both of you while I do this."

Cody was led to a bed. Brady belted out instructions, and after the sedative was administered, Cody felt himself unwillingly start to fade. He finally let go into the dark when Nina touched his forehead gently and urged him to go to sleep.

When he woke later it was to searing pain on top of deep, throbbing pain and a very dry mouth. He moved and for a second thought he was in a dark room before he remembered—oh right, he couldn't see.

He was in bed and there was something warm and soft next to him. It moved.

"I really hope this is Nina and not my brother," he said, wincing at the pain in his throat and how ragged he felt.

"What about Shay?"

Cody shifted uncomfortably. "I said Nina, didn't I?"

Nina made a considering noise, but she didn't move away from him. She snuggled closer. "How are you feeling?"

"Dandy."

Her laugh was soft, muted, but it made him feel marginally better. "How long have I been out?"

"A couple hours. It's about midnight. You should try to sleep more if you can."

"Did they ever look you over?"

"Yes. Brady rebandaged my stitches, and a few other scrapes I got from the accident, but he said I was fine."

"You're not lying to a blind man, are you?"

"Not right now."

He relaxed some. She was okay and that was what was important.

"Sleep," she ordered.

"Have you been sleeping?"

Nina sighed. "I'm trying."

"You're worried." He could hear it in her voice—the tightness, the exhaustion. She was trying to hold it all together for him, because he was hurt. But hurt or no, blind or no, he would do everything to keep Nina from suffering.

"Do you think she's scared?" Nina asked after a long, interminable silence.

She didn't have to say *Brianna* for him to know who she was talking about. "She has everyone but us rallied around her. I'm sure she's worried about you, but she's safe. That's the important thing right now." He tried to believe that instead of thinking of all the ways she was only unsafe because of him.

"She loves you, Cody."

It was dark—or he couldn't see—but it felt like the very same thing, and Nina was curled up beside him like they hadn't lost seven years. Like those years didn't exist. Part of him didn't want them to.

But they did.

He wanted to believe there was some magic connection between father and child—so that he could believe Brianna had just loved him on sight, but that only meant there was something connecting him to Ace.

He didn't love his father. Maybe his feelings had been complicated as a child, but he'd never *loved* Ace.

"If she loves me, it's only because of you."

"I tried to give her everything I would have wanted her to have. I wanted her to have you, but I didn't think she could. So I did the best I could, but they were just stories."

"Stories that gave her a foundation of trust. We both know how hard trust is when you grow up in a dangerous situation, and you gave that to her."

Her breathing hitched, but when she spoke, her voice was steady even if there was fear behind her words. "Cody, what if—"

"No what-ifs. One step at a time. We're going to get through this. It'll be hard, and yeah we might get hurt in the process, but we're going to get through to the other side safer and better off."

She was quiet for a moment, but he could feel her fingers curl around his hand. "And together," she whispered.

"Yeah." Together. A family. He wasn't sure quite what to do with that yet, so he slid back into sleep instead.

Chapter Thirteen

When Nina woke up she was achy. Not just from the stitched-up wound in her stomach, but all over. Her neck throbbed along with a pain at the base of her skull. When she slid out of bed, she nearly collapsed at the pain in her knees and feet.

She managed to steady herself and glanced at Cody in the dim light of the room. It had to be morning, but he needed his sleep. The white bandages had spots of blood bleeding through, and his complexion was so waxen.

Brady had assured her he'd come through, but it was hard to believe looking at him like this.

So she couldn't. She slid out of the room and headed for the kitchen. She'd get some coffee hopefully, try to remind herself of all she'd fought for and would continue to, and when she returned to Cody's side she'd be ready to have a determined outlook.

Nina stopped abruptly at the sight of the woman in the kitchen. She didn't know what to make of Shay or the way Cody talked to her.

Or how the similarities between them made even *her* uncomfortable. Same color blond hair, same color blue eyes. Shay was taller, but they had the same kind of build.

"Morning," Shay offered. "Coffee's on. Help yourself."

"Thank you."

"And ibuprofen," Shay added with a small smile, pushing a bottle toward the coffeepot.

"Bless you." Nina fought off discomfort and moved into the kitchen. Shay shoved something into a big duffel bag and then hefted the strap onto her shoulder.

"You're leaving?" Nina asked, surprised and maybe a little afraid they were losing this woman who seemed so sure of everything.

"I have to get back. North Star controls my life, and this was a blip they're not going to easily forgive. I've got some major groveling to do."

"But you helped us. You saved us."

Shay's lips twisted wryly. "It wasn't part of the mission I was supposed to be involved with."

"Then why did you help us?"

The woman shrugged. "Cody's a good guy."

Something uncomfortable turned in Nina's stomach, but she didn't have a right to that, so she tried to push it away. "I…"

"I'm going to go out on a limb and guess he's been pretty tight-lipped about everything, but nothing ever happened between us."

"Oh. Right. I didn't…" It was none of her business. She hadn't been with Cody. She had absolutely no hold on him those seven years she'd been hiding. Jealousy was dumb, feeling relieved by Shay's words was worse. Shay seeming to read her thoughts was embarrassing. Still, it didn't seem to shut her up. "Why not?"

"We would have gotten kicked out of the group." Shay raised her shoulder as if that was that. "Neither of us could afford to lose North Star."

"Then you didn't want each other very much." At the look Shay gave her, Nina turned a deep shade of red. "It's none of my business. I'm sorry."

"No, you're right. I suppose we didn't. Never really thought of it that way. Anyway, I've got to go or I'm canned for nothing."

"It wasn't for nothing. Thank you."

Shay nodded, slinging a bag over her shoulder. "Ace is a dangerous man. Don't underestimate him."

"I don't."

"Sometimes they do," she replied, nodding toward the back of the cabin where Cody was asleep and presumably so was Brady. "A guy thing or a being-his-son thing. I don't know. But Ace underestimates them too, so I guess they're even. Unfortunately when men get even, women often get the shaft. No matter how good some of the men involved are. Watch out for yourself, Nina."

Nina nodded, even as the words settled uncomfortably on her shoulders—a scary, truthful weight.

Shay left the cabin and Nina was left alone in the kitchen. She got her coffee, took the painkillers and listened carefully for Cody waking up while her thoughts of Ace, Shay and Cody being blind whirled in her head.

"How's our patient?"

She looked up at Brady and tried to smile. "Still sleeping." She sipped her coffee. "Will you be honest with me and tell me how bad it really is?"

He pressed his lips together. His eyes were sad, but he held her gaze. "I don't know how bad it is. Truthfully. I wish we could get him to a hospital, and maybe we'll be able to soon enough. But we have to make sure Ace doesn't know. Ace can't know."

That had been a tenet in her life for so long, and it turned out it didn't matter. Ace *had* known about Brianna.

Nina swallowed against the way that realization just kept *hurting* like a brand-new wave of pain. She looked at her coffee. "As long as Ace's alive, Brianna isn't safe. None of us are."

"You know, you could take Duke's suggestion. Move to some remote area. Disappear. Ace has reach, but not that kind of reach."

"He'll find a way. Maybe not for ten years, but he'd find a way. The only answer is Ace's death."

"We can't make that happen while he's in jail."

"Unless he gets the death penalty." Nina looked up at Brady, a desperate hope clawing through her. "He could, couldn't he?"

"What he's in jail for right now involves trafficking. No death penalty there."

"But he's killed people. We know that."

"We know that, but we can't prove that. Gage and I have talked about this some. We'd need a lot more evidence to make a bigger charge stick. Ace is careful, and he has a lot of men doing the work for him. It's nearly impossible."

"Unless we get one of those men."

"And do what? Torture some answers out of him?"

Nina lifted a shoulder. "To save my daughter? Yeah. I've killed two men, and it may have been self-defense, Brady, but I'd kill a hundred more to keep her safe."

She could tell she'd surprised him, but motherhood had changed her. Ace had changed her. She'd do whatever it took, with no moral qualms, to keep her child safe.

"One hundred won't be necessary."

At Cody's voice she and Brady immediately jumped into action, moving to help him to the table—though somehow he'd made it out of bed and the bedroom.

"You can see?" Nina demanded, her heart beating so hard with hope.

"No. I can feel the walls and move toward voices,"

Cody replied wryly. "Even over the lovely pounding in my head. I smell coffee."

"I'll get it," Brady offered.

Nina led Cody to the table, helping him get settled on a chair and Brady put a mug in front of him. Nina gently placed his hand around the handle.

"I'm not used to being waited on," Cody finally said when no one spoke.

"I wouldn't plan on getting used to it," Brady replied.

Nina frowned at Brady, but he only shrugged, and Cody's mouth curved upward. She supposed the warped way the brothers were hard on each other was some comfort to Cody right now.

"Shay left?"

Nina nodded, then remembered Cody couldn't see. "Yeah, just a bit ago."

"Good."

"Is it?" Brady asked.

Cody shrugged. "For her. For North Star. I can't keep leaning on them for help."

"I don't understand why not. If they're trying to bring Ace down, I don't understand why you just get kicked out and left in the cold."

"Because they're trying to bring the Sons down, not Ace in particular. I had a use and now it's done. Look, this is our fight. Ace is our fight."

"You're blind, Cody. And stuck in this cabin… Who even owns this place?"

"It's fine," Cody replied.

Nina could tell Brady wanted to argue, but he clamped his mouth shut and scowled instead.

"It occurred to me while listening to you guys talk, we're so focused on Ace, we're missing an important part of this puzzle." Carefully he lifted the mug of coffee to his mouth and sipped, Nina and Brady leaning more and more forward as they waited for him to finish that thought.

"The men he's getting to do his dirty work?" Brady supplied impatiently.

Cody slowly lowered the mug and shook his head. "Not his goons. They don't have access to him, but someone does who's passing along information."

"It could be a guard, I guess?" Brady suggested.

"Or one of his lawyers."

"Weren't they court appointed?"

"One was, and North Star couldn't find any information passing, but Jamison said he had lawyers coming to visit him—plural. He was looking into them, but we got sidetracked with the whole go see Ace thing. We need to look into these lawyers. And the great thing about lawyers is they know just how to twist the law."

"Okay. But what do *we* do? Right here?"

Cody lifted the mug again. "We give them what they want."

"THIS IS HIS head injury talking, isn't it?" Nina demanded, her voice leaning toward shrill. "He didn't just say that."

It was strange to have to live in this world of only gray. To depend on his hearing and his touch to understand what was going on around him. But something about that kept him calm. Kept him centered—not in fear, but in the reality of the situation. He couldn't see the hurt in her blue eyes, so he could breathe. He could think. "Nina. Hear me out."

"How can you be so calm?" she demanded. "You're sitting there blind and hurt. I've been shot. My daughter is—"

"Safe," Cody and Brady interrupted in tandem.

"They hurt both of us. Why should I believe she's safe?"

Her voice broke at that. He couldn't reach out and touch her. He'd come up with nothing but air, because even though he knew she sat to his right he couldn't *see*.

"There is nowhere she'd be safer than at the ranch, with both our families watching out for her. I think you know that. There's no place we could hide her that he couldn't reach. So we have to protect her. And we all would do anything to keep her safe."

"It isn't enough," Nina said, though her voice had roughened into a whisper.

"We're all still alive. Still here. We have scars—all of us—Jamison, Dev, you and me. But we've survived. Because we believed we could and fought to. We just have to keep fighting."

"By giving them what they want?"

"Ace wants us hurt. Weak. Rattled. He wants us afraid, and he wants us to make a mistake. So he can punish me. It's all part of it. He likes the game as much as the punishment—it's why he can wait so long to enact it."

"So, you let him believe you're hurt, weak and rattled?" Brady replied. "I hate to break it to you, brother..."

"I know. We are those things, but we'd usually try to hide it. What if we didn't. What if, instead of hiding everything beneath pride and some desperate need to show him up, we let him believe he's getting what he wants?"

"He *is*," Nina replied, but her voice didn't break. She sounded more contemplative than angry or terrified.

"It doesn't matter. Not in the long run. The mistake I made in that jail? It was getting mad. It was reacting. It was trying to show him up. He made that comment about Brianna to trick me into admitting I knew about her, and he won because I wanted to prove to him he would never touch her."

"Okay," Brady said, and Cody knew he was trying to sound thoughtful instead of dismissive.

"Let's go with this thread. How do we use Ace knowing you're hurt to our advantage?"

"We need to catch him in the act. Which means, we need to have him thinking it's the time to strike, and we see how he's getting messages out of the jail."

"This second lawyer."

"Exactly. I'll want Jamison, Dev and Gage at the ranch with Brianna and the girls. We want the most presence there. But Tucker can look into this lawyer, while you find a way to get someone from the Sons to suspect you're helping patch me up."

Cody wished he could see his brother's face. Brady was good at keeping his feelings close to the vest, but Cody would know his response to the plan.

"It won't work."

Cody frowned in Nina's direction. "It could."

"Not if you have three of your brothers stationed at the ranch. Ace won't make a move for Brianna when she's that protected. He'll wait. He'll wait it out."

"She has a point," Brady offered. "He doesn't want you dead. He wants you hurt. He wants to punish you. Dev's still alive for a reason. He'd leave you alive for the same."

Cody wanted to shove away from the table. He wanted to pace. He wanted to *act*. But he couldn't in his condition.

He could just hear the words his brother wasn't saying rattle around in his head.

He'd leave you alive for the same...but he'd kill Brianna and Nina to hurt you.

No. He wouldn't allow it. "If he thinks we're weak, he'll make a mistake." Cody believed that wholeheartedly. Ace *had* made a mistake yesterday, or at least a slipup. He'd admitted the first man Nina had killed had blundered the kidnapping. Ace would have never wanted them to know he failed—even if he did blame it on an underling.

But how long could they wait around for Ace to make a move? Ace had the gift of time. Cody didn't—because he had a little girl who deserved a real life.

He heard Nina take a sharp inhale, then slowly let it out. He wanted to place his hand over hers. Offer some kind of comfort, but he didn't know where to reach and he couldn't bring himself to fumble.

"He's not going to act just because we're weak," Nina said quietly. "Surely we've been weak before. He wants a specific thing. He wants to use Brianna to hurt you."

He'd worked very hard not to blame himself for his father's vices, for his father's evil. Sometimes he was so afraid he had that evil in him, but he chose to turn away from it. Which meant he wouldn't lay blame on himself for Ace's choices.

But Brianna being in the crosshairs of this hell *was* his fault. There was no getting around that. Being his daughter meant she'd always be Ace's target.

"I don't say that to hurt you," Nina said quietly.

"It's the truth. Regardless of hurt," he replied, trying to keep his emotions out of it. Harder when he had nothing to look at but gray, when he remembered what it had felt like to read Brianna a story while she curled up next to him.

He heard Nina sigh, and could almost feel her wanting to argue with him. But maybe that was all wishful thinking. It wasn't as if he could examine her expression and see what was going on there.

"Fine. Regardless of hurt. We let Ace know we're weak. We give him the leeway to make a mistake, but he has to be motivated to use that leeway now. Which means he has to think Brianna is weak too. Obviously, we can't ever let her be, but maybe we can make him *think* she is.

What if he thinks we have Brianna? Here. Unguarded. Just the two of us, hurt and on the run. What would he do if he thought we were trying to run with her?"

Chapter Fourteen

Just the idea made Nina sick to her stomach, but if yesterday had taught her anything, it was that this had to end.

End.

"He'd send someone after you," Brady said. "But... It'd require a lot of subterfuge to make it actually look like you guys had Brianna. It would take... I'm not sure it's possible."

"It doesn't have to be possible," Cody replied, nodding along with what Nina had said. "What does trying lose us?"

"I want to point out you're both hurt. Severely. Nina's gunshot wound might be last week's news, but that's still a serious injury. There's a lot to lose."

"As long as Brianna is safe, we haven't lost anything," Nina replied.

"But what will she lose?"

What would Brianna lose? Nina tried not to think that far. If she started counting all the things Brianna had already lost, she'd be crushed under the weight of it.

"Nothing," Cody said, his voice harsh even as his unseeing eyes stared straight ahead. "I won't allow Brianna to lose a damn thing."

It wasn't that the violence in his tone surprised her. She knew Cody had all sorts of violence in him. She knew, simply from watching them together, that he loved Brianna with no reservations. She knew he would protect her, because his own honor demanded it. But she was starting to realize that no matter the years she'd kept Brianna's existence from him, he would protect her not just because he had to, but because he loved his daughter unreservedly.

If she let herself linger in that wonder, she'd have to look too hard at her own parents' failures and be buried under the weight of *that*. So she studied his face—bruised and bandaged.

That bandage needed to be changed. He needed a real doctor and probably some kind of scan to look at the damage to his brain likely causing the loss of sight. He needed this to be over.

They all did.

"So, how can we make that happen? How can we make Ace think we have her, and that we're running away?" Nina asked, turning her gaze to Brady.

They spent the next hour or so coming up with ideas, rejecting most of them. Brady went about changing Cody's bandages and examining his eyes as they plotted.

But no matter how many plans they came up with, they kept running into the same problem.

"How is Ace going to know we're doing this? We keep working under the assumption he's watching our every move. I don't think that's true. Clearly there are limits to what he can accomplish—at least with time constraints," Brady said.

"We have to find out more about this attorney," Cody replied to his brother. "Use that angle. We need to go at this from multiple fronts."

Nina watched them. Both men seemed to pulse with excess energy—Cody unable to pace like she was almost sure he would be doing if he could see. Brady keeping still whether out of deference to Cody or because it was simply his personality.

"The more fronts we go after, the more we leave Brianna unprotected. We can't all be on the ranch if we're pulling on these threads."

Cody rubbed a hand over the side of his face that wasn't bandaged.

"So, we have the attorney thread," Nina said, holding up one finger. "Jamison is the one most likely to tackle that."

"Making it look like someone got Brianna to you guys, or you got Brianna from the ranch—all while making it look like we're trying to be sneaky," Brady said, adding another finger to the list. "You'd need more than one of us. Likely me and Gage."

"Tuck should also look into these men who've come after us. Maybe he can get someone to talk. Bodies are piling up. You really want to be next while Ace cools his heels in a cell?"

Nina held up a finger for him since he didn't know they were silently counting.

"That only leaves Dev at the ranch to protect Brianna." Brady shook his head. "We can't go after all those threads at once and leave her that open."

"That's insulting."

Brady raised his eyebrows at her. "How so?"

"You're underestimating everyone who doesn't have a magical genital gift between their legs."

Brady tilted his head toward Cody even though Cody couldn't see. "Did she really just say *magical genital gift*?" Brady asked, his voice tinged with both horror and amusement.

Nina didn't have time for either. "Grandma Pauline is probably just as good a shot as any of you boys, if not better. Liza held her own in the Sons for years. Cecilia is a police officer, for God's sake. You're ignoring the fact we have very capable women able and willing to keep my daughter safe."

"*Our* daughter. *Our* daughter safe," Cody returned, his voice so cold she almost shivered. "Excuse me if I trust my brothers first and foremost."

Though she felt the sting of that rebuff, and guilt that she *had* used *my* instead of *our*, she kept her response to the point. "Excuse *me* if I trust my sisters just as much."

"She's right," Brady said, though his voice was quiet, almost as if he was trying to talk to Cody without her hearing. "Liza and Cec and Dev, plus Grandma and Duke? She'll be protected."

Cody was quiet, and whatever he was thinking or feeling, Nina couldn't read. So she didn't try. She let silence settle around them, everyone waiting for Cody to talk.

"You'll have to go," he finally offered in Brady's direction.

"Excuse me? I'm not leaving you guys."

"Gage can't cause a diversion *and* make it look like he got Brianna out all on his own. He needs help," Cody returned.

"Rachel, Sarah and Felicity."

"A half-blind woman, a timid park ranger and Sarah— who'd chop off Ace's nose to spite all our faces?"

Cody's mouth curved. "Say that to their face?"

"Not a chance in hell," Brady muttered, shoving away from the table. Irritation simmered off him in waves, and Nina had to resist the urge to return with exasperation in kind.

Rachel, Sarah and Felicity could take anyone Brady threw at them. Unfortunately, they weren't the answer here.

"Let's think like Ace for a second," Nina replied, ignoring the disgusted snorts from both men she was stuck in this little cabin with. "We know he doesn't think much of women. I think he might be afraid of Grandma Pauline, but mostly he sees the rest of us as pawns. Pawns to get to you boys. It'll be you boys he's watching, and it'll be you boys he expects to do the work. If we really wanted to get Brianna out of there, we'd go with people he wouldn't expect. But we're trying to play into his hands."

Brady heaved out a sigh. "Play into his hands without him seeing through it."

"Yes," Nina agreed. "But we've talked about Ace's weakness being his pride. His focus, his obsession, is his children. He wanted me dead." This time, she couldn't quite suppress a shudder. "He made that clear back there in that prison. I should be dead. Because I don't matter to him." She forced herself to say the next part. "But Brianna does."

"*Matter* isn't the word I'd use, Nina."

"Well, I don't want to argue semantics, Cody. I want this over. We all do. So, Brady. You'll go. You'll lay out the plan for everyone. Once Jamison has a few leads on the lawyer, and can be sure he'll be watching or having someone watch so he can feed messages to Ace, you and Gage enact a plan to make it look like you're bringing Brianna here."

"And if some of his goons find you first?" Brady returned.

"We can protect ourselves, injuries or not," Cody replied. "We've gotten this far. Besides, this is a North Star property. There are weapons and security measures here."

Nina frowned. "Shay made it sound like she might get kicked out for helping. But they'll let you stay here?"

Cody shrugged negligently.

"That is *not* an answer, Cody Wyatt."

Brady snorted. "That is *some* mom voice."

Nina glared at him and he held up his hands in surrender.

"I can't get into it. It's North Star business, but we've got this place for a few days. While we're here, we can use their security systems and their weapons."

"You'll want it to look like you're getting ready to move. To run. You'll need a vehicle," Brady mused.

"I'm guessing it won't be my truck."

"Make it part of the fake getting Brianna to us," Nina suggested. "Come in two cars. Leave one."

Brady nodded. "What about communication?"

"We've got to be careful. No texts. Phone calls should be all right, as long as they're in safe locations. I don't think Ace has the power right now to do much more than follow and threaten. Tech's going to be beyond his reach, but we should still be careful."

"I think you're right, and we'll all be careful. I guess we should start."

Cody nodded. "Thanks for the patch up."

Brady scowled, studying Cody's damaged face. "You need a real doctor."

"You do in a pinch."

Brady shook his head in disgust. "Let's end this quick so someone can check out that head wound, huh?"

"I'm all for quick as long as Brianna's safe."

Brady grunted, nodded toward Nina. "I'll get my stuff together and head out." He walked back into the hallway and to the room he must have stayed in.

Nina knew Cody couldn't see, but his gaze was on his clasped hands in front of him. Some of his stoic surety had faded—likely in knowing Brady would be gone and she'd be his best hope for survival. Probably not a pleasant thought.

But she'd protect him, just as she'd protected Brianna.

Love swept through her, a painful reminder that for these past seven years she had existed in a kind of cage. She'd kept moving forward, kept protecting her daughter, but on the inside she was the same woman who'd loved this man.

She opened her mouth to tell him she'd keep him safe, but then thought better of it. That would be no comfort to him. She didn't know what would be—so she did the only thing she could think of.

She got out of her chair and leaned close to his face. She'd only meant to kiss his cheek. A kind of reassurance, a sign this was as okay as it could be. But he angled his head, as if he heard her next to him. She could have stopped herself, if she'd wanted to.

But she didn't want to.

So she brushed her lips against his instead.

LIPS BRUSHED HIS and Cody's heart seemed to shudder to a stop, like a car slipping a gear. He thought maybe he could have handled it somehow if he could see, but blind there was only sensation and that was very, very dangerous.

So he held himself still. As much as he wanted to reach out, how could he? He didn't know exactly where she was. When he could think, puzzle out what they would do, he didn't panic despite the loss of eyesight.

But in *this*, a sensation he'd missed for seven years no matter how often he'd told himself he didn't want or need it, seeing nothing was only panic.

He could hear what were presumably his brother's footsteps even over the beating of his rioting heart.

Nina didn't move, and all Cody could seem to do was wonder how she looked. He wasn't even sure if she was standing or sitting—he only knew she was close enough to touch—and he didn't know how to reach her.

"For the record, no one is going to like this plan," Brady said. "I'll be lucky if I even explain it to them before the arguing takes over."

"Get lucky then." Cody tried to aim a smile in Brady's direction. "Watch your back, brother."

"Let Nina watch yours," Brady replied.

Cody didn't say anything to that, didn't say anything at all until he heard a door swing open and then click shut.

He heard Nina's expelled whoosh of breath—a kind of release of tension even as a new one settled around them.

They were alone. Their hands were tied until someone else acted.

She had kissed him.

He was blind.

Brady's words *let Nina watch yours.*

It scraped him raw. It wasn't that he didn't trust her, didn't believe her capable. She'd kept Brianna safe from Ace—whether for seven whole years or just stabbing a man after she'd been shot—it was quite the feat.

But he wanted to be the one saving. He hadn't saved her seven years ago. If anything, by disappearing and never telling him about Brianna, she'd saved him then.

What had he ever done for her except bring her here? Away from their daughter. Injured. With a man who couldn't fully protect her.

The scrape of chair against floor interrupted the quiet, the table wiggling underneath his arms.

"I don't understand this North Star group," Nina blurted out, clearly agitated. "How can they threaten to fire Shay when she's helping you? How can they not help you when they want to bring Ace down?"

"They don't want to bring Ace down," Cody replied

calmly. It was easy to be calm when talking about facts. And ignoring that a kiss so sweet and featherlight made him feel like he'd been asleep all those seven years he thought he'd been doing the most important work of his life.

"I thought you said…"

"They want to end the Sons," Cody explained, as he'd had to explain to all of his brothers at one point or another the past two months. "It's their mission to demolish the group. So, yeah, taking Ace down is part of it sometimes. But while he's in jail, their focus is the Sons—not Ace, and certainly not his actual children. Personal vendettas aren't their problem."

"Personal vendettas? Is that what you'd call it?"

"No, I'd call it a psychotic episode. It certainly isn't simple sociopathy. Regardless. It *is* personal. It's not about the Sons. That group and their drugs and weapons, and trafficking of all that, *and* their attempts to get into human trafficking are the real target of the North Star group. By abandoning my mission and helping Jamison and Liza *over* the North Star mission, I got myself kicked out."

"Did they expect you to turn your back on your brother?" Nina demanded incredulously.

"No. They didn't. But expecting me to turn my back on my brother and being able to use me for their missions are two different things. I'm too personally connected now. They can't trust me to do what *they're* trying to do. Which doesn't just jeopardize their mission, but the lives of everyone on any one of my teams."

"It isn't fair," Nina replied, and it eased some of the tension in him that she sounded somewhat petulant. "It isn't right."

"It is to them, and for them," he replied, his tone gentler than he'd intended.

He heard a sound—maybe her plopping back onto the chair—and a harrumph. "I hate when you're all detached and reasonable," she muttered. "I don't know how to do that."

"Because you haven't been trying to take down anyone. You've been trying to keep our daughter safe."

"She's safe," Nina said quietly, but there was a tremor to her voice. As if she was saying it to reassure herself. To seek his reassurance.

Which was the only reason he pushed out his arm, held his palm up. He didn't know how to reach for her hand, or her. He didn't have words. So he had to reach out and trust she would too.

Her hand slid into his. He squeezed it. "She's safe. Our families will keep her safe."

He wished he could see her. Judge if that gave her any reassurance. Was she pale and exhausted like she'd been back at the ranch? She hadn't been knocked out like he'd been…maybe she hadn't slept.

He opened his mouth to tell her to do just that, but she spoke first.

"How come nothing ever happened between you and Shay?"

Embarrassingly, he jolted. It was a pointless question, with an easy answer, and yet the way Nina asked it into this gray mist that was all that existed around him right now… It knocked him back.

Nina's hand closed tighter around his, as if she was afraid he'd walk away.

If he'd been able to see, he would have. But of course he couldn't. So he had to sit there.

"It would have risked our jobs."

"That's what she said. She brought it up. The whole you two not ever… Well."

Cody *really* didn't know what to say to that.

"I don't buy it."

"Excuse me?"

"On her end, maybe. But if there'd really been something there—something enough for Shay to mention it, and you to act tense about it when I do—there has to be something more than your jobs."

"North Star wasn't just a job. Not to me." Which was true. Beside the point, but true.

"Maybe not." She was quiet for so many seconds he thought he'd be able to pull his hands away and escape. He thought wrong.

"I know you, Cody. Maybe you've changed. I haven't. I've been stuck in the same place, where everything I am is survival. The only parts of me that have changed are the lengths I'm willing to go to protect the people I love. But that's not change. Not real change. I still know the boy you would've been when you joined North Star and it doesn't add up."

"You've always been bad at math," he replied.

"I want a real answer."

"Why? What does any of this matter?" He tried to ignore the simmering irritation, but this line of conversation, plus the throbbing pain in his body, and the situation that required him to sit here and *wait* made that very difficult. "What would it matter if Shay and I had a relationship? This has nothing to do with the task at hand."

"The task at hand is to sit here and wait to see how we can make your father think we have our daughter," Nina replied. "We can't do anything until wheels are set in motion."

"So…you want to what? Take a tour of our romantic detours the past seven years?"

"No," she replied, the reasonableness in her tone setting his teeth on edge. "I'm asking you a specific question about a specific woman."

"What do you want me to say?" Cody demanded, his frustration with *everything* bubbling over at this *one* thing she kept poking at. "That she looked like you? That sometimes out of the corner of my eye it'd be like a ghost was there. That I was never certain if that attraction I felt was her, or still wanting you? Is that what you want to hear?"

She was wholly silent. He didn't even hear her breathe until she spoke. "I only wanted the truth," she said quietly, a pinched quality to each word as if she was in pain.

As if *she* was in pain.

"Well the damn truth is it was still wanting you. It always will be. You're the only one I've ever wanted."

Chapter Fifteen

Every word Cody spoke seemed to strike her with such force that her breath got caught in her lungs. She couldn't move for a good minute or so as she absorbed the words. Then it took another minute for her body to stop reacting to each blow.

She didn't know why she'd suddenly felt she had to understand the whole *Shay* thing. The woman had said nothing had happened. That whatever attraction there'd been had been incidental, unimportant. So, why should Nina care what Cody had rightfully done in the seven years they'd been apart?

She didn't care.

Okay, she didn't *want* to care. And it turned out Nina didn't care what Shay felt or thought or said about nothing happening or why. She only cared what Cody felt. Not then. Here and now. Was there any of *this* left over inside of him too? Could that be what had really held him back when it had come to Shay?

She'd wanted it to be true, but knew it couldn't possibly be. She'd had to hear him say it to get rid of all that awful hope.

Maybe she'd secretly believed he'd say something about her being hard to get over or something vague but comforting.

She hadn't expected anger.

She really hadn't expected being the *only* one.

He'd said *you're* like it was present tense. Like in this moment, she was his only one. It washed over her and through her, all that terrifying hope she'd been trying to avoid.

Wasn't everything she hoped for always too good to be true?

Not Brianna.

Six years with that beautiful girl. They'd been terrifying years—always afraid the next move would mean she'd lose her. Because Brianna was too good to be true, and yet for six years she'd been true—and now Nina had so many people working to make sure it would be true. Period.

Brianna was still here. Still hers—and now theirs. Brianna finally got to have Cody, and Nina wanted to have him too, no matter how unfair it might be.

You're the only one I've ever wanted.

"You're going to have to let a blind man know if you walk out of the room, Nina."

"I didn't walk out," she managed to reply despite how tight her throat felt. "I'm trying to…" Her breath shuddered out, betraying all the emotion battling it out inside of her. "I don't…"

"You don't," he said flatly.

"No! No. I… Cody." She raked her hands through her hair trying to get a handle on the here and now and not her circling thoughts. She could cry if she wanted to. He wouldn't see it. She could indeed slip out of the room and never have this conversation. She had all the power here.

But hadn't she already lost seven years? Why wouldn't she use her power to do something about *that*?

"You're telling me after I left you the way I did," she said, wincing at how her voice shook, and how much the memory still hurt. "After I *lied* to you the way I did, I'm still the only person you've ever wanted? We lost all that time. I kept Brianna from you."

"Yes. You concealed her. We lost. Seven years passed." He said that all in his detached way, but emotion was creeping into his expression, into each word. "Too much has changed and passed, and I can tell myself that from here to eternity. It doesn't seem to change how I feel."

"I never stopped," Nina whispered, despite the fact that tears burned her eyes, that her throat felt as if someone was squeezing the breath out of her.

All he'd mentioned was want, not love.

"Stopped what?" he muttered, clearly irritated with the conversation, with himself, with being unable to leave.

But he actually couldn't leave. Not easily in this unfamiliar cabin with a brand-new loss of sight. Which meant she got to say whatever she wanted. After seven years of not being able to tell him *anything*.

"I never stopped loving you."

It was his turn not to speak, even as she waited, desperately wishing he'd say something. Anything. But his unseeing gaze was straight ahead and his expression gave nothing away.

There was just the oppressive silence in this weird little cabin that wasn't theirs. This life that hadn't felt like her own in seven years. How was it she was sitting next to him—both of them injured—having this conversation? Brianna secreted away on the ranch with Duke and Liza and all the girls and Wyatt boys and…

Now wasn't the time, or the place. Brianna should be their focus. They should hatch a million plans until they were all safe and home.

Home. What's home anymore?

She wasn't sure she ever knew. It hadn't been the trailer

she'd grown up in. It hadn't even been the Knight house, no matter how much she'd loved it. She'd been too afraid, always, to believe in home. A little too afraid to believe in a future—there, with Cody, with anyone or anything. She'd taken everything one day at a time—always so cognizant of how it could be lost.

Or that home was not for her.

And here she was, with so much to lose, every day. Every breath. She had lost these seven years with him. Because she hadn't told him.

She stood by that decision. Neither of them had been ready for the threat of Ace back then. Not really.

But things were different. They were older. They'd weathered storms, and even a small taste of parenthood together for the last few days. Maybe seven years ago had been the time for caution.

And maybe now, with everything falling around them, but with their family sweeping it all up and stitching it together to protect them, out of love, out of duty.

Maybe now was the time to forget caution. Who knew what tomorrow would bring.

"There was no one else. There's been…nothing else. My life stopped in that moment. A new life was born with Brianna, a new humbling, blinding love. But when your life is changed like that, taken over like that, it's like… I don't know what I'm saying. I don't know what I'm trying to say. It's always been you." She leaned forward, sliding her hands slowly over his, then up his arms. "That hasn't changed. I stopped thinking it could, or even should. It is what it is."

"You still love me." He sounded so shell-shocked. Beyond disbelief, as if he'd been thrust into a new kind of blindness. "We were…young."

"And dumb. So, so dumb. I don't think being young

matters. I felt what I felt—I didn't know how precious that was, or how hard it could be. I didn't even know how hard *life* could be then, and it wasn't like I'd had such an easy life. I don't think age changes love. It just changes how you deal with it."

His face was tilted toward hers, but he couldn't see. Because he would do whatever it took to save Brianna. Just like she would—and she had the bullet wound to prove it.

"Cody." She cupped his cheek with one hand, studying his face. Bruised. Scratched. Bandaged.

Yes, she had always loved him—which made her think she always would—but more than that, here was a man who'd lay down his own life, not just to protect her, but to protect anyone he loved—most especially his daughter.

He shook his head against her hand, though she refused to take it away.

"Maybe you don't know the man I've become," he said, his voice hoarse. "What I did with the North Star group..."

"Cody, I've killed two men in the span of a week to save my daughter. Killed. Ended lives. I don't know how I did it. I never thought I would." She used her other hand to hold his face in place. She knew he couldn't see her, but maybe he could feel what she meant if she held on. "It hasn't changed us because we were *born* survivors. We have had to do what needed to be done ever since our doomed parents brought us into the world. So, no, these seven years haven't changed who we are. And as long as Ace has a hold over us, we can't change. We're stuck here."

"I should have killed him."

He said it with such disgust she could only feel sympathy for him, and not wish so much he had. "Maybe that *would* have changed you, Cody. And for whatever reason you didn't, or couldn't. There's no blame for that."

"I've got plenty."

Since she could see the misery on him, the guilt, and she understood that he couldn't end Ace's life, even when he'd wanted to, she brushed her mouth against his again. "I don't," she said against his mouth.

CODY DIDN'T KNOW what they were doing—what Nina, specifically, was doing. Talking about love and guilt and all manner of things that didn't work to keep their daughter safe. Which was all he wanted to do.

Liar.

Something about the way she'd said *survivors*, the way she put the two of them on the same plane as such, the way she laid everything out and it somehow made sense.

They hadn't changed. Love still wound around them, strong and true. Love pulsed here in this cabin, just as it had when he'd seen her being lifted into that ambulance.

Because he'd always known it was his job to survive, and so had she. They would do whatever it took—to survive, to protect.

Would they do whatever it took to love?

Maybe he'd blame all the emotions on being blind and walk away. Or ask to be led away since he wasn't oriented enough in the room to know which way was which.

But Nina's mouth was soft and gentle and it undid him, no matter how he tried to harden himself against it. Nothing had been soft and gentle for seven years, since she'd cut things off. He'd told himself he hadn't missed it. The Wyatts didn't do soft and gentle, and God knew North Star really didn't.

But the longing of someone putting their arms around him, taking some care with how they touched him—it undid everything. He couldn't think past Nina. Couldn't worry that he was the reason they were here, and Brianna wasn't. He couldn't wallow in all that guilt and pain and the horrible, horrible impotence at not being able to end Ace.

Even when he'd had the chance.

Except that reminder pulled him out of the little dream her kiss could provide. He hadn't done what he could to protect Brianna or Nina—even if he hadn't known what would happen at the time.

He eased his mouth away from hers. "Nina. What is this?" He found himself trying to study her face, still oddly confused at the fact he couldn't see. But that persistent gray shadow was all that was in front of him.

Her hands still held his face, her fingers tracing his jaw and the corners of his mouth. "I don't really know. What feels right, I guess. We lost…seven years. Even if we had to, they're lost. But this moment isn't."

She kissed him again, and it turned out kissing her back was one of the few things he was capable of doing easily even without his sight. The sense that he wasn't completely helpless was a comfort. Just like she was.

And no, she hadn't changed. She felt and tasted exactly the same—the softness of her mouth a ghost that had haunted him all this time.

Maybe it had been some kind of subconscious penance to refrain from being with anyone else, and if it had been, didn't he deserve what she so willingly offered?

It was a kiss, and it was comfort they could give each other. A distraction while they waited. It wasn't wrong.

"Make love to me, Cody," she whispered against his mouth.

He wanted to, his body pulsed with the need to have her—and a heart he didn't want to admit was so soft desperately wanted to be with her again. "I… I can't see." A travesty to have her back, even if it wouldn't last, and not be able to see anything.

Still she tugged him to his feet as she chuckled. "Last time I checked eyes weren't a necessary body part for this."

He stood—off-kilter not just because of his lack of sight as she led him forward, but because for all the talk about not changing—she had, in some ways. Maybe not *who* she was, but what she was willing to do and reach for.

Maybe she was nervous and he just couldn't see it, but he wasn't getting the feeling she was unsure or timid. She led him somewhere, and he'd follow her anywhere.

"I always wanted to lead." She put gentle pressure on his shoulders until he sat on the edge of what turned out to be the bed. He scooted himself back, curious how far she would take this.

"So, why didn't you? I probably would have been rather amenable to the idea."

She laughed again, and the sound eased the black tension inside of him. She'd always been able to do that. Soothe, without even trying. She made him believe there was good, light, hope.

Then. Now.

"I didn't know *how* to lead back then. I can't say I'm glad for the past seven years, that we were apart when we didn't have to be. I can't say I'm in any way grateful for what Ace put me—*us* through. But it gave me something I didn't have before, and probably never would have found."

"What?"

She slid over him—a soft, enticing weight as she straddled him. "Courage. Strength."

"You were always brave." He found her hips with his hands. "You were always strong. You just hid it."

She paused above him, but he didn't. He let his hands

roam. Had he ever taken his time with her? They'd been teenagers, forever in a rush toward that magic adulthood when things would feel settled, make sense.

What a joke.

But maybe that just meant it would never feel that way, and for once in his life he had to hold on to the now and enjoy it, believe in it.

He slid his hands up her sides, gentling as he felt the bandage under her shirt. "We're pretty banged up."

Fingers traced the bandage on his face.

"Weren't we always?" she whispered, before kissing him as if the admission they'd been bruised and broken internally all those years ago was too much to bear, even after they'd borne so much these past few years.

"I love you," she murmured against his mouth, her body moving against his in blissful agony.

He knew he didn't deserve that—her love, or this, but the same love was inside him, and they had lost so much time. "I love you too."

Chapter Sixteen

Nina woke up to a throbbing in her side and the feeling that she'd actually slept for more than a few fretful hours. The bed was warm and aside from the pain she was getting used to as being just an everyday part of life, she felt surprisingly good.

If it was a nice day, she and Brianna could…

Reality crashed down not just as she remembered she was in a strange cabin far away from Brianna, but as she realized she was naked.

And so was the man next to her.

She couldn't roll over on her side, because it would hurt, but she turned her head to study Cody.

He was still fast asleep, one arm thrown above his head showing off the impressive muscle of his bicep. At some point between *then* and *now* he'd gotten the tattoo he'd always talked about—the cattle brand Grandma Pauline used at the ranch. *A P* and an *R* intertwined, because until Cody's mother had broken the tradition, everyone in the Reaves family had been given the initials *P* and *R*.

Nina had always loved the story. Grandma Pauline bucking societal convention and refusing to take her husband's name, refusing to act as though he ran the ranch when it was *hers*. Nina had always been fascinated by the man she'd never met who'd agreed to it—purely out of love.

They'd named their only daughter Patricia Reaves-Henderson. She'd broken Grandma Pauline's heart by refusing to use the Reaves and going only by Henderson, by refusing to give the name to any of her children.

By loving a madman.

Nina sighed. So many sad stories in the world and she was in the midst of her own, but it didn't feel sad with Cody next to her. It felt like hope. Life was hard, but there were good things to reach for, hold on to.

Good things to fight for.

The room was dim and Nina realized they'd completely screwed up their sleep schedule and spent most of the day asleep.

The sound of a phone going off in the midst of sleepy silence had Nina jolting and Cody's arm flashing out grasping for the phone. But his instincts were off as he pawed through nothing but air.

Nina's heart twisted as she reached over him to the nightstand where his phone vibrated. She took his hand and placed the phone into his palm, sliding her finger across the screen to answer the call for him.

"Hello," Cody muttered, voice irritated and sleep rasped. Then for the next several minutes he didn't speak as whoever had called him spoke, the volume too low for Nina to make out any of the words.

Cody kept his expression perfectly neutral. She wanted to touch him, stroke away some of that iron tension inside of him, but she was too afraid of whatever news he was getting.

"All right. Tomorrow then," he said, not giving away if *tomorrow* was good or bad. He held the phone to her and she ended the call for him, then set the cell on the nightstand.

He let out a breath. "They've been busy." He turned his face toward her. Then he frowned, whether something new occurred to him or...

"Can you see?"

He blinked a few times and shook his head, making hope launch through her like a spring.

"No," he said. "But it's...something is different. Lighter, maybe."

"Is that good?"

"I don't... I really don't know."

Nina would pray that it was. "Who was on the phone?"

"Brady. Tuck's got a tail every day, so he's going to be in charge of making it look like he's bringing Brianna to us."

"Won't he be in danger, like we were, of someone trying to attack him? Especially if they think he has Brianna."

"They've got a plan for that. They've got a plan for everything." He didn't sound happy about it. He sounded frustrated.

Nina reached out, rubbed her hand against his arm. "You feel...superfluous?"

He shrugged, but it was an irritable move masquerading as ambivalence. "I am superfluous. We wait. They move. The end." He moved restlessly, inching his way out of bed as he painstakingly felt around for furniture to guide him.

"Let me help you."

"I don't need help for every damn thing," he replied, inching his way down the bed. And he could probably make it out of the room all right, but he was missing a particularly important aspect of getting out of bed.

"You're going to walk around naked all day?"

His scowl deepened and he said nothing.

"I wouldn't complain if you did."

That *almost* got a smile out of him.

"Let me make you some break... Well, I think it's past dinnertime. I'm not sure what you'd call this meal. Post-sex sustenance, I guess."

"Stop trying to make me laugh," Cody grumbled.

She slipped on her clothes before going around to his side of the bed. She took his hand.

"Why? You probably need a laugh." She picked up his discarded clothes and helped him into them.

"You've had plenty of laughs these past seven years?" he returned.

"I've tried. For Brianna. We both know bad things happen, terrible things really. We were born knowing that, right? So yeah, I had to figure out how to laugh in spite of it. For Brianna." She placed her hands on his shoulders and brushed her mouth against his. "So, I'll do the same for you."

With only a little fumbling his hands closed over her elbows. Though she knew he couldn't see her, he stared hard at her as if he could. Maybe his sight was coming back—whatever injury was healing and... Maybe this would all be okay.

Hoping for okay seemed so dangerous. Could Cody really get his sight back, could they be some kind of family, without the threat of Ace? Ever?

It was too much to hope for, but all that hope filled her up until she couldn't breathe. It didn't smother the fear inside of her, but it tried.

"Come on. We need to eat something," she said, her voice tight with all those emotions swirling around inside of her.

Still he stared or whatever it was he was doing, holding her in place. It made her heart beat too hard and her pulse scramble for purchase. What was going on in that head of his?

He opened his mouth as if to say something, something serious and important and she held her breath.

Which allowed her to hear a muffled sound that came from outside. Cody frowned, inclining his head where the sound had come from.

Before Nina could ask what he thought it was, or even make a move to look, Cody's phone beeped.

"Get my phone, Nina," he said with a gravity that had her jumping to do just that without asking why.

"There's a gray box, but it's blank."

"Tap it." He talked her through opening some app that made no sense to her, but once he had walked her through it, four squares appeared on the phone screen. Clearly they were video feeds from some kind of surveillance camera.

"What do you see?" Cody demanded.

Nina shook her head trying to make sense of the boxes. They were black-and-white and she could make out trees on one. She didn't remember there being very many trees around the cabin when they'd walked up. Maybe in the back there'd been a cluster? But the memory was hazy because she'd been so focused on Cody and getting to the cabin and help.

"I don't see anything that makes any sense," she finally said as she could sense Cody growing more and more impatient. "Four squares. One has trees, the rest just look gray."

"Ironic," Cody muttered. "Watch the screen."

"What am I looking…" She trailed off as a shadow appeared on the screen. She couldn't make it out, but she could tell something was moving just out of sight of the camera.

"What is it?"

"I don't know. I just could tell something is moving out there, but it's not on the screen. Where are these cameras pointed?"

"You've got four quadrants. A, front. B, left side. C, right side. D, back. Where was the shadow?"

"D."

"That's back. Which area is the shadow in?"

"I… I don't understand all this."

"North, east, west or south, Nina?"

"I don't know!"

"Give me your hand," he ordered.

She wanted to be petulant and refuse—he couldn't see her after all, so he couldn't *make* her. But there was a shadow, and a noise, and a million other fears pounding through her.

She slid her hand into his. He gripped her hand, pulled her toward him, his other hand finding her other arm. His palms moved up until he gripped her shoulders and then he rested his forehead against hers.

"We're okay. I'm frustrated because I can't see. Not at you. Okay?"

She nodded, even if he couldn't see the movement, he could feel it.

"Just describe to me everything you see, and if I snap about something just remember you can take it out on me later if it makes you feel better."

"Did you just make a joke?" She was incredulous, not because of the timing—God knew you had to laugh even in awful times or you never would—but because *he* of all people was joking. Period. Let alone about sex.

"I don't want to add to this…" He made a vague motion with his hands. "I don't want to be a jerk, but I can't see and I'm frustrated so I probably will be. The situation is bad enough without me adding to it, so I'm trying to rein it in. This is my—"

"It isn't your fault. If it was your fault you'd be purposefully hurting me and Brianna and you're trying to save us from the man whose fault it is," she returned, gripping his arm in turn even as he still held her shoulders.

"He's part of me, Nina. I can't escape that."

"Of course you can. If I believed that, I'd have to believe my addict, negligent parents were a part of me I'm helpless to resist, and I've *never* been helpless."

He shook his head, whether to argue or in exasperation that she had an iron-tight argument, she didn't know.

"We can talk blame later. Explain the shadow."

NINA EXPLAINED WHAT she'd seen on the monitors. Cody bit back his impatience with how hard it was to understand what she'd seen when he couldn't see.

He couldn't let himself hope that the fact he seemed to make out some light and some shadow now pointed to the fact he might be healing, the fact he might heal. Because he could just as easily be stuck in this place forever.

And now was not the time to deal with either scenario.

"Do you think someone is out there?"

Cody considered. "Maybe. There are blind spots on the cameras. If someone is out there they don't want us to know and they know how to avoid detection." His father's men hadn't been that smart before now.

At least the men he could get. Cody had to wonder at that. The Sons were a well-oiled machine. Sure, Ace had lost some of his best men in the explosion a few months ago—including his right-hand man. In fact, the death toll included many of the Sons highest-ranking members.

Who had stepped into that power vacuum? Could it be someone who was happy Ace was in jail?

Was it possible Ace had *some* reach from prison, but not a particularly large span because the Sons had gone in a different direction?

He and his brothers had been so focused on Ace in particular, had they considered that Ace might not have the Sons full support now that he was behind bars?

Maybe it had taken him time, or his messenger time, to get someone worth a darn.

And maybe they were here *now*, which would be the problem at hand he needed to focus on. Not what-ifs about the Sons.

"So what do we do? I should call Jamison. I should—"

"We're not calling anyone."

"Cody. Teamwork. We have to be a team. We have to be. For Brianna."

He had been a part of a team for years, but that wasn't what she meant. She said *team* and what she really meant was *family*.

He'd kept himself isolated from his family until two months ago. Visiting infrequently at best, convinced it was necessary to remain secretive about his work with North Star. That had been part of it, but much like why nothing had ever happened with Shay, there was more to it.

He hadn't wanted to depend on anyone. Hadn't wanted to be the littlest Wyatt. He'd wanted to do something on his *own*—for pride and whatever else.

But now he had a daughter, and his pride would have to be swallowed.

"All right. I still want to try and handle this ourselves, but we'll let Jamison know we've got a visitor."

"Or visitors, plural," Nina pointed out.

"Yeah, well. I'll call Jamison. I need you to get the weapons." He explained to Nina where she would find them and how to unlock them. She connected with

Jamison's name in his phone for him and he held the cell to his ear as he listened to Nina retreat to where the weapons were hidden.

"Cody."

"J. We think we've got a visitor." He didn't mention there might be more than one. "I don't think we'll need help, but I wanted to let you know."

"But you might need help."

"We can't afford to mess up the plan."

"I'll tell you what we can afford."

"No. You won't. This is my kid at stake. My…" He didn't know what to call Nina, so he didn't finish that sentence. "I call the shots."

"You can't see."

"Everyone keeps reminding me of that as if I don't know very well what I can't do. I've still got a brain."

"A stubborn one."

"Yeah, well, welcome to life with the Wyatts, Jamison. I want to try to capture him and get him to talk."

"How on earth do you think—"

"Have you noticed? How sloppy this barrage of Ace's men are? They're making mistake after mistake. Have you thought about what that could mean?"

There was silence on the other end of the line for a while, so Cody kept talking. "We don't have time to look into it right this second, but it's something to start looking into when we can. It's very possible Ace doesn't have the power we think he does."

"Cody…"

"I'll check in every thirty minutes or so. Don't send anyone out unless I don't check in."

"Cody. That's—"

"It could be a trap, or worse, a distraction. Give me time to handle this. Give *us* time to handle it."

"Twenty minutes. A check-in every twenty minutes," Jamison said, his voice hard, which meant he didn't exactly approve, but he'd go along with it because in the end, Jamison trusted all of them.

Cody had to wonder why. After Dev nearly getting himself killed, Cody couldn't *fathom* why.

But he'd take it. "Fine. Twenty. Is… Brianna close by?"

"Hold on."

It took a few seconds before a young girl's voice filled his ear. "Daddy?"

It was amazing, the fierce sweep of love and longing that swept through him. He'd known her for a few days, and yet her voice steadied him, strengthened him. "Hi, Brianna. Everything going okay at the ranch?"

"Yeah, I guess. I miss Mom."

"I bet you do. Here, I'll have you talk to her in a second, okay?" He could hear Nina approaching. "Are you wearing the necklace I gave you?" he asked quietly into the receiver.

"Uh-huh. Gigi wants one too. Can you make her one?"

"Sure. When I get back. Here's Mom." He held out the phone in the general direction he thought Nina was.

Her fingers brushed his as she took the phone from him. "Brianna?" There was a pause, the faint sound of a sob being swallowed. "Uh-huh. I miss you, baby. I'll be home as soon as I can, okay? Okay. I love you, baby. I love you." Another pause, and then the croak of a goodbye.

"Come here."

He'd barely gotten the words out when Nina filled his arms. He held her tight and she held him back just as strong. She didn't make much noise, but he knew she was crying into his shoulder.

"I just miss her. I can handle it when I don't hear her voice, but…"

"I know. I know." He pulled her back, trying to squint himself into being able to see her face, but it was all still shadows. "So, let's see if we can get back to her sooner rather than later."

Chapter Seventeen

Nina explained the guns she'd found to Cody, and he seemed to file the information away. Then she watched the security footage for a while. No more shadows or hints at anything out there.

It was worse, somehow, the nonthreat after a threat that had never materialized. Worse, with Brianna's voice echoing around in her head from that too-brief phone call. She wanted to be back on the ranch, curled up with Brianna on the couch, reading a book or even watching one of the obnoxious kids shows she loved. Nina wanted her daughter.

And, if she was honest with herself, she wanted to know if anything that had happened with Cody was actually real. Or if it was just the dregs of the past and this whole awful situation.

She knew she loved him still. She had no doubts about her feelings… She frowned over that. If she didn't doubt her own, was it fair to doubt his?

"It could have just been a scouting mission," Cody said into the oppressive silence when still nothing appeared on the screen. They'd been whiling away *hours*.

"What would that entail?"

"See what we've got here and determine what they'd

need to successfully breach and attack. Go back and plan, gather, attack later."

It was an awful thought. He no doubt knew what he was talking about, but to wait here patiently while they planned an attack had her pulse hammering in her neck, panic and fear twining deep inside of her gut.

"The problem is," Cody continued, his eyes cast toward his folded hands on the table. "I'm not sure about the endgame. These men who've come after us have been careless. As if they don't care whether we live or die."

"I'm sure they don't."

"That doesn't read as Ace's MO. He wants me alive, so I can suffer. He might want you dead, but it'd be in a way that would make me suffer the most."

"I love being the pawn in some psycho's mind game," she muttered, that edgy feeling after adrenaline wore off making her particularly irritable.

The timer went off and she sent the all clear text to Jamison. It had been hours, so it was just rote now: Set alarm again. Text Jamison 'AC' for all clear, then sit and wait and wait and wait.

"I know this is hard," Cody said after she hit Send. "Waiting is the hardest part. It's a mental game. You have to be tougher than the wait."

"Well, I'm not."

"You are," Cody returned. He held his hand out and she slid hers into it. He gave it a squeeze. "I think you're tougher than anyone has ever given you credit for."

She wanted to cry because she'd had to be tough for seven years without one person telling her she was doing a good job at it, and to have some kind of reassurance, someone believing in her, it mattered. But there was no time for more crying. There was only getting out of this. "How long do we wait?"

"Not much longer. It's possible whoever you saw is already gone. That'd be the smart thing. But these men Ace has had after us... They haven't acted in a way that denotes much intelligence."

"You think he's still out there." The thought gave her a cold shudder.

"I think it's possible there's someone waiting. Setting a trap, maybe. If they have any inclination Brady might come back, or someone else is going to...well, they have a lot of options."

Too many. Too many for them to sit around waiting, that she understood. But he *was* waiting, not acting. He wasn't bringing his brothers into it, and it dawned on her now that it was because he was worried they'd be ambushed.

So, he was waiting. But for what? She studied him, his eyes unseeing, his hands folded so tightly together his knuckles were white. He didn't want to wait. He *had* to wait. "What would you do if you could see?" she demanded.

He shook his head. "It doesn't matter."

But it did. He was holding back because he couldn't see, and because whatever *he* would do if he had his sight, he didn't trust *her* to do. "Tell me."

"I've been trained to neutralize threats, Nina. Take down crowds of men with lethal weapons. I have been trained to deal with all these kinds of situations, these kinds of men."

"Yes, and while you were being trained, I actually dealt with these kinds of situations, these kinds of men. For our daughter. So, you will tell me. What would you do if you could see?"

His jaw worked, and when he spoke it was pained. "I can't risk anything happening to you."

She wanted to be touched, and she supposed somewhere under the fear and panic she was. But there was too much else going on to spend time on it. "We have to risk *something*. Or we'll never get anywhere. We'll sit here and wait for them to finally rub two brain cells together. If you don't tell me what you would do in this situation with full sight, I will make my own plan, and enact it on my own."

He stood abruptly, then seemed to remember he had nowhere to go without risking running into something or tripping and falling. He balled his hands into fists, but he breathed slow and calm.

"If I could see, I would put to use the many skills I've been taught and slip outside, sneak up to wherever he's hiding—if he is in fact still out there—and I would either fight or threaten him into submission, then bring him in here and demand answers."

Nina thought about it. She could maybe threaten, but she was no expert with a gun and surely the man out there would be. Cody could no doubt overpower someone. Her? Not so much.

So, maybe it was a mistake to expect she could think and act like Cody. She'd saved Brianna. Ace had sent someone to kill her and she'd fought him off. She'd survived.

So, what would she do if she was here, with Brianna? What steps would she have taken to keep her daughter safe?

"If we can't fight them, we can run from them."

"I'm blind. Both of us are banged up from the crash. Running isn't an option, and it doesn't solve anything."

"If we get far enough away, the injuries don't matter. They will keep watching the cabin, hatching their plans, and we'll be long gone."

"And then what?"

Then what? When it had been just her and Brianna, the "then what" had been disappearing and rebuilding a new life. But there was no rebuilding now. There was only keeping Ace behind bars.

And she had help. Regardless of sight, she had Cody. All the Wyatt boys. Her sisters. Duke. She had everyone.

"We get out of here, and then *we* set the trap."

NINA OUTLINED HER PLAN. It clashed with his, which was to wait until dark and then do a little explosives work. But with his sight issues that would be even trickier than he and Nina sneaking out of here.

Cody was starting to see shadows more clearly. He still couldn't see, but he was almost certain he could tell where light was shining from. He hoped it was a positive sign, but since he didn't know for sure, he didn't tell Nina.

"It's a better plan," Nina said as she finished.

"Define *better*."

"Four against one instead of two against one."

"You're assuming there's only one, Nina. That's a dangerous assumption."

"Everything we do is a dangerous assumption, Cody," she returned, irritation straining her voice. "And your plan, if you could see, would be to go out there assuming there's only one you could somehow capture."

"Not necessarily."

Though he couldn't see her roll her eyes, he got the distinct impression that's just what she did.

"Set aside the fact you want to do this on your own. Set aside the fact you want to be in control. Think of my plan from all your angles, and then, if you still don't agree, come up with a better one."

If she hadn't pegged him so dead-on, he might have smiled at the demand in her voice. But the way she picked apart all his trepidation over her plan, made it about his own stupid feelings that didn't matter... Well, it scraped.

And it was exactly what he had to do.

Truth was, if he had a better plan he would have thought of it by now. Waiting was dangerous. It gave whoever was after them too much time to plan, and with time and planning came preparation—which led to an alarming lack of mistakes.

These men after them had made a lot of mistakes so far. Cody had to keep the momentum going in his and Nina's favor.

"We can't head toward the ranch. It opens up Duke and the others too much, and despite my precautions, puts Brianna in the crosshairs."

"Does North Star have some other kind of place like this?"

"Not for me to use." He could probably finagle it, but he'd likely get Shay kicked out once and for all, and that wasn't his place.

"Let me see that map we used to get here."

He got out his phone and walked her through finding it. There weren't the normal map markers, and her explanation of directions and the markers on the map weren't exactly clear. It took longer than it should have to give him an idea of where they were.

"We're close to the National Park," he said, mulling it over and hoping he'd understood her verbal explanations. "Felicity knows the park better than anyone."

"I don't want to drag her into this."

"She's already dragged, Nina."

"No, she isn't. The only time I've seen Felicity since I've been back was our one whole-families meeting. She didn't even speak to me."

"That doesn't mean Ace won't eventually go after

what's yours. His focus is on me, but if you piss him off enough, it could be on you. Which would then extend beyond just Brianna and yourself to Duke and the girls."

For once, he was glad he couldn't see. He didn't want to have to witness what he could already imagine—the color draining from her face, maybe a little horror. She'd never fully understood what getting herself mixed up with him meant.

He supposed none of them had—always thinking they could stay one step ahead. Even after Dev's run-in, Cody had been sure he only needed the *means* to take down Ace. And that was what North Star had been for.

And still he was here. Right here in this awful situation that felt harder and harder to win.

"So, we, what? Hike to the Badlands?"

"More or less. Felicity can give us a clue where to go, and she can either get help to us or be the help to us without drawing much attention. Even if they're following Duke or the girls, they'll get bored real quick trying to traipse around the Badlands after Felicity when it will look like she's just doing her job as a ranger. She's our best bet for help without detection."

"You should be the one to call her. She won't speak with me."

"You underestimate what Felicity would do to help you, Nina. No matter what kind of hurts are running through, they all have your back. They came and took care of our little girl."

He heard her suck in a shuddery breath, but the one she blew out after it was even. "I still think you should call her. You understand the map better. I'll…pack us up with whatever I can find."

"We'll need dark, so you've got time, but we can get a good start. I'll call, you pack. You'll have to carry some guns, supplies. You'll have to study the map and know where you're going. Everything is up to you leading a blind man."

"Not all that different than carrying around a baby, Cody."

"I'm heavier."

"So make sure I don't need to carry you."

She was trying to make light of the situation, feel in control of it, and it fully dawned on him how often she'd been in this exact spot—but alone and with their daughter depending on her.

It awed him—she *awed* him—and some of the anxiety at letting her lead smoothed out. Because she'd kept their daughter safe and alive for *years*.

And what had he done but fail at getting rid of Ace completely?

He wanted to fix that, and maybe he'd get the chance yet, but for now he was still blind and he had to rely on her. Hopefully, he'd get the chance to return the favor.

He held out his phone in the direction he figured she was. "Dial Felicity for me?"

She didn't take it from him immediately, and he got the sense—both in listening to her move and the shadows he seemed to be picking up—she was moving toward him, phone ignored.

She pressed her lips to his, featherlight and sweet, but with a heft to it. "Cody. When this is over—"

He didn't know where she was going with that, had a bad feeling it was something like letting him down easy. Sleeping together had been a one-off, born of panic and fear. She didn't want him to get ideas. "One step at a time."

"When this is over," she repeated, more forcefully. "I need to know Brianna and I have a place in your life.

I know she does. I *know* she does. But I need a place there too."

The thing about being blind in a dangerous situation that threatened the life of his daughter and the one woman he'd ever loved was that it stripped all the mental gymnastics he would have done otherwise. He couldn't sit here and worry about if they were the same people, if he could forgive her keeping Brianna from him, if any good thing in life would ever last for him with Ace Wyatt's blood running through his veins—because in the here and now it mattered not at all. Only life mattered. "There's no *place* for you two, Nina. You're both my life."

The phone slipped out of his hand, then back in. "There," she said, her voice oddly calm and solid. "I'll go pack."

Chapter Eighteen

They waited for dark like Cody had suggested. Cody wore the biggest pack, but since she was the one who could see, she needed to be the one with easy access to light and weapons. She had a smaller pack strapped onto her back, a gun holstered to her side and a headband with a light on it on her forehead.

Cody had taken her through how to use the gun, but there'd been no place or opportunity to actually practice. She prayed to God she wouldn't have to use it. Maybe she'd been able to take out the last guy, but that had been in broad daylight.

They had a plan to sneak out the side window—betting that even if there was more than one person out here, they were looking at the exits—not including windows.

They'd had an argument about who would go first. Cody couldn't seem to get it through his head that not being able to see meant he couldn't be the first into danger anymore.

But what impressed her, once she got past her irritation, was that he was trying. He had to be reminded he wasn't Mr. Call-the-Shots, but he'd swallow down that silly pride or whatever it was that made him determined to be in charge, and try to give her room to lead.

Try being the operative word, but not all men would.

Especially men like Cody—trained in this kind of thing. He'd spent years with some mysterious group trying to take down one of the most notorious biker gangs in North America. He *knew* what he was doing—he just couldn't enact it.

Meanwhile she was nobody. She could remind herself all she wanted that she'd kept Brianna safe for almost seven years, but as she slid out of the window, doing everything in her power to be stealthy and quiet, the backpack caught on the window and then she banged her knee on the side of the cabin. She held still, half hanging out of the window, holding her breath and listening for sounds of someone coming.

She could hear the sound of an engine, maybe even the faint strains of music. She looked up at the window where Cody was standing. "Are they…listening to music?" she whispered.

"Probably trying to stay awake. Which makes me think there's only one, and he's watching the door. Keep moving."

Nina nodded and took the short jump to the ground. Even without his sight, Cody managed to make climbing out of a window look graceful and easy.

They moved straight back, as they'd planned. They needed to get far enough away that turning on a flashlight didn't give them away. Nina had to admit the moron with the running engine and music playing didn't strike her as the type who'd notice a light *behind* the cabin.

Still, she stuck to the plan. Move forward in a straight line. Wait for Cody, who claimed he had some inner sense of how far they'd gone, to give her the signal.

So she walked, picking her way through the dark as she led Cody. She heard the night go strangely still and Nina paused.

"He cut the engine. Keep moving," Cody whispered. "No lights."

She did so, but something in the air changed and she looked back over her shoulder and stopped dead.

"What is it?" Cody demanded, his body tense and ready to fight no matter that he couldn't see.

"The lights in the cabin just went on," Nina whispered, watching the glow spread—one window, then two, then the window they'd crawled out of.

"It's okay. Keep moving. It'll take him time."

Not enough time, Nina thought, but she swallowed at the panic in her throat and wrenched her gaze away from the light and back to the dark. She needed a minute for her eyes to readjust to the complete dark before she could move forward again.

They walked, on and on. She tried to avoid it, but every once in a while she looked back. The cabin's lights were almost completely gone now, but a new light had joined them. Headlights pointed in the exact direction they'd gone.

"Keep going. Just keep going," Cody urged.

Then she saw a new swath of light moving. A flashlight.

"He's following us."

"Let him."

"We could double back. Leave him to get lost. If he's stupid, he'd get lost out here, surely."

"If he's following us, he won't get lost. He'll just double back too and we're where we started. He might be alone now, but if he's following, he's not *acting* alone. We have to stick to the plan."

"He could—"

"Stick to the plan, Nina. Your plan, remember? Think about what you'd do if you had Brianna."

She'd keep moving. It would be the only choice. She wouldn't like keeping going with someone following, but she'd do it.

So she did.

Then there was the other element of danger that formative years on an isolated ranch in South Dakota made her all too aware of. She knew what lurked in this kind of night. She knew nature could swallow you whole simply for taking the wrong turn or tripping over the wrong animal.

One scary threat at a time.

She managed to put some distance between them and the moving light, which gave her some hope he wasn't following tracks so much as looking for them.

"Still no light, but let's get the map out," Cody suggested.

Bringing out the phone would put off a small light, but she'd be able to mitigate how brightly it shined. Cody had showed her how to bring everything up, talked her through how to follow the map—just as he had the first time they'd had to use it. She paused just long enough to grab the phone and bring up the correct app.

Cody held on to her coat so she no longer had to hold his hand. It made it harder to lead him around potential tripping hazards, but aside from a few stumbles he quickly righted himself from, they were doing okay.

They had a hell of a long way to go though.

Nina focused on the end result, just as she would if she was with Brianna. Get to the meeting point Felicity and Cody had agreed upon. That was all she could worry about right now.

Get them to the agreed upon area, then wait till morning. Without their little friend back there catching up and finding them.

She let out a shaky breath, but kept moving. She forced herself to only look back every once in a while, was gratified each time she'd put more space between them and the moving light. She wished they could lose him completely, but she had to follow the map.

They'd initially planned to stop every hour or so, get a drink and a snack, but there'd be no stopping now. Just cold, endless hiking.

Cody fell once, nearly brought her down with him but managed to release her coat just in time. She looked up at where the light was. She could barely see it now, but she could sense he'd stopped too. The light didn't move.

She helped Cody up, one eye on that light. "Maybe we should—"

"Follow the map," Cody interrupted, getting to his feet. "Follow the map, get to the spot. Felicity might not be there yet, but we can hold off whoever this is until she gets there. Then we'll have help. Any help we'd get here is too long off."

He was right, of course, which was irritating. But irritating didn't matter when you were running—or walking quickly—for your life.

By the time she reached where the interactive map told her to stop, there was the faintest hint of light on the horizon. Morning was coming. She didn't think they'd lost their stalker, but she couldn't see his flashlight anymore.

There were signs that they were entering national park land. Not much cover, as the Badlands wasn't known for its forests.

"Now what?" Nina asked, tired and achy and starving.

"Felicity said we should be able to find some shallow caves around here."

"Caves." Nina shuddered. "Great."

"It'll keep us out of sight. We can sit, eat, rest."

Nina hefted out a sigh. "I'll need my flashlight then. I don't see the guy, so it might be safe." She looked at Cody, standing there. It'd be so much easier if she could search for caves without having to maneuver him around the rocky, uneven ground.

"Leave me here."

She frowned at how easily he read her. "I wouldn't leave Brianna here. I thought we were doing—"

"Leave me here, Nina. Find a cave. I'll shout if I get scared."

She nearly snorted. He wouldn't shout, because he wouldn't get scared—even if he should.

"Just go, Nina. I might be blind, but I'm not a small child. Give me *some* credit."

It wasn't about credit, but she didn't have time to argue with him. She'd go search for a place to hide for ten minutes tops, and if she didn't find one she'd come back and get him. But she wouldn't tell him that.

"All right. Stay put. Give some kind of signal if you need me, Cody. Promise me that."

"Sure," he replied.

Because of course him admitting he needed someone was as likely as him admitting he was scared. Wouldn't happen.

"I'll be back," she said, and hoped it would be as easy as that.

CODY HEARD THE APPROACH, knew it wasn't Nina's. He held himself tense, ready, and listened closely to the sounds. Careful but confident, a lighter footfall could be Felicity or someone being careful to sneak up on him.

Cody listened, angled himself toward the noise, and hoped to God Nina was being careful wherever she was.

Though he knew it was likely still dark, he could tell

his vision was worse again. Mostly grayness with no sense of light or shapes and his head ached and pounded. But that only served to give him *some* hope. If when he'd been well rested and calm he'd started to be able to have some concept of light and shadow, he'd been healing and his sight had been coming back. The walk and the handful of stumbles he'd taken had made the healing regress.

But he could heal.

He would heal.

Another set of footsteps approached from behind him, and he could tell those were Nina's. "I think I found—" Nina stopped her whispered sentence on a sharp intake of breath.

"You two look like hell."

It was Felicity's voice and Cody felt a relief so wide and deep he nearly stumbled. "You're early," he managed to rasp. He'd told her to wait. Give it until park hours started and make it look like she was just doing part of her job coming to this isolated area of Badlands National Park.

He hadn't wanted her followed or involved and God only knew what Ace had up his sleeve. But with a man following them and his vision worse, he could only be utterly grateful for Felicity ignoring his orders.

Two sighted women with his instruction against one stalker was far better odds.

"I have a program at nine," she replied, her tone still oddly detached and cool when usually Felicity was timid but sweet. "I couldn't get out of it, and I figured this would take a while." There was a long pause. "God knows I was right. We've still got a way to go on foot. I couldn't take my vehicle back here."

"Someone might have followed us," Nina said, her voice hesitant and unsure. "This whole way. Someone was following us. I'm not sure we lost him completely."

Cody had almost forgotten that's how she'd been at first, with everyone else. She'd always been fierce and determined with him. Or sad, which was worse than anything. But those initial meetings with Duke and the sisters—she'd had this timidity to her.

Felicity's pause made him wonder if Nina hadn't been closer to the truth on Felicity's feelings regarding Nina, but Felicity was here, to help. That was what mattered right now. Not what they needed to work out about the past.

"Well, then let's get going," Felicity said at length.

"Did you tell anyone?" Cody demanded as he felt Nina's arm twine with his. She urged him to step forward.

Again Felicity's pause was telling.

"I told you not to."

"You did," Felicity agreed. "I'm sorry, I thought it best if someone knew. Not just for you, but for me too."

"They need to protect Brianna."

"I'm sure they'll find a way to do both," Felicity said gently.

Admittedly, if not for her job, Felicity never would have been his first pick for help. She was gentle and shy. Liza and Sarah were all sharp edges, and Nina and Cecilia were wary edges, but Felicity and Rachel were sweet and soft and not fighters of any kind.

But Felicity worked at the park, and that's where they'd been. He really hadn't expected her to go against what he'd told her.

Cody grumbled his displeasure as Nina led him forward. "We can't just walk. He's tracking us at this point. If we just go to your vehicle, he'll see what happened. He'll mark you too."

"And as far as you know he doesn't have a vehicle on hand, so what's it matter?"

"I don't want him making you, Felicity. We've got enough people in danger. I called you as a last resort, and because I'd have the best chance of keeping you the hell out of it."

"None of us are out of it, Cody. Doesn't anyone understand how this all works? We're a family. We take care of one another." There was a fierceness in her voice he hadn't expected, but appreciated in the moment.

Still. "The point isn't what we are, the point is who Ace targets."

"Right now, he's targeting you two."

"And our daughter."

"And your daughter. Don't you trust your family to protect her, Cody?"

He shut his mouth, because there was no good answer for that. He did. But that didn't mean it wasn't terrifying to put his daughter's life in someone else's hands no matter how much he trusted them. Especially when they were up against Ace.

But they'd gotten this far, and Cody continued to believe Ace was incapacitated in *some* way.

Nina stopped abruptly, and neither woman spoke.

"What?"

"Rattlers. We're going to have to backtrack and go around the other side."

Since Cody couldn't see he didn't know what "other side" Felicity was referring to, but Nina turned him around and started leading him again.

Backtracking was no good, rattlers or no. Surely dawn was beginning to streak across the sky and surely their stalker was closing in.

"Look around, Nina," he said in a low voice, hoping Felicity was far enough ahead of them she couldn't hear. "Keep your eyes peeled for our friend."

"I am," Nina returned easily. "Sun's rising. He won't need a flashlight anymore, but the trees and rock formations are still dark. He could easily hide in the shadows."

"I've got binoculars. Do you want to stop behind some cover and check?"

As much as Cody preferred science, reason and technology, sometimes a gut feeling was all a man had, and the way the hairs on the back of his neck stood on end, something was coming.

"Give Felicity a gun, Nina," he ordered, trying to figure out which way the threat was coming from.

"I can't have your gun, Cody. I'm a park ranger. It's illegal to—"

"Take the gun, Felicity. We're going to need it."

Chapter Nineteen

"Let's get situated first," Nina said, nodding toward a rock outcropping that would hopefully hide all three of them.

Felicity moved in first, and without saying anything, Nina helped Cody into the spot before scooting in herself. Tight fit, but they would be mostly hidden from the direction their stalker had been coming from.

She unzipped her pack and handed Felicity one of the guns they'd packed and then the magazine.

"This is illegal," Felicity muttered, though she took the gun and put it together with some ease.

"Write yourself a ticket later," Cody muttered. "You see anything?"

Felicity lifted the binoculars to her eyes. She was quiet and scanning, and Nina had to close her eyes and inwardly count to five to try to find some center of calm. "He's coming. Far-off, but on his way."

"We should just go." She couldn't help saying it. How could they sit here and wait around for a threat to appear when they could be fleeing it? "He doesn't have a vehicle. How is he going to know we got one from a *specific* park ranger?"

"How did Ace know where *you* were?" Cody countered.

She didn't have a good answer for that, so she kept her mouth shut.

"So, what are we going to do, Cody?" Felicity asked.

She wasn't exactly as Nina remembered her. The Felicity she remembered had been shy to the point of running and hiding in her room when the Wyatt boys were around. She'd had a stutter for a while. Nina had always believed Felicity would grow out of that shyness a bit, but figured she'd always be more on the anxious, high-strung side of things.

This Felicity was calm. There was something regal about her, and it wasn't the drab brown park ranger uniform with a badge that gave that aura. It was self-possession and confidence.

"Nina, you remember my idea back at the cabin?" Cody asked, though she knew it wasn't a real question. He was going to lay out this plan like it was what they had to do.

"No," she retorted harshly. Not because she didn't remember, but because there was absolutely no way the three of them were going to endanger themselves to try and capture their stalker.

"The more information we have, the better chance of keeping Ace out of our lives better. Longer."

Which was tempting. She had to get Ace completely and utterly neutralized, though she didn't know how that was going to happen without ending his life. Which was why this felt like an unnecessary risk. "What about the risks?"

"We mitigate them."

She hated when he responded with those nonanswers spoken with such surety and conviction—both things she couldn't muster now. She was exhausted and aching and starving.

"For every moment we spend talking, he's getting closer," Felicity informed them, her binoculars trained somewhere beyond the rock.

"Good. We want him close."

"*You* want him close," Nina returned. "You don't even know he has any connection to Ace. If they're all this bad at coming after us, surely it's because there's some kind of conduit hiring them."

"Yes, and wouldn't it be good to know who that conduit is?"

She couldn't argue with that. Still, this felt like putting their lives in danger for a chance instead of a sure thing.

"I could pick him off. Shoulder or thigh or something," Felicity said, still intent on the binoculars. "Slow him down."

Nina blinked at Felicity. "Could you really?"

Felicity smiled over at Nina a little sheepishly. "A lot happens in seven years, Nina." She turned back to the binoculars. "You'll get caught up."

It was the first encouraging thing one of the sisters aside from Liza had said to her.

"I don't want you to shoot him," Cody said. "Too risky."

"I'm a good shot. Ask Brady."

"Some things haven't changed," Nina muttered, hanging on to that same hero worship in Felicity's voice that had always been there when it came to Brady.

Felicity gave her a wide-eyed *don't you dare* look that reminded Nina of old times so sharply she wanted to cry.

But there still wasn't time for that.

They all swore in an echoing kind of unison, ducking farther behind the rock they were all huddled behind as a gunshot rang out and crashed into the rock in front of them.

Cody's face went grim, icy. "Okay, Felicity, shoot him. Try for the leg. We want him alive and able to talk. But make sure he's stopped."

Felicity handed Nina the binoculars then lifted the gun

Nina had handed her earlier. Nina watched in fascination as her shy, nervous sister calmly lifted the gun to rest on the rock. She waited with the rest of her body still hidden behind it before she carefully inched her way back up, clearly testing if their stalker would shoot again.

"Easy," Cody murmured, and Nina supposed it was just a general comment since he couldn't see.

"Distract him, Nina," Cody ordered. "Stick the back-pack up or something he'll shoot at or look at, but won't hurt."

Nina scrambled to follow the order, and Cody kept giving clear, precise orders. "He shoots, you shoot, Fee, got it?"

"Yup."

They were so calm, and Nina tried to find her own. She'd run away from men with guns before. She'd saved her daughter—and at least mentally that'd been easier. Because all she'd ever thought was *how do I keep Brianna safe*.

There were too many people, too many layers now. She believed Brianna was safe at the ranch because she had to, but her, Cody and now Felicity were all in danger. Immediate, gunshot danger.

But Cody had given her a job. She shrugged the lighter pack off her back. With shaking limbs she lifted the back-pack slowly up so it was visible over the rock. The sound of a gunshot was almost immediate.

"All right," Cody said, each word cold and forceful. "Shoot."

THE SOUND OF the gunshot next to him had Cody flinch-ing even though he'd expected it, braced for it. Ordered it, so to speak.

Felicity let out a little *yes*, and he took that as success. "Got a sense of where you hit?"

"Thigh. Fell right down, but he's trying to get back up."

"Nice aim. Okay, let's get him."

"Let's?" Nina demanded. "You can't see."

"I love how you keep reminding me of that, Nina." He stood to his full height, then ducked when a gunshot farther off slammed through the air. Judging by the sound as it impacted the rock not that far from his head, it was way too close.

"He's still got a gun, Cody," Felicity said drily.

"Gee, you don't say."

"You should stay here," Nina said next to him. "You can hardly walk over there *not* being able to see."

"And you two can hardly walk over there getting shot at," he retorted. He thought he'd been handling his loss of sight pretty well, but right about now he would have sold his soul to be able to see and *accomplish* something.

"I can sneak around behind him," Felicity said.

"No," Nina and Cody replied in unison.

Felicity huffed out a breath. "I know the landscape better than either of you—and God knows you can't see, and Nina…"

"I can handle it. I can do it."

Though it went against everything he wanted, Cody knew what had to be done. "You'll both do it."

He'd expected immediate retorts and arguments, but there was nothing but heavy silence in response.

"You hate that I keep reminding you," Nina began softly. "But how can we leave you here when you can't see?"

"I'm the distraction," Cody replied. "It doesn't matter if I can't see if I can distract."

"It does if he gets to you," Felicity pointed out.

"Not if you guys are right behind. Listen, I don't think he'll kill me. Ace wouldn't want him to kill me."

"That doesn't mean he won't. He kind of sucks at his job, if you haven't noticed."

"Unfortunately, we don't know what his job is. Now, you guys have to take off and get behind him. If he starts coming for me, no matter how slowly, you need to get going."

Though he couldn't see, he had no doubt Nina and Felicity were sharing a wordless look as they decided what to do.

He heard shuffling. Then Felicity spoke. "He's up, but he's moving slow. If we hurry, I think we can get around him before he makes it here."

"You have to make sure he doesn't hear you."

"And what are we going to do if we *do* sneak up on him? Tackle him?" Nina demanded.

"Why not?" Felicity replied with a shrug in her voice. "It wouldn't be the first guy I've had to tackle out here."

"Really?" Nina replied, clear awe in her voice, which didn't make any sense to Cody, considering Nina had done way more than tackle a guy.

"Get his gun off of him. And any other weapons he has. Whatever ways you've got. Then we want to know who sent him, how he's getting orders from Ace. Once he's incapacitated enough, someone come back here and get me so I can question him."

There was another silence that Cody had no doubt included silent communication between the women. He couldn't say he trusted them to follow his orders word for word, but he didn't have other choices.

"All right," Felicity said at length. "Nina, follow me."

There was shuffling and rustling and as Cody tilted his head toward it, he realized he could make out shadows again. There was even almost a hint of color when he held his head just so.

Nina's mouth brushed his. "Be careful," she whispered.

He gave a nod, his vision going back to gray then everything too bright so he flinched back. He tried to play it down. "You too."

She didn't move for a second, but she didn't say anything else. Then he could hear them moving out. Situated in rock the way they were, it made an awful lot of noise. Though he imagined a man who'd been shot would make a lot of noise on approach.

He was counting on it anyway.

He felt around for the backpack, made a lot of noise drawing it onto his lap. He blinked three times when he realized he could see the shape of it.

He took a deep breath, willing himself not to get overexcited that his sight might be coming back at the exact right time. He felt around in the pack, because though he could see it he couldn't make out the details of what was inside. That was all shadow. Out of focus.

But he found what he wanted and pulled the sheathed knife out of the pack. He set the pack aside and then moved onto his feet, crouching low. He reached out, felt the cool, jagged rock in front of him, slowly inching up and up until he found the top of the rock.

He held up the tip of the knife, bit by bit, higher and higher, keeping his breathing even so the pounding of his heart didn't interfere with his hearing.

Once he'd extended his arm fully, he moved the knife back and forth, hoping it would catch in the sun.

Because it was daylight. He could *tell* the sun had risen. *Focus.*

There was still no response to him holding up the knife, and it made him nervous that he wasn't being the distraction he needed to be. Still, he couldn't stand just yet. He strained to listen over the wind whistling through the canyons.

He thought about banging his knife against the rock, but that would be an obvious attempt for attention. He had to do something that might draw fire without actually getting caught in said fire.

Then Cody heard it. The distinct sound of rubble crumbling under careful pressure. As if someone was climbing up the other side of the rock.

A tough climb with a gunshot wound to the thigh, but when he heard a pained grunt that definitely came from a man, he knew that's exactly who was trying to make the climb anyway.

Cody positioned himself farther back, hoping he was facing the right direction to have a sense of when the man first saw him. He held the knife loosely at his side. If he trusted his sight more he'd try to look for the man, get an advantage and knock him down, but it was too risky.

Besides, Nina and Felicity were supposed to be sneaking up behind the man. They'd have time—and guns—Cody would be fine.

There was a low chuckle, and Cody kept himself still and poised. He couldn't make out an exact outline, but he could sense the position of the man, get a sense of light and shadow. He only needed another sound cue and he could reach out and land a blow.

God, he hoped.

Chapter Twenty

Nina and Felicity didn't talk. Felicity walked at a break-neck speed through rock formations, pausing only when they had to cross fields with no cover. She'd look, then cross at speeds faster than breakneck.

Nina didn't complain, though she was out of breath and had a stitch in her side as she hurried along after Felicity. The longer they left Cody alone, *blind*, the more she worried.

There'd been a sense that maybe he'd been able to see for a moment, but he hadn't said anything. So she hadn't. Besides, even if he did regain his sight it wouldn't just magically appear right when it would come in quite handy.

"Crap," Felicity muttered, coming to a quick stop. She pointed to a ridge. Nina was all turned around after the fast-paced, zigzagging run Felicity had taken her on. In front of them rock and grass stretched out as if fighting each other for purchase, but there was a man climbing up that ridge, and Nina had no doubt it was the outcropping of rock they'd been on the other side of.

The gun the man held in one hand glinted in the ever-increasing sunlight.

"Run," Nina ordered. They both did. Because on the other side of that rock Cody was a sitting duck.

Just as they reached the bottom of the rock the man was scaling, he fell straight back with a howl.

All Nina could do was watch him fall, and wince when his body landed with a thud.

"He's still got the gun," Felicity warned, already leaping forward. Nina did the same even as he brought that arm up, struggling to roll over and point it at them.

They both lunged at the same time, and the weight of two women had no problem knocking the gun out of the man's grasp. It skidded across scrubby grass and rock and Nina sucked in a breath as pain had her seeing stars. But she quickly scrabbled to her feet as Felicity did—though Felicity did it much more gracefully in Nina's estimation.

Since the gun was closest to her, Nina hurried to pick it up. Then looked up at the rock the man had been climbing.

In wordless agreement, Nina handed Felicity the gun, then turned away from her and the moaning and thrashing man. Felicity would handle him while she attempted to climb up and check on Cody.

It was a hard climb, and she was shocked the man had done it with a bullet wound to the leg. Still, despite a few slips and slides she managed to get to the top.

Cody was slinging one of the packs onto his back. He turned slowly, blinked a few times. "Where's Felicity?"

"Can you see?" she breathed.

"Not…exactly. I don't know. It clears up then goes back. Where is he? I assume he's alive from all that racket?"

"He fell. Straight down. Felicity's got the gun on him. How…"

"I hit him. Didn't mean to knock him over, but it'll do. Get me down there."

She shouldered the bag she'd left behind earlier and

then took his hand. She looked dubiously down the sharp rock. "We could go around—"

"Quickest way, Nina. Let's end this."

She liked the sound of the word *end* too much not to do her best to help him down the climb. She figured he had to be seeing at least a little bit because he didn't stumble.

They made it to the bottom where Felicity stood over the man, who was still lying on the ground but was mostly still except for the rapid rise and fall of his chest. Felicity had both the gun Nina had handed her earlier and the gun they'd gotten off the stalker pointed at him.

Cody studied him before he said anything, but his gaze wasn't directly on the man—it was a little to the right. So whatever pieces of sight were back, it wasn't total.

"Gotta name?" Cody asked.

The man's moaned response was vulgar.

Cody's response kick to the ribs was vicious—and surprisingly on target for a man with limited sight.

"We could just leave him," Felicity offered casually, studying the man on the ground as if he were an interesting piece of roadkill. "Rattlesnakes. Bobcat. Coyotes. Hell, the elements'll get him before any of the animals start nibbling."

Cody's mouth quirked. "We'd have to tie him down or something though. Just to make sure he couldn't crawl his way out."

"Or you could shoot his other leg," Nina offered.

This time Cody smiled, though it was sharp and feral at the edges. "Bloodthirsty. I like it."

"You think I'll live if I tell you anything?" the man demanded, but his eyes went back and forth between them and then to the harsh surroundings.

"I could make sure you do."

The man snorted. "You don't get in my position and live. So shoot me."

Cody held out a hand and both Nina and Felicity stared at it.

"You can't—"

He sent Nina a glare that had her snapping her mouth shut. On a shrug, Felicity handed one of the guns to Cody. He held it right to the man's skull and Nina sucked in a breath, bracing herself for the sound of a gunshot even as her brain screamed that this couldn't actually be happening.

The man tried to scoot away, eyes widening and sweat popping up on his forehead. "Okay, okay. Wait. Just… wait."

"Name."

His eyes darted around to all three of them, then beyond, as if calculating his chances of survival. He licked his lips.

"How exactly can you make sure… How are you going to protect me? *Why* are you going to?"

"If you give me the information I want, your identity will cease to exist. I'll get you a new one. I don't need your life. We both know you're a low man at best. I don't care about *you*. I care about information."

The man gestured helplessly at where his leg was bleeding pretty profusely.

"You'll get medical attention and a new identity. Or you're dead. So, make a choice."

"I don't know anything. I just get orders and I follow them."

"Who from?"

He looked around again. "I don't have a name."

Cody stepped closer, crouched down, got the gun right

up in the guy's face. "I don't have much patience left. You will give me his name. Now. Or..."

"Fine. Andy. Andy Jay."

Nina watched as Cody immediately stood, still with the gun pointed at the man. His expression was rage. "Don't lie to me. Andy Jay is dead."

The man started to shake, held up both hands in supplication. "That's the name I got. That's the only name I ever heard. Andy Jay. I swear it."

Cody didn't lower his gun, and the cold fury in his gaze made Nina shiver. But then something mechanical echoed around them. It was coming from the rocks. She supposed it was Cody's phone, though she would have thought it would be on silent. But the look on his face had her body going cold.

"What is it?"

Cody's expression had changed, turned to that stone that only meant trouble. Deep, horrible trouble. "We have to go. Now."

THERE WAS ONLY one reason his phone would make that sound—especially if it was on silent.

Brianna had pushed her necklace button.

He shoved the gun into Felicity's hand. "Call...one of my brothers." He swore internally. If something was going down at the ranch, they should all be there. "If you don't get anybody, just call the sheriff's department."

"Hey! You said you'd get me a new identity. You said—"

Cody aimed a killing look at the man—what he could make out of his sprawled-out body. He'd been planning on helping the guy, but Cody was almost certain the name he'd been given was bogus. And he was quite certain Brianna was in trouble, so he didn't concern himself with the lowlife who would have happily killed all of them.

"Never trust a Wyatt," he told the guy flatly.

He turned back to the tall, willowy shadow that he knew was Felicity. His brain was scrambling. He couldn't leave her alone with this guy. Sweet, nervous Felicity, who'd handled all of this without even the hint of a qualm.

Maybe she could handle it. She had to. Brianna was in trouble and that came above everyone else. He looked over at the figure that was Nina. Some of his vision sharpened, and he swore he could make out the bright beacon of blond hair in the sunlight.

He wanted to leave her with Felicity, but he didn't have enough of his sight back to drive. And he knew she wouldn't appreciate being left behind without good reason. Protecting her would not be considered a good enough reason.

"What is it?" she demanded again.

"Trouble at the ranch. We need to—"

"Here," Felicity interrupted. He heard a jangle, got the impression she'd tossed keys that Nina had caught. "Drive my truck. I'll take care of this guy. You guys go. Once you get to the other side of that ridge, there's a trail. You'll catch it and follow it to the trailhead. Once you're there, my truck's in the lot. Should be the only one. I'll handle this here. I've got my phone plus radio if I can't get ahold of who I want to—I can get another ranger out here. You go."

Cody nodded. No time to argue or think of a better plan. He needed to get to Brianna.

Nina's hand curled around his arm and she began to lead him, presumably where Felicity had instructed. He still couldn't see much of the ground except a broad swath of light, with the occasional blip of something he assumed were the rock outcroppings the Badlands were known for.

He wanted to hurry, but hurrying would likely end in him tripping and falling flat on his face, probably bringing Nina with him. No time for falls or stumbles, even if it meant the walk was slow and steady.

He hadn't had time to climb back up and get his phone, so he could only hope to God it had been a mistake, or his brothers were taking care of it. But he couldn't gamble with the time it would have taken to recover the phone and be sure.

The walk seemed to take forever, and even once Nina helped him into Felicity's truck—then climbed in the driver's seat herself—they still had a forty-five-minute drive to the ranch.

But Nina started to drive, and he doubted she was paying much attention to the posted speed limits.

"Who's Andy Jay?" she asked.

Cody shook his head. "He's dead."

"Okay. Who *was* he then?"

"I'm not sure exactly. Part of the Sons. One of Dad's main guys back in the day. I don't particularly remember him, but I know of him from stories. When Brady and Gage escaped to Grandma's… He caught them and let them go instead of bringing them back to Ace. Then he was found dead a few days after Gage and Brady made it to the ranch with Jamison. The twins always blamed themselves. So, that guy's lying about Andy Jay."

Nina was quiet, but he could hear and feel how quickly she was driving. Still, she was calm. Probably because he hadn't mentioned the alarm would have come from Brianna—not one of his brothers.

"If the guy out there with Felicity was part of the Sons,

or involved, he'd know Andy Jay was dead and that you'd know who it was."

"Yeah. Probably Ace trying to twist the knife."

"Or someone purposefully using that name."

Cody shook his head. He couldn't work it out, but he could only think about Brianna. Who was in trouble. "When we get there…" He trailed off, because he didn't know how to broach the subject. His sight was coming back. Not near what he needed though. But he could hardly send Nina into a dangerous situation to yet again handle the saving of their daughter all on her own.

"When we get there what?"

He blew out a breath. "We have to be careful."

"What did that noise mean? It was some kind of signal from the ranch?"

Cody shifted in his seat. He didn't want to lie to her. Even if he'd be in the right, she'd blame him for it. Which struck him as ironic, considering she'd kept Brianna a secret from him.

But a secret was different than a lie. Especially when it involved their daughter's life.

"I don't know what exactly is going on. That sound from my phone just means someone was alerting me to an emergency."

"Help, you mean. Someone at the ranch needs help. They're in danger. And, knowing all they knew about where we were and what we were doing, they still need help from you."

"Presumably."

She didn't say anything to that, but he could sense the increasing speed of the vehicle. Not being able to see clearly made that a heck of a lot more nerve-racking than it would have been otherwise.

"You can't go careening onto the property. We have to see what we're up against first."

"Our daughter is in that house. Screw what we're up against."

Since he'd felt that echo through him at first, he didn't immediately argue with her. Maybe he should have told her back with Felicity exactly what that sound had meant—because he'd had a chance to walk off his excess anger and fear and find some clearheaded focus.

Whatever was going on at the ranch, they had to be careful. They had to get a sense of it before they ran in guns blazing. Most especially because Brianna was in danger—and any wrong move could risk everything.

Andy Jay. The man was dead—Cody was sure of it. That was how the story went, and he doubted his brothers would beat themselves up over his death without knowing for sure it was him who was dead.

Or had they all been too young to be that cynical?

He had no phone to warn Brady or Gage. No way of finding out what was really going on at the ranch. He wanted to believe Brianna had touched it out of curiosity, or as an accident… But she was too bright, too cognizant of the trouble she'd grown up in to be careless.

Eventually he could feel the truck begin to slow. His vision was still mostly a blur, such a blur he had to close his eyes half the time to ward off dizziness.

"Don't go to the front gate. You remember the side one? Back off Frank's Lick Road. Let's ease in there."

"Too late for that," Nina muttered darkly.

"What do you see?"

He felt her pushing his head down. "Duck."

Chapter Twenty-One

The gunshot shattered the windshield and Nina had to swallow a scream.

She should have slowed down earlier, but she'd been desperate to get to Brianna and then surprised to drive past a very large SUV with two very large men fiddling with something along the fence of Grandma Pauline's property.

When she *had* seen them, it hadn't been much of a surprise to see a gun lift and point in their direction.

Nina peeked up, saw she was careening for a utility pole and jerked the wheel. "Any weak spots on the fence I can bust through?"

"No. We'll have to do it on foot."

"What?" she demanded.

"Stop the truck."

"We can't—"

"Stop the truck," Cody insisted. She thought it had to be insanity. She'd rather bust through the fence with Felicity's truck and worry about the damage later.

But she trusted Cody, so she stopped. "You still got a gun?"

She nodded, patting her side where she'd strapped it back at the cabin what seemed like forever ago. "Yeah."

"You run for the house. I'll go for them."

"You can't see—"

"I can. Good enough anyway. Go!" He started pushing at her and she didn't have time to think. Brianna was in the house. That could be her only thought.

So she got out of the truck and started running. With every step she reminded herself Cody could handle himself. Would handle himself.

The important thing was Brianna.

Damn it, he better come out of this alive or she'd kill him herself.

She ran and ran, ignoring the horrible pain in her side and her struggling breath.

Brianna. Brianna. Get to Brianna.

No one shot at her and she didn't see anyone, though she didn't have time to look around and scan the surroundings. But nothing stood out to her as being off. No other SUVs. No big men in black. Jamison's and Gage's trucks were outside the house in the distance, and Tucker's SUV was parked near the barn.

Maybe those two men had been it. Maybe somebody inside had somehow seen or…

Keep running. Keep breathing.

She continued across the yard, half expecting another gunshot or someone to jump out at her, but no one did.

She made it to the door and burst in, horrified to find it unlocked. Even more horrified to find four men, Duke and Grandma sitting around the kitchen table. "What on earth are you all doing? Where's Brianna?"

"She's out in the barn with Gigi and Dev," Grandma Pauline returned, rising to her feet. "What's going—"

"Cody's out front. Someone's shooting. Big black SUV, two guys, a few yards before the front gate on the road." She was already running out the door. Maybe Cody was the one in real danger, but she had to be sure that her daughter was safe.

She knew the Wyatt brothers would go help Cody, and she would too as soon as she knew for sure Brianna was fine.

So, she ran for the barn. She skidded to a stop outside the barn when she heard voices. Not ones she recognized. Well, she recognized Dev's voice, but not the other person's.

Heart rioting in her chest, she inched closer and closer, trying to see what was going on. Trying to see where Brianna was.

The barn door was open, but all she could make out was Dev talking to someone. He seemed calm as he came into view. Just standing there, attention on someone out of view, but the closer she got, the more she recognized the banked fury in his voice. He wouldn't talk to the girls like that. Ever.

Trying not to gulp for air, she changed her angle to see where Dev was looking. Sure enough, there was a large man, with a very large gun, pointed right at Dev's chest.

Where was Brianna? And Gigi?

She took a slow, quiet deep breath. Okay. So, it seemed like there were three men. Six Wyatts, Grandma Pauline and Duke, plus her and Liza—they could take three men. Even ones with big guns.

So she needed to focus on her daughter. Where would Brianna be? Surely Dev would do anything to keep the girls from getting hurt.

She reached for her weapon as she heard soft, careful footsteps behind her. Hand on weapon, ready to draw and shoot, she whirled.

Then scowled at Tucker, who held his hands up, but not without the mocking lift of an eyebrow.

Like any of them had time for *mocking*.

He didn't say anything, only pointed up. She turned back to the barn, didn't see anything, but she wasn't meant to. It was a reminder there was a hayloft. The girls must have hidden.

Relief swamped her, not that it took all the fear away. But the man with the gun must not know where those two precious girls were.

Please God.

She looked at Tucker, seeking some kind of guidance. With two of them, surely they could take out the man in the barn. She didn't see a gun on Tuck, but that didn't mean he didn't have one.

He made hand motions, circling a finger then pointing to the ground. It took a few times through for her to get he was saying he was going to walk around to the other side and she should stay right here.

She nodded, and Tucker began to walk to the back of the barn. There was another door on the other side, but from what Nina could see it didn't look to be open. But it *was closer* to the ladder that would lead up to the girls.

But how did Tucker know they were up there? He was just making a guess. They could have run. They could be lost in the fields and—

One problem at a time.

She kept her gaze on the man talking to Dev. Actually *at* Dev was a better description since Dev's mouth hadn't moved once. The door on the opposite side of the barn didn't move—so what the hell was Tuck doing over there?

Nina sighed, rolled her shoulders in an attempt to keep her body from going tight after the crash a few days ago plus all this running and hiking and climbing. She couldn't let the tension centering between her shoulder blades keep her from being agile.

Finally Dev spoke, making a gesture toward the house—which was a gesture toward the open door and Nina herself.

Nina froze.

Dev's gaze met hers, and though she thought he hid his surprise at seeing her rather well, the man with the gun trained on Dev began to turn.

Nina didn't think, didn't aim, didn't worry. She simply reacted—and pulled the trigger of her own gun.

CODY HAD MISCALCULATED GRAVELY. He'd gotten out of the truck and run, but the running made his vision worse to the point he started to question if he was even going in the right direction.

Everything was gray again, though he could make out the difference between light and dark. Barely. He swore inwardly, standing God knew where, with absolutely no clue how to move forward.

Well, you have to. He reached out his hands, tried to find something to give him a clue as to where he'd run.

Then he heard voices and froze. Two men were talking as if they didn't have a care in the world.

"Always had to be a show-off," one man said, sounding vaguely amused. "I kinda hope they knock him around a little and we have to swoop in and save him."

"I wouldn't care if we didn't save him," the other man said. "I don't like dealing with kids." This one sounded gruff and irritated.

Cody could keep moving toward the sound, but he couldn't see well enough to move toward shapes or shadows anymore. He wouldn't know if they drew a gun or came charging. And worse, they would know he was having problems seeing and take advantage.

But he supposed as long as they were here, talking casually, they didn't know Nina had run across the yard a mile or so down the road. They didn't know if there was any trouble at the ranch. Maybe they figured their gunshot had scared off whoever.

"Ace can only do so much from behind those bars. He's going to have to name someone. We can't keep on like this. For all we know, that truck we shot out is going to the cops as we speak."

"If they're smart. We'll be gone by then though. Besides, what if Ace names this moron we're lackeying for?"

"A moron leader is better than no leader at all. Might get dumb orders, but no infighting."

"Boy, there's always infighting. Even under Ace."

Cody tried to determine where they were, based on voices alone, but when he didn't know where *he* was, it hardly mattered.

"You hear that?" one of the men asked.

Cody didn't have the first clue what to do, but he heard something too. An engine?

"We better move."

Then a gunshot pierced the air. Since Cody hadn't been expecting it, he jolted.

"We got company," one of the men said, and Cody knew he was screwed. Just. Screwed. He had to hope they didn't shoot him, or that if they did, he'd survive it. Surely they'd know he was Ace's son and not...

"That's one of Ace's, isn't it?" the more irritable man asked. "A Wyatt boy, aren't you?"

Cody hoped to God he was smirking in the right direction since he had a sense of where they were based on the sound of their voices. "I guess that depends."

"What's wrong with your head there, boy?"

They were getting closer, but they weren't shooting. Maybe Cody would have a chance to fight them off.

Two was going to be a lot harder than the one back at the Badlands, but he could do it. Surely he could do it if he had to, and with Nina off to save Brianna, he *had* to.

"Where'd he come from?" the one asked, and though he said it quietly, Cody still caught the words.

"Cat got your tongue?"

Cody wondered if the man had lifted a gun to point at him. There'd been menace in those words, a threat. Surely the threat was backed up with some kind of weapon.

So he held up his hands. "Not looking for any trouble, gentlemen."

One snorted.

"Better be careful screwing with a Wyatt until we know—"

"Would you shut up," the other man snapped.

"But see…why screw with one Wyatt boy, when you can screw with four?" a very welcome voice asked.

Cody couldn't see his brothers, but that was Gage's voice. Of course if they were here, where was—

"The house?" Cody demanded.

No one responded, and there was a bit of a tussle before Cody could hear Jamison reading the men their Miranda rights.

"You can't arrest us," one of the men argued, clearly still struggling to fight off Jamison. "We didn't do anything."

"I'm sure we'll find something," Gage said casually.

"One of them shot Felicity's truck." Cody didn't know which brother took him by the arm, but it didn't matter. "Brianna? Nina?"

"Everything was fine at the house when we left. We heard the gunshot and Brady backtracked just to make sure, but Tuck's back with Nina and Liza. I'm sure it's fine."

"I'm not," Cody returned. "Take me back to the house."

"Still can't see?"

"Comes and goes. Get me back."

Someone's phone chimed. "It's Liza," Jamison said, voice flat. "We all need to get back to the house."

Chapter Twenty-Two

The man was writhing on the ground, swearing and cursing at her.

Nina still held the gun trained on him, and Tucker had slipped in the opposite door and retrieved the gun the wounded man had dropped.

"Guess I shouldn't have insisted Sarah take my dogs to the Knight property." Dev looked down at the man with a sneer. "And just who do you think you are?"

"Wouldn't you like to know?" the man gritted out, holding on to his leg.

The shock started to wear off and Nina practically lurched for the ladder up to the hayloft. She could hear Tucker and Dev talking, but it was a kind of buzzing. She couldn't pay attention to the words. She had to get to her daughter.

She made it to the top of the ladder, scrambled onto the board of the hayloft and then looked around in heart-pounding panic. Where were they?

Then she heard the faintest sound, like a rustle. A whisper. She turned toward it, then moved toward it, right before a hay-covered tarp shook, moved, and two little heads stuck out from behind it.

Nina nearly sank to her knees, but instead she moved for them, grabbed them and held them to her. "Aren't you good, smart girls? You hid so good. You were so quiet. Oh, I'm so proud of you." She hugged them both, kissed their heads, tried and failed not to shed a few tears.

"There was a big noise, but I told Gigi we had to stay quiet," Brianna said solemnly.

"And we did!" Gigi said excitedly.

Both girls grinned, and it soothed something inside Nina. Terrible things could happen, these little girls could know they had to hide from bad men, but then they could stand up and be proud of themselves because they kept themselves safe.

They saved themselves, and maybe it wasn't fair they had to live in a world that made that happen—but wasn't it a miracle they could find some pride in it just the same?

"Uncle Dev saw the bad man and told us to hide. I knew just where to hide. Just like you always told me." Brianna snuggled into Nina's arms. "Where's Daddy? I pushed my button just like he told me."

Nina closed her eyes. Cody had known all along Brianna was the one who'd sounded the emergency alert. She couldn't work up anger over it. They were safe, and he was out there…

"We'll go find out." She stood, taking both their hands and helping them out from under the tarp and hay. "Come on now. Let's get you down."

"But where's Daddy?" Brianna demanded.

"We'll get him. Jamison and the boys are out getting him right now." *Please God.*

Nina helped the girls climb down the ladder, found Brady and Liza had joined Tucker and Dev standing over the increasingly weakening man bleeding on the barn floor.

"Come on, girls," Liza said, expertly positioning herself between their little gazes and the man's bleeding leg. "Cookies in the kitchen for being such good hiders."

Nina looked back at Tucker, Dev and Brady. "Where's—"

"I've called the ambulance to come pick up this one," Brady said, nodding toward the man. "I'll accompany him to the hospital. Jamison has the two guys you, er, ran into and is taking them to the jail. Gage has Cody and is bringing him back to the house."

"What about Felicity? We left her—"

"She already called. Everything is good there. She's got it handled. You go on with Brianna. We've got it here."

Nina nodded, grateful that someone had it. That it was over.

God. Please let it be over.

She trudged after Brianna, pain and exhaustion and the wearing-off adrenaline making every step feel like wading through lead.

Gage had Cody. Cody was safe. All the men who were part of this were being taken care of. For now, anyway.

She looked at her daughter bopping along with Gigi as though nothing horrible had happened. *For now* was okay. *For now* was better than okay.

CODY WAS SURPRISED at how long it seemed to take to drive back to the house, irritated that he had to be led into the ranch house, and then thrown into a world of pain when he felt two sets of arms squeeze around him.

He hissed out a breath, but bit back the groan of pain. "There's my girls."

And it felt good, even with the pain, to have them both back in his arms. Here in his grandmother's kitchen.

Everything would be okay. He *felt* that now.

"So, what on earth happened?" Liza demanded.

Everyone got situated around the kitchen table, and

someone led him to a chair. Brianna climbed up into his lap and though he couldn't see her, he held her there, smelled her hair. She was fine. She was alive.

If he never regained his sight permanently, that was worth it right there.

"From what we figured out through the guys Jamison arrested, the man…" Cody stopped himself from saying *shot in the barn* in the nick of time. Brianna and Gigi didn't need to hear the full details even if they had to live through them. "The man in the barn was Andy Jay. Junior."

Gage swore under his breath.

"Obviously he blames the Wyatts for his father's death. It's not clear if Ace had twisted him to use him against us, or if he was using Ace to get to *us*. But either way, the lawyer was getting messages to Andy, who was leading parts of the Sons in Ace's absence."

"So… Nina shot the new head of the Sons?"

"Not exactly."

"Mom? You *shot* someone?"

He heard Nina's strangled response, which wasn't words so much as the sound a person makes when they don't know what to say.

"Brianna, can the adults have some time to talk by themselves? Is there something you and Gigi can go play?" Cody asked.

"I'll take them. Jamison can clue me in later," Liza said.

Brianna slid off his lap, and Cody knew he'd be having to talk to her about when it was appropriate to shoot someone, but first he needed to tell his brothers and Nina what they'd figured out.

Once he thought they were gone, Cody continued. "Andy Jay wasn't the new leader. They don't have a new leader. In fact, it sounds like the Sons are on shaky footing. I heard the two guys out front talking before they noticed me. The Sons are waiting for Ace to name a successor, and he hasn't. Infighting. Power vacuums. They're self-destructing."

"Well, then it's not a bad thing Andy Junior and his cohorts will be in jail for quite some time," Dev said gruffly.

"And with all three being taken care of, and Brianna occupied, I'm going to take Cody to the hospital," Nina announced.

"I don't—"

"You need a doctor," Grandma Pauline interrupted. "Let your woman take you to the hospital."

Your woman. He couldn't see, but he grinned in what he hoped was Nina's direction. "You going to take that label?"

"I'll take it," Nina replied, and her slim hand wrapped around his arm and tugged him back to his feet. "All the way to the hospital."

He grumbled, but he let her lead him outside.

"You don't have to do this, you know. I know I need a medical professional, but one of my brothers—"

"I'll take you. Because I love you." She stopped, brushed her mouth against his. "We're safe, Cody. And together."

"And we will be." He'd make sure of it.

Epilogue

It took a few days of rest, to the point he was going near crazy, but when he woke up a few days later his sight was back just as the doctor had predicted.

Not just the blurry in and out he'd had the first few days of healing, but full-fledged seeing.

His head injury had only needed to heal, and then his sight would too. And so it had. Thank God. He was really tired of being led around, even by the people he loved most in the world.

He sat up, looked around. Nina was curled beside him, clear as a picture underneath the big blue comforter. She was sound asleep.

Gorgeous. His.

Brianna bounded in, as was her current routine. She jumped right on the bed and grinned at him. "Can you see yet?"

"Looks like today's the day, B."

She gave a whoop of triumph, then launched herself at him.

Nina rolled over and yawned. "Now, you two. You still have to be careful. Healing takes time."

So much time. Time he was tired of. "You know, Jamison and I had a long talk last night."

"About bad guys?" Brianna asked, bouncing.

"No." He pulled Brianna onto his lap, slid his arm around Nina and brought her close. "See, Jamison and Liza and Gigi they all live in a town called Bonesteel. It's a short distance from here, not far. Liza's going to home-school Gigi, and she thought your mommy could help her. So, you and Gigi would be in school together, taught by Aunt Liza and Mom."

Brianna's eyes got big as saucers. "I could go to school *with* Gigi?"

"And what will you do?" Nina asked, frowning up at him.

"Jamison said there's a computer repair store for sale. Owner would sell the building, the supplies, outright. I've got some tech skills."

"You're going to run a store?" Nina asked skeptically. "In Bonesteel?"

"A store. A front for some other things. Potato. Po-tahtoh."

She snorted out a laugh, and it was like in this very moment his world righted. Nina and Brianna were his. He had a plan for what he could do to help bring down the Sons—without being involved in North Star, though he planned to offer his services when they were needed.

And he could keep his family safe, because they *were* a family. "We could buy a little house. Have some slice of normalcy. Stability. Together."

Nina looked up at him, a considering look on her face, so he gave Brianna the signal they'd practiced, tapping his nose three times.

She let out a little squeal, then scooted off the bed and ran out of the room.

"What are you up to?" Nina asked, skepticism still in place.

Cody dropped a kiss to the tip of her nose. He enjoyed

the skepticism, Brianna's excitement, and as much as he didn't plan to do anything so sedate as run a computer repair business in a tiny town, he liked the idea of stability.

Of family.

Brianna scooted back in.

"You got it, B?"

Brianna nodded excitedly and jumped on the bed again. "Here, Mama." She shoved the box at Nina.

Who stared at it, eyes wide, much like Brianna had looked when he'd mentioned going to school with Gigi.

"Well, open it."

She flipped the lid, and there it was. The ring he'd bought all those years ago. Because Nina had always been right, and they'd already lost enough time.

"I love you. Both. With everything I am. We lost seven years. I don't want to lose a second more."

Nina looked up from the ring, tears swimming in her eyes. "I don't either."

"So. Marriage. House. Settle down in good old Bonesteel, South Dakota. Keep each other safe."

Nina reached up and cupped his face. "And happy," she said, as a tear slipped over.

"A family," Brianna shouted exuberantly, flinging her arms around both of them.

Because they were finally a family, just as they always would be from this moment forward.

* * * * *

COMING SOON!

We really hope you enjoyed reading this book. If you're looking for more romance, be sure to head to the shops when new books are available on

Thursday 2nd April

LET'S TALK
Romance

For exclusive extracts, competitions
and special offers, find us online:

 facebook.com/millsandboon

@MillsandBoon

@MillsandBoonUK

Get in touch on 01413 063232

For all the latest titles coming soon, visit
millsandboon.co.uk/nextmonth

MILLS & BOON

THE HEART OF ROMANCE

A ROMANCE FOR EVERY KIND OF READER

MODERN

Prepare to be swept off your feet by sophisticated, sexy and seductive heroes, in some of the world's most glamourous and romantic locations, where power and passion collide.
8 stories per month.

HISTORICAL

Escape with historical heroes from time gone by. Whether your passion is for wicked Regency Rakes, muscled Vikings or rugged Highlanders, awaken the romance of the past.
6 stories per month.

MEDICAL

Set your pulse racing with dedicated, delectable doctors in the high-pressure world of medicine, where emotions run high and passion, comfort and love are the best medicine.
6 stories per month.

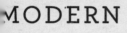 *True Love*

Celebrate true love with tender stories of heartfelt romance, from the rush of falling in love to the joy a new baby can bring, and a focus on the emotional heart of a relationship.
8 stories per month.

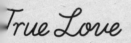 *Desire*

Indulge in secrets and scandal, intense drama and plenty of sizzling hot action with powerful and passionate heroes who have it all: wealth, status, good looks...everything but the right woman.
6 stories per month.

HEROES

Experience all the excitement of a gripping thriller, with an intense romance at its heart. Resourceful, true-to-life women and strong, fearless men face danger and desire - a killer combination!
8 stories per month.

 **DARE**

Sensual love stories featuring smart, sassy heroines you'd want as a best friend, and compelling intense heroes who are worthy of them.
4 stories per month.

To see which titles are coming soon, please visit

millsandboon.co.uk/nextmonth

JOIN US ON SOCIAL MEDIA!

Stay up to date with our latest releases, author news and gossip, special offers and discounts, and all the behind-the-scenes action from Mills & Boon...

 millsandboon

 millsandboonuk

 millsandboon

It might just be true love...

MILLS & BOON

HISTORICAL

Awaken the romance of the past

Escape with historical heroes from time gone by. Whether your passion is for wicked Regency Rakes, muscled Viking warriors or rugged Highlanders, indulge your fantasies and awaken the romance of the past.

MILLS & BOON
MEDICAL
Pulse-Racing Passion

Set your pulse racing with dedicated, delectable doctors in the high-pressure world of medicine, where emotions run high and passion, comfort and love are the best medicine.